SECRETS
ARE
Chancey

SECRETS ARE CHANCEY

7

KAY DEW SHOSTAK

August South
PUBLISHING

ISBN: 978-0-9991064-7-1

Library of Congress Control Number: 2019904582

SOUTHERN FICTION: Women's Fiction / Southern Fiction / Railroad / Bed & Breakfast / Mountains / Georgia / Family/ Small Town

Text Layout and Cover Design by Roseanna White Designs
Cover Images from www.Shutterstock.com

Published by August South Publishing. You may contact the publisher at:
AugustSouthPublisher@gmail.com

Dedicated to Book Clubs

They seem to be filled with my very favorite kind of people—
People that like reading and like talking about reading.

Especially want to thank my Books Plus Book Club
who enthusiastically wait for, read each of my books,
and then discuss them with me.

Sue, Carmen, Nancy, Kay, Betsie, Mary, Eugenia, and Maggie.
You can't imagine how you feed my writer's soul

Character List at end of book

Hello,

This is Peter Bedwell. I wish to extend my heartfelt appreciation for your kind thoughts during the hard days in the recent past. My father's death was unexpected for me, and for many others, I'm sure, so it continues to seem unreal. Your thoughts and kindnesses have truly helped and are much appreciated. I would like to say I am also speaking on my mother's behalf, though she informed me she had responded to the many kindnesses our family received via handwritten notes on appropriate stationery, also addressed by hand, each personally affixed with a plain stamp (no cartoon or cute or sentimental stamps) and mailed at her local post office. She did not wholly approve of this note to people we don't have relations with. Please extend your grace and understanding to her. (Whether she deserves it or not.)

Francis Marion Bedwell, better known as F.M., leaves a painful hole in our town of Chancey. I know he would be thrilled to hear his granddaughter, Anna, and her husband, Will, are naming their daughter Frances Marion after him. Maybe Anna and Will getting along better lately is due to him smiling down on them. However, at the same time I know he would be dismayed to find out Susan is moving back to town without her husband, Graham. Seems just as one couple finds their way, another begins to come apart at the seams, doesn't it?

Hard to believe I'd be writing this, but my relationship with Shannon seems to be going rather well. She was such a rock during my father's passing. She also, well, stands up to... no, never mind, I've mentioned my mother enough already. Anyway, Shannon is enjoying living in town, even though we are so close to Gertie's moonshine basement and my mother's house. We walk together to work each morning, and it appears something new is going into that perennially empty space next to Ruby's. They are doing a lot of remodeling as well as replacing the windows that poor little Zoe Kendrick broke. (I have a soft spot in my heart for children with crazy parents.)

Carolina seems to know more about the new business than she lets on. She becomes anxious when the topic comes up in conversation. But then she's got a lot on her plate with her brother-in-law moving into Anna's old apartment and his girlfriend visiting. (I know there's a story there. She's quite, uh, different.) Plus, Carolina and Jackson are becoming grandparents in less than two months while still dealing with their two high schoolers. Just glad we're not them, right?

Back to the new business in that dumpy junk store, all I can say is more business downtown will hopefully help my bistro. Not that I need help. Please don't tell Mother I need any help. Just, more business is good for everyone, right?

I'm sorry. Excuse my inexcusable rambling. This was supposed to be a short note of appreciation, and here I am talking on and on about a thousand other things. Pardon me—since moving back home to Chancey I seem to become more Southern by the minute.

With much gratitude for your warm thoughts,
Peter Bedwell

CHAPTER 1

"Sounds like school to me," Savannah says from her perch in the living room. My seventeen-year-old daughter, almost eighteen, sits on the arm of the living room chair next to the window. Her feet are in the seat of the chair and on her knees is a book. An open book. A book she's been reading for months. I'm not joking. It's her summer reading book, and we bought it the last week of school in May. She's carried it around since then and looking at where it's open to, she's nowhere near done. She half lifts the book, looking at it in disgust. "Who reads for fun?"

"I do," I answer as I open the wooden front door and look outside. "And speaking of reading, shouldn't you be about done with that book? School's been in well over a month. Two months almost. It's the second week of October." Late afternoon sunlight pours in through the screen door, and I lower the sliding window to let in some of the fresh breeze.

She collapses her head onto her knees. "Teacher said my report on it sounded like I hadn't actually read the book, so he's making me redo it."

"Did you read it?"

"Not exactly." She flips her head up and shakes out her long, dark hair. "It's just so boring to sit and read a made-up book.

What's the point? Like I said, this book club you're going to sounds like school to me. Do y'all read interesting books, or just made-up ones?"

"You mean fiction? Honestly, well, I don't know. I haven't seen the book list yet. But I like using my imagination." As I sit on the couch, I smirk as I imagine telling her I think that math is what is stupid. Savannah loves math. She is her engineer daddy's daughter. However, there is a little alarm running in my head that's got my attention. What if in the book club they don't just read fiction? Our realtor Retta didn't say exactly what kind of books they read, and I didn't think to ask. I'm not joining this book club to read about sad things, which are what non-fiction thrives on in *my* opinion.

Savannah slides down into the chair. "But you had to take math and read real books in college, didn't you?"

"Of course. I can *do* math, I just don't like it. And while I read lots of non-fiction getting my degree in library sciences, it doesn't mean I have to do it now. Unlikely I'll be working at a library again anytime soon."

We moved here a little over a year ago, and everyone, especially my husband Jackson, wanted us to open a bed and breakfast for railfans. Railfans are people who like to watch trains, and we have a spectacular train-watching venue in our front yard. I, however, did not think opening a B&B was a good idea. I was very vocal about my opinion.

Well, despite my protests, we opened the B&B, and still in avoidance mode, I got a job at the local library. That was an even worse idea. The head librarian and I did not get along, and within a matter of weeks after our arrival in Chancey, I had an enemy for life, no job, *and* the B&B to look after. But I eventually ended up with a used bookstore downtown. So, score one point for me!

Blooming Books is a bookstore and florist. The book part is doing better than anyone, including me, ever thought. We still have Crossings—the B&B, here in our house—but I have help with that, and the bookstore lets me get away from here. Tonight we, the store and I, are starting a new venture. The local book club asked to meet in our store, and I asked to join. My first book club! I'm excited, but nervous. Joining is not usually my thing.

Savannah twists around and puts her legs up over the arm of the chair. She opens her book and sighs as she stretches her neck.

"That doesn't look comfortable," I say as I get up. "You could go read on the deck. It's still warm enough, and the backyard is beautiful with all the leaves starting to change."

"I can't get comfortable or I'll fall asleep. I have to finish this today." She spreads the book on her lap and stares at it, tipping me off that I'm supposed to be quiet now.

"Good luck. When's the paper due?"

With another long sigh, she says, "Tomorrow. That's why I have to finish."

"Tomorrow?" Shaking my head at her, I walk back into the kitchen. As a parent of three, I chose to drop the homework battle long ago. The only way a parent wins a homework battle is if you do it for them, and that ain't happening. At the doorway, I stop and turn to her. "Dinner is easy tonight. Corn dogs, salad, and green beans. I'm also going to make a pan of fries to try and fill Bryan up. You can eat whenever you want, so you can keep reading."

She doesn't answer or acknowledge me. She's depleted the words required to speak to her mother.

Savannah's a good student, I think as I pull corn dogs out of the freezer. She's done well with our move from the Atlanta suburbs, where we left the big, well-appointed schools and high-pressure parents. There, her mostly all As in regular-level classes were to be expected. The really smart kids were making all As in Advanced Placement classes for college credit.

Honors classes were also expected, even looked down on. At Chancey High, Savannah's the smart one. Everyone thinks she's an aggressive student, or at least they did last year. This year, she seems to just not be interested. I'm a bit worried it's due to the rough few weeks we've had.

Over fall break, kind-of boyfriend tricked her into going on an all-expenses-paid cruise with his family. She didn't realize it came with strings, strings even his religious parents agreed with. (And his father is a local pastor!) When she cut those strings before they even got on the boat, his parents left her at a hotel on the way to Florida. It truly shook Savannah's confidence not only in others, but also in herself. She stays home more and isn't dating anyone. She doesn't seem bothered or upset. Mostly it feels like she's figuring things out, thinking through it all. She has been talking to the counselor at school, so that's good. After talking about it when we first brought her home, she's not wanted to talk to her parents about it since.

After turning on the oven, I put a half-dozen corn dogs on one end of the baking sheet and frozen French fries on the other. Jackson's job takes him out of town most of the time, and this week is no different. With the kids on such varied schedules we rarely have sit-down dinners during the week, which does *not* break my heart. The salad is left over from last night, and I put the green beans on this morning to cook all day. Southern vegetables need to cook a long time. If they are crisp or snap, they are raw.

This mess of late green beans came from my co-worker Shannon's father. Shannon runs the florist part of Blooming Books. Her father came into town to bring us all some of his end-of-harvest overflow yesterday. At least that was his excuse, but I believe he wanted to see Shannon. Her parents won't go to Peter's house where she's now living due to lack of a marriage license in the house, so they have to do all their visiting at the store. Makes things a little crowded at times, but

I do love vegetables fresh from a garden. Especially when the only work I have to do is say, "Thank you."

The banging of the front screen door tells me our youngest, Bryan, is home from football practice. I listen but can't tell if he's alone. His "hey" to Savannah only garners a grunt from the armchair, then he lumbers into the kitchen. "Hey, Mom. Dinner ready?"

"Will be by the time you shower. Where's your uncle?"

He shrugs as he opens the fridge and grabs an orange Gatorade.

"Did your uncle bring you home?" Jackson's younger brother Colt is the assistant coach at Chancey High and usually gives Bryan a ride home.

"Yeah, but I guess they got pretty much everything moved into the apartment, so he was going there."

He's out of the kitchen by the time his sentence is over. He's left behind a waft of sweat and freshly cut grass. He's also left a knot in my stomach. Can't believe Colt's girlfriend, Rebecca, is moving here and opening a dance studio next to Ruby's Café. I have nothing against dance studios. I don't even have anything against ex-strippers teaching pole dancing. However, I will admit to some concern to the studio-to-be's big, plate-glass windows on Main Street in my little town. There's also a twinge of nerves caused by the physique of said ex-stripper and her love of revealing clothing. However, the real knot has to do with her being here because of us. Colt followed us here, and she followed Colt. It's seems an awful small town to share with family to me.

You've heard that old saying, "Good fences make good neighbors," right?

Well, my motto is, "State lines make happy families."

Chapter 2

"You understand the only reason you are allowed to join us is because we want to meet in your store, right?"

As our realtor, Retta Bainbridge was the first person from Chancey we met last year. Apparently in addition to her real estate duties, she's the gatekeeper of the book club. Her gate is apparently under repeated threat of attack as this is the third time since we've sat down that she's told me why I was allowed to join.

"Yes, I understand. I mean, is it really something you need to worry about? Keeping your numbers down? Seems to me you'd be happy people want to join."

Retta huffs as she looks around the circle of seven people gathered in the sitting area of our shop. The closed sign is on the door, and it's quite cozy. Retta is a large lady and always fashionable, if by fashionable you mean that her ropes of plastic beads match her lipstick, or that she rushes fall by wearing wool (and a nice sheen of sweat) in September, or that her color wheel is stuck on "colors not found in the natural world."

But she did let me join the book club.

Because, lest we forget, they want to meet in my store.

Retta expels her last huff and shoves up the sleeves of her

chartreuse sweater. It's long, and underneath it she has on a pair of patterned leggings. On their black background there are all manner of neon falling leaves. Yes, some of them are chartreuse, and it's a perfect match. See? Fashionable. "Carolina," she says, "it's not to keep our numbers down. There are some we'd gladly welcome into our little group. It's those *others*. The ones we don't want to spend time with, who are champing at the bit to be a part of this group."

"Oh, Carolina," Pearl Bennett Something says.

I say Something because the whole family is known by their maiden name of Bennett, even the next generation. They say it's because they all share and run the beauty shop, Beulah Land, out near the highway, so it's easier to just use their maiden names instead of their married ones.

She repeats herself, sounding even more condescending this time. "Oh, Carolina. In the beauty shop, Crystal and I have to put up with listening to everyone who walks in the door. And poor Retta can't refuse a real estate listing just because someone is annoying. Same with Sally since her husband is a pastor," she says as she flourishes a hand toward Sally, a woman about my age whose husband is apparently a preacher somewhere. Her other hand flourishes to indicate the other women I don't know. "Dot and Helena can't be open if the parents of their students show up here clamoring to join." She leans forward and smiles at me with sad eyes. "You understand, don't you? There are just some people we don't want to put up with."

Oh, I understand. I *so* understand. "Okay. So, Pearl and Crystal, you two are sisters, right? Beau is your daughter, right, Crystal?"

Crystal smiles and nods as Pearl speaks up. "Oh, yes, and I'm Beau's aunt and great-aunt to Brittani who still has your youngest boy wrapped around her finger!"

"Law, they aren't even dating! Or *are* they?" Crystal says

this with a wink and a giggle. I look away to avoid having to respond.

Speaking of my boys, sitting next to me is the woman my married oldest boy wrapped his finger, and God knows what else, around this summer. "So, Rose," I extend an olive branch to her. I'm trying to be more generous with my olive branches. "How did you come to be a part of this group?"

"Inherited it from grandmother." She shrugs and crosses her long legs. She's wearing old jeans and a Dalton State sweatshirt. She never wears makeup and her hair is plain brown, but she has a shine to her. I want Will to be with his wife and the mother of his soon-to-arrive daughter. That's what I want.

Until I'm around Rose. Rose seems like whom Will would be with if he and Anna hadn't gotten pregnant then eloped. But it is what it is.

With a sigh, I turn to Retta. "Inherited?"

Retta wrinkles her nose at me. "Lavada was one of our founding members, so when she could no longer come to the meetings, she asked to send Rose in her place. Now Rose is one of us. Do you know Dot and Helena? They teach elementary. So you might not know them."

"No, I don't. Hello."

Dot and Helena are close to my age and look to be good friends. They make a lot of eye contact and roll their eyes at the same time. Funny, but I think I could've picked them out of a lineup to be elementary school teachers. Not sure why. Maybe it's their seasonally themed jewelry and clothing. I'll have to think on that.

Dot waves her hand at me. "We've been in your shop, but we never really talked. You always seem busy or preoccupied."

"Yes," Helena continues the thought, "but it is a lovely and comfortable shop. You know, the other lady would be welcome to join us also since, again, we are meeting in her shop." The others nod in agreement.

"Who? Shannon?"

There's a visible recoil around the circle and Dot says, "No. Oh, most assuredly not. I think Helena means the tall woman. Bonnie, I believe, is her name. She was a teacher over at Darien Academy?"

"Oh, yes, she was, but she lives up in Laurel Cove. I don't believe she'd be interested." I refrain from telling them Bonnie's exact feelings on the club. Feelings she accented with a shudder.

Pearl holds her hand out, palm facing me. "Do not ever let on that Shannon is welcome. She is not. It would be a shame to have to find another place to meet, which would also mean you would be out of the club before you actually joined."

I know it's completely disloyal to Shannon, but I roll my eyes and join in the laughter. Call me cruel, call me heartless, but well, I really, really want to be in a book club. Plus, I never got to be in a sorority in college and, well...

Maybe we can get T-shirts or something.

"Now. Our book for November is *The All-Girl Filling Station's Last Reunion* by Fannie Flagg. It's been out a few years, so you should have no trouble finding copies." Retta lifts her copy of the book out of her satchel and shows it to us, me in particular. "Carolina, see if you can round up several copies, then shoot out an email to the group."

Up until this moment, book club was going great. They'd read an Agatha Christie mystery, *Murder on the Orient Express*, for October, and unlike what I'd heard about some book groups, they actually discussed the book the whole time! I was pleasantly surprised.

"Wait, I don't know if I can get that book," I say. "I usually just get whatever Andy finds, unless we order new books."

Retta pushes herself up on the knees of her leafed-out leggings, then slowly unbends to stand over our circle. "Could you please just try? Missus always complains about your lack of initiative. Now I see what she's talking about. Would you like me to assign someone each month to help you with refreshments?"

"I'll do next month, Carolina," Helena says as the rest of them begin standing. "Discussion does go easier with a glass of wine," she says with a wink. "So you do that and I'll bring some Chex Mix since I'll be making it from the beginning of November until Thanksgiving for everyone. Any wine will do."

"I don't drink," Sally says, "so some cider would be nice." She smiles and gives me a little wave as she heads to the door.

"In public," Crystal says behind her hand to Pearl and me.

"What?" I ask, watching as the sisters giggle.

Crystal darts her eyes toward the door and says under her breath again, "In public. Sally and her husband Pastor Coler don't drink in public. They drink at home. They buy their wine and beer down in Canton at the warehouse store. Everyone knows." The two women giggle again.

Alcohol is a funny thing in the South. Some religious denominations don't believe in imbibing at all, and since we don't tend to wear our denominations on our shirts (unless you're on the softball team), no one is sure who drinks and who doesn't. One of my parents' best friends was a deacon in a church that didn't agree with drinking, so in his refrigerator his beer was kept in a brown paper bag. What God can't see, God can't judge, I guess.

"Oh, don't look so concerned," Pearl says to me. "Their church doesn't mind it. They're a drinking denomination."

"It's about setting an example, they say," Crystal explains as she wraps a scarf around her thin neck. "Why is it so cold already? I don't know if I'll make it through this winter! I just freeze to death."

I follow the ladies out the door and turn off the lights. On the sidewalk I turn to lock the door so my back is to the group when I hear one lady exclaim, "What in the world!" Another one gasps as she says, "Dear God in Heaven!" Leaving the keys hanging in the door, I step back and look through their group down the sidewalk.

Bright light spills toward us. Toward the street. Toward the houses at the corner. Bright light everywhere, spilling out of the new glass windows next to Ruby's. It's like someone replaced Chancey's Main Street with an Atlanta Airport runway.

Shaking my head, I walk back to the door and retrieve my keys. By the time I rejoin my book club friends, they are farther down the sidewalk, the lights drawing them like bugs. Now that I think about it, the quality of light does remind me of the charm of one of those electric bug zappers. Walking behind them, my head bowed, I join the growing crowd. We're not the only people on the sidewalk looking in, and our group is welcome to join in on speculating about what exactly is going on.

My right arm is grasped and pulled just as my left arm is grasped and pulled.

"Carolina!" Missus demands at the same time that Gertie also says my name. The big, well-lit, windowed room is empty of furniture or fixtures. However, there are lots of workmen and one rather attractive woman in nothing but a leotard.

From up near the window, Retta calls my name. "Carolina? Isn't that your brother-in-law? Isn't that Coach Jessup?"

"Yes," Missus growls. "Isn't that your brother-in-law?"

"Yes. Yes, that's Colt. They're opening a dance studio, I believe." Like tossing a rare steak calls off a pack of wild dogs, tossing a bit of new info can distract a rabid small-town crowd.

"I've got to go." I shake off their hands and back away from the group.

As I turn around and pick up my scurrying, Gertie cackles and says with a shout, "Never seen no skin-colored leotard before. Looks like that woman is right there in the window nekkid."

I've heard "naked" is when you don't have any clothes on. "Nekkid" is for when you don't have any clothes on—and you're up to no good.

Yep, Rebecca's nekkid.

Chapter 3

"In the window. For all of creation to see! I'm serious, Jackson. You have to talk to Colt." I take a sip from my water bottle, but almost spit it out when I realize my husband is laughing. "Jackson!" I yell into my phone. "I'm serious. It was completely embarrassing. Luckily everyone from book club were so busy staring that I got away without having to admit I knew all about it days ago."

I walk out on the back deck to report the latest Chancey happenings to Jackson. In the living room all three kids are watching some horrible movie I should probably stop them from watching. However, they all have schoolbooks scattered around them, so maybe they're studying while they watch. Don't roll your eyes at me.

I tuck my free hand up against my chest and pace in an attempt to stay warm.

With nary a laugh, he asks, "So how was book club?"

"I really liked it. It's apparently fairly exclusive. You have to be invited to join, and they really do talk about the books. They all like books like I like books. Maybe even more." I ramble on a minute more, telling him who all's in the club, but then I hear him yawn. "Sorry if I'm boring you."

"No. Not at all. Just been a long day."

"Where did you go for dinner?"

"Picked up a sandwich and ate it here doing some work. But back to the dance studio, what could I possibly tell Colt? He and Rebecca are embarrassing us? I honestly didn't think they'd get things moving on the studio this fast, though. What if she bails on him? I hope he's not too tied into it all."

"Tied into an ex-Vegas stripper who used one man to get to Kentucky and then dumped him as soon as your brother came along? At least Colt doesn't have a wife to abandon like the judge he stole Rebecca from."

"He didn't steal her. She, well, she came willingly. They might actually be in love, you know," says my husband, who has turned into a hopeless romantic at the idea of a stripper leading exercise classes in downtown Chancey.

"Yeah, sure. But you're right. How did they get things moving along so fast? She just showed up on Saturday." I shiver and tuck my phone hand inside my sleeve so that I'm holding my phone precariously between my ear and shoulder. This was so much easier with big, old thick cordless phones.

"Well, I think Colt might have been working on things with the dance studio before. Making some arrangements."

This gets my attention. "Wait. Did you know about all this? When did you know?"

"Not really. I mean, not much, but you know how you say I don't listen to you real good?"

"Yeah...?"

"Apparently I didn't listen to my brother either," Jackson says. "Didn't really dawn on me what he was talking about until they told us Saturday night."

"So this is basically your fault. You could've slowed Colt down. Told him it wasn't a good idea!"

"Don't know that it's *my* fault," my husband says, "but yeah, I probably could've said something other than what a neat

24

place Chancey is to live. And how accepting folks here are. And how I thought that building would rent for a song." He pauses and thinks about all of this. Yeah, maybe it is my fault, but it's all too late now, right?"

"Whatever. I'm going inside where I won't freeze. I have to try to erase the vision I have of Rebecca in a nude leotard. It's burned into my brain. I'll also try to forgive you for bringing this plague to our town."

"Okay, bye, and I love you. Remember that, okay?" He's laughing again, and it makes me laugh, too.

"Okay, I'll try. I love you, too."

"Wait!" Jackson says. "I just thought of something. Maybe you should check to see where one might buy a nude leotard. I will be home Friday, you know."

"Oh, really? Now, that's something to think about. Hmmm." I let my voice fall into the sexy-voice range and purr, "Sure thing, Mr. Jessup, I'll see if I can find out. I'm all a fluster just thinking about seeing you in one." I hang up before he can say anything. My smile is big as I step into the warm light of the kitchen.

Now that I think about it, maybe I should check on buying stock in latex. There might be a run on leotards around town.

Before I can cross the kitchen, my phone rings and Susan's name pops up on the screen. I've kind of been avoiding her calls, but I think I'm getting close to the unspoken number of calls sent directly to voicemail before a friendship ends.

Taking a deep breath, I answer. "Hi there."

"Hi. What are you up to?"

"Nothing much. What about you?"

"Painting at the new house. Want to come over and help? I have wine."

Susan only told us all on Saturday that she and Griffin are divorcing. While we're all still processing that strange, crazy thought, she's moving full steam ahead. It's either get on the divorce train or get ran over. "How's the house coming along?" I say.

"Great! You should come see it. Did I mention I have wine?" She laughs then rushes on. "Seriously, though it's so cute. So much more me than that monstrosity up in Laurel Cove. Ugh. I mean, who lives like that? Come see it. You don't actually have to paint. You can just talk to me."

"I don't know, Susan. It's a school night, and I just got home from book club."

"Retta's book club?" She seems impressed. "How did *you* get in?"

"I do own a bookstore and love to read, you know."

"Oh, you're letting them meet there? They don't let new folks in, you know."

"I know. I know. But listen, I've got to go. Have fun painting."

"Wait! Don't hang up. Seriously, I miss talking to you. Laney still isn't talking to me, and Mother is stuck in mother-mode, which is no fun. Come out to the Lake Park tomorrow for lunch. It's gorgeous with all the leaves turned right now. I'll bring lunch. Okay? Noon?"

I sigh to myself. "Okay. Sounds nice. See you then." We hang up, and I lay my phone on the kitchen table before walking into the living room. I also turn off the ringer. "Hey kids. Movie over?"

Will stretches and rolls over on the floor in front of the television. He has books spread in front of him and a pen in his hand. "Mom, can I use your van tomorrow?"

"Why?"

"Anna and I are going to buy some baby stuff when I get out of class."

I sit on the end of the couch. "Sure. What do you think you'll need? Should you get a portable crib for here?"

He puts his arms behind his head and nods. "Probably a good idea." He keeps his eyes focused on me and waits.

"You're waiting for me to mention you moving back to the basement, aren't you?"

His grin is so much like his father's, that it brings a grin to my face. He says, "Only if *you* want to talk about it. Colt is officially moved out and into the apartment with Phoenix."

Bryan looks up from his notebook he's writing in. "Who? I thought his girlfriend was Rebecca."

I groan. "Please tell me she's not going back to being called Phoenix."

Will's grin is enhanced with a shrug from his prone position on the floor.

"Erghhh," Savannah growls as she stands up from her end of the couch. "I'm trying to read here!" Holding the same book as earlier, she picks up her phone, a half-empty bag of microwave popcorn, and a bottle of water. "I'm going upstairs."

"How's the paper coming along?" I ask. Maybe that's not very supportive, but she's the one who was reading while watching a movie.

Above her stomping up the stairs, she shouts, "With all the noise in this house, who knows if I'll ever get it written." She's completely disgusted and glad to let us all know.

When I look back at Bryan and Will, they're grinning. Bryan singsongs, "Good luck, Savannah. Let me know if you need any help."

The slamming of the door to her third-floor room is his only answer. The boys start laughing.

"What's so funny?" I ask.

"She's reading *To Kill a Mockingbird*. How can she *still* be reading that?" Will says as he sits up. "She was so ticked off when she found out Bryan and I have both already read it. It's like the best book out there, and she hates it."

"You've read it, too?" I ask, looking at my youngest.

Bryan nods. "Brittani read it last year and told me to read it."

Let's ignore the fact that his ex-girlfriend told him what to do and he did it. I shake my head a bit to forget that part, then say, "I don't think I've ever heard of anyone who didn't *like To Kill a Mocking Bird*. I kept thinking it would click with her and she'd start liking it."

Bryan fold his legs under himself as he shares his fourteen-year-old wisdom. "Girls don't like to be told what to do. That's the secret to mine and Brittani's relationship. I never tell her what to do." He goes back to his homework while Will and I share an eye roll.

Wait… he and Brittani are back together?

CHAPTER 4

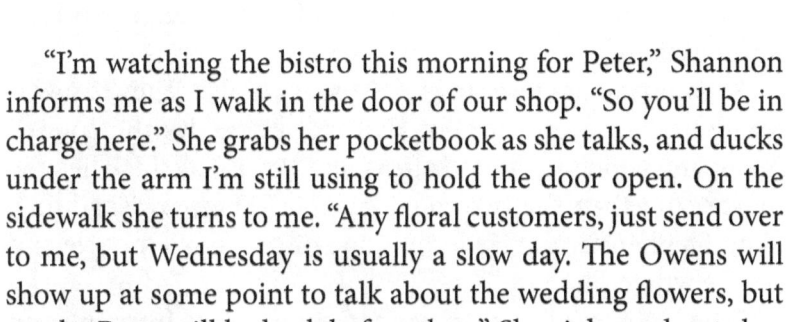

"I'm watching the bistro this morning for Peter," Shannon informs me as I walk in the door of our shop. "So you'll be in charge here." She grabs her pocketbook as she talks, and ducks under the arm I'm still using to hold the door open. On the sidewalk she turns to me. "Any floral customers, just send over to me, but Wednesday is usually a slow day. The Owens will show up at some point to talk about the wedding flowers, but maybe Peter will be back before then." She sighs and puts her hands on her hips. "Don't get all caught up in some book and forget to talk to the customers, okay? Sure would feel better is Bonnie was here this morning."

"I'll be fine, Shannon," I say. "That only happened once."

With another sigh/huff combination, she flounces around, her brightly patterned skirt flaring around her legs and boots. Cute boots. Not the little fairy slippers in fanciful colors she used to wear. Living with Peter is definitely improving her fashion sense. Pushing on the door, I step out onto the sidewalk and shout after her. "Where is Peter? He's okay, isn't he?"

She steps to the bistro door and puts the key in, but before she turns it, she scurries back in my direction. As she approaches me, she puts one hand over her mouth, only slightly moving it to let her words out. "You can't say anything. Anything at all. To anyone, okay?" When I nod, she takes a deep breath, and her hand can't hide her smile. "A movie. There's going to be a movie made right here! You know how Peter took Griffin's spot on the city council? He's meeting with the film people this morning!" She nods her head towards the end of the street at Missus' house.

I look where she indicates. "Who? Movie people? Where?" Nothing looks different to me. Missus' big old antebellum house sits in stately shades of gray, white, and salmon. Next door to Gertie's home and Andy's Place sitting in stately shades of acid green, dark purple, and neon orange. Nothing unusual there.

Shannon steps closer to me. "Missus's house. They're meeting there so no one at City Hall will know. It's the council members, which includes Missus and Peter, Jed since he's the mayor, and then the two movie people." She scowls, adding, "And Stephen Cross. He knows one of the movie people and set the whole thing up."

"Hey! Where's Peter?" a woman shouts at us from in front of the bistro. "He left his keys hanging in the door."

Shannon whirls halfway around and shouts back, "Be right there!" Then to me she says, "Nothing to no one, right? It's all so exciting." Then she rushes back down the sidewalk, making apologies to Peter's first customer of the day.

It's a quiet morning, as usual, and I turn to look around and take a calming breath before getting to work. I like opening the store. It's the quietest part of the day and lets Bonnie have breakfast with her retired husband before he heads off to the golf course.

Very few leaves have fallen in the square, but we're closing in on peak leaf color. We've not had a frost yet, so while the flowerbeds around the gazebo look tired, they are still pushing out blooms. Of course there are the new bunches of fake flowers in Ruby's window boxes, which look as fresh as ever. They still will even with a coating of ice and snow. Our line of stores on this side of the square are all old, dark-red brick, and then there's the line of antebellum homes at the end of Main Street leading to the library at the other corner. The gray stone of the library forms a backdrop for the square and makes the red, orange, and yellow leaves stand out even more. Chancey sits on a long curve in the railroad, which forms the last boundary of the town center. We are sitting in the foothills of the Smokey Mountains, so in each direction mountains form a frame. A colorful frame this time of year.

Yes, I could see a movie being filmed here.

With a chuckle, I step inside and let the heavy door close behind me. Yes, I could definitely see a movie being made here—except the movie people haven't met Missus yet.

"Took all of ten minutes for the first person to call about the movie," I tell Jackson on our own late-morning phone call. "And every single person—including your daughter, who texted me from class—said not to tell anyone! It's a huge secret! Bonnie got here a bit ago, and she knew all about it, too. But I've got to go. I'm meeting Susan for lunch out at the lake."

"Good luck with that. Did I tell you Griffin wants to get together with us sometime?"

"What? No, honey, we cannot get dragged into the middle of this divorce or separation, whatever it is. Hopefully they'll work things out and get back together, but until then..."

"Until then I just ignore a friend? I didn't say anything when you invited Susan to dinner after church on Sunday."

"But we always do that," I protest. "It wasn't like we were picking sides."

"Exactly. It would be the same if we went out with Griffin, right?"

I say, "Right," but I don't mean it. "I better go. I'll keep you updated on the movie stuff. Love you."

We hang up. Bonnie stands at the counter looking at me, one eyebrow raised. "Men just don't get it."

I spin my phone in my hand. "We've never had close friends divorce. His parents' divorce hasn't caused much friction for Jackson because his dad was messing around with Shelby, and we still have their wedding to deal with, but his mother is so happy at the beach. There's no real competition or hate between them. Other divorces were people one of us knew, so again, there was no competition or dividing of loyalties." I step around the counter and pull out my purse. "And then there's the kids. Bryan is best friends with Grant, and Grant wants to stay with his dad." I growl and shake my head. "It's just a mess."

Both of Bonnie's eyebrows jump. She straightens her hip. "Uh-oh. Looks like the mess has found you." Her wide eyes leave the windows and alert me to look in that direction. Which I do, just as our front door flings open.

"You are not going out to lunch with my sister! Right? Tell me I'm right," Laney Conner demands as she explodes into the store.

Move to a small town, they said. It'll be fun, they said.

Before I can even lock eyes with Bonnie, she's turned and walking to the back. She doesn't excuse herself or lie about needing to do anything. She just leaves me staring at her back as she hurries to the exit. What she's going to do in the back alley is beyond me. I mean, wouldn't you have just gone to the other side of the store so you could listen in?

I whirl around. "Laney. Hi! What was that?"

Her eyes dart to my purse on my shoulder. They move to my face and narrow to accusatory slits. "Going to lunch? With my sister?"

"What if I am? She's still my friend. Maybe she needs someone to talk to."

Laney throws both hands up in the air. "Exactly! Like her husband! That's who she should be having lunch with. Not crying and moaning to me or to you. We have to work together if we're going to help them." Lowering her arms causes her shoulders to sink, and her whole face follows. Of course she's fully made up and her hair is perfect, but through the makeup, her eyes are red, puffy, and tired. Her lip liner is still in place, but she's chewed off her bright red lipstick. Matter of fact, she's doing it at this very moment. In the few moments it's taken for me to examine her, she's slumped even more. Now her eyes are filling with fresh tears. Laney walks toward me and then rests both palms on the counter, then rests her weight on them.

"I'm just so tired," she says. "Cayden is back to getting up three times a night, and I'm too old to do this. And my sister cannot be getting a divorce. She and Griffin are who we all look to as examples. That's what a marriage is supposed to look like. I won't accept it. Mother is devastated. She might be crying more than Cayden these days. And Susan? Why, Susan's as happy as a pig in slop!" She collapses her arms so that her elbows rest on the counter. Soon, she's a Laney-shaped lump, with her head slumped on her crossed arms.

I pat her back, though I take a peek at my watch. I'm going to be late meeting Susan. We stand like that for a few minutes, then Laney rises up. "Think I nodded off there for a moment." She straightens and steps back. "Go to lunch. See if you can talk some sense into her." She begins walking toward the back of the store. "I'll tell Bonnie the coast is clear." Over her shoulder she says to me, "Oh, did you hear about the movie?"

"Yes. Me and everyone else in town apparently. Some secret. Speaking of secrets, not that it actually was one, but how did you know I was going to lunch with Susan today?"

Laney turns around, and I see her beauty queen smile for

the first time today. "Everyone knows everything you do. Remember when Missus synced all our calendars on our phones for the Desserts Festival? Well, you never un-synced yours, so…" She shrugs and laughs. "Oh, yeah," she says loudly as she continues toward the back door. "Everyone can't wait to hear how that nude leotard works out Friday night."

Chapter 5

"Sorry I'm late. I had to fix my calendar," I say as I sit down at the picnic table and swing my legs over the bench.

"About time! Why in the world would you put that you were buying a nude leotard on your calendar?" Susan pauses and reconsiders. "Now that I think about it, Missus did have those communal shopping lists. I need to make sure I'm unlinked from her on everything."

"Who knew a smartphone could be so dangerous in the wrong hands?" I say. I take in the spread. "This looks delicious. Chicken salad?"

"Yes. One of my old neighbors from Laurel Cove makes delicious salads. I'm hooking her up with Peter and his store. I know he could sell her stuff in the bistro. She also makes a shrimp salad and designer deviled eggs. You know they're all the rage right now." Susan hands me a paper plate and fork, then opens and holds out a plastic container holding two big croissants. "She didn't have any deviled eggs ready this morning, so you'll have to try them another time."

"You went by her house this morning? All the way up in Laurel Cove?"

Laurel Cove is the well-to-do community up on the mountain. Gated driveways, hot tubs with mountain views, lots of stone and wood, and money. Lots and lots of money. While they have all of the possible amenities, they don't have a town, so Chancey is their own little quaint mountain town. They enjoy visiting for a day down here, but Susan will be the first in history to actually move down the mountain. *No one* moves down the mountain.

Susan shakes her head at me, but then looks at her plate. "My house here isn't ready yet. I'm still living up there. I promised Grant I'd wait until, well, that I'd wait."

"Grant still doesn't want to move?" I say this quietly. I take a bite out of my croissant to give her time and to give me a chance to think about her still living with Griffin.

"Grant doesn't understand how hard it will be without me there to take care of everything. He can't actually imagine his dad and I are really through." She tears off a small piece of her bread and rolls it between her fingers.

"He's not the only one having a rough time imagining that." A sudden gust off the lake blows over us, and we both lift our heads. I take a deep breath. "I love that smell of the lake mixed with the leaves that have fallen. Can't believe this park wasn't even here last year this time."

Susan nods and looks around. "We were all so opposed to the power company building out here, but it turned out all right, didn't it? We got a park, and I got a good job."

"But it also led to Griffin's new job, y'all moving, and now you're separating. I don't think everything turned out all right."

She shakes her head. "No one understands. Griffin and I are good together as friends, but not as a couple. We're fine living together, even now. We've not, well, it's been a long time since… I mean, we don't have what you and Jackson or Laney and Shaw have." She throws the piece of rolled-up bread off to one side and rips off another, bigger piece. "I was furious when I read that entry of yours about a nude leotard. Furious and then jealous. I want that! I want to be wanted! I want to share everything with someone. Griffin and I are so far apart, and have been for years. We put on a good front, but that's it. Grant is too young to realize what's missing. Leslie and Susie Mae, though, they know. They don't say, but they know." She shoves the piece of croissant in her mouth. Then, lifting her plastic fork, she digs into her chicken salad.

"I had no idea," I say as I reach for my bottle of water. "What changed to make you want to move out?"

She chews, then swallows. "Honestly, I was fine before we moved. Griffin was depressed, but a lot of people's lives don't turn out like they dreamed." She rolls her eyes at me and smirks. "I saw him becoming another Missus, running Chancey with an iron fist, knowing all the time he was meant to run bigger, better things. But I was fine, the kids were fine. Lots of people feel suffocated, right? They just suck it up and move on. I never thought he'd do anything about it. When the power company offered him that job, he took it without even telling me. Accepted the house, too." At my stunned look, she smiles. "Yeah, nobody knew that. I acted like I was on board with it all because what else could I do? And I really thought if we move and he's happy, maybe it will all be okay."

We both work on eating for a moment and I think back to how fast everything happened. Laney surprised us all with being pregnant around that time. Will and Anna also announced they were married and pregnant. There was Andy and Patty's wedding and then the reception right here at the lake park. Add to all that just normal living craziness, and I don't feel that bad that I didn't pick up on what Susan was going through. Plus…

"But you didn't seem unhappy in the new house," I point out.

"I wasn't at first. But even there, we just kept moving in opposite directions. Can you believe he's running for the homeowner's association up there? He wants to have dinner at the club most nights. He's golfing or playing tennis all weekend. He wants that whole life, and why shouldn't he? He's always worked hard. He was top of his class in college."

She looks around at the pine-straw-covered ground and the other picnic tables. We're alone in the park, which is a shame since it's a glorious fall day. Then she looks back at me like she's made a decision. "Can I tell you something?" She waits for my nod before saying, "I tricked him into moving to Chancey. Told him it was just until he got his master's, that I would need help with the baby while he was studying. We got pregnant with Leslie basically on our honeymoon, which was not in the plan. Well, not his plan. I was ready for babies and settling down. He thought I was on birth control, but well, I knew better, right? I was on birth control some, but…" She shrugs and sighs. "By the time he got his master's we had a house here, a toddler, another baby on the way, and I was happy. My sister had just had twins, my brother's boys were toddlers, and my parents watched all the kids any time we asked. How could he even suggest taking our children away from their cousins and grandparents? He did suggest it, often at first. But, well, you've met me."

She picks up her plate, still half full of food, and shoves it in one of the empty grocery bags. "I can't eat anymore." She doesn't look my direction, but adds, "You're awfully quiet."

"I, uh, I didn't even guess at all that," I confess sheepishly. "No idea. Jackson and I went through some of us not wanting the same thing when we moved here, and it was awful. I can't imagine doing that for years. It must've been so hard for you both."

"I guess at first it was, but then there were the kids and we were so busy. Plus, I was happy, and Griffin is one of those people who just want others to be happy. You've heard me talk about his mother and what a demanding person she is.

38

He grew up keeping her happy, so keeping me happy wasn't that difficult. It just meant *he* wasn't happy." She takes a long drink of her water, then looks me square in the eye for the first time today. "Honestly? I'm actually a little proud of him for grabbing the brass ring when it came close enough for him to grab."

"Wow, that's really something to say."

"Yeah. He and I will be fine. The kids will be, too. We'll make sure of it. Even if…" Her voice catches. "Even if Grant stays with his dad. He loves Darien Academy, and he'll miss my being around so I know I'll see him a lot. It won't be long before he's driving, and I wouldn't be surprised if he's down here every evening for supper." She laughs as she stands up. "He *is* a growing boy, and the club does not fry okra, cream handpicked corn, or make my biscuits."

We collect everything from the table, then I stand up, too, saying, "You need to tell all of this to Laney. She doesn't understand. Plus, she's so tired from having a five-month-old."

"I know, but I'm not sure I can make her understand. She and Shaw never even entertained the thought of moving away. They came home from their honeymoon to Shaw's grandparents' house and have lived there ever since." She turns to walk up toward the pavilion and her office.

"I'm going to walk by the lake for a minute," I say as I reach out for her empty hand, "but I do want to thank you for talking to me. I think I understand. It still makes me sad, so sad, but…" I shrug and then we move together for a hug.

We part and start in opposite directions, but then she turns and asks, "Did you hear they're shooting a movie in Chancey?"

I laugh. "Of course."

She turns back around, dead serious. "Well, don't tell anyone. It's a secret."

CHAPTER 6

"Why in God's good name are you working in your stocking feet?" Missus says as soon as she walks in our store. She's wearing a blue suit in a subtle plaid. Her blouse is also blue, and it makes her silver hair appear blue. She's thinner since FM's death a month ago, so her blazers look even more boxy than usual.

"My loafers were muddy, and I'm not going to be here but for a minute."

She marches to one of the high-back chairs and points to the couch next to her. "Sit here. I need to talk to you. You've apparently disconnected your phone calendar from mine for some unknown reason. Was it a mistake? Do you need me to fix your phone?"

"No," I blurt out. "It was a mistake still having it connected!"

She waves her hand, half beckoning me to her, half dismissing my bizarre need for privacy. "Whatever. It was much easier when I knew where to find you."

Bonnie mumbles as she passes me. "Kind of like belling a cat."

Missus clears her throat, then says, "Sit, Carolina. Unless

you have some important thing to rush off to which wasn't on your calendar as of this morning."

Plopping onto the arm of the couch, I keep my back straight and my chin up. "What?"

She has to tip her head upward and to the side to see me. "Your shoes became muddy at the lake, I assume? How is Susan? Has she come to her senses?"

"Susan's fine. What do you want?"

"I have a business proposition for you. For Shannon also, I suppose, but I know she's still at the bistro with Peter. Since that girl has moved in with my son she's got an air of superiority that is a mite off-putting. You should mention that to her. For goodness' sake, sit down here like a normal businessperson and not some shoeless waif that doesn't know how to act in public!"

It's business, plus I completely agree about Shannon's air of superiority, so I slide down onto the couch.

"There. That's better. I'm assuming you have heard we are to be hosting a movie crew here in Chancey."

"Yes, of course."

"Good. Sometimes you get preoccupied with whatever nonsense is going on your mind, and things get past you. However, this is very important for our town. It's the fourth in a made-for-TV series of movies, like those on that Hallmark Channel. So there could be future filming here They were all set to start filming over in Welling until they had a measles outbreak. The lead actress, whose name I can't say right now—"

"Can't say because you don't know or can't say because she's a big actress and it's a secret?" I can't help it; this is really exciting.

"I, uh, I just can't say at this moment," she says, without a look of I-know-something-you-don't-know.

I sigh and sit back. That means she doesn't know of or has never heard of the actress.

Missus blinks at me. She's not used to being interrupted, so I help her get back on track. "You were saying there's a measles outbreak over in Welling."

"Yes, and the lead actress has young children, unvaccinated young children, who will be visiting the set, so they needed a new location immediately. Stephen Cross knows one of the producers and brought them here over the past weekend. This morning we signed all the paperwork. You'll be happy to hear that your store was one of the deciding factors."

"My store? Why?"

"They need a bookshop to film some scenes in. I told them you'd be happy to work with them. And don't worry, they pay rather handsomely, as I found out when I offered them my house to use."

I'm already on board. "What will we need to do? What about the florist area? Shannon has several big weddings coming up."

Once again, she waves her hand. "Peter is handling that as we speak. That's how I knew she wasn't here. This is a grand opportunity for our town, and we must do everything possible to see it through to a successful conclusion." She stands up, smoothing her skirt down. Clasping her gloved hands, she looks down at me. "It might be a bit crowded for you at times, but it will all be for the good of the town, right?" She doesn't wait to see if I nod before she turns and heads for the door.

Bonnie comes up to the sitting area as I stand. She waits until the door closes behind Missus, then grabs my arm. "This is exciting! Filming right here? In our store! I wonder what kind of movie it is."

"I don't know, but I don't believe it'll get crowded in here like Missus said, do you? Look at all the open space in the back of the store. We can move the shelves apart and back some if we really need to."

The bell over the door alerts us to look as Shannon comes bustling in. "Did Missus tell you? Filming right here in our store! Peter hopes they'll want to use the bistro at some point, but so far they just want to use our place, Missus' home, the Methodist church, and the Piggly Wiggly. Guess they are also looking for a restaurant near here." She holds up a hand. "But no one is supposed to tell Ruby. They don't think her place will work out." She puts her hands on her hips and looks around her side of the shop. "I'll need to do a lot of the floral work somewhere else, but apparently I'll be paid plenty for my trouble."

I jump as I realize the time. I head toward the back to collect my muddy loafers. "Oh, I need to go. I need to stop by the store, and I have sheets to change at the B&B. Strange to have reservations on a Wednesday night." Then it hits me. "Maybe they're movie people! The party made their reservation on Sunday night!"

Shannon squeals. "Oh, how long did they make the reservation for?"

"Just a couple nights because we're full this weekend. We are full on the weekends all through the fall. They said just Wednesday and Thursday nights were fine." I say all this as I step outside and bang my shoes together to knock off some more of the dried mud. Stepping back inside, I set my shoes down and slide my feet into them. "Now I'm excited to get home and see who shows up!"

Shannon is standing near the counter, freshening up one of the arrangements she'd pulled from the cooler. "Wait, take this with you. It won't last past tomorrow, but it'll be nice when they get to the B&B tonight." As I take the arrangement, she wipes her hands and says, "Carolina, you don't seem very worried about being crowded."

"No, I'm not worried. This space is so big. We rarely even use the back, and Patty and Andy can use the back door to come and go to their apartment." I step back, hands full, so that Bonnie can open the heavy glass door for me.

As I step onto the sidewalk and turn toward the store, I notice a small smile on Shannon's face. "Missus wasn't talking about the store being crowded. She was talking about your house. Her house is going to be a main focus of the filming, so she and Anna are moving in with you."

I'm still staring at Shannon when the door slowly shuts between us.

So.

It's going to be a horror film.

CHAPTER 7

Jackson is preoccupied. I know he has this job thing, but seriously, this is the most important thing in our lives right now and he needs to be paying attention to me! I shift my hips, standing against the minivan I'd just parked in our drive when he finally answered my call. All right. My *calls*.

"Okay. I'm back," he says. "But just for a minute, honey. These inspectors can't be kept waiting. We were lucky to get them out here on the site today, so we can move forward before cutting out for the weekend. Having to pour that concrete again was nearly a disaster—"

"If you only have a minute, then quit talking about all that. Missus and Anna are moving in here while the movie is filming. Did you hear me?"

"Yes. I heard you. What do you want me to do about it?" he snaps at me.

"Don't snap at me! Missus. Living in our house. And Anna. Will's pregnant, estranged wife. In our house."

"For how long?" His calm I'm-being-rational-while-you're-on-the-crazy-train tone is worse than him snapping at me.

"I don't know."

"So it could be only for a couple days?"

"I didn't get that feeling."

Jackson pauses for a moment before asking, "Is Will okay with Anna moving in?"

"I don't know."

"Well, maybe this will help them get back together."

Hmmm. Maybe I was a bit on the crazy train. "That's a thought. Okay, I'll let you go."

"You sure you're okay?" He laughs.

"I'm sure. We'll talk tonight. I had a long talk with Susan today that I have to tell you about."

"All right. I better go. They're looking my direction."

"Okay. Love you and good luck with the inspections."

"Love you and good luck with Hollywood South."

I hang up my phone, throw it in my purse, then actually look around me.

Only a third of the leaves on the large maple next to our house are still green. At the top, orange has taken over, and in the afternoon sunshine they practically gleam. In the autumn light, the white of the house looks brighter than it is, and everything has a touch of gold. Along the edge of the woods, a collar of goldenrod is fluffed full beneath the tall, dark-green pines, and as the sun hits it, it also touches the red sumac and makes it come afire. Across the river, the hills are turning, but the mild days have left even the dead leaves in place, so there aren't the empty spots, which will appear later, after we have more storms.

Yes, it's near perfect today, but I have movie people to get ready for. Maybe. It may be just regular ol' people, but they deserve clean sheets, too.

"I don't know," I whisper into my phone as the doorbell

rings. Speaking up over Bonnie's groan in my ear, I say, "Someone's at the door. I'll text you if I find out anything."

As I walk toward the front door, I glance down the hall where, in two of our three rooms, our new guests are unpacking. Through the screen door I see our mayor, Jed Taylor, beaming at me with a huge basket in his arms.

I open the door and am back to whispering. "Jed, I don't know if they're from the movie."

He frowns, his big, round face topped with slicked-down red hair reminding me of a sad Mr. Kool-Aid. "Well, I have to sit this down somewhere. It's heavy." He bustles past me and into the kitchen, where he sits the basket on our kitchen table and drops himself into one of the chairs. His whisper is gruff and not that quiet. "How can we not know if they are with the movie? What did they say when you asked them?"

Jed is younger than me by ten years. He is universally liked because he's kind, doesn't boss everyone around, and genuinely likes Chancey. He also has a really nice wife and kids, so he's generally a happy guy, but not today.

As I answer, I turn away to get him some water. "I couldn't just come out and ask something like that. They came in, I showed them the rooms, that's all. Here. Drink this. You look hot."

"I am hot. I ran all over town getting donations for this basket, got Shannon to wrap it up like this, then came up here as fast as I could, and now you don't even know if they are with the movie." He takes a long drink of water and then sputters it when the front door is thrown open and Laney shouts, "Hey y'all!"

Jed whirls around, almost falling out of his chair. With a sigh, I step to the doorway between the living room and the kitchen. "We're in here."

"Everyone?" Laney asks as she sashays our way.

47

I don't think she means Jed. "No, not everyone," I snarl. "Hush! They're in their rooms."

Her eyes dart down the hall, but she adjusts her smile and pushes past me into the kitchen. "Hey, Jed. Oh, look at that basket. I bet you about worked your poor ol' self into a heat stroke gathering up all those goodies. Has she introduced you to our guests yet?"

"No, she hasn't." After staring at Laney, he takes a quick moment to scowl in my direction, but taking more time than that away from gazing at the beauty queen is asking too much.

Her heels are the tallest. Her hair is the biggest. Her suit is the pinkest. Her skirt is the tightest. Her silky blouse is white and enhances how white her teeth are. The lace on her bra is a shade lighter pink, and we can see that because she's leaning forward on her elbows, which are on the back of one of my kitchen chairs.

I sit in the chair across from Jed as I say, "Laney, why don't you quit posing on that chair and sit in it?"

"You don't think they'll be coming down the hall soon?"

I shake my head at her.

She moves around the chair. "Okay, but let me know if you hear them coming." She lowers herself slowly into the chair. "Oh my, I don't know if I can even sit down in this skirt. There's tight and then there's 'five months after having a baby' tight." She kicks off her heels under the table. "And who knew you could forget how to walk in heels?" She sighs and leans back so she can get her breath. "But the baby thing does make my boobs look even better." She looks at our mayor. "Don't you think so, Jed?"

Poor Jed's mouth falls open, and he is once again sputtering water. "Oh, oh, I have to go. Maybe I could go knock on their doors? Introduce myself?" He stands, purposely not looking at Laney.

"You could," I say. "But what will you say if they're not with the movie? That's what I couldn't find a way around. Don't want to insult anyone just because they're regular people like us."

"Speak for yourself," Laney says with a snarky look at me. She then adds, "However, I know for a fact that they are definitely from the movie because I googled their names. I do all the computer work for the B&B, so I just looked up their reservations. One is a producer and investor type. The other does a lot of directing and filming."

"Oh," I say. "I didn't think of googling them. Shoot. Now I'm getting nervous. I'd convinced myself they weren't the movie people."

Jed stands up. "Then I definitely believe I should go welcome them."

Before he can, we hear the doors open down the hall. Laney and I jump up, and Jed picks up the heavy basket. The two men are deep in conversation as they walk down the hall into the dining room. Jed's hearty "Welcome to Chancey!" startles us all.

Both men look to be in their mid to late thirties. As a matter of fact, they look a lot alike. They are about the same size, for one thing. Both have their hair cut short on the sides, but longish on top, and sport closely shorn beards. They are attractive in a very cool way, and the only way I could remember who was who earlier is that one has a lot of tattoos and one doesn't. Lucky for me the one with the tattoos is Tyler. T for tattoo, T for Tyler. I step forward. "Tyler. Leif. This is our Mayor Jed Taylor and one of our partners in the B&B, Laney Conner."

Jed sits the basket back down to shake their hands, and Laney waits for a clear path to them. When Jed moves to pick the basket back up, she moves in and it's like Scarlett O'Hara is welcoming them herself. It was over the top, of course, but didn't take long. However, when Laney finally steps back, she looks like a rain cloud getting ready to burst. These men deal with actresses all the time, and one more décolletage in a tight pink suit doesn't appear to phase them. Laney's not used to un-phased men when she's pulled out all the stops.

Tyler peeks into the basket. "This is quite a haul. Thank you, Mr. Mayor."

"Oh, call me, Jed. We'll be working closely together, I'm sure. There's some wine and sparkling water. Lots of little munchies along with maps and flyers about the attractions in the area. We just want you to know we are thrilled you're here!"

Laney has moved around to the other side of the table. She leans on the back of the chair like she did earlier. No one, not even Jed, looks her way. I frown at her with my eyes and tight mouth to try to get her to straighten up and quit acting like a spoiled brat.

Leif, I see now, has lighter hair, and his beard, which really just looks like five o'clock shadow has a golden tint. His eyes are a light blue, unlike Tyler's dark ones. They don't look that much alike now that I'm really looking. Guess I was just excited earlier. Leif reaches into the basket, which Jed sat back on the table, and pulls out the maps and flyers. "These will come in handy. We're going to drive around before it gets dark. Thanks," he says as he reaches out to shake Jed's hand again. Then he looks at Laney, nods, and says, "Nice to meet you, too."

Laney beams. "I've lived here my whole life. Just let me know if you need any help with anything." She's answered with another nod and a wave as the two men walk into the living room. She frowns and then pushes Jed and me ahead of her to follow them. Then she says loudly, "Are y'all going to be needing any extras?"

Tyler stops and turns around. He grins when he realizes we are all three right behind him. "Yes, we will. It always makes a set seem more realistic if we have some of the actual people from the area involved." He tips his head and smiles at Laney. "You'd be a lovely addition to any set. Be sure and come around."

Back in the limelight as she fully intended to be, Laney preens. "Oh, that's so nice of you to say."

I'm a bit behind her, so when I roll my eyes, Tyler and Leif both catch me. But no worries, their grins could *only* be because of the hidden Southern beauty they'd found in Laney.

Just ask her, I'm sure she'll tell you.

CHAPTER 8

Jed and Laney left soon after Tyler and Leif, both with stars in their eyes. Jed had invited the two men to Ruby's for muffins and a tour of town hall tomorrow morning, and they'd been *very* enthusiastic in their acceptance. Although most folks here like Jed, he doesn't get a lot of admiration or respect. I think our movie guys might have picked up on that and realized it was a small price to pay for keys to the kingdom. As for Laney, she was already busy rehearsing her Oscar acceptance speech. Seriously. She got into her big SUV muttering, "Thanks to the Academy and all the little people."

With a half-hour before the kids come home, I grab an apple and my book and settle in one of the front porch rockers. The back deck gets chilly in the shadows, but the sun keeps the front of the house warm. I quickly immerse myself in my latest cozy mystery, and everything swirling in my head falls to the side. The heroine in my book is alone in a dark warehouse parking lot, hiding from the killer, so it's hard to focus on my own little problems when so much is at stake.

I'm so absorbed in the plot that when Savannah's car bounces over the railroad tracks, my heart catches and I gasp. (And not because the way she hits the tracks isn't good for the car and she's been told and told about it. It makes me eager for the days when it'll *her* car and *her* repair bills. I have the feeling I might be a vindictive old lady, but if that happens, it'll be the kids fault.)

I take a shaky breath and mark my place in the novel. The kids are home earlier than usual. It seems every other Wednesday they get an early release day.

Wednesdays are church night in the South. Used to be that no one had any sports or school activities on Wednesday nights. Now, that's more relegated to small towns in the South like Chancey. We don't really participate in the Wednesday night activities at church, but I like having the night free for the kids, when I actually remember it.

Savannah parks, and I can already see she has a car full of kids. Bryan crawls out of the back seat along with two of his sister's friends. In the front seat with Savannah is a surprise. Susie Mae, Susan's daughter, jumps out and runs around to where Savannah has just slammed the driver's door. As they walk up the sidewalk, Susie Mae is on Savannah's hip, whispering with her like they are best friends, which, last time I checked, they are not.

"Hey," I say to all of them.

"Hey, Mrs. Jessup. What are you doing out here?" Susie Mae asks as she skips up the porch steps ahead of the others and sits in the rocker next to me.

"Just reading. What are y'all up to?" I speak to Susie Mae, but shoot a quick glare at my daughter. Savannah's eyes open wide in innocence before she gives me a small eye roll to say she's appalled at how I don't appear to trust her.

"We're planning senior night, and I'm the junior representative for the cheerleaders. Whatcha reading?" Susie Mae is tiny with big eyes framed by a short-shag haircut. Behind her, Savannah and her friends walk on into the house. Bryan parks himself in one of the rockers on the end of the porch near the sidewalk. Savannah's friends wave and smile at me as they follow her in, but clearly they know who the boss is.

"It's just a mystery, set around Halloween. I like seasonal mysteries. Do you like reading?" She's taken the book from me and is reading the back cover. She's already shown, like, a million percent more interest in a book that I'm reading than any of my kids ever have.

"I bet I would if I read books like this. That sounds interesting. I don't think I've ever read a mystery." She scrunches up her nose, sits back in the rocker, and sets it in motion.

I can't believe that. "Not even Nancy Drew?"

"Nope. Can I borrow that when you finish?"

"Of course, but it's not the first in the series. I have that one at the shop. Why don't I get that for you? I think you'll like it."

"Okay." She rocks and looks around. "It's nice out here."

Bryan slides me a look from his end of the porch. He follows it up with a shrug like he can't figure out why Susie Mae is still out here either.

All three of us rock for a few minutes. Then Susie Mae stops her chair and scoots up to sit on the edge of it. "Guess I better go inside." She stands, then turns to face me. "Will you be in the shop tomorrow?"

"Um, Thursday? Yes, just before lunch until three or so."

"Perfect. I'll come see you—you know, to get that book—at lunchtime. Juniors get to leave campus at lunch."

She swings into the front door, and we can hear her pound up the stairs leading to the second floor and to Savannah's tower room beyond.

"That was weird," Bryan says.

I agree with a nod. "So, what's up with you?"

Lugging his book bag, he comes to the chair vacated by Susie Mae and sits down. "Can I camp out down at the lake this weekend?"

"What lake? The lake park?"

"No. Our lake. Guess I meant the river. There's a big, empty area over near the bridges by the water."

"I guess. Just you?"

"And some of the guys," he says.

"Which guys?"

"John, Brendan, Kyle, and me."

"No Grant?"

He leans over and lifts his backpack to his knees. "Grant's over us." He looks at me. "Seriously. That what he said. He's over us."

I wince. "He's really going to live with his dad up in Laurel Cove when his mom moves down here?"

Bryan sighs and then stands up, hauling his backpack over one shoulder. "Yeah, I guess. He's shooting to make the golf team at Darien, so that's all he has time for."

"I'm sorry. That stinks."

"Whatever. What are we having for dinner?"

"Spaghetti and garlic bread. I'm making lots, so if any of your friends are around…"

He nods. He just looks so sad. Grant and he hit it off quick when we moved here. It's hard making new friends at any age.

Halfway in the door, he leans back out. "Brittani will be here soon, so I'll tell her she can stay for dinner." He heads on in the house looking much happier.

Shoot. I fell for the sad teenage boy thing again. Guess it's a good thing I didn't date that much in high school. Apparently all it takes is sad eyes and some sighs to soften me up.

"Sure there's enough," I say, "but I've got to warn you, it's just sauce out of a jar."

When I heard Leif and Tyler come into the living room

from outside, I left the kitchen where I was finishing dinner to greet them. Mom-sense said the young men looked hungry, so I'd invited them to join us, with my standard lecture on the difference between home-cooked and homemade.

Tyler grins and says, "Jar sauce... just like my mom used to make! But we really don't want to impose. We were going to head back out toward the interstate and grab something to eat. I just needed to come back here and change my jeans. I slid down into a ditch and came in close contact with some of your famous red Georgia clay." He turns around, and I see that the back of his jeans are caked in red. "I've tried to brush it off so I don't get it all over the room, but it doesn't seem to want to brush anywhere."

I laugh and shake my head. "Nope, it's not going anywhere. When you take them off, bring them to me. I'll put them in some water to soak and then run them through the wash. I have some of our jeans to wash anyway."

"Oh, no. You don't need to do that. Feed us *and* do our laundry? We may not ever leave," Tyler says as he raises his eyebrows at Leif, who grins. Right on cue, Leif's stomach rumbles, and they both laugh. "Seriously, you don't have to—"

"Hush," I say. "Go change. We're eating in about ten minutes."

They both head down the B&B hall, and I return to the kitchen. Pulling open the freezer door, I reach in and bring out the extra-large bag of frozen meatballs I'd opened only a little while ago. I fill a dinner plate with the frozen balls and pop it into the microwave. In only a minute they are thawed, and already being fully cooked, they go straight into the big pot of sauce on the stove.

I'll boil another pot of spaghetti noodles while we eat the first batch and make another sheet of garlic bread from the freezer, while we eat the hot pieces I just put into a basket. The salad is already waiting in the fridge in the big bowl and ready for the table. I don't have any extra salad ingredients, so that'll have to do.

Besides, filling up young people on salad is a modern urban fantasy.

It can't be done.

Chapter 9

"You did *not* tell me there was a movie of *To Kill a Mocking-bird*," Savannah says for the nine hundredth time since dinner last night. She's sitting at the kitchen table eating cereal, and I'm getting my first cup of coffee.

"That's right. I want you to fail senior English so you never leave. Just stay here with me for the rest of your life trying to finish that book." I roll my eyes. "I'm going out on the deck."

It's chilly out here, but it's quiet. Dinner was crazier than usual last night. With their many movie stories, Tyler and Leif were the center of attention. At first Brittani and Savannah were full on drama trying to impress our guests, but then they relaxed. Will came in while we were eating and, as older siblings will do, let it drop that Savannah hadn't even finished her summer reading. That led Tyler to say that *To Kill a Mocking-bird* was his all-time favorite movie and that he'd actually been in a performance of it in a summer theatre outside of Chicago a few years back.

Savannah heard that, and the accusations of our intentionally keeping her in the dark began. The meal got louder the longer it lasted until I finally sent them all out to walk on the bridge while I cleaned up. Tyler and Leif opposed that idea, wanting to help clean, but I finally convinced them that I could use the peace and quiet.

Hence, tonight we are having a showing of *To Kill a Mockingbird*. Will went online and found out that his college has it on DVD. In my defense, I did at one point toward the end of the summer tell Savannah there was a movie, but I didn't push it because I was afraid she'd never finish the book. Now, I'm way beyond caring about that.

Heavy dew still coats the outdoor cushions, so I stand at the railing and breath in the damp, chilly air. When the door behind me opens, I look back and smile at Tyler's questioning look. "You're fine. You're not bothering me."

He shivers as he comes to stand beside me, cupping both hands around his own steaming cup of coffee. "Should've put on a coat. Didn't think it'd be this cold out here."

"There's a coatrack full of jackets inside the office down the B&B hall. Feel free to use one of Jackson's or Will's."

"Thanks." He bends his head sideways to look at me. "And thanks for last night. We really enjoyed it. Makes me wish I was going to be on this shoot with Leif more."

"Oh, you won't be here?"

"Not much. I'm more on the production and administration side, so I spend a lot of time in the office in Atlanta. The sudden change in shooting location is what got me up here at all. It's been a good reminder of why we started shooting in small towns. It's fun to get to really know the people. My girlfriend has some time off later this month, and I'd love to bring her up here. Do you have any rooms open the later this fall?"

"Not on the weekends, but midweek, sure."

"I also hear you're the bookshop owner. We'll be filming there quite a bit. That's all okay with you?"

"Well... we get paid, right?" I look up at him.

"Oh, of course. I actually have all the paperwork ready for you to look at. I didn't realize it was you I needed to talk to

SECRETS ARE *Chancey*

until last night after I was back in my room. You and your partner, Ms. Chilton, run the bookshop?"

"That's Shannon. She's already on board and very excited."

"And a Ms. Samson? She's the owner?"

I shiver and groan. "Gertie." I rub my hands along my cardigan-covered arms. "Did you see Andy's Place? The brightly painted house right off the square at the end of Main Street?"

Tyler's eyes bug out of his skull. "How could I miss that? What is it, exactly?"

"It's also Gertie's. Andy is her son-in-law. You have to go inside to believe it. It's a cross between an antique store and eBay, with a moonshine cave in the basement."

He pulls back and squints at me to see if I'm joking. I shake my head at him. "I'm telling the truth. You have to see it to believe it."

Tyler reaches into the pocket of his skinny corduroy pants and pulls out his phone. "Let's see," he says as he opens his calendar. "How about one o'clock at the bookstore so I can meet Shannon, and then we can all go over to Gertie's, if she's available. I'll reach out to her this morning. I've got to see this moonshine cave."

"Sounds good to me. Now I've got to get back inside and see what the kids are up to."

As he pulls open the door, he says with a laugh, "Teenagers are a trip, aren't they? I keep thinking I want kids... and then..."

"They are not for the weak of heart," I say, just as a chorus of "Mom!" greets us.

And I do not mean "greets" in a good way.

CHAPTER 10

What's that saying? Two wrongs don't make a right? Well, we're about to see what two "Yeses" make. In the twenty minutes of quiet after everyone left the house this morning, I got all my housework—okay, *some* of my housework—done. I wiped the kitchen table of cereal bowl rings and muffin crumbs and poured myself another cup of coffee before looking through my phone. That's when the first text came through. Susan wanted to meet at Ruby's. Before I could answer that another text popped up. Laney wanted to meet at Ruby's. Hmm…

I responded only "yes" to both, got dressed, and now I'm almost there. I only have about thirty minutes before I need to get to the grocery store so I have time to take the groceries home and get back to the shop by noon. I park across from the downtown shops of Chancey, and then I get out and take in a deep sniff of the dying leaves in the square. With a turn, I scan to see if either Susan or Laney are in view yet. Nope. Good, maybe I beat them here.

I pull open Ruby's door, and a blast of warmth and deliciousness greets me. Ruby's looks like a throwback to a couple of decades ago. Maybe more than just a couple decades, now that I think about it. There's chrome and fake leather seats and sparkle-encrusted laminate tables which harken back to a *Happy Days* version of the fifties, even if the cheap blonde paneling and glass trophy cases makes me think of my childhood in the seventies.

However, the smell is all NOW. Pumpkin spice, with a touch of pumpkin spice, layered over undertones of pumpkin spice. Then I see why there's a polar vortex directed my way. Laney is seated in a booth halfway up the wall on my right, and Susan is seated in the booth in front of her. Both of them are facing the front. Both of them are facing me.

There's some low talking at a couple of the tables, but those on the stools at the back are fully turned, also looking at me. Ruby catches my eye, shakes her head, then turns back to her ovens. Libby crosses the middle of the restaurant with a half-full coffee pot. She gives me a sick smile as she goes. Okay, I should've thought this out a little better.

Laney raises her hand and waves at me. "Here I am, Carolina."

Susan also waves her hand, but she looks so mad she can't talk. Her tanned face is turning red, and her lips are pressed so tight together that I can't even see them. Uh-oh, what has Laney done now?

"Laney," I say. I march back toward the two sisters with my head held high and my shoulders back. I need to show them I'm not messing around. "Laney, what did you do? Your sister looks awfully mad. Let's all sit together and talk this out." I stop at Susan's table and point to the booth bench across from her. Then Susan explodes.

"Her? She's not the one that tricked me. She's just her normal obnoxious self, always thinking the world revolves around her. *You* are supposed to be my friend. My sister and I will work things out in our way. No need for you start acting like Dr. Phil!" She pushes out of the booth, causing me to jump out of her way. After a steely glare at me, she picks up her untouched muffin and shoves past me to the door. She opens it with such force that she sets the bell above it to dancing.

Guess I'll sit with Laney then.

In two steps I'm at Laney's booth. I check to make sure she's not mad at me. She rolls her eyes as she continues buttering her muffin, and with a nod motions me into the booth. "Ignore my sister. She's having some kind of mental breakdown. She'll snap out of it."

"I'm not so sure, Laney," I fret. "She's really upset. We talked yesterday, and I think she might actually know what she's doing with the divorce." I sit real still and wait. I know Laney heard me because she quit buttering her muffin. She looks up at me through squinted eyes, then moves her hand into a more solid grip on her butter knife.

"What?"

"You need to listen to her. Hear what she has to say. Oh, thanks, Libby," I say with a smile as she turns over my coffee cup, settles it into the saucer, and fills it.

Libby leans close and whispers, "Everything is pumpkin spice this morning. Ruby burnt a whole batch of chocolate muffins waiting for you to get here, and then in the stress from these two sitting here talking out loud about each other she put double, possibly triple, salt into the apple muffins. If I were you, I wouldn't look back that direction for a bit." Libby straightens up, gives me that sick smile again, and pats my shoulder.

With a small laugh I pick up a pumpkin spice muffin. "Guess it's good we both like pumpkin spice."

Laney spits. "Whatever. I really don't care, but there was no way I was leaving with *her* here. How could you make arrangements with both of us? Did it not dawn on you we were both sitting here when we texted you?"

My jaw drops. "No, not at all. Why would I think that? Why

were you both sitting here by yourselves? No wonder Ruby is in a tizzy. You texted me over thirty minutes ago."

Laney pushes her covered-in-butter pumpkin spice muffin away from her, then wipes her fingers on a napkin. "Mother tried the same thing you did. She invited both of us to meet her here without telling the other one. Mother was sitting over there at that table in the middle when I got here. When we *both* got here. We arrived at the same time, and when we came in the door we both ignored Mother and sat in our booths. That's when we began talking at each other. At some point, Mother left. I'm not sure exactly when and I'm ashamed of that."

Apparently she's had enough of her family feud because she switches to more pressing matters. "But enough about all that. Didn't I really hit it off with Tyler yesterday? Did he say anything about me? Did he say what part he has in mind for me?"

"This muffin is to die for," I say, trying to change the subject. "So moist. The perfect balance of sweetness and spice. You really should try it."

She wrinkles her nose, then tries again. "What are Tyler and Leif up to today? Did you see them this morning?"

"Anna had a doctor's appointment yesterday, and everything is coming along with great with her pregnancy. How's Cayden?"

"He's fine." She snorts. "I get it. You're not talking about the movie. Fine. I'm not talking about Susan." She puts her phone into her pocketbook and grabs her sweater as she bustles out of the booth. At the end of the row, she stops long enough to pull on her olive-green sweater. Securing her pocketbook on her shoulder, she looks at me and sticks out just a bit of her tongue. Then suddenly sunshine and innocence fill her face as her eyes lift toward the door. "Missus, so good to see you! Carolina was just saying how she hoped you'd stop by. I've got your seat all warm."

She leans and tries to kiss Missus' cheek, but Missus stiff-arms her.

"You are insane. Go calm down your hair a bit. It's big to-day even for you." She sidesteps Laney then slides in the booth across from me.

While she's doing that, I stick my tongue out at Laney. Laney gives me a simpering look as she exits the diner. I look back down, self-satisfied, until I see Missus' highly unamused face.

"Good morning, Missus," I say. "I don't have much time. I have to go grocery shopping before I come back to work at noon. I need to finish my muffin while we talk."

She stares at me. "First you hide your calendar from my phone, now you force me to listen to you drone on about all your sundry daily duties? If you want me to know everything about every minute of your day, just reconnect your calendar to mine. Obviously it would make your life easier." She doesn't look to see where Libby is. Instead, she just raises her right hand from where it was laying on the table to say she needs a new cup and needs it filled with coffee. Libby's dart to our table happens before Missus' hand can return to the Formica top. Happens every time.

"Good morning, Missus," Libby says. "Let me take Laney's cup. Either of you want that poor muffin she suffocated in but-ter? Didn't think so. Pumpkin spice is the only muffin flavor we have right now." She shifts her eyes toward me as she sighs. "We had some interference this morning."

Missus cocks her head back and I prepare for the great pumpkin spice tirade she regales us all with each autumn. However, with a little nod, Missus says, "Yes, that will do nice-ly. As a widow, I'm trying to keep my mind open and not be so judgmental. Thank you for your suggestion, Libby."

Libby backs away, fake smile pasted on to hide her confu-sion. Missus with an open mind? Missus not being judgmental? And here I was just thinking she'd gotten meaner since FM's death.

With my mouth full, I make a big show of checking the time on my watch, then smile at Missus. She's wearing a teal turtleneck sweater with gray slacks. Her matching suit coat is hung on her shoulders. It stays there, like a cape, nothing holding it together. I've tried that and usually end up dropping mine in a puddle. Hers stayed even as she slid into the booth. Maybe it has something to with her having bony shoulders.

I don't have anything bony. Everything on me is full and rounded. Whatever. Capes are a stupid look, anyway. But I always did want to wear a cape...

"Carolina," Missus says, "I'm sure by now you've heard that Anna and I will be moving into your home tomorrow—"

I nearly choke on pumpkin spice. "Tomorrow? Why so soon? They haven't even started filming in town yet."

She heaves a long-suffering sigh. "If you'd listen, I'd tell you why. Are you ready to listen? I thought you were in some sort of a time crunch."

"Okay. Sorry. I'll eat and listen."

"We are moving into your house tomorrow, but I will only be there through the weekend. Anna doesn't know—actually, no one knows that part of the arrangement." She waits for Libby to set her warm muffin in front of her and to fill her coffee cup. "Took long enough," she says. "Especially when there's only one choice in both coffee and muffin."

Libby doesn't even acknowledge her. It's better to act dumb sometimes. I need to learn that.

"So where will you be staying next week?" I ask.

She tilts her head up at my question. "Giving up on listening so quick, Carolina?" She tsks to herself, then lifts up one half of the rich brown muffin. "Where I will be is of no concern to you. However, my granddaughter, who is carrying your son's daughter, is who you should be much more concerned about.

66

I've delivered her to your doorstep, and it will be up to you to get them back together before she is meant to move out."

She takes a bite of her muffin and concentrates on chewing. After swallowing, she says, "I possibly have been mistaken. This is quite delicious." She raises her hand in beckoning, and it works yet again.

"Yes, Missus? What can I do for you?" Libby says as she comes to an abrupt stop at our table.

"Tell your boss these are very good. We'll want them for the B&B this fall." She barely lifts her hand and says, "That will be all."

"Thanks for ordering for *my* B&B," I say.

My sarcasm was wasted. "Tell me that you, you who like everything, don't think these are the perfect taste of autumn?" she asks.

"Whatever. Welcome to the bandwagon. Now tell me how I'm supposed to get Anna and Will back together."

"I could, but I refuse to do all of your thinking for you. I've set things up for you. Now are you going to help, or not?" Her eyes pierce me, and I am nodding before I can even think about it.

She nods once. "Of course you are. Now, I can't sit here with you all day. I know I have other things to do and you seem to think you do also." She puts a five-dollar bill on her saucer and slips out of the booth. Her coat only swings a bit, but stays in place.

I try to finish my coffee and last bite of muffin so I can show her just how busy I am. But the quick swig of coffee chokes me and I'm in the midst of a coughing fit as I try to also struggle out of the booth. "I'm fine. I'm fine," I croak to Libby as she comes up to pat me on the back.

Missus waits for just a minute, rolls her eyes, then swishes out the door. Libby pushes down on my shoulder. "Hon, sit right back down here for a minute. You've had a hard morning." She laughs a bit as she starts cleaning up our table. "Most folks like to ease into their mornings, but you, Carolina, you jump in with both feet. With Susan, Laney, and Missus for friends…"

"I know. I don't need enemies."

"No, hon. I was going to say with them three for friends, you need to look for some new friends, but what you said is probably true, too."

CHAPTER 11

"I'm here!" I yell as I come in the front door of Blooming Books. "Bonnie? Shannon?" It's just before noon, and there's no one to see that I got everything done and am here just as I said I would be. Stepping farther into the empty shop, I say "Hello?" again.

Pounding steps on the back stairway catch my attention. "Carolina! Oh, it's you," Andy says as he slows his pace. At the bottom of the stairs that lead to his apartment, he stops to take a breath. "I just went upstairs for a minute. Just one minute, and of course that's when you'd come in and catch me. I really don't like to use strange bathrooms, and with ours just upstairs, well, you know..."

"Where's Bonnie and Shannon?" I ask, as much to cut off his TMI train of thought as for any other reason. I check the counter to make sure the cash register is still closed. He says he was only gone a minute, but who knows how long he left the store wide open.

He comes over and flops onto the couch. He's a big guy, and when he flops, the couch actually seems to groan. He lays his head back and smiles at me. "Not sure. When I came in to get some lunch, they grabbed me and said they'd be back in a minute. Gertie doesn't believe in diet food and me and Patty are trying to lose some weight. They said they'd be right back, but that was a good ten minutes ago." He bounces up from the couch. He's big, but young and limber. "So, you're here now. I'm going to make our lunches and get back to work. I hear you and the movie people are having a meeting at Andy's Place later. Do you need me in that meeting?"

"I don't think so. It's more for them to meet Gertie since she owns this place and they want to film here."

"Good," he says. He shakes his head, and his red hair flops down into his eyes. "I'm not into the Hollywood scene. Think it'll turn too many folks' heads, you know what I mean?"

"Not really," I frown. "It's just fun for a bit, and it'll be nice to make some extra money."

"Money and fame. Why can't we just enjoy what we have and not try to be something we're not?"

"I don't think we will. It's just for a few weeks, right?"

Andy's halfway to the back stairs when he turns and says to me, "That's how they suck you in. It's only temporary. It's only for fun. It's just some extra money. Mark my words, Miss Carolina, this won't end pretty. Won't end pretty at all." He walks up the stairs, shaking his head and muttering to himself.

Well. That's the thirty-year-old town curmudgeon heard from.

Andy's still upstairs when Shannon comes pushing into the front door, backside first. I hurry to help, and she holds out a plate wrapped in aluminum foil. "Thanks. Those are for you." Shannon follows me to the counter. "Andy tell you where we went?"

"Of course not. He just said you left for a few minutes. He's still upstairs making lunch for him and Patty. What's in here?"

She pulls off the foil. "Deviled eggs. Best you've ever eaten."

"Oh, are these from Susan's friend up in Laurel Cove? She was telling me she was going to talk to Peter." There are four half eggs on the plate, each filled with varying shades and consistencies of yellow. The toppings on each also vary.

"She brought a huge sampler platter down for Peter, so he called for us to come get some. He also had some little cups of chicken and shrimp salad, but those were already gone when I snagged these for you. Word got out quick that there was free food at the bistro."

"No worries. I had some of the chicken salad yesterday, and it was delicious. So, what flavors are these?"

Shannon frowns as she studies them, then she shrugs. "I don't know. The plate got turned around. There's a blue cheese one, a spicy one, one that's regular, and then I can't remember the other one. But they were all good. Well, I didn't try the blue cheese one because I don't like blue cheese."

The door opens while we're studying the plate and we look up to hear Susie Mae say, "I love blue cheese. What are y'all looking at?" She's wearing jeans and a dark-green, long-sleeve T-shirt from the youth group's ski trip last winter.

Shannon points at one of the eggs. "Deviled eggs. I'm pretty sure that one is the blue cheese one. Maybe Carolina will share with you."

"Of course, Susie Mae," I say. "It's all yours."

"Aren't you supposed to be in school?" Shannon asks.

Susie Mae picks up the egg and says, "Juniors get lunch off campus. Just started this year because of the renovations in the atrium where most everyone eats lunch." She takes a tiny bite, and I'm reminded of the way her mother eats.

I pick up the one that looks the most normal and take a normal-sized bite. It's delicious and so creamy. I can taste everything I put in mine: pickles, mayo, maybe a touch of mustard, but they are so much better than mine. Maybe because I didn't have to peel them first.

Shannon marches away from us toward her big flower cooler along the side wall. "I have work to do. This morning has been an entire waste of time. You're good up here, Carolina?"

Just as I say that I am, Andy comes pounding down the stairs again. He's got two loaded grocery bags in his hand as he breezes through. "Hi again and bye again. See y'all later, gotta get lunch to my lady!"

We all smile and wave. When the door closes, it's just me and Susie Mae and two more eggs. "Which one do you want?" I ask. She shrugs. "One is supposed to be spicy. Do you like spicy stuff?" She wrinkles her nose and shakes her head. "Okay, then I think this one looks like it has red pepper flakes. I'll take it."

We lift our chosen eggs, and I walk toward the sitting area. Susie Mae follows. "How are things going with school this year?" I sit on the couch, and she takes the chair that faces the front windows.

"Good, I guess. You know about my mom and dad, right?"

"Yes. Sure hated to hear that."

She nods and takes another little bite. "This isn't the spicy one. How's yours?"

"Perfect," I say and pop in the last bit. I swallow, then lick my finger and thumb. "Just the right amount of spice. How's your dad doing? Your mom seems okay."

She nods some more. "I think they're both okay." She stops talking as she looks around her at the books, the flower displays, and out onto the street.

I try again. "Did you get everything planned for Senior Night yesterday? I didn't even hear y'all leave."

"I guess. They didn't really want me there. I invited myself."

I wrinkle my forehead. "Why did you invite yourself?"

She shrugs and looks at me. "I don't know. Where's that book?"

"Oh." I stand up and take a couple steps into the shop. "It's still on the shelf. I haven't had time to pull it out." I take the small paperback off the mystery shelf, which is right beside the sitting area. "Here you go. My treat. Always good to meet another reader."

She stands up, too. "Thanks, but I can pay you for it. How much is it?"

"Nope, I'm serious. It's yours."

She hesitates, staring at the front cover. "Okay. Guess I better go then. If I'm late, all the parking spaces at school will be taken." She turns and walks to the door. She grips the handle and pulls as she asks, "Are there other days you're here at lunch time?"

"Monday and Thursday usually. Why?"

She grins. "Just wondering. This was fun." She lifts the book and waves it at me as the door closes. "Thanks again!"

"This was fun?" I mutter to myself as I retreat to the counter. "This was *weird*."

Chapter 12

"This is amazing," Tyler says in a low, awed voice. "The crew is going to love this place." He's creeping around Gertie's moonshine cave like he's in a real cave where something might jump out at him. Shannon and he talked at the shop while she arranged bridal bouquets of sunflowers, tiny dark purple flowers, and white lacy ones for a wedding tomorrow evening. She signed off on me and Gertie doing whatever we needed to do and said she'd make it work with her business. She's not faking how busy she is, and even Tyler was impressed with her skill.

Gertie beams as she saunters behind the counter. "Do you have a favorite dessert? I already know what Carolina wants."

"Carolina wants nothing," I say. "I have a house full for dinner tonight. I still don't actually know what we're having, so no thanks."

"It's just a taste, and it was your idea…"

Gertie holds a small, half-filled glass out to me. "Carolina, you always have creative suggestions. Peanut butter cookie? Moon pie? Krispy Kreme?"

Tyler laughs as he walks up the bar. "Wait. You've suggested all those?"

I shrug. "Maybe. What is it?" I ask as I take the glass from her.

"Guess."

Sniffing brings up an immediate recognition, but I can't place it. "It's something I know." My first sip is sweet, but that's to be expected with dessert-flavored moonshine. It's a certain familiar sweetness. Makes me think of… of fire. No, being at a fire. "Toasted marshmallow!"

Gertie squints at me. "Try another sip. You're close."

Tyler motions for her to give him a taste, so she pours him a sample also. He says, "More than marshmallow, there's—"

"Chocolate!" I shout. "S'mores, right?"

"That's it. Want another sip?"

"No," I say, then drain my glass and move over to the closest table. "Is here okay?"

Tyler nods as he gets his glass refilled from a different bottle. Gertie then pulls out two bottles of water from the fridge behind the bar and carries them out, handing one to me, then twisting the top off the other for herself.

"I taste blueberry in this one. Delicious," Tyler says, staring at his glass as he eases onto the gray, cushiony chair he's pulled up to our table. "My girlfriend and I are definitely coming up here for a night during filming." He sits his glass down and lifts his briefcase onto his lap. "Okay, let's get this taken care of." He goes over the details with Gertie like he did for Shannon. I half-listen as it all sounded good to me the first time. They will do a lot of shooting in the store after hours. Sometimes they'll be there while we're open, but there will also be days we will need to be closed.

Tyler leans back as Gertie says everything sounds fine to her. "Good," he says. "Didn't think there'd be any problems. Except I'm going to need to find someone to play the bookstore owner since Carolina refuses."

Gertie cocks her head at me. "Not up for a bit of stardom?"

"Nope, they've explained it's just background with only a couple lines. I'm not interested in seeing myself on TV." With a nod and a grin towards Tyler I say, "You better hope Laney doesn't find out or you'll never have another peaceful moment in Chancey."

He coughs and sits up straight. "Mrs. Conner is definitely enthusiastic, but she's a bit too..."

"Stereotypical?" I say at the same time Gertie says, "Big for her britches?"

We all laugh, albeit a bit uncomfortably. Tyler says, "We'll definitely want to use her. I'm sure she lights up anything she's in, but we're looking for something more understated for the bookstore owner. Carolina, you'd be perfect. Easy to get along with, nice-looking, Southern enough... sure you won't reconsider?"

I wave him off. "Absolutely not. Are we through here? I've got dinner to think about. You and Leif are welcome to join us again. My husband will be home tonight. He's looking forward to meeting you." I stand as I extend the invitation.

"If you're sure and if you'll let us clean up tonight. What time should I tell Leif to be there?"

"We'll eat at six. Where is he today?"

Tyler takes his glass over to the bar as Gertie struggles up from her low, soft chair. "Leif is setting up our campground in the parking lot out at the lake park. We needed a big paved area without a lot of traffic for the cast's trailers. It's a the fourth movie in the series so the lead actors and their families have become friends and like living close to each other on the shoot. They'll be ecstatic with the location at the park. Much better than a closed-up mall parking lot in a not-so-good neighborhood. Some of the crew may end up at a hotel at the interstate, but most will be in smaller campers out at the park, too." He reaches across the bar to shake Gertie's hand. "Good to meet you, Mrs. Samson. What do I owe you for the drink? I'd also like to purchase a bottle of whatever moonshine Carolina prefers."

She pumps his hand up and down. "It's Gertie, and I believe a bottle of this peach cobbler is what Carolina would choose, right?"

"You don't have to do that, Tyler," I say, but he waves a hand at me and nods for Gertie to put the bottle in a bag.

"Least I can do for all your help and for taking us into your family. Besides," he drawls with a wink at Gertie, "I hear there's the matter of your husband coming home tonight? And seems earlier at Ruby's I heard something about a nude leotard?"

Gertie laughs out loud. Tyler grins and shrugs. I try for a nonchalant, mysterious look over my shoulder as I head up the stairs. Peach cobbler moonshine and that box delivered this morning, now stashed in my closet, *will* go well together, if I do say so myself.

So glad Amazon Prime finally made it to Chancey.

Crockpot to the rescue. I put in a whole bag of frozen chicken breasts along with broth and cream of chicken soup like the internet recipe for easy crockpot chicken and dumplings said to do. That's been cooking now for a couple of hours, and I'm beginning to get little whiffs of the good smell due to the chopped onions and poultry seasoning one of the commenters suggested. An hour before we eat I will roll thin and cut up three containers of refrigerator biscuits and drop them in, too.

There's something I like about cooking in the fall. The cooler air blowing in the open windows, darkening skies in the early afternoon, and the honking of geese as they head south all cause me to pull out cookbooks. You don't have to actually cook to accumulate cookbooks, right? Just like you don't have to enjoy cooking to know hungry kids are not fun to be around. My fall cooking repertoire is pumpkin bread, ginger cookies, and apple crisp. A quick run to the Green family's farm stand outside of town left me with two bags of apples. One for eating whole and one for cooking so we can enjoy apple crisp while we watch *To Kill a Mockingbird* tonight.

Along with the beginning smells from the crockpot, the apple peels and a stick of cinnamon on a low boil on the back burner of the stove are making the house smell delicious. Jackson will think he's come home to heaven when he gets here, which should be any minute.

And he doesn't even know about the box from Amazon.

Chapter 13

"You'd be perfect!" Tyler says. Then he looks at me and says, "Wouldn't she be? Wouldn't she be perfect as the bookstore owner?"

Keep smiling and don't look down. That's what I say to myself as I nod and croak, "Absolutely."

Jackson's eyes are big, almost as big as his brother's, except Jackson isn't smiling and Colt is.

Colt exclaims, "She *would* be perfect! She's a natural on stage, aren't you honey?"

Impossible as it might seem, Jackson's eyes get even bigger. Will laughs, but quickly covers it with a fake cough.

Phoenix—she's completely dropped the name Rebecca—smiles and strokes the long braid hanging over her shoulder. "Why, really? Do you all think so?" With a sweet, demure smile she acquiesces. "Then how could I refuse?"

Leif hasn't weighed in. I look at him in panic. Please see how insane this is. She's a stripper! Her name is Phoenix! She can't play me! But watching the smile grow on his face, I see that he's a lost cause, too.

Fine. I don't care. "If we're going to watch the movie, guess I better get the cleaning up started," I announce. Looking around the table I see that my supposed cleanup crew is too busy fawning over their new star to remember to intervene. In the kitchen I dump the dishes in the sink in a loud complaint, but then realize these are my good dishes which could actually break.

"Did they really ask you to be in the movie?" Savannah hisses in my ear as she comes up beside me carrying only her plate.

Giving her a little side-eye, I snarl, "Going to take you a long time to clean off the table one dish at a time."

She twists to lean on the counter and sticks her head closer to mine. "Did they?"

"Yes, but..."

She huffs at me and then dashes her plate into the sink. "Why would you say no? You know I'm dying to be involved. Did it ever occur to you that you could help me out? Did you think of me for even one minute?"

I see her daddy coming into the kitchen, arms loaded with dishes and eyes creased in sympathy as he mouths, "I'm sorry."

I drop my eyes to our daughter. "No. Just because you want to be an actor does not mean I do." I chuckle, trying to calm us both down. "Besides, do you honestly think they'd take you seriously once they saw how bad I would be?" She rolls her teary eyes at me and crosses her arms tight. I lay my hand on her forearm. "Honey, go back in there and tell Tyler and Leif you want to be a part of the movie. Any part. That you want to pursue acting and you'd love to learn the business from the inside out."

She looks down at her feet, and my heart hurts. I tuck my hand up under her chin and lift her face to look into mine. "So you trusted Isaac Rivers and his parents. Of course you did, why wouldn't you? You've been raised with people you can trust. Just because there are people out there not deserving of your trust doesn't mean a thing, except now you are even

80

more ready to take on the world and be the amazing person you are meant to be. Don't let them have one more minute of you. I miss the old Savannah. Don't you?"

Jackson, close behind her, had placed his hand on her shoulder while I was talking. She smiles and lays her head on his hand for just a moment as he squeezes her shoulder. Then she laughs a little. "I actually do miss me."

She tips her head as if she's looking inside herself. "Yeah, why wouldn't I take care of this myself?" She looks at me, and there are no tears in her eyes now. "You're right. The Rivers are not worth me wasting my life on." She hugs me, then reaches out with one of her arms to include her daddy, too. As she pulls away, she says, "Thanks, Mom." She strides towards the dining room and at the doorway says loudly to those still around the table, "I agree. Phoenix will be so much better than my mom."

Jackson wraps his arms around me and pulls me into his chest where I can feel him laughing. After a minute, he looks at me. "Well, you wanted the old Savannah back."

Colt stacks the two Styrofoam bowls covered in aluminum foil and filled with apple crisp in his big hands. They aren't staying for the movie so I gave them dishes to take home.

"Dinner was delicious, Carolina," he says. "It was fun to be back up here with everyone. Isn't it crazy that Rebecca, oops, Phoenix is going to be playing you?" he asks me. "You'll get to spend a lot of time together. I'm real glad about that."

"Yep. Well, enjoy the crisp."

Phoenix sticks her head into the kitchen. She has her white belted coat on with a white knit hat from under which her red braid hangs down. "Thank you again for dinner, Carolina. What an interesting evening it turned into."

"Sure did. Y'all drive home safe."

She comes on into the kitchen and makes a beeline for me. She hugs me and says, "It's so good to be here with family." I'm not sure I can make my smile bigger. It feels frozen, but I try. She takes one of my hands into her gloved hand, which is cream knit to match her hat. "I've always wanted a sister."

"I sent you some apple crisp for home. Y'all drive safe." I pull back from her and step behind Colt. I corral them into the living room and towards the door. Every seat around the television is taken as we get ready to watch our movie, and goodbyes are expressed until they are actually walking out the front door. Then one last goodbye sounds from the stairs as Savannah comes down ready to watch the book she's been trying to read.

"Bye, Mom," she sings.

"Bye, daughter," Phoenix answers back.

Yeah, Savannah got a part in the movie.

She's the bookstore owner's daughter. Imagine that.

CHAPTER 14

"I have things to do later," Missus explains as she holds open the screen door in the predawn dark for Will and Jackson to carry her things into our house. She turns sharply as she shouts behind her, "Anna! Put that down. Will can carry that for you. Come inside and sit down!" She sighs as she turns back to me and lowers her voice, but it doesn't really lose its shrillness. "That girl keeps telling me, 'Exercise is good for pregnant women.' It will be so good to have another person of my generation explain to Anna she needs to not exert herself!"

"Well, we're not exactly the same generation," I say, but my protest gets lost in the commotion of Anna coming in, her coat flapping in the breeze. She looks like she has a basketball under her sweater. The rest of her looks normal, but the beach ball will not let her coat close. She doesn't speak to her grandmother as she pushes past her. She gets to the nearest chair and lowers herself slowly.

"Anna, good morning," I say as I step to her. "Do you want some tea or decaf coffee? Anything?"

She shakes her head and then lays back in the chair. "Some more sleep might be nice."

"Quit complaining." Missus explains—again, "If you'd

packed last night like I told you to, then I wouldn't have had to get you up so early."

Jackson comes through the door. He's as unhappy as Anna about the hour. "I can't see why any of us should be up this early."

"I told you," Missus emphasizes, "I have things to do later. After all, it's Friday. A workday. It's not the weekend."

She slams the front door loudly after Will brings in the last load.

I hiss, "Missus! We do have guests, you know."

She shrugs. "It's a workday for them as well. You can't tell me they could possibly still be in bed when it's almost seven a.m." She turns to Will. "Where are you putting Anna's things?"

Her question makes all of us stand still and listen for the answer. Will and Anna's shopping trip for baby earlier this week things seems to have drawn them closer. Jackson meets my eyes, and we try to not look like we're waiting. However, when Anna clears her throat, Jackson, Missus, and I all turn our attention to her.

"Will is giving me the basement bedroom, and he's going to sleep on the pullout couch down there." She looks up at Will who is still near the front door and adds, "For now. We'll see how things go."

Our son looks at me and then at Jackson from underneath his bangs. "Is that okay with y'all?"

"Of course," we both say.

Missus' beaming is almost too much. "Of course it's all right. It's as it should be." She claps her hands once. "Jackson, take my bag upstairs please, to the room next to yours and Carolina's. Where's Savannah? Doesn't she have school today?"

As I give a nod to Jackson to just do what she wants, I say, "She hasn't come down yet. She's still getting ready. Honey, make sure Bryan is awake when you're up there."

Jackson growls in answer as he climbs the stairs. I *assume* it was a growl of acquiescence.

Missus straightens her gray leather gloves and pulls open the front door. "I'll go get the muffins for you this morning, Carolina, since it appears things are not as organized as they should be for a work and school day here. This weekend we will look into how you can develop a smoother schedule going forward. However, I will only be here this weekend, so you will have to put in your best effort to make it happen."

She leaves, and when the door shuts, I ask Anna, "So where is she going to be staying next week?"

Anna lifts her head and stares at me. After a shrug and a deep breath, she says, "Does it matter as long as she's not here?"

Nope. Good point. Doesn't matter at all.

"You think maybe she's got a boyfriend?" Laney asks as she tucks in the corners of the fitted sheet on the bed in the Chessie room.

"No! Absolutely no way," I say between teeth holding onto the pillow case I'm trying to fit a pillow into. "FM just died."

"Quit playing with that pillow and do your side," she instructs as she unfolds the flat sheet. "So where else could she be staying? Why wouldn't she just stay here with you?"

"That's why I'm trying not to appear that interested, but, well, it's hard..."

"'Cause you're nosy like me. Well, maybe not as much as me, but yeah, I get it."

In a matter of minutes we have the bed done, and I lay the soft gray throw across the bed. The room is the smallest of our three, and the coziest. Tyler checked out first thing this morning, and now we're getting his old room ready for our weekend guests. Leif left really early from the Southern Crescent room, but he's not checked out so we can't do his room yet.

"If you need to go," I say to Laney, "I can do Leif's room when he gets back."

She stalks around the end of the bed in her high-heeled patent leather shoes and doesn't answer me until she's almost out the door. "No, I'll stay around. Mother is watching Cayden this morning."

"But you said she was watching him for you to do errands," I say, following her down the hallway. "You can go ahead and get those done."

She can't see me, so I grin. Ahead of me the black polka dots on her Sunday dress flounce from side to side. She's once again dressed to the nines with her hair fluffed beyond all reason. Her makeup looking like she should be asking for donations on TV.

She stops and whirls around. "I know you know I'm up here to see Leif, so you can just hush up with your funny, funny comments." Just as she finishes, we hear the front door open. She turns to strut into the living room.

"Why, Mr. Leif, you sure got an early start this beautiful morning. Did you sleep well?"

The young man grins and nods. "Yes, ma'am, I did. I need to get my things so you ladies can get my room ready for tonight's guests." He ducks past us into the hallway and then into his room.

Laney says, "Shoot!" then stomps into the kitchen. "He didn't even notice me. I don't want to be just some run-of-the-mill extra lost in the crowd!"

Again following her, I reject her opinion. "No, he most definitely noticed you. It is not possible to *not* notice you in all that. Maybe there's not a part for a Southern belle in this movie."

She takes a banana from the fruit bowl. "You're funny. It's

being shot in Georgia. In a small town. Of course there's got to be a Southern belle even if she's just walking by on the street."

"So you want to be a streetwalker, now?" I ask with another laugh and a leer.

"Hush. I just don't plan on missing out on the biggest thing to happen in Chancey in forever. I mean, you're going to be in it as the bookstore owner, right?"

I also grab a banana and sit down across from her. "Nope. Not interested."

Her exclamation is muffled by a mouthful of mashed banana. "Did you tell them I could do it?"

I keep my mouth shut, look down at the table, and half shrug, half nod. Then I let out a squeaky "Sure."

She swallows and sits up straight, preening. "I'll be perfect."

"But, Laney—"

Before I can finish my sentence, Leif's door opens and she's out of her chair like a shot.

She hits him full force. "I know this outfit wouldn't be right for working in a bookstore, but no worries, I can dress plain like Carolina does. Here let me help you with that." She grabs his laptop bag and leads the way into the living room. "When will you be shooting in the bookstore? I just love being there. I'm there practically all the time, aren't I, Carolina?" She says this with a huge smile as I come into the living room from the kitchen.

Leif's smile isn't quite as huge or quite as genuine as hers. Matter of fact, it looks more like a grimace. Poor guy. I intervene. "Laney, they've already gotten someone to play the bookstore owner. Leave Leif alone."

She pulls on her pouty face—and she has a *really* good pouty face. She stops right in front of the outside door. "Who? I'm perfect."

Leif shoots a pleading look at me, and I speak up. "Phoenix."

Laney's pout is transforming into anger as she stares at our guest. "Where did you meet Phoenix? Does she even look like she reads books? You know she's a *dancer*, right? Isn't this a family movie?"

"Laney! She'll be fine. Let Leif by."

"I'm sorry, Mrs. Conner," he says. "We needed someone a little less, less, you know." He puts his head down and barrels on out the door. I hold it open for him as he struggles. His face is red, and he can't get out of here fast enough.

Turning to look at Laney, I shrug. "Don't give it a second thought. They just wanted to go in another direction."

She no longer looks pouty or angry. She's thinking, which is probably not any better. Then she remembers his laptop on her shoulder. "Oh, his computer. Can you take it out to him? I'm not feeling like I want to be in the vicinity of someone who wants me to be *less*." Her nose lifts, and she swings into the kitchen like she's Scarlett O'Hara wearing curtains for a dress.

With his computer again in his possession, Leif's car crosses the railroad tracks out front, and I head back inside. Obviously Laney didn't wait for him to cross the tracks before she kicked off her heels and removed her hairpiece from the top of her head. I can hear her in Leif's abandoned room, but I could also find her due to the trail of her discarded clothing and personal items. I also notice, but do not plan to mention, the bundle of panty hose and a girdle stuffed into the top of her purse.

As I turn into the room she says, "I don't want to talk about it. I'll figure something out. Now grab those pillows."

We work in silence, and then, while she runs the armload of bedclothes downstairs to start another load of wash, I check the laptop in our tiny office. There's nothing new in the B&B's email box other than ads. However, on my personal email, I'm curious to find a party invitation, one of those that you open and RSVP to online. I open it before I put together who it's from. Mere seconds after opening it, though, I'm cringing and wondering if the sender can see that I've opened it. Can I pretend I never got it?

"What are you groaning about?" Laney asks as she closes the door to the basement stairs. She takes the few steps to our office door on the B&B hallway.

"Shelby's having a bridal shower. I'm invited."

Shelby is a perfect example of why families should be separated by state lines. Her fiancé is, too. Of course, her fiancé is my father-in-law, Hank. Make that Hillbilly Hank of the senior citizen do-it-yourself books and retirement home speaking circuit. Shelby is younger than me and was married for like one day to my husband back in the eighties. It was some crazy thing that happened when they were kids. Last Christmas, when Jackson's still-married parents were here, Hank and Shelby's affair came to light. It should've ended worse than it did, but his mom ended up living on the beach and Shelby ended up with Hank, so I guess it was a win-win for everybody.

Laney is mentally reminding herself of all those connections and disconnections in that part of my family, so she shrugs. "But that's in Kentucky, right? You don't have to go." She then gets a smarmy look on her face and says, "*However*, she was such a good nurse for poor old Hank when he fell off that ladder, so maybe you *should* be a little nicer."

Rising from the office chair, I give her a good eye roll. "Whatever. I've got stuff to do." I push past her out into the hall.

You'd think with her girdle off she'd be a nicer person.

CHAPTER 15

I come downstairs happy to see the afternoon sunshine filling the house. "Where's your grandmother?" I ask when I find Anna studying at the table.

"She's down at the bistro helping Peter." She looks up at me as she swipes her brown hair away from her face. "Grandmissus thinks he's neglected his store lately, all due to Shannon moving in with him. She want to get things spruced up so maybe the movie people will shoot some scenes in there."

I slide into the chair across from her. "Do you like him and Shannon together?"

"I guess. It's his business, you know."

I nod, but I don't mean it. Oh, the luxury of being young, when you are the center of the universe and above discussing other people's lives.

Then I stand up, and she clears her throat. "Really I thought they'd never make it, but Missus is seriously pushing for them to stay together. That kind of weirds me out, you know? If Grandmissus likes it, can it really be a good idea?"

Sitting back down, I sigh. "I know. But then again, she's a big fan of you and Will."

Anna stares at the pen in her hand. Meanwhile, I look at the notebook and for a way to change the conversation. "Wait," I say. "I'm so used to the kids studying it didn't dawn on me to ask what you're studying. Oh!" I straighten up and smile at her. "Are you taking classes? You're back at the community college?"

She begins her answer with a straightening of her lips and a deadening of her eyes, then she lifts up the book she's been reading to show me the cover.

"*Retail Management the Dollar Store Way*," I read out loud. "Oh, that's right. Good for you!" I try, but I can't get my enthusiasm pumped back up. FM and Missus set aside plenty of money for her to go back to college full time. FM managed to even make it so the money's completely in her control as long as it's used for her to go to school.

"I want to work and be independent. The Dollar Store has been really good to me, and I want to be a manager there. FM's money can go to the baby's college fund because I don't want it." She dismisses me with a stern "I have to study." She bends back over her books, and I quietly leave the kitchen. I walk through the dining room and to our little office where do some B&B work at the computer.

The three weekend couples arrived within an hour of each other from different Atlanta suburbs. None are big railroad aficionados, but they are here for a fall getaway in the mountains. One couple dumped their bags in their room and left for a quick hike, another is taking a walk down at the river, and the last couple, the Nortons, are the ones I identify with most: they are taking a nap. They made no bones about it. They announced they were taking a nap with just as much passion as the hikers told me their plans. You have to admire intentional nappers, right?

We're not hosting a wine and cheese gathering this afternoon like we do some Fridays. The freshman high school football game is actually before the varsity game today since there is no JV game this week. So, Jackson and I will be headed out in a while for Bryan's game.

I pull up the bridal shower invitation again and stare at it. Shelby has been a real trooper taking care of Hank. Savannah is invited, too. Maybe we could take a girls' road trip? I click on the guest list. It's really short. Anna? I guess she is in the family now, isn't she? Hmmm.

My phone rings, and I see it's Susan. "Hello?"

"Hey. You still at home?"

"Yep. Bryan's game is in an hour, so we'll be leaving soon. What are you up to?"

"Wellll…" She draws out the word and then pauses. "Well, I'm at the house. My house. In Chancey." She pauses again, then spills it all out. "Can y'all pick me up? Susie Mae has my car. Mother and I got into a huge fight, so she won't come get me. Laney isn't answering my calls. Everyone I've tried is either already at the game or not going."

"Your mom and you are fighting about the divorce again?"

"Yes. It's so insane. I'm a grown woman, and it's best for everyone. Can you give me a ride?"

"Of course, but we're going to the freshman game at five. You sure you want to go that soon?"

"Yes. Thanks so much, I really appreciate how you and Jackson aren't angry with me. So many folks here seem to be taking Griffin's side. I better go change and try to wash off some of this paint. Wait 'til you see the walls in my bedroom. See you soon."

We hang up, but I keep the phone in my hand and stare at the text Jackson just sent me from upstairs.

"Griffin and Grant coming to game to see Bryan play. Meeting us there. Leave 4:30?"

"Sure," I text back. I'll tell him about Susan in person. Guess there'll be no doubt that the Jessups are not taking sides in the

Lyle divorce. Now, if we can manage to not get a divorce our-selves over the whole thing, that'd be great.

"I'm going to pass," Jackson says with a tight smile, not dar-ing to look at Susan who has poked her head into my car win-dow. "We don't want to be late to the game."

I pat his arm and jump out to follow Susan into her new house, which she wants—no, demands—that I see. She actu-ally wouldn't get in the car until I came inside.

"What do you think?" she asks, but her huge smiles tells me what I'm supposed to think, so I'm going to go with that.

"It's awesome! It's so bright. You did it yourself?" Her bed-room is purple, each wall a different shade. Yes, it sounds like it should be her teenage daughter's room, but that room is just a plain old pink. Medium pink. Every wall. It's next door. Across the hallway from that room is a tan, room which is Grant's. She wrinkled her nose as we came by it saying he wouldn't tell her what color so she's creating a camo room for him.

"I always wanted a purple bedroom growing up, but Moth-er said that was for hippies. Plus, I always had to share with Laney, who said purple didn't go with all her blue pageant sashes. And well, you know Griffin, he's absolutely not a pur-ple kind of person. Isn't it divine?"

"Absolutely, but we need to go now." I walk back down the hall. The house is small and plain. The living room and kitch-en make up the main room, then there's a short hall with the three bedrooms and a bathroom off of it. "Does that go out to the carport?" I ask, pointing at a door on the outer wall of the kitchen.

"Yes, and the laundry room is out there, too. Want to see the backyard? There's not much out there yet. Mom's last renters had two big dogs. They pretty much tore up any plants, so I have a clean slate to start with."

Her enthusiasm about a dog-ravaged, bare yard is endearing. Wonder how long she can keep it up? I roll my eyes at Jackson as I climb back into the front seat. Susan chatters about the house all the way to the football field. Jackson clears his throat in a low way that is directed at me, and he motions me with his eyes to tell her about Griffin and Grant.

"Hey," I start, "just to give you a heads-up, Jackson and Griffin were talking… He and Grant are coming to Bryan's game. We're meeting them there."

Well now, that sure stopped the home and garden update. As a matter of fact, Susan says nothing as we find a parking spot, park, then get out of the car.

I motion for Jackson to go on ahead of us, and I thread my arm through hers. "You okay? Sorry, but Jackson didn't tell me until right before we left."

"No, it's fine. Don't be silly. It's just the first public place we'll be in at the same time since we split up." She squeezes my arm with hers, then releases it. We catch up with Jackson at the gate, and he hands us both tickets.

"Here you go. Went ahead and got yours, too," he says to Susan with a small smile as we all walk through the gate and towards the concession stand.

Griffin is standing at the corner of the building and as we turn he waves. "Hey, guys. Hey, Susan."

It's awkward. Very awkward. We stand in a little circle, then Susan steps away asking, "Grant down at the student section? I'll go say hi. Didn't get to see him this morning before I left the house." She scurries down the sidewalk, and we watch her go.

"Sorry, Carolina," Griffin says. "It's awkward, isn't it?"

"That y'all are still living together? Or that she's leaving that mansion for a Cracker Jack box? That your kids are going to live in different houses? Why in the world would all that be awkward?"

Yes, of course you know I only shouted all those things in my head, but I absolutely did shout them. At both him and Susan. Covering the head-shouting with a pressed-on smile, I shrug and say, "No. It's all fine. Let's get to our seats before the game starts." Then I dart down the sidewalk and up the first set of steps. Which do not lead to the section we sit in.

Chastened, I go down the next set of steps where Jackson waits for me, shaking his head. He puts his arm around me and whispers in my ear, "Griffin went to get us each a cup of hot chocolate. Are you okay?"

A shiver runs over me. "Hot chocolate will be nice. I'm fine. It's just so sad and, well, so close to where we were headed last year. Oh, and she's painted her bedroom four shades of purple. Can you believe it? Purple!" As I start up the correct set of steps, I turn to look at him. "Just imagine what Laney is going to say about that!"

He laughs and shakes his head. Then says, "Uh-oh," and jerks his head toward our usual seats. "Looks like you can find out what Laney will say sooner rather than later."

Laney is waving frantically at us and patting the seat next to her. On her other side is her husband, Shaw, rocking their son Cayden's baby seat. Laney yells, "We're here to support Bryan! Dawned on me we hadn't been to one of his games yet. Hurry, they're getting ready to start!"

We sit down just in time to see Griffin coming up with our drinks in a carrying tray. Then Susan stalks toward us down the row, coming from the student section. I look away from watching their separate approaches and turn to watch Laney's eyes narrow and her lips thin. Susan wiggles her skinny behind between me and Jackson so that, joy of joys, I'm sitting between the sisters. Jackson scoots but not much because Griffin is claiming the spot on the other side of him.

"Here's your hot chocolate," Griffin says. He leans forward to pass it over my husband and his soon-to-be ex-wife. "I didn't get you any, Susan, because it seems I really have no idea what makes you happy."

"You can say that again," Susan snipes.

And to think I used to like football.

CHAPTER 16

"Susan used to be able to ignore Laney's comments, but not anymore," I lament to Jackson. We're waiting to cross the street in front of Ruby's for post-game coffee and pie. I'm tucked under his arm trying to stay warm. The day was so warm that I didn't dress appropriately for the drop in temperature when the sun went down and the wind picked up.

"Hope it's toasty warm in Ruby's," I add as I dash the remaining feet to catch the door before it closes. However, when I hold it open for my husband to follow, he's not behind me. Stepping back into the cold, I see him a few feet to my right. He's staring at the big, illuminated windows of his brother's dance studio.

Letting the door fall shut behind me, I walk toward him. "See how awful it is? Lights up the whole street."

He welcomes me back underneath his arm as he says, "Yeah, but what are they doing in there?" We move closer, and when we come flush with the front window, we can see cubicles. Little rooms built right up next to the windows. Jackson shakes his head, then wonders, "For the movie, maybe?"

I walk away from the warmth of his arm to see the first cubicle. There are three tables, with chairs at each, and I see

97

a box of salt shakers, dishes, and table linens. "I think you're right. This would be for a restaurant scene. That looks like an office, maybe? The last one is just a counter, like maybe a doctor's office?"

"Bingo!" Tyler says as he comes up behind us. "Since Phoenix was in the middle of renovations, she suggested we use her space as a big soundstage. Much easier than running all around town looking for appropriate settings and adapting them."

"So this is why you don't need to film at Ruby's," I say, pointing to the first set.

"Yes, good thing, too." He lowers his voice. "Between you and me, Ruby's Café would've required a ton of work and, well, Ruby, she's… let's just say she's not exactly on board."

"But you still want to use the bookstore?"

"Absolutely! It's perfect. Are you guys going into Ruby's? I'm freezing."

We all dash in that direction and finally enter into the warmth of the bright and crowded café. Tyler is claimed by the first table beside the door. Then Jackson's brother hails my husband to join the freshmen team's coaches, and he's gone. The left-hand corner has Susan at its center while the right-hand hosts Laney and their mother, Gladys. I see all that with an innocent sweep of the room, ending with me focusing on the table on my right. At least, I hope it looked innocent.

"We saved you a seat," Retta says as she pats the chair beside her. "Book club always sits together."

With a mental sticking out of my tongue at the feuding Troutwells, I sit down in my reserved seat. "Why, thank you. I didn't realize that about the book club."

Pearl Bennett shakes her head and speaks from behind her hand. "We don't want people to know that's what we're doing. We act like it's accidental." She tucks her chin as she looks around the table, then shrugs. "We've found we just have so little in common with those that don't read."

I laugh. It's a moment before they join me, and I get the feeling they aren't joking. "Are you serious?"

I'm ignored, and they move right back into their discussion. Luckily, my seat faces the interior of the café so that I can watch everyone. Laney has a crowd interested in whatever she's talking about. Susan is laughing with a handful of younger moms she probably knows from the lake park activities. There are most of the men, gathered around the coaches who aren't still at the school. There are no teenagers, even younger ones. There was a bonfire after the game sponsored by the Baptist church, so I assume that, like mine, all the young people are there. Just as I realize I don't see Missus, the door opens and she strolls in. I say stroll because she isn't storming in as usual, with her hair on fire about something or other.

She acknowledges me with a small nod, then turns to speak to the person following her. Oh, it's Phoenix. The dancer turned actor strolls in, too, but then again, she strolls, or slinks, everywhere she goes. She's just so cool and above everything. Here I didn't think Missus could become even more annoying, but watching her with Phoenix proves me wrong.

Colt excuses himself out of the men's center ring to hover around his woman. "Honey, there you are! Sit right here. They're only using that end of the table, I already checked. What can I get you? Missus, can I get you anything? I hear the apple pie is delicious."

Missus lifts her face, as if to speak to my brother-in-law, then I see her check to see what Phoenix says first. What?! Talk about out of character! Phoenix nods, and Missus directs her attention back to Colt. "Yes, please. Apple pie sounds lovely."

Colt only has to turn around and give the order to Libby who had been on her way to the table. Libby screws up her face looking at the two women at the table, then back to Colt. He practically shoos her back to the kitchen area, then turns and kisses Phoenix's flawless cheek. "I'm going back over to talk to the guys, okay? Need anything else?"

Missus shakes her head, only after a quick glance at her table partner. My jaw drops open, but any fly looking for a landing spot would have his pick. There are more than a few mouths hanging open watching this spectacle.

"You're staring," one of the two schoolteachers in the book club says to me.

I can't remember either of their names, so I nod as I close my mouth and look down. "Is this coffee for me?"

Retta says, "Yes. We assumed you'd be here, although you did take long enough."

"We had to drop off a carload of kids at the bonfire."

"Wasn't Susan riding with you? She rode with you to the game," Brittani's mother, Crystal says as her sister Pearl nods.

"Yes, but she got another ride here with—"

"Her husband, I hope," says Sally. "We have their marriage on every single prayer list at church. He was at the game, but I don't see him here."

"No, he had to go home. His son has an early tee time," I explain, though my brain is telling me to stop talking.

Crystal rolls her eyes. "Griffin Lyles is enjoying that club life a little too much is what I hear."

The two teachers turn their heads to each other and telepathically make a decision. They turn to face me and Retta. The one wearing a black and red scarf whispers, "And *where* is Rose?"

Each of us look around the table. I know she was at the game. She is part of the book club, so I assume they expect her here. At our table.

Retta clears her throat as she lifts her coffee cup. "Well. She *is* a Webster. And Griffin Lyles, mind you, is an unattached man."

I jerk back, first in understanding, then in objection. "Griffin? Oh, no. Plus, I don't think Rose is like that. She really is a nice girl."

Retta smacks her lips as she resettles her cup in its saucer. "Really? I'm not sure you daughter-in-law would agree." She clears her throat again. "What can you tell us about getting our books for next month's meeting?"

I'm relieved to not be discussing Rose anymore, so I'm a little more chatty than usual. "Nothing. I haven't had time to check. We had midweek guests, and that threw off my schedule. Then, Missus and Anna are moving in so that took some time." As I ramble my excuses, I try to stop, but they just keep spilling out. "Besides, I only found out about me getting the books a couple days ago."

From beside me, Retta puts her arm around my shoulders. "Carolina, Carolina! My, but you do like the excuses. It's all fine. Just let us know by Monday." She squeezes and shakes me, and there are smiles all around the table.

"Okay," I squeak then I take the chance to jump up. "I need to go talk to somebody." I escape, but I can't help but feel that they just *let* me leave. Not that I don't appreciate them letting me go, but why did they let me go? What's going on? Do they still want me in the book club? Surely they wouldn't kick me out. I'll get them their books, or do whatever they need me to do if they'll let me stay.

Okay. Even I'm ashamed that I thought that.

I've run out of words. Jackson and I are sitting in the parking lot of the Baptist church waiting for Bryan and his friends.

I'm in the driver's seat because Jackson looked beat as we left Ruby's. I doubt he's heard a quarter of the words that have washed over him. He occasionally grunts when his head snaps to the side, and he wakes up for a minute.

Sure, I complain that he doesn't listen, but if he actually listened I might have to deal with his input.

It doesn't matter. Our kids are on their way out.

"There they are," I say. I flick our headlights to get Bryan's attention.

Scanning the crowd for his sister, I finally see a gaggle of white cheerleading skirts flared out over the girls' warm-up uniform pants. I spot Savannah and see she's walking with a boy who looks familiar. They don't look like they're together, just talking to each other. One of her friends grabs her hand, and they jog off toward the other end of the parking lot. The boy waves and yells something at her. When he turns, I see his face in the lights from the cars around us. Parker Garrison? Her old boyfriend from Marietta? What is he doing up here?

The doors of the van fly open, then the van rocks as it fills with boys. Laughing, yelling, smelly boys. They bring sweat, mown grass, campfire smoke, and heat with them, and I can't help but smile—and expand. Relax. Noise rocks the car as much as their jostling to find seats. Their hair is sweaty, their clothes too big, their voices cover every octave, and the energy rolls off them in waves.

Being the mom of a teenage boy is too big, too real, and too consuming to be contained.

Chapter 17

Voices in the kitchen draw me down the stairs. The door to Savannah's tower is still closed, but Missus' door is open and the bed made, another reason I've been dillydallying this morning. I hope she left to do some of those important things she's always braying about. Bryan's door stands wide open, so I take a closer look inside. Bedclothes and sleeping bags are strewn across the floor. The boys opted out of sleeping in the tent beside the river when the temperature took a nosedive last night. Even inside, we were glad to have a couple of his friends spend the night since he and Grant are no longer best friends. That thought pulls a sigh out of me as I step off the last step and head toward the voices.

Two of the B&B couples are in the kitchen with mugs of coffee and a plate of muffins. As I walk in, they're heading out the open door to the deck.

"Good morning," I say. "You're welcome to sit out there, but the cushions might be wet."

"Oh, hi," the younger woman says. "Your son and his friends dried everything off for us. The cushions were inside when we got up, so it's all good."

Jackson steps into view from down the B&B hall. He waves

at me, then tiptoes into the kitchen. "The Nortons are still sleeping, I believe. Good morning," he says as he gives me a kiss. "All's good down here."

"Your husband and son took good care of us. Hope we didn't wake you," the gentleman still holding the door open says.

"Not at all. Needed to take a shower this morning. I was just too tired last night. Go," I instruct with a smile. "Drink your coffee before it gets cold. Sunshine on the deck should make it perfect." The four leave, and I pour coffee for me and Jackson. We take our cups into the living room. "Where are the boys?" I ask him.

"Down at their campsite. Although it was too cold to sleep out there last night, they wanted to get down there and make a fire first thing this morning. I told them they could take some food if they helped me with the deck and cushions. They took a pack of sausages and a pack of Hawaiian rolls."

"What if they don't cook the sausage all the way through? I better…"

He stops me with his hand. "I gave them a pack of those little smoked sausages that are already basically cooked. They just have to warm them up is all. Enjoy your coffee. Relax."

This helps me relax. "I do have a few minutes before I have to leave. What's your schedule for the day?"

He squares his shoulder and smiles. "Fixing the back stairs and the deck off our bedroom."

"What? How?"

Jackson has put that off since we moved here, and I'm a tad leery about him taking it on. We might actually want to use those stairs. He's an engineer, but that's more on big things like bridges.

"Colt has a crew for the dance studio, but they're not busy right now since they're going to use it for the movie first. He said he noticed our deck and stairs were unusable when he was living here, so the guys will work for a couple hours' wages and food as long as he and I help."

I smile. "That's really nice. I gotta tell you, your brother was a huge help when he was living here. Even though he's the reason Phoenix and her studio are in town, I'm kind of glad he moved here."

"Me, too." Jackson stands up. "Need a refill?" he asks as he reaches for my cup.

"Sure."

We wait to continue talking until he returns as some of our guests are still sleeping. He sets my cup down and then walks to look out the front window. "Looks like Colt is already here. He wanted to do some measuring and get out to the Home Depot early."

"I'm excited to see what they do with the stairs, but I won't be home until this afternoon. You said we were providing food. What are you thinking?"

He looks at me and gives a bit of a pause for me to jump in and make a suggestion, before correctly reading my face and asking, "Pizza?"

I don't nod. I don't smile. I just wait. It's hard, but I'm relearning what it means to be a working mom. I cannot take care of everything.

He asks, "Do we have beer? I mean, enough beer. Or soda?" He's asking with both his words and his expressions as, with a couple quick knocks, Colt walks in the front door.

"Hey, y'all! Ready to get started, big brother?" he booms. Jackson and I both shush him just as the third B&B couple enters the living room.

"Oh, you're up? Hope we didn't wake you," I say as I stand up. The Nortons are a little older than Jackson and I, which makes them a couple decades older than our other guests. You guessed it, these are the intentional nappers from yesterday.

"Not at all," Mrs. Norton says. They move across the room

as she speaks. "We understand there are muffins, but we're going to head out for breakfast to a little place we love near Dalton." Just as they reach the door, Mr. Norton's stomach growls loudly.

We all laugh, and Colt pats the older man on his back. "I feel ya! I'm hitting the Hardee's for a couple biscuits as soon as I get some measurements out back. I'm Colt Jessup, Jackson's brother." They all shake hands, but hungry stomachs spur the Nortons out the door and Colt towards the kitchen deck.

Jackson follows him. "Speaking of food, what should we feed the guys this afternoon? Can you pick up a bunch of biscuits to feed them this morning?"

I stay a little ways back. They can handle this, but I do want to hear them handling it.

"No worries!" Colt declares. "Already planned to pick up some biscuits in case they show up hungry, but then Rebecca—I mean Phoenix—is bringing lunch. She was up cooking when I left. Marinating chicken to cook on your grill if that's okay with you. She had our little kitchen full of fixings for stuff I've never heard of, but she was right excited and it was already smelling good."

I'm still in the living room, but I can practically see the awe in Jackson's voice. "Really? That's an awful lot of work to cook and bring up here, isn't it?"

Colt's half out the door—yes, I can see because I've followed them into the kitchen—when he shrugs. "Naw, she likes cooking. With the studio not opening, she needs something to keep her busy. That girl doesn't like just sitting around."

The door shuts behind them without either noticing me.

You know, I really dislike people who need to keep busy. When did just sitting around go out of style?

106

With the exception of Ruby's, the square is not really awake yet. I leave my car on the side street beside Peter's bistro and walk around the corner to Blooming Books. We had a real freeze last night, so it seems like everyone is having a hard time getting going. Yes, yes, I know—everyone except for Phoenix. Hunkered down inside my jacket, I jerk to a stop to avoid hitting a person leaving the bistro.

"Carolina!" Susan exclaims. "I thought you were getting to work early. I came down looking for you and your shop is all closed up. Want some spider webs?"

I resist lifting my face out of the neck of my jacket and push past her to our front door. Once I unlock it, dart inside, and motion for her to follow, I ask, "Why would I want spider webs?"

She shrugs out of her coat. "Halloween? Aren't you decorating this morning? I found out I can't use these fake spider webs at the park. Apparently birds and butterflies get trapped in them if you use them outside. You should've heard those young moms at Ruby's last night. Thank the Lord I didn't have them put up yet. I was waiting until closer to the Halloween party out there this weekend. Of course I also didn't tell them those cobwebs in Ruby's are not fake. They'd have thrown up right there." She frowns as she rips open the packages of spider webs. "Anyway, I gave Peter a couple of packages, and you can have the rest." I wait, but apparently her rapid-fire monologue is over. Someone has had more than their share of morning coffee.

"Slow down," I say. "You're wired. Yes, I was going to get some of those webs, but they were sold out at the Walgreens over in Collinswood. Thought they'd be easy and cheap."

"I'm not wired. I've always had a lot of energy." Then she slumps back onto the couch. "Actually, I did have one of those energy drinks this morning."

"You did?" I come back around to face her. "Those aren't good for you."

"Neither is sleeping on the floor," she says without looking at me.

I sit on the chair across from her. "Why did you sleep on the floor?"

She looks up, and her eyes are shiny with tears. "Like I could go stay up at the Laurel Cove house after the way Griffin acted last night. I'm not spending another night up there. I'll get a blow-up mattress or something. Who was I fooling that we were going to be mature about things? That we weren't going to be like those other people," she says with a sniffle.

"Oh, Susan. Y'all were just sniping at each other last night. You didn't say anything really awful." I don't add that, just listening to them go back and forth, Jackson and I felt they still care about each other. However, as we learned last winter, it doesn't take much to push a marriage off the cliff when you get too close to the edge. "Griffin and you just need to sit down and talk."

She leaps up. "Maybe. But I've got things to do. Want help with the spider webs? I know you said Bonnie doesn't like Halloween decorations."

Bonnie has the store awash in gold, red, and orange leaves. Baskets of pumpkins and nuts are tucked here and there. The pumpkins are topped with plaid ribbons or raffia, but not a single pumpkin has a face. There are no witch hats, black cats, or bowls of trick-or-treat candy. Shannon and I noticed this only when a customer last week pointed it out to us, asking if we had a religious problem with Halloween. Bonnie told us later that her aversion to the holiday has nothing to do with religion and everything to do with teaching elementary school the day after Halloween for years and years.

Understandable, but we are running a store. Before Bonnie

comes in, my job is to pay homage to All Hallows' Eve, so, as I stand, I accept the help of my sad, energized friend.

Susan pulls on the white cotton of the artificial webbing, separating and spreading it, then drapes it over a collection of pumpkins. I open up the grocery bags I'd brought from the house and begin placing my personal decorations around the store.

"What was up with that Phoenix and Missus last night?" Susan asks as she works on webbing the front window.

"Okay, so it wasn't just me that thought that was odd?" I reach into the window to help her. "How do they even know each other?"

"I saw Missus in the studio talking to her yesterday morning."

We step back to look at the window, and then I sigh.

Susan turns to me. "You don't like it? I think it looks good."

"No. I mean, I like the window. But this Phoenix woman. I honestly thought that if I just ignored her she'd end up going away. I like Colt, and he needs someone nice, someone his age, you know…"

"Someone who's not been a stripper?" Susan whispers with a grin.

"Exactly! She's been here barely a week, and she's everywhere. She's making this huge meal to bring up to my house later. For Colt's work crew. We're finally fixing our stairs," I explain.

"That's great," Susan says. "And since you don't like to cook it's even better, right?" She moves around the store picking up stray pieces of cotton and the empty packages.

I ignore her remark. "And she's playing me, the bookshop owner, in the movie."

"You turned that down, right?"

"Savannah is playing her daughter, and so now she's calling her 'mom.'"

Susan has one hand on a hip, and she's grinning even bigger. "So when you say she's 'everywhere,' you mean she's everywhere in *your* life. Honestly, just last week Missus was *your* best friend. Poor Carolina, Missus isn't playing with you anymore." She sticks out her lower lip in a pout then laughs out loud. "You are too funny."

I laugh a bit in hopes that maybe she'll go away. When that doesn't work, I say, "Thanks for the help and the webbing. I have work to do. Just put all that in the garbage can behind the counter. I'm going to make some coffee."

She comes up behind me before I can get to the coffee pot and wraps her arms around me. "Lighten up. Enjoy your vacation from Missus. It looks like Phoenix is going to be around for a while. Get used to it." She squeezes me tighter. "And thanks. You're right, it was childish of me to sleep on the floor last night. Griffin and I were both being silly. We *are* going to handle things like adults!" She releases me. "I'll see you later."

She's back near the door by the time I turn around. We wave at each other, and she leaves.

I feel a lot better. Phoenix is making dinner for my family, occupying Missus, and taking a role in a movie I didn't even want to be in.

With another chuckle, I take the empty coffee pot to the bathroom to fill with fresh water. Yes, Phoenix seems to have all the answers. Hmm, that's a thought. I wonder if she knows where Missus is going to stay when she leaves our house on Monday.

Chapter 18

I walk into the house midafternoon, after spending most of the day in the bookstore. "We're carving pumpkins tonight!" I announce. Even though I can hear the television, music from somewhere, and power tools in the backyard—no one hears me. I punch at the remote control lying on the end table to turn off the TV and walk on into the kitchen. No one there either, so I walk out to the deck.

"Hey, hon," Jackson yells from the yard. He's surrounded by wood and tools and men. "You're home. Surprise!"

The surprise is that the deck off of our bedroom is almost done, and it's huge. "Wow!" I say. "That's almost as big as this deck!"

"Yep. Isn't it great?" Jackson bounds up the couple steps to where I'm standing. "Colt had checked everything out already and drawn it up. Isn't he good with stuff like this?"

Colt waves at me from where he's cutting boards in the yard with two other men. There are even more men working on the stairs themselves, and they sure have gotten a lot done.

"Thanks, Colt," I yell. More quietly, I say to my husband, "I had no idea you were thinking of something like this. What will we do with all that space?"

"Put chairs out there. Another table, maybe." He turns to look at me. "You don't like it?"

"Oh, no, I love it, I guess. I'm just surprised. Is that another set of stairs they're putting up?" I point to the far end of the house. The small balcony that needed to be replaced had a slim set of rickety stairs that led to the ground at the edge of this deck. Now that set of stairs is wide and has a landing that looks like it's going to join onto this deck. Then the stairs turn and end up in the yard. On the complete opposite side, there is a completely new set of stairs coming down to the side yard near the woods and the river.

"Yeah, Colt has this great idea of joining the front to the back. Those stairs will lead onto a wooden walkway that goes around to the front of the house. We can connect it to the front porch later. Colt has a lot of new ideas for us to fix up the place."

"Okay." I fold my arms. "I'm just not sure I like the idea of our bedroom being so accessible, you know?"

He does me the favor of at least pretending to look critically at the stairs for a moment. Then he squeezes me in a quick hug. "I think we'll love it. Better get back to work."

I'm sure I'll like it when they get done, but I'm remembering something I've heard Jackson's mother say about Jackson's father many times. "Hank doesn't do anything simple." She would then sigh and say again how much she loved her completely renovated laundry room that now featured an ironing nook, drying racks, more windows to clean, and a front-loading washing machine she hated.

Or she would sigh and say again how much she loved her new kitchen cabinets with glass door fronts, which showed all the old plastic drink cups and mismatched plates. Glass doors that were so much harder to clean than her old wooden ones, which she'd merely mentioned having painted.

Or she would sigh and say again how much she loved her

all new wooden floors when she'd made plans to only replace the carpet. Wooden floors she thought were too hard and too cold, that required throw rugs she kept tripping over.

Or she... Did I mention Etta and Hank got divorced last year?

Jackson didn't have that redo everything-bigger-and-better bug like his father had, and I've been so grateful. However, now Colt is here, and as it turns out, the little brother is being a little too influential. I like small, slow changes. I don't need bigger, better, newer, and neither has Jackson. Before.

"Look at that! It'll be wonderful, won't it?" Phoenix says as she steps out the door behind me. "You're going to love it, aren't you?"

"It's something, all right. How are *you*?" I ask with an extra dose of sincerity. "I hear you've been cooking." She's wearing tight, fawn-colored leggings tucked into tall brown leather boots. Her white dress shirt is hanging down past her hips, and she's wearing a medium blue sweater vest, which also hangs low, covering her behind. Her red hair is smooth and partially pulled back. She looks elegant, sexy, and that's just not fair.

"Oh, I love to cook. I may have cooked too much, so..." She looks at me and bites her lower lip. "I invited some others to come eat. Hope that's okay."

"Sure!" My extra dose of sincerity is beginning to feel fake. "Who?"

She turns back into the kitchen, and I follow. She says, "Of course, Missus and Anna are living here, so they didn't need a special invitation, right? But Peter and Shannon are coming. The mayor and his wife, too... I don't know her name."

"Betty," I supply the answer. "Are their kids coming?"

One of her perfect eyebrows rises. "Oh, I would think not. Or will they? I didn't plan on having children here."

I suppress an eye roll. "They have five."

Her other eyebrow has joined the first. "They have five children?"

"Hello!" We hear the shout along with the front door opening. "Heard there's a party here!"

I smile in all sincerity, and as I step to look into the living room, I say, "That would be Laney. Looks like she brought all the cheerleaders from the competition this afternoon with her, too."

Both of Phoenix's eyebrows have now fallen and flat-lined. She squeaks, "*All*? How many is all?"

I shrug, then lean to look farther into the living room. "Not sure, but there's a line of them going up to Savannah's room."

"I did not expect this to turn into a children's affair." Phoenix's face is flushing to a tomato red. She puts her hands on her hips like she means business. When Cayden lets out a squall from where Laney is changing him on the living room couch, Phoenix lets out a huff and flings herself around to face the counter near the stove. She's mumbling, so I step closer. You know, to offer a hand.

"What can I do to help?" I say when I can't understand what she's saying under her breath.

"Nothing!" she blurts. Then she stops, takes a deep breath, and says, "Yes. Can you please turn on your grill?"

"Sure."

Actually, I feel kind of sorry for Phoenix. She had a lovely dinner planned. Grilled chicken, fresh green salad with apple slices and pecans, roasted butternut squash tossed with sautéed spinach, mashed cauliflower (which I only tasted so I could complain about it and ended up loving), and beautiful flatbreads she grilled alongside the chicken. I can only comment that the flatbreads were beautiful. The kids and men devoured them before she could get them to the table, and I never got a taste.

Folks in Chancey may show up uninvited, but they don't show up empty-handed. The old tried and true crowd filled the kitchen and, though they enjoyed Phoenix's healthy offerings, they presented offerings of their own. Laney brought two packs of hot dogs and two packs of buns. She didn't bat an eye at the grill being taken, just filled a big pot with water, and boiled all the wieners herself.

Betty and Jed sat a huge bucket of fried chicken from KFC right in the middle of the table, at which Missus raised a disapproving brow. Betty found bowls in my cabinets, which she promptly filled with mashed potatoes and gravy. Gravy found a place right between the two mashed vegetables. I'm not sure mashed cauliflower is all that healthy when it's flooded with KFC gravy. I turned Phoenix away just in time so she didn't witness that particular desecration.

Anyway, like I said, I feel kind of sorry for her. Anybody that's spent time planning and cooking a big meal knows that feeling when, in a matter of minutes, the table looks like a flock of seagulls were let in the house to have their way. I know that's how I feel after any family meal, and I'm actually trying to keep alive the ones I brought into the world. To do all this for strangers? Ungrateful strangers who wouldn't even give you time to list the salad ingredients? Who groaned when you followed the word "mashed" with "cauliflower"?

With the football game on loud in the living room and all the kids—I think each of the mayor's kids brought a friend—it was a steady roar. I don't believe it was the dinner party Phoenix had imagined, so when I find her in a corner of the dining room, eating a piece of angel food cake with blackberry sauce by herself, I sit down with her and say just that.

"Everything you brought was so beautiful and looked delicious," I start. "I absolutely loved the cauliflower. You have to tell me how to do it. Sorry things got out of hand, but it seems to happen like that up here."

"So I've heard." She looks up at her angel food cake sitting in the center of the dining room table with only a couple slices taken. "But how can a homemade cake compare with boxes of ice cream sandwiches and Oreos?" She makes a disgusted face and takes another bite.

As I jump up, I say, "I haven't had a piece yet, but I can't wait to try it. Just getting a plate." In the kitchen I find a small paper plate, grab a fork, then make sure there are no Oreo crumbs still on my mouth. "That blackberry sauce looks delicious. Did you make that, too?"

She smiles and looks up at me. "I did. Bought fresh berries and everything."

I cut a slice of cake and then ladle two spoonfuls of the sauce over it. As soon as I sit back down, I take a bite. "This is delicious, too. Have you always enjoyed cooking?"

Phoenix is silent as she stares at her plate, then she runs her fork through the sauce on her plate and licks it. "I don't know. I'm jealous of people who say they knew what they wanted to do when they were kids. I was always too busy keeping my head above water to *want* to do anything." She tries to laugh, but it comes out more like a sigh. "I always just did the next thing." She stands up. "I guess the next thing now is to clean this up."

As she stacks some of the dishes, I finish my cake. "That cake and sauce is really, really good. Thanks for everything. Why don't you go relax in the yard? I'll get this. I can round up some help."

From the other side of the table she says my name and I look up. She's staring at me, and then she gives her head a tiny shake. "But that's not what the ladies do, right? I mean, is it okay if I stay and help clean up?"

"Of course it is. Why?"

"Nothing. Just want to do the right thing." She smiles as we gather some of the bowls.

Phoenix takes a stack into the kitchen just as Missus comes in from the living room. "Let's get this mess taken care of," she says with a look around. Then she focuses on me. "Now, did you get some aprons like I asked you to, or am I left to ruin another good outfit after another one of your dos?"

I ignore her and take a load of dishes into the kitchen, mainly so she can't see the dressing I just spilled from the big salad bowl onto my shirt.

If only someone had told me to get some aprons.

CHAPTER 19

"But we always carve pumpkins together," I say again. "How about tomorrow afternoon? Tomorrow night?"

Savannah shrugs as she puts her small, square purse over her shoulder. "Okay, I guess." She does not sound like she plans on actually putting pumpkin carving on her calendar.

The front door still stands open from when Will and Anna left for a movie moments ago, and Jackson is barely awake on the couch in front of another football game. The house is empty of all non-family people. Our B&B guests are all out to dinner. Missus is up in her room—reading she says, but I think she didn't want to admit she was going to bed this early. I wouldn't blame her, though. It was an exhausting afternoon with the big dinner and then cleaning it all up. This means it is the perfect time for a family activity like carving jack-o-lanterns. Except…

Savannah, keys in one hand and the other hand on the screen door handle, says, "I agree with Will. Aren't we a little old for all that?"

"Bryan isn't! Why should he miss out on special family traditions just because he's the youngest? You'd've died if I'd tried cancelling pumpkin carving when *you* were a freshman. It would've been the end of the world!" I'm standing at the door trying the same pleas that fell on her older brother's deaf ears right before he walked out the door.

"I don't think so, Mom," she says and her hand moves on the door handle. "Besides, Dad's here, so y'all do it with Bryan. I've got to go." She's gone before I can roll my eyes and explain how much Bryan would *not* like carving pumpkins with just his parents. Which she knows already.

"I refuse to let those two out of this. They loved carving pumpkins!"

Jackson answers with a snore, so I follow my daughter out the door, pulling the big door closed behind me. I know she's already gone, but I feel like getting a breath of fresh air. After the cold last night, humidity built up this afternoon, so it doesn't feel refreshing like fall is supposed to feel, but it's still fresh air nonetheless.

The guys worked another couple hours on the deck while the rest of us sat around chatting and watching the kids come and go. We played a couple rounds of some guessing game on our phones. It was fun, and we laughed a lot. Phoenix did a lot of watching, which was a little odd. It wasn't like she was judging us, more like she was studying us. Naw, it sounds creepy when I say it like that. In all honesty, it didn't feel creepy.

At the end of the porch, looking down toward the river, I see a fire is lit down at Bryan's campsite. He's staying down there with one of his friends that couldn't stay over last night. He wouldn't have even wanted to have carved pumpkins tonight, anyway.

Guilt. The realization hits me. That's what's behind my drive to make jack-o-lanterns tonight. Today at the grocery store, when I passed the huge pile of pumpkins, I realized I couldn't remember if we had carved pumpkins last year. I'm trying to hold onto making memories with the kids and enjoying these few years we have left together, but is it supposed to be this hard?

They are constantly going in a million different directions. It feels like I'm the only one that misses the pumpkin carving, watching *It's the Great Pumpkin, Charlie Brown* together, going to the Apple Barn on a Saturday, and having a picnic. (I mean I miss it if I remember it. Cue guilt.) They are all in such a hurry to do what they want to do. I want them to do what they want to do, but does this mean those sweet childhood traditions are really over?

Staring at the little fire way down on the riverbank and seeing Bryan's shadow as he moves around makes me smile and sniffle a bit. All three of my kids are happy, healthy, and busy. That's the goal, right? I turn to go back inside and then shove the heavy wood door shut. Jackson comes awake with a start and sits forward, saying, "Doing pumpkins? I'm ready."

My laugh makes him look around, then he shakes his head to help himself wake up. "Where is everyone? Did you already cut the jack-o-lanterns?"

I pat his head as I walk past him toward the kitchen. "Go back to sleep. We'll do it some other time."

He falls back but argues, "I wasn't asleep. I'm watching the game."

"Sure, sweetie. Whatever you say."

"I saw it! Everybody saw it!"

Brittani Bennett is yelling at the top of her lungs in the church parking lot after the main church service. She's yelling at Zoe Kendrick. The two of them are encircled in the noon-time sun by the rest of the youth group. Scurrying down the back stairs of the fellowship hall, I try to spot Bryan on the edges of the circle.

My bad. There he is, right in the middle of the argument. I rush into the group at the same time some other adults do. "Brittani, Zoe! What's going on?"

Brittani has a real presence for a sixteen-year-old. Of course, she lives in a family of women who could give lessons on having presence. She throws her shoulders back and flips her red curls with the hand not glued to her waist. Then, with the hair-flipping hand, she points at Zoe. "It's on that blog. She spent the night with your son in his little camping tent!"

"What?" I screech as my focus shifts from the girls to my son. I grab the sleeve of his jacket.

"Mom. No! That's not right." He tries to explain but not before another girl has handed Brittani a phone with a picture pulled up. It's a picture of my son and Zoe wrapped up in a kiss in front of a fire. A fire that looks very much like the fire I was watching last night from my porch.

"What's going on? Carolina?" I turn to see Jackson making his way to me.

Just the man I need to talk to. I start in. "I told you to check up on them last night before you came to bed!"

Brittani now flashes her angry eyes at me. "You knew they were down there? Mrs. Jessup, I thought you liked me! You're one of my mother's closest friends!"

"Wait. No, not them," I say, pointing at Zoe and Bryan. "Bryan and John. And your mother and I—never mind. Jackson?"

"I did!" my husband protests. "I did go down there. Didn't I, Bryan? It was just him and John. I swear!"

Bryan nods, but still seems to be trying to fade into the crowd. There is a crowd now, more adults than kids. I clear my throat, tighten my grip on my son's jacket, and pull him towards me as I growl, "Where is this picture from?"

With his head tucked, he whispers, "Last night."

Jackson's mouth is hanging open, and mine matches his. Brittani shuts them both when she says, "See? Told you she spent the night there."

With our mouths shut, we go into action. I release Bryan into his father's control while I put an arm around Zoe and start walking. "Are your parents here?"

She shakes her head, then mutters, "I'm supposed to get a ride home from somebody."

"We'll give you a ride home. We need to talk anyway, don't we?"

The four of us walk quickly to the van. Susan comes up even more quickly to catch up with us. "What's going on?"

I close the side door after Zoe gets herself settled on the seat next to Bryan. With a questioning look and lifting of my hands, I whisper at Susan, "Bryan and Zoe? I had no clue." I lean against the car, which reverberates when Jackson slams his door. "I guess I have to go."

She pats my arm and smiles. "I'll call you later."

In the van, I wait to speak until we are out of the parking lot. "Okay, guys, what happened?" I turn in my seat to eyeball them. "Bryan?"

He just shrugs.

"Where was John?" This gets him to look at me.

"He was there."

"He was there? In the tent?" My voice and eyebrows raise, and I hear a groan from Jackson.

Both kids shout, "No!"

Zoe shakes her head and leans toward me. "I never went in the tent. Never. What Brittani said, that didn't happen. No, we just—"

Bryan turns even redder. "She didn't go in the tent." His voice lowers. "We just kissed. Just, that's all."

Zoe nods at me. "Promise, Mrs. Jessup. That's all. You know

122

I like to walk down by the river. I saw them out at the fire pit, and I joined them."

"That late?" I ask. "What were you doing out that late at night? Your folks were asleep, I guess? I thought they were trying to do a better job watching you." After her mother's hands-off approach to raising Zoe and her father's attempts to get hands on with my daughter-in-law, I'm not surprised this happening with the Kendricks. Not surprised at all!

"Oh no, it was way before bedtime. It wasn't dark." She points at Bryan's phone, which he is holding toward me. "See? It's not dark."

I take the phone and study the picture, trying to not focus on their faces mushed together. It *is* light in the background. The fire is in the foreground so it shows up brighter, but they are seated on a couple of camp stools. I drop his phone into my pocketbook and dare him to complain with just a look. "Okay, so you didn't, um, spend the night?"

They both shake their heads and again look embarrassed.

"Are you dating?" I hate when I am the last to know what's going on in my kids' lives.

They again shake their heads, but this time there are small smiles.

"Well, you were obviously kissing."

"Just happened," Bryan mumbles, and Zoe agrees with more nodding. Holding back a grin he says, "John kind of dared us."

Jackson speaks up. "No one was down there but Bryan and John when I went to check. I hung out down there for a while and then helped them put out the fire. When I left it was all quiet and they were in the tent."

"So, Zoe, you were only there for a little while, and then you went home? And it was before dark?"

"Oh, yes, ma'am," she says. "Definitely before dark because

now the little kids have to go to bed at seven. It gets dark after that."

I shift to face forward. I fold my arms and stare out the windshield. Zoe's parents are supposed to be taking some of the load off of her caring for her small siblings. Of course, her parents can't be trusted at all. I will definitely be having a talk with Kyle and Kimmy Kendrick. With a crisp click of my tongue I ask, although I know the answer, "So you *still* have to put the three younger ones to bed?"

Her sweet voice pipes up from the backseat. "No, ma'am. I just wanted to get home early because we were carving pumpkins. We did one for each of us. They look really good sitting on the front porch all lit up. You should drive by and see them one night."

"Hey," Jackson drawls. "I thought *we* were going to carve pumpkins last night. Why'd you change your mind?"

If I wasn't wearing church shoes, I'd get out and walk.

Chapter 20

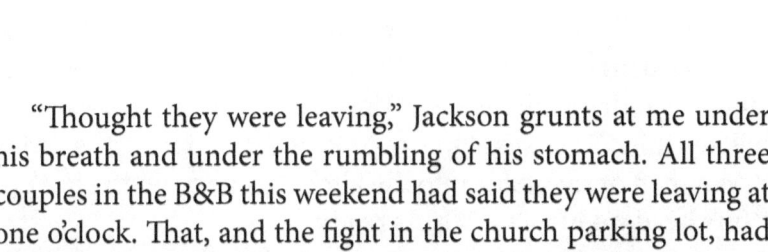

"Thought they were leaving," Jackson grunts at me under his breath and under the rumbling of his stomach. All three couples in the B&B this weekend had said they were leaving at one o'clock. That, and the fight in the church parking lot, had us rush home and not go to lunch. Now our last couple, one of the young couples, is sitting in our living room talking to Will about becoming a teacher. The couple is seated on the couch and Will is leaning toward them, all ears, in the nearest chair. Jackson and I are settled together on the love seat. It is truly a love seat as it bows toward the middle and mushes us together.

I elbow my husband, trying to get a little space, and mutter, "At least he's listening to them. Everything we say goes in one ear and out the other."

Jackson's stomach growls really loud. It catches the couple's attention, and we all laugh.

"Honey, we should go. I'm getting hungry, too," the husband says as he stands and then offers a hand to his wife. "Good luck, Will. I'm sure you'll find a job when you get done with school if you keep your options open and aren't too picky. Those first-time jobs often are where other people don't want to work. Like the area of Atlanta where we teach."

His wife reaches out to shake our hands. "We've had a lovely time. So good to just get away. This is such a beautiful place!"

We all smile and walk toward the front door. Before they are across the front porch, Jackson is in the kitchen pulling out eggs and a big, bone-in slice of ham.

"Will, how do you want your eggs?" I ask as he flops on the couch and I go to help his dad.

"Over easy, if that's okay." Then he yells, "Dad, I can cook the ham if you'll turn on the grill."

"Perfect," Jackson says as he runs out to the deck to start the gas grill. When ham steaks are on sale I get several because they are delicious on the grill. And fast, with zero clean up. Jackson comes back inside. "Want to eat outside? It's warm in the sunshine." He steps to the foot of the stairs and yells for Bryan then dashes back into the kitchen, smacking the back of Will's head on his way. "Grill's ready."

Before long we are seated on the deck with our boys. Jackson and Will have their over-easy eggs, and Bryan and I have ours scrambled with cheese. Will even brought the toaster out, so as the English muffins pop up, he grabs them and passes them around the table. Savannah went out with her friends for dinner after church, so it's just us four.

My back is to the new deck off our bedroom, but the smell of fresh wood is stronger even than the smell of the ham straight off the grill. There are pieces of wood lying in the yard, boards still on sawhorses, and tools scattered around. "Guys coming back to work this afternoon?"

Jackson shrugs and chews.

Will studies the new deck and shakes his head. "That sure is big. It might even be bigger than this deck."

I sigh and eat some more eggs. Mouth half full, I say, "Colt sure is Hank's son. Make everything bigger and more complicated whether it's a good idea or not. Speaking of Hank, I got an invitation to a shower for Shelby. Me and Savannah. Anna, too."

"Anna?" Will says with a look of confusion. "Oh, yeah." He grins. "Forgot."

I give him a mom look. "It's not funny how often you forget she's your wife. Where is she anyway?"

"Missus wanted to go the mall right after church and wanted her to go with her. They're eating down there. And I don't forget she's my wife, I just forget she's like part of the whole family, you know."

"I know," I have to admit with a sigh. "Honestly I was confused that she was invited at first, too. Anyway, I'm thinking of us having a girls' weekend, driving up, spending one night, and heading back the next day. The shower is late Saturday afternoon two weeks from now."

Jackson shakes his head as he cuts off another piece of ham for his plate. "Can't get my head around them getting married. Just can't. Are you sure we have to go?"

Bryan speaks up, "Yep! I am the best man, you know."

"What?" the rest of us demand in unison.

"Yeah, Paw Paw called me and asked." Bryan keeps on eating, not a care in the world, having fully informed us of everything he knows.

"Nope. Not good enough," I say. "When did he call you?"

"A while back."

I wave a hand to prompt him further. "What did he say exactly? When were you going to tell us?"

My son shrugs. "I don't know. He said he didn't feel like choosing between his sons. Will and I are his only grandsons, but Will has his hands full with that new wife and a baby coming." He scrunches up his nose. "What else did you say you want to know?"

"Were you going to tell us?"

He shrugs. "I don't know. Figured Paw Paw would tell you.

I mean, all I've gotta do is be there for the wedding, right? At least that's what Paw Paw said. 'Just be here for the wedding.'"

I won't say what I think, but I give Jackson a look, one that says, "Your FATHER!" I'm sure you can picture it.

Jackson smiles at me and spreads some strawberry jam on a bite of English muffin. Before he puts it in his mouth he says, "Guess we're going."

"Just as your father planned it."

He chews through his confusion, then says, "You really think he did it on purpose?"

I stand and roll my eyes as I start collecting empty plates. "Have you talked to Emerson lately?" Emerson is Jackson and Colt's oldest brother. He lives in Virginia and has three girls. We don't see or talk to them often.

"No, why? I'd bet money they aren't going to the wedding. Don't they spend every Thanksgiving with her family?"

"Every Christmas, too," I say under my breath. "But if Hank found a way to make sure we'd be there…" I shrug at him, then say to the boys, "Don't you two run off until this table is completely cleaned off and you've wiped it down, too."

Jackson leans back, lifting his glass of orange juice away from the cleaning. "I'll just sit here and watch," he says with a laugh.

From the kitchen I yell, "And call your brother, right?"

He stands up. "Oh, right."

Once they've cleared the table, I toss the dish rag to Will and he goes back outside. That leaves me and Bryan loading the dishwasher, just like I planned. "So, you and Zoe?"

"What? She's nice."

This is certainly not my first rodeo, so I just wait and rinse dishes to hand to him.

"I guess I like her. She's kind of different since," he looks at me, "since you know."

"Since the vandalism?" I ask. "How is she different?"

He leans against the counter and thinks. "She's not so perfect. Not so hyper. And she has more time because her parents aren't making her do everything."

"Good. But you know you shouldn't kiss someone just because someone dares you to."

"He dared me because he knew I liked her."

"Oh. Okay. What about Brittani?"

He goes back to loading dishes, then washes his hands. As he grabs a kitchen towel off the oven door, he just raises his eyebrows and lets out a puff of air. I guess that's all of the answer I'm going to get.

He tosses the towel onto the counter and asks, "Can I be done?"

"Hang the towel back where you got it, and then, yeah."

He takes care of the towel and heads out onto the back deck. "I'm going down to the campsite. Some of the guys are going to come over before youth group. You can drive us right?"

"Sure. One of us can take y'all. Be careful with the fire." Stepping to the door, I yell, "And no girls down there, you hear me?"

Will laughs from where he is sprawled out in one of the deck chairs. "Heard y'all talking so I thought I'd just wait it out here."

I grab my dish rag from his hand but stay. Might as well see what I can get out of him. Men with full bellies are so much easier to talk to. "How are things with you and Anna? Sharing the basement and all?"

He doesn't open his eyes, but that space between them creases. "It's all right, I guess."

I step to the edge of the deck and pick off some dead leaves from the geraniums. As I said, this isn't my first rodeo. Waiting kids out is a good way to—

I turn just as a snore comes from my supposed-to-be-thinking son.

Never mind.

CHAPTER 21

"Where are you?" Missus asks sweetly when I answer my phone.

Sweetly? Yeah, right. She yelled at me like she was my mother telling me I'd broken curfew at two a.m.

"Ask me nicely and I might tell you," I say with a smile and a wink at Susan.

"Carolina, must you play these silly games?" Then there's a click.

I pull my phone away from my ear. "She hung up on me."

Susan leans back from where she's painting trim along the bottom of her living room wall. Ever the perfectionist, she's touching up problems that I can't even see. Which is why I'm not helping. "Really? She just hung up? Maybe you should turn your phone off before she can call back."

"But what if she really needed something? Maybe I should call her back. She's not been acting right lately."

Susan pauses as she starts to dip her brush back into the white paint. "She did just lose her husband. I mean, I doubt she really needed something, but you never know..." She looks up at me where I'm seated on a step stool and sighs.

"But she's just so rude sometimes," I say. "She doesn't even say 'hello' or 'how are you?' She just starts demanding things."

Susan goes back to painting as she asks, "Did you ever find out where she's going to stay tomorrow night?"

"No. Nobody knows anything. Except Laney was wondering if she has a boyfriend."

Susan laughs out loud. "Stop, you'll make me mess up." She finishes one particularly complicated brushstroke, then leans back onto her knees and lays her brush down. "I sure do miss my sister. Any softening you've noticed? Is she ready to forgive me for my marriage failing?"

I shake my head. Laney and Susan fighting isn't too unusual, but it never lasts more than a few hours. Usually Laney rants and raves, but this time she's saying nothing. Nothing at all.

"Maybe I should call Missus back. Make sure she's..." I stand and see a car pulling up in front of Susan's house. "Oh. You've got company." The scraggly bushes hide my view until I walk to the front door. I get a glimpse through the tiny window of Missus striding up the short driveway with my pregnant daughter-in-law following her.

"It's Missus and Anna. Guess she wanted to talk to you, too." I pull open the thin wooden door, its varnish peeling, and can't help but think of the massive, thick oak door on Susan's house in Laurel Cove. Everything here feels so thin, cheap, and worn out.

Might as well face Missus head on, so I step out onto the concrete stoop. "Surprise, here I am! Did y'all have a good time at the mall?" I grin at them.

Missus stops on the sidewalk, then throws a corner of her peacock-blue wrap over her shoulder. Her leather gloves are the same shade of blue, which really complements the blue in her gray—

"Missus!" I can't help saying. "What have you done to your hair?"

Anna stands behind her grandmother with eyes wide, mouth shut. My exclamation makes Susan hurry to the door. I step aside so she can see.

"It's blonde!" Susan says. She walks outside and down the steps. "It's really blonde. It wasn't like this in church, was it?"

Missus turns for us to see the back, and I can't believe how much hair she has. It's all fluffy and styled. She doesn't wear her hair fluffy or styled. It's short and easy to take care of and gray. Oh my stars, she *must* have a boyfriend!

Susan says, "I knew it had gotten longer, but I thought that was just because, well, you just weren't back into your routine. The color is really good on you."

Anna grins. "Isn't it? We went to this really fancy salon at the mall. It had lots of great reviews."

"So this is why you called me?" I step down to join the three of them on the sidewalk in the late-afternoon, shadow-dappled sunshine.

"No. Anna and I have something to discuss with you, Carolina." Missus pointedly looks at Susan like she's interloping on our conversation, which just happens to be taking place in Susan's front yard.

Susan scoffs. "Why did you come to my house if you didn't want me around?"

Missus folds her arms under the front of her throw and then, with her blonde head, nods in my direction.

I'm confused. "You knew I was here? How did you know I was here? I just stopped by after going to the grocery store." I take a step back. "Are you tracking my phone?"

"Possibly, but that is neither here nor there. Susan, if you'll excuse us. I'm sure you have *something* to do to your *home*." She may look more glamorous, but the nasty spin she put on that last word was vintage Missus.

Susan swallows as her head drops and she backs away a step.

I reach out and hold onto her arm to keep her from leaving. "Missus, you can't talk to Susan like that. Apologize now."

Susan shakes her head at me. "No, it's fine."

To her credit, Missus looks chastened. She speaks up. "Carolina is right. It's not fine. I was, well, I was ugly, and I apologize."

Susan says, "Thank you," and gives me a wide-eyed look of wonder as she goes back inside.

I'll have to amend my earlier thought. Missus has a boyfriend... *and* he's good in bed.

That's the only possible explanation for her apologizing and actually sounding like she meant it.

"She's having a face lift!" I hiss at Jackson.

I grabbed him by the shirt front when I came through the living room and practically dragged him onto the deck. We seem to have most of our private conversations out here. Except...

"Who's having a face lift?" comes from above me. Above me and to my right. My grip on Jackson's shirt loosens as I see Colt and Peter standing on the new deck in the waning light of day. See, I knew that new deck would be problem.

"No one," I say. "What are y'all doing?"

Jackson points to the light Colt is standing under. "Colt's putting up some solar lights, and Peter is helping because he wants to put some on his deck. But seriously, who's getting a face lift?"

I give him that look married couples share that says, "Shut

up, I'll tell you later," but Jackson's never been good at that look.

He wonders out loud. "Laney? Not Susan, she already looks like a teenager." I give him the look again, but Peter laughs, so I swing my glare to him.

As I do, I notice that the new steps come down to the old deck, where they took out the railing. The entrance is right in the middle, so now where is our table supposed to go?

"Jackson," Peter says as he comes down these irksome new steps. He steps toward us as he laughs and says, "Jackson, I think your wife wants you to shut up."

I'm grateful to him for a minute, until he looks at me and says, "So, who is it?" He takes a drink from a water bottle he's holding. "Have you seen my mother?"

"Yes!" Then I clear my throat and lower my voice from that screech so I sound half bored, half unconcerned. We know how good I am at hiding what I'm thinking—not. "Why?"

Jackson reopens the kitchen door I had slammed behind me when I came outside. "I was inside getting us coffee. Decaf. You want a cup?" he asks me from the open doorway.

Peter's eyes go from squinted in confusion to wide in amazement. "My mother!? My mother is getting a face lift?" he yells.

Peter and I have shared a special friendship since we met, back when he was playing the ghost on our riverbank. At times it was a little too special, and we both pulled back. However, we are still on the same wavelength. Jackson would've never guessed who I was talking about in a million years, Peter didn't hardly even have to guess.

"Missus? Missus is getting a face lift?" Jackson says, and then his words are echoed by Savannah, who sticks her head out the kitchen door.

"Really?" she says. "That's brave of her, but I mean isn't it dangerous to have surgery when you're *that* old?" Savannah is braced behind her by a couple of cheerleading friends, including Susie Mae.

I try to squelch this conversation before it can go any further. "No! No, I was talking about someone else. Someone from Marietta, from our old neighborhood. Absolutely not Missus."

Colt laughs, Jackson looks confused, Savannah rolls her eyes, and Peter strides through us and into the house. I follow him and catch him on the front porch. I pull the front door closed behind us as I ask him to wait.

"Your mother only told me because Anna has an online test she has to take for her manager training tomorrow. She can't be there when Missus comes out of surgery, so she asked me to do it. Please don't tell her I told you."

"Why shouldn't I know when my mother is having surgery?"

"It's not like a full old-fashioned face lift," I say. "It's a, um, a procedure! That's what she called it. Just a procedure. She doesn't even have to stay overnight at the hospital. She's staying at a hotel place there with someone to watch out for her. Then she's staying at a little inn for a couple of days. She didn't want anyone to know. Please."

He slumps to half sit, half lean on the porch railing. He's looking down at his hands, then he laughs. He looks up, still laughing.

"Please, Peter, you won't tell her? Or try to stop her?"

He takes a deep breath, stands up, and sighs. "I won't tell her or try to stop her. Honestly, I'm relieved." He starts down the porch steps.

"Relieved? About what?"

Halfway turning, he smiles and says, "I was afraid she had a boyfriend."

Chapter 22

"Why did Savannah wish me 'good luck' as she headed out the door?" Missus asks as she comes into the kitchen Monday morning before the sun has fully risen.

Missus and Anna went over to her house last night after Susan's to pick up some things. I made sure that by the time they got back to our house I was tucked upstairs behind our closed bedroom door. Savannah was watching *To Kill a Mockingbird* again on the living room couch, but I'd sworn her to secrecy. Of course, she couldn't keep her mouth completely shut, could she?

"I don't know," I lie. "Can I fix you some breakfast?"

"Surely, Carolina, even you know I can't eat before a procedure. You do remember you're coming to the center at three, correct?"

"Yes, I remember. I'll make sure you get to the inn and get you tucked in. You know you are perfectly welcome to come back here and recuperate." I turn to face her and am taken aback by the kerchief she has tied around her head. "Why are you wearing that?"

"To hide my, you know, my new hair. That way when people see it, they won't even notice my face. And of course, think,

Carolina. I can't come back here because then people would know. I'm not one of those attention-grabbing Hollywood stars who wants everyone to know everything. I'm a rather private person."

Will had come up the basement stairs in time to hear the end of her statement. He catches my eyes, winks, then smiles. "Good morning, Mom. Missus. I'm just grabbing a yogurt to eat on the way to school. Anna will be right up." He's gone back down the stairs before we can say anything.

Missus frowns and suspicion fills her voice. "He said nothing about this kerchief. Why would he not ask, unless he knows and doesn't want me to know that he knows?" She whirls around at me. My heart stops when she scowls at me. "Do you think Anna told him? I expressly told her she was not to tell him or anyone else. As you agreed to do, or not do."

I open the refrigerator door to put a little space between us. "Of course Anna didn't tell him." I clean out the bottom drawer of three stalks of wilted celery, knotty baby carrots, and one soft apple, but I don't stand up. At this point I haven't actually lied to her. I am sure Anna didn't tell Will because I accidentally told Will. Yeah, don't ask.

I stay in the fridge when I hear the basement door opening again, but watch with a sideways stare as Anna pulls herself to the top and into our view. She locks eyes with me and rolls her eyes. Looks like Will told her that his mother is the absolute worst at keeping a secret. "Ready to go, Granmissus?"

"Carolina, can you please move out of there and let my granddaughter get something to eat? What in the world are you doing in there anyway?"

"Just cleaning things out." I move out and to the garbage can. "There you are, Anna. Do you want me to make anything for you?"

"No, I came upstairs and ate earlier. I'll just take some snacks, but I'm ready. So you'll be there by three, right?"

"Absolutely." I reach over to give Missus a hug, expecting her steel shoulder and withdrawn chin as she looks down at me with disdain. Instead she leans into me and hugs me back. Maybe she is learning to appreciate others more, like when she apologized to Susan last night. I pat her back as we pull apart and I smile at her. "That was nice."

She shrugs. "Well, I *am* going under anesthesia. I understand how unsettling that can be for some people. I've always tried to be sympathetic when others are in distress. You'll be okay to drive later, won't you, Carolina? I would not enjoy having to call a cab because you are too emotional."

Gritting my teeth, I still manage to say, "I'll be there. Good luck." I follow them out the front door and onto the porch, then enjoy a couple breaths of fresh, cold air while they get in her big car. Anna pulls around to drive across the railroad tracks.

I do feel bad about letting her secret out. I feel even worse about how bad it'll be when she finds out.

And she *will* find out.

Walking back into the house, I'm greeted by the ringing of my phone. I dash into the kitchen and pick it up to breathlessly say "Hello" to Jackson.

"Hey, I pulled off to get a biscuit. Forgot to tell you I talked to Emerson last night after you went up to bed. Just a minute, let me give 'em my order."

I pour another cup of coffee while I listen to him talk to the drive-thru speaker. He left early this morning, heading to the job site in South Georgia. Georgia has a very stern cell phone usage law, so he doesn't call me while driving. He doesn't think he'd like a Bluetooth system. "I'm not wearing one of those things on my ear," he always says, but what he doesn't know is that Santa will soon be bringing him one anyway.

"Okay, I'm back. Anyway, you were right. Dad has all three

of Emerson's girls in the wedding without him or Abigail knowing a thing. Just like Bryan. Just a minute."

I wait for him to pay and get his food.

"Back again. I'm going to pull over here to eat."

"Where are you?"

"Down around McDonough. My usual Chick-fil-A stop. So, Dad has one of the girls doing a reading, one singing, and, get this, one doing a dance."

"What kind of dance?"

Jackson takes a moment to chew and swallow. "Irish dance, I think. Isn't that what they were all doing back a while ago? Emerson himself wasn't too sure."

"Where are they staying?" I ask as I sit at the kitchen table.

"In town. He said Abigail was making the arrangements. He's going to have her email you the details. It could be fun staying at the same place with them."

"I guess." I can wrinkle my nose because it doesn't make any sound. Abigail and I are just so different. She's polished and aristocratic, like her well-to-do family. The girls are beautiful and very, uh, charming. Yes, that's a good word for it. Charming.

"Did Missus get off to her surgery okay?" he asks.

"Yes, they just left. She had her hair hidden under a kerchief, and she actually let me hug her. I wish she'd just slow down with everything. FM hasn't been gone but a few weeks."

"But remember," he says, "unlike the rest of us, she knew they were on borrowed time. Plus she's not really the sentimental sort. I wish she wouldn't insist on staying in that inn and would come back to the house."

"I tried again this morning," I say, "but she insisted she didn't want anyone to know."

He pauses. Not to eat or sip his coffee, but to try and not laugh out loud. He's coughing low in his throat, and when he finally speaks I can hear the laughter in his voice. "So, I take it she didn't find out you let the cat out of the bag?"

"Yet. She didn't find out yet. She's going to kill me."

"Possibly. But maybe she'll be in a weakened state."

"Did Emerson say if Abigail is going to the shower?" I ask to change the subject.

"He didn't mention it. But I doubt it. Honestly, I'm surprised you're thinking of going."

"Well, I'm thinking of it more as a trip with Savannah before she goes off to college. I don't think Anna will go, being pregnant and all. Plus, she's working hard on her management course. She did finally say she'd be okay with a baby shower after her course is over. Maybe I'll see if Susan and Laney will throw it together. Maybe that would help their relationship."

"Possibly." He takes a minute to chew or swallow, then says, "Well, whatever I can do to help you be able to go to Kentucky, just say. I know we'll have guests that weekend. It'd be nice for you and Savannah, though. She's seemed more like herself since she got the part in the movie, don't you think?"

"I do. Who would've guessed we would miss her bossiness?"

"Seriously," he says. In the background I hear him wadding up paper. "I'm ready to get back on the road. What are you up to today?"

"Andy's bringing in a lot of new books this morning. He ran into a big liquidation sale where he picked up a bunch of them. Oh, and I've got to try and find the books for book club. Then over to the surgery center this afternoon. I want to get there early so I have a few minutes with Anna. She and Will seemed awfully happy yesterday."

"Maybe they're turning a new page. Sure would be good, wouldn't it?"

"Yes. Drive safe and I'll talk to you later. Love you."

"Love you. Let me know how Missus is."

We hang up, and I can't help smiling. My husband just such a good man. Just a good person and I really like him.

But now I want a chicken biscuit.

Chapter 23

"So far it's all good. Sit here," Anna says. She moves her backpack over to the chair on her other side.

I managed to get out of the shop early, so I stopped and picked up lunch for her. "Here you go. I ate in the car. No word yet?"

"Nope," she says as she opens her sandwich and takes a bite. "Thanks, I'm starving," she mumbles trying to keep her chewing mouth shut.

I look around to let her eat in peace. The surgery center has a huge waiting room and is very bright, with sunshine coming through big windows that face onto a little garden. Most of the garden is choked with brown weeds, killed by frost, but a beautiful crimson tree fills the window. There are probably another dozen people in the chairs around the room. Some are watching quiet televisions, some are reading, and one older man is sound asleep.

"That was delicious," Anna says. "Thank you. I don't know why I thought those snacks would hold me over. Isn't this a nice place?"

"It is. That's just what I was thinking. Not a bad place to have to wait. How was she on the way here?"

"Pretty good. Still so insistent that no one know." She shrugs at me. "Even Peter, although I may just go ahead and tell him. It's his mother, for crying out loud."

"Well…" I smile at her and cringe a bit. "He might already know."

"How?" Her face crumples in disappointment. "Oh, did you tell him, too?"

"I didn't know he was outside when I told Jackson. He said he wouldn't tell her, but I agree with you. He should know."

She shakes her head at me. "And so how did Will find out?"

"I tried to get up to my room before I could tell anyone else, and before you two got home last night, but Will was in the kitchen and asked if he could use the van today. I blurted out that I thought Missus would be more comfortable in the van than his little car. Of course, then he wanted to know why I was driving Missus around, and well, I had to tell him. Sometimes I'm good at keeping secrets, and sometimes, like this time, I'm not."

"Maybe she won't find out," she says, but there's no conviction in her voice.

Of course her grandmother's going to find out. A long sigh escapes me, and I lean back in my chair. "You and Will enjoyed the movie Saturday night?"

"Yes, we had a good time. We're taking things real slow for now, so I appreciate you not asking too much." She settles back, too, one hand resting on her stomach. Her hand jumps as the baby kicks it. "Francie loves when I eat. Put your hand right here."

"Francie? So that's what you're going to call her?" My hand lifts a bit as a little foot or hand jabs at it.

We both stare at my hand and laugh. "Think so. Granmissus isn't sure it's a dignified enough name. She prefers Frances or Marion."

I nod. This baby under my hand is a powerful reason for

Will and Anna to come together, but that's a big burden to put on a tiny baby. Hopefully they'll find more to keep them together if that's where we end up. "I think she's settled down."

Anna smiles and tucks her long bangs behind her ear. "That's usually her pattern. Guess it's time for me to head home. My webinar starts before long. Thanks for taking care of her." She struggles up and begins collecting her books and notepads into her backpack. "The nurses said they'll come get you when they are ready for you in recovery. Should be about another half-hour to an hour."

"No worries. I brought a book. I was thinking, why don't I stay with her tonight? There's no need for you to come back over here. She'll mostly be sleeping." I pull my wallet out of my purse. "Here, you and Will order a pizza for everyone to eat tonight. We don't want you to get too worn out."

Anna squints at me. "Really? Are you sure? She has a nurse reserved at the inn. It's a place for surgery patients, so I wasn't going to stay the whole night."

"I know, but I brought some comfy clothes and another book, so I'll be fine. I'll let you know how things are going. She'll probably be so out of it she won't know who's there."

Anna finishes loading her backpack, then swings it onto one shoulder. "Okay. I do need to do the follow-up work pretty soon after the webinar ends, so it really would be a big help." She takes a deep breath and turns away for a moment, before turning back to me. "Are you sure? I mean, she's not like your family or responsibility, you know."

I stand and step toward the young mother-to-be. I brush her bangs back and lay my hand on her cheek. "But you are. You're my family. And I'm so very glad you are."

Her gray eyes relax, but only for a moment. Then the squint is back. "I don't know how... how..." She shrugs and pulls away. "I better go."

She walks away, her head down and her steps slow. Poor thing. Learning to trust is not easy. Not easy at all.

Creeping through my front door a little after eleven p.m., I'm surprised to find a quiet house. One lamp left on shows me a straightened living room, and a cleared-off table and empty counters greet me in the kitchen. I should stay out late more often.

Missus did fine, and the inn and nurse were ready for her as promised. I mostly sat in the background, read, and answered texts about her from Peter and Anna. Okay, and everyone else in town. (She's going to kill me.) Around ten, the nurse said Missus would be asleep the rest of the evening, so I left. Anna is going there first thing in the morning, and then we'll play the day by ear.

Missus' face was swollen and wrapped in bandages. She plans on being all back to normal by the end of the week. I'm not too sure about that, but the nurse said the procedure usually heals quickly. She called it a "mini-face lift" and said more and more older women are having it done to tighten up the jawline. I'd never thought of Missus' jawline as needing tightening, but apparently she felt it did. Her reservation at the inn is through the next weekend, so she's planned ahead.

I turn out the living room lamp on my way to the stairs. I've done nothing strenuous today, but I'm exhausted and tomorrow is a big day.

It's Movie Day, and it'll be lights... camera... action for Chancey!

Chapter 24

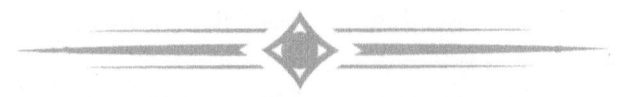

"This actually works better than the bookstore in Welling," Leif is saying to Gertie and some people I don't know when I enter the shop. "A lot less for us to clean and decorate. Set folks love this place. Hey, Carolina."

"Hi," I say and look around. "Looks like y'all got an early start. Look at all this." There are two big cameras and lots of black boxes and lights along with those big reflecting screens that look like something you might put inside your car windshield to block the sun.

Leif nods. "Gertie let us in here last night so it's all ready to begin shooting. Let me introduce you. This is Jenny Walker-Hall and Silas Pendersen. They are our two lead actors."

I shake hands with the attractive man and woman as they thank me for letting them use the store.

Jenny holds onto my hand with both hands and leans closer. "This store is so nice. No musty smell like books sometimes have, you know?" She's adorable with blonde waves curling around her face. She's really tiny, and I can't imagine how much I would've looked like a horse on camera next to her. Good decision to stay off-screen. Silas shakes my hand and goes back to reading the sheets of paper in his hand.

Even with all the equipment and the praise for our shop, I'm still a bit disappointed. I don't know either of these actors from any movies or TV shows I've seen.

Leif directs my attention to the area beside the front windows where a sturdy table sits along with two wooden chairs like you'd find in any library. "Here's the only thing we had to really add. The scene of the crime."

"Crime?" I shake my head. "I thought this was a romantic comedy. Like a Hallmark movie?"

"Oh, it is. By crime I meant where our couple meet, fight, and fall in love. They are researching opposite sides of a Civil War battle. This bookstore is where they meet and do battle—before falling in love. The movie bookstore has an extensive and highly rare collection of books pertaining to the battle." He looks up across the room and then points. "There, Herbert Fisk plays the owner of the collection." He points out a stout, older man with a full, white beard.

"But is his collection for sale?" I ask. "Why is it in a bookstore?"

Leif shrugs. "It's another love tangle. His character has been feuding with the local librarian for two decades, so he won't allow his collection to be housed there. Of course, by the end of the movie, the two of them have made up. And more."

My eyebrows can't help but spike up. "Library? Are you by any chance using *our* library?"

He laughs. "No, we are not. We met with your librarian, but she thought it was beneath her and her establishment to be involved. Honestly, it's too dark and scary-looking to shoot in there, so we're using the one in Welling for a day. Jenny isn't in those scenes, so no fear of measles. Herbert's librarian love interest is really a minor role. That actress lives in Atlanta so she won't be in Chancey at all."

They'd moved a few bookcases around to frame the table. I could also see the old books they'd added to a special, glass-fronted case—the rare collection, I'd bet. When the bell over the door chimes, we look that direction. Three ladies stand there gazing around, then one asks, "Can we come in and watch?"

Leif rolls his eyes at me. "I'll handle this. Believe me, in a couple days us being here will be completely normal."

I walk back to get a cup of coffee and am surprised to find tables of food and big urns of coffee along with pitchers of several kinds of juice. There are bowls of fruit, boxes of cereal, trays of Danish, tubs of yogurt, and more. A woman in a blue apron arranging the tables welcomes me.

"You're Carolina, I bet," she says. "I'm Margery. I'm in charge of craft services. Gertie said this would be the best place to set up. She's a doll!"

"A doll. Okay." I turn around and see Gertie lumbering my way.

"Carolina," she grunts. "I see you've met Margery. Figured it worked best to have this set up here."

I step fast to meet her halfway. "Gertie, couldn't Peter have provided the food? Helped his bistro out? This is supposed to help the town."

She tsked. "That soft spot you have for that Bedwell boy is showing again. You think he could do something as nice as this?" she says with a sweep of her arm as she marches past me. "Margery has worked for Leif on several locations. Just let Peter worry about himself."

"I don't have a soft spot for Peter," I say under my breath. Scowling at her, I add, "I'm getting some coffee."

As I pour my coffee and look over the table, I have to admit Peter probably wouldn't have pulled something like this off. Matter of fact, ever since Alex Carrera, our northern transplant, went out on his own with his food truck (paid for by his uncle, I'm sure) the food at the bistro hasn't really been very good. I turn and survey all the people in what used to be our quiet little shop. Bonnie comes in the door and makes a beeline for me.

"Pretty exciting," she says. I notice her hair is a little fluffier and she's wearing makeup. I didn't think she'd be the type to get all caught up in this, but she's positively giddy. "Look at all this food! Ooh, and hot water for tea." She asks Margery if she can have a cup of tea, and I walk away to lean against one of Shannon's flower coolers.

Bonnie soon joins me with her steaming cup, its tea bag label hanging out. "Have they started filming?" she asks quietly.

"No. They said later this afternoon. Phoenix and Savannah are supposed to be working in the background while the two stars are seated at that table in the front. That man there is also in the movie." I point out the older man with the beard. "I can't remember his name."

Bonnie blows on her tea. "He looks kind of familiar. We'll have to look him up." We stand and watch for a while, then the lights are turned off and people begin packing thing up.

Leif comes striding back towards us. "Okay, we're done here until later. Just in time for you to open. Hope it's okay we set craft services up in here. Since you're open all day, we thought it made the most sense. Don't want people coming in and out of the Bedwell house, and there's too much going on over at the dance studio. Margery will wrap this all up when we finish shooting each afternoon. For the evening shoots she'll set up something outside for us. But I do have a favor to ask. Can we serve some sit-down meals here? There's plenty of space." He looks around while Bonnie and I meet eyes.

"Here? But..."

"Margery will get tables and everything she needs. There's plenty of room."

"I don't know. Let me think..."

He smiles at me with a little squint and a head tilt. "Gertie already said it was okay. I was just hoping you'd be on board."

His grin says that he's too cute to argue with. I'm surprised he's not an actor. I'm beginning to find out the people in charge of a movie have to be more charming than the actors.

"Sure, then. Gertie's the boss," I say with a shrug and a smile back at him.

He grabs me, kisses my cheek, then winks. "Perfect!"

Bonnie and I watch him plunge back into the crowd of people that all seem to want to talk to him. She sighs. "Guess I'll go turn over the open sign. You know we'll be busy today, but I'm not sure anyone will be buying books."

As she does, I seem to remember wanting this shop as an escape from the craziness of the B&B and our house.

Yeah, that didn't work out so well, did it?

"Hi, Anna. How's Missus?" Pointing to my phone and then to the back door, I let Bonnie know I'm stepping away from the register. It's been a crazy day, and Bonnie was very, very wrong. We've sold a ton of books! I'm so happy I might even offer to cater the meals for the movie crew. Except that part about me not being a good cook.

"Wait, I can't hear you in here," I say as I push open the back door onto the alley. "It's been crazy here all day. Okay, it's quiet out here. So how is she?"

"Sore and really sleepy, but the doctor said that's all normal and she's healing just fine. He took out her stitches. She only had a few behind her ear. She keeps asking me how it looks, but I never thought she looked bad before so…"

"Where are you?"

"At the inn. She wanted something warm to drink, so I'm in the kitchen area. This is really a neat place. There are two other patients here, another one with a personal nurse like Grandmissus, the other with her husband. They live way out in the country, so staying here made going back to the doctor easier."

I smile. "Sounds like you're making new friends."

"It's just such a laidback place, and the owner is so sweet. This house has been in her family for years, and she lived here most her life. When her husband died, she had the thought to open the inn for folks going to the hospital. She calls it a Ronald MacDonald House for old people since most of her patients are from the plastic surgery center." She lowers her voice, and I can hear that she's cupping her phone with her hand. "Get this, though. She says she first talked to Grand-missus a few years ago! She said FM wouldn't let Grandmissus have any plastic surgery. Sounds kind of like she's been waiting for him to die." She pauses then says, "Makes me kind of mad."

"Well, I understand, but you know it's hard to know what goes on in any marriage. I guess I can see FM not wanting her to, you know, change her appearance like that. But it surprises me her even wanting to, you know?

"Yes. I couldn't wait to talk to you and tell you. Knew you'd find it interesting," she says with a bit of a laugh. "I better go. Our tea's ready. Um, I'm not sure if I can ask, but are you doing dinner tonight? If so, can I eat there?"

"Of course you can ask! You're welcome anytime. And of course I'm fixing dinner. That's one thing they do not stress enough when they hand you that precious bundle at the hospital. It's going to need to be fed several times a day for the next couple *decades* and that's all on you."

"Don't scare me any more than I already am!" she says, but she laughs again as we say goodbye. That conversation felt great and gives a lift to my hope for mine and Anna's relationship.

Before I can turn around to go back inside, a car pulls into the small lot in front of me. We don't park back here because it's a pain to unlock the back door, plus the little lot has a lot of potholes in it.

Alex Carrera steps out of the car. "Taking a smoke break, Carolina?" He laughs and winks at me.

"Sure, Alex." I try to not be bugged that this twenty-year-old calls me by my first name. He can't help he was raised up north. I tuck my phone into the pocket of my long shirt and turn to open the door.

"Hey, just a minute," he calls. "Can I ask you something?"

I turn to face him, and his dark good looks strike me again. He knocked Savannah for a loop when he showed up in town last summer. She chased him and chased him, but he was actually caught by the least likely girl anyone could think of, Angie Conner. Quiet, black-eyeliner-addicted, creative, non-flirty Angie Conner. "I need to get back to work, but sure, I've got a minute."

He stops, plants his feet, then sinks his hands into his jeans pockets. "So, I was wondering if you could put in a good word for me with your friend Laney."

"What about?"

"She's dead set against Angie moving in here with me. Won't even talk about it with Angie."

My eyes are bugged out, and my mouth hangs open. It takes a moment for me to laugh. "You're joking, right? She's still in high school!" My voice cracks, and he takes a step back.

"Yeah, but she's going to be eighteen in a couple weeks. She should be able to do what she wants, but she doesn't want to make her mother mad. I don't want you to convince her it's the right thing to do, just convince her to talk to Angie about it."

I clear my throat and try to speak calmly. "Alex, I'll be honest with you. I don't think there is any amount of talking that will make Laney, not to mention Shaw, okay with their high school daughter moving in with her boyfriend. Not to mention you live right here on the town square, in front of God and everybody!" Okay, so I didn't end that calmly.

He throws up his hands and starts backing up towards the stairs to his apartment above the bistro. "Whatever, Carolina. Like everyone doesn't already know we're together. We're out with the food truck every weekend, and she's over here all the time." He swings around and runs up the stairs. Halfway up, he stops and looks down at me. "This place is delusional!" Then he dashes up to his back door and slams into his apartment.

Delusional? Why, yes, sir, we are. And we are right proud of it. Like California works to develop wine, New England strives to perfect clam chowder, and Washington, D.C. prides itself on crafting more confusing legislation daily, the South has spent years, decades even, creating a tapestry of delusion that cannot be matched anywhere in the world.

Our football is better, our women prettier, our peaches and pecans the best, and our daughters do *not* have sex before marriage. There.

Glad I could straighten that out for you.

Chapter 25

You know what happens when your life is going smoothly? You become the depository for everyone else's woes.

I found myself scowling as I was driving home to get something started for supper. I wanted to finish up early in order to get back down and watch the shooting of the first scenes in Blooming Books. Savannah won't get there for another forty-five minutes, so that's my goal. To be there when she gets there.

Anyway, back to my scowling. As I realized my brow was furrowed and my jaw clinched, I did a review of why I was setting my own self up for a round of plastic surgery—and none of it has to do with me! So, waiting for the ground beef to thaw in the microwave, I sat down at the kitchen table to list what all's on my mind.

There's Missus and her wanting plastic surgery and FM forbidding it. That doesn't sound like the relationship I thought they shared. Plus, what's going on in Missus' mind with her new hair and surgery? And do I really want to know?

Angie wanting to move in with Alex. She's just too young, but how can Laney stop her without it being a total meltdown of their relationship? I wonder if Laney actually knows how far this has gone? Should I tell her?

Susan and Griffin. The very idea of them getting a divorce deepens my scowl. It just doesn't sit right with me. And what in the world is up with Susie Mae acting so strange? Of course, I don't think Susan even realizes her daughter hangs out with me on the occasional lunch period. Laney and Susan fighting also makes my eyebrows descend deeper. They need to get over themselves. And how do I get out of the middle of it?

Jackson's father marrying that Shelby is just yuck, mostly for Jackson and his brothers. I'll go, stand in the background, and smile when appropriate. But still… Yuck, right?

Will and Anna of course involves me and my family, but as I try to give them some space, I'm able to relax and let things happen there. They are adults. Breathe. But what if…?

Savannah and Bryan are not on the front burners as far as I know with anything. Bryan kissed Zoe and Savannah needs to make a college decision, but those are normal worries, right?

Maybe I just feel out of sorts because Halloween came and went, and no one seemed to notice. We never did carve pumpkins. I mean, the kids went to parties, but we didn't have even one trick-or-treater. I sat here all alone with a bowl full of candy. Maybe I'm out of sorts because my blood sugar is probably still off the charts. Midweek Halloweens are never good, especially in this kind of weather, which drizzles and spits day after day.

Standing, I stretch my back and then walk to the kitchen counter. It's another gray November day with more rain expected tonight. Reaching into an upper cupboard, I pull out two boxes of Hamburger Helper Cheeseburger Macaroni to make up into a large casserole to put in the refrigerator. Later I'll cover it with shredded cheese, bake it for twenty minutes and dinner will be once again mastered.

Hamburger and onion is frying and macaroni boiling when

I hear a knock on the front door followed by, "Yoo-hoo! It's me. Carolina?"

I step to the kitchen door to see Laney carrying Cayden's carrier and her big satchel inside. "Hey, come on in."

"Smells good in here. What are you cooking?"

"Supper for later. I want to go back downtown and watch the filming when Savannah gets there. What are you up to?" Stirring the meat allows me to stare at it and think about how to broach the subject of Alex and Angie.

Laney comes into the kitchen only carrying her satchel. "He's asleep, so I'll leave him in the living room. I went to the bookstore looking for you."

That gets me to turn around. "How was it? We were crazy busy this morning, but things had slowed down when I left. Guess they started filming down at the dance studio, so people moved there."

"Bonnie said it was much calmer. Plus, Shannon was there, so Bonnie said for me to tell you there's no hurry to get back." She pulls open the refrigerator and takes out one of the diet peach teas I bought over the summer but keep forgetting to drink. "Can I have this?" she asks as she's opening it. "You want some of it?"

"Naw, I don't really like it."

She grins at me as she closes the refrigerator. "Figured. They've been in there for months."

"So what did you want me for?" I go back to browning the meat as I try to decide if it'll be about Susan or Angie. Both have to be dealt with, and I'm sure both are on my friend's mind.

"This movie. I need some more details like time of year and weather. Is it set nowadays? Is it a happy movie, or would a more somber appearance be best? Leif obviously has too much on his plate to answer these things for me, but I need to know so I can fulfill my duties."

"Duties?" I shake my head and bite my lips, but I don't turn around. Silly me thinking she was concerned about the actual things she should be concerned about.

"To set local color! You know, you heard Leif and Tyler. I've done some research—well, googling—and that is a very important part of filming in small towns." Her voice dims as she looks into the living room. Then she comes back and sits down at the kitchen table. "I feel as if it is my responsibility to Chancey, my hometown. Who else can do this?"

Clicking off the burners, I finally turn around and look at her. She's wearing leggings and a long, burnt-orange tunic sweater. Her hair is a normal size (which is still bigger than for most folks), and her makeup is normal—again, normal for Laney Conner. I'm relieved. "You look nice."

"You're sweet. So give me the details. Then I can adjust my wardrobe and makeup. Hurry before Cayden wakes up."

"Honestly, I don't know anything other than the fact that Phoenix and Savannah were told to wear their normal clothes. That if anything else was needed wardrobe could take care of it."

A thundercloud rolls over her face. "See! That's what I want. Wardrobe to take care of things. I want to be in this movie!" She shouts the last line, and it's punctuated by a wail from Cayden. She jumps up with a huff, and I'm left standing beside the oven in astonishment. I hear her talking in low tones to the baby, so I give her some space as I put together the casserole. With that done I walk into the living room where she's sitting on the couch feeding Cayden a bottle.

"Hey there," I say as I pat her shoulder and then sit in the chair nearest her. "You okay?"

"Sure." She doesn't look up, but stares at the sweet boy in her arms. She sniffles, and it hurts my heart. She's always so vibrant and enthusiastic that I think we forget that having a baby is never easy, especially not when you are over forty and totally caught off-guard by said baby.

"You have a lot on your plate."

She nods and sniffs again, then says, "And a lot of it looks like Brussels sprouts," she says with a little laugh. "And I hate Brussels sprouts. My life has gone by way too fast. The girls were this size not a minute ago," she says then looks up at me. "I was young and beautiful just yesterday! You know, if these movie people had been around here when I was eighteen, well, they would've been *begging* me to be in their stupid movie."

"Absolutely," I state, but then sigh. "I know what you mean about life going fast. Maybe it's just that our kids are doing things that we remember so well. It feels like I was deciding on colleges last week, and here my daughter is. Not to mention Will having his first baby. It does all move awfully fast."

She sits Cayden up to burp, and he laughs and talks to me. It's impossible not to feel better with a happy baby on your lap, and soon Laney is laughing and there's no thunder on the horizon. She says, "About that full plate. Susan is most definitely a huge ol' pile of Brussels sprouts. Huge! I tried talking to her, but she doesn't want to hear one good thing about Griffin or Laurel Cove or that amazing house. She's all about Chancey and that dump of a place made mostly of cardboard. She tell you she painted her bedroom purple? I just have no idea what's gotten into her!"

"So... you talked?"

"Not really. I tried, you know I tried a couple times, but like I said, she wouldn't listen. She's playing make-believe. Like some teenager whose parents are out of town." She hands Cayden to me. "Hold him while I get stuff to change him. It's in my satchel. Like she's actually going to divorce Griffin. Split up the kids. Live in that tiny house. Give me a break!"

She bustles around getting the changing mat laid out on the

couch, finding a diaper and wipes, and then takes her son from me. While she's talking to him and getting his onesie unsnapped, I bravely venture into the pile of Brussels sprouts. "But what if they *do* divorce? They are both moving that direction. She's pretty sure… you know…"

And it hangs there while Laney talks to her cooing boy. He's cleaned up, pants re-snapped, sitting back in his carrier when she finally turns to me. "Susan? Don't worry. She'll come to her senses." She stands up. "And ignore all that about the movie. I'm just having a bad week. I'll check with Leif, and I'm sure he'll let me know what I need to know."

As she moves toward the door she says, "Check with Savannah if you want to go on any college tours with me and the girls. Angie is excited about Georgia College, so we'll be going down there. Jenna has her heart set on University of Georgia, but between you and me, I don't think her grades are good enough."

I follow her onto the porch where the damp greets us. "Savannah is talking about schools closer to home right now, but I'll let you know. You say Angie wants to go to Georgia College? Way on the other side of Atlanta?"

She stops on the top step, and her head twists so she can stare at me. "Yes. Have you heard something different?"

There's that delusion staring me in the face. It's shouting, "Do *not* say anything that will challenge what I have just said!"

But, well, I like to live dangerously so… "Aren't she and Alex serious?"

Laney shrugs and looks away for a minute. "Not as a couple. It's all about their business. That's all."

Her eyes meet mine again, and, well, I don't like to live *that* dangerously. "Oh, okay."

With a small nod she acknowledges my acquiescence and continues down the steps. "Looks like more rain," she says. "Y'all stay dry."

"You, too." I yell from the porch.
Guess what?
I'm scowling again.

Chapter 26

"Can I go with you?" a voice pipes up as I'm walking down the sidewalk away from Blooming Books. I turn around to see Susie Mae walking toward me. Her big eyes and neck are both stretched in question.

"Where?" I ask as I slow for her to catch up.

"Where you're going. You know. To see Missus."

I goggle at her. "Why do you think I'm going to see Missus?"

She shrugs and shivers a bit.

"Where's your coat?" I ask, fully expecting another shrug. Asking teenagers about their coats is a practice in futility right up there with dusting. Or sweeping. Vacuuming. All of those useless pursuits.

However, she points behind her. "I saw you on your phone in your shop. I wanted to catch you before you left. My coat's in the shop."

The filming in the bookstore was tedious in my opinion. We couldn't hear what the actors were saying to each other, and we kept being shushed when we tried to talk. Phoenix and Savannah walked to and fro in the background whenever they were told to. They didn't seem bored at all. When my phone rang for the second time after a couple of text notifications, I was practically shoved out the door. Anna wanted to know if I'd go check on Missus as Dollar Store needed her to work late. I grabbed my coat and purse and left gladly.

I dismiss Susie Mae. "No, you can't come. Go back inside."

She shivers longer as she turns and looks at the door. "Can't. They've got it blocked to keep people from going back and forth." It's not raining yet, but it's misting and her dark, spiky hair is limp with the moisture. She sniffles, and I move toward her and put my arm around her.

"Well, you can't stay out here." Peter's is closed, and my car is parked right on the corner. "Okay, come on. But you have to stay in the car," I warn. "You can't come inside."

She grins and nods, so we dart to the car.

The afternoon is dreary and damp, but the car warms us up quickly. "How did you know I was going to visit Missus?"

"I guess I just assumed someone needed to go see her, right? How is she?"

Instead of answering her questions, I ask more. "Don't you need to let your mom know where you are?"

"Mom'll text me if she wants to know. Think she'll look good when she's all done?"

"I thought she already looked good. Anna says the doctor took the last couple stitches out today, and she's doing really well." I take a look in her direction. "So what's new in your world?"

"The movie."

"Do you want to be in the movie?"

She shakes her head briskly. "No. I'm much more of a be-hind-the-scenes person. I like being involved, but you know. Not right up front."

I nod. I know exactly what she means. "Things with your family, you're okay?"

She bites her lip and turns toward me. "I think so. However, it's a very interesting time to be alive, don't you think?"

With a little laugh I meet her gaze. "I guess. Why do you say that?"

"Just a lot of interesting things happening in Chancey." Her phone chimes. She settles back into her seat and begins studying her phone.

When my phone chimes, I look over to see a text from Will. "Dinner?" As I pull up to the stop sign, no cars in sight, I quickly text back: "yes 6"

I see Susie Mae's eyes switch toward my phone, but she doesn't say anything. I pull across the intersection and drive on into the gloom, trying to decide if Susie Mae is up to something or if she's just odd. Something definitely feels weird.

"You weren't in there very long," Susie Mae says when I open the car door.

"The nurse seemed put out that I had disrupted their schedule," I tell her as I get in. "Missus was getting ready to eat. She's off the pain meds now, and she's getting grouchy. Neither she nor the nurse looked pleasant. They've been together more than a week now. I'd be cranky, too, I guess."

I crank the heat up and pull out of the small parking lot behind the inn. "So give. Why did you want to come with me?"

She shrugs, then sets her phone in the cup holder between us. "I wanted to see this place where Missus is."

"Why?"

"I just think it's interesting. It's something different. People think living in a small town is boring, but they just don't understand that there is always something going on."

"Really?"

"Yeah. Maybe it was us moving up to Laurel Cove, but this summer I really got to noticing how much happens in Chancey. I wonder if it's the same in other small towns."

"I imagine."

"Can I turn on the radio?" she asks even as she leans forward to press the button. We drive through the gray day as it turns to black, and when we pass the Welcome to Chancey sign, I smile. Small towns are still not my favorite, but maybe it's all according to perspective. Maybe I should try Susie Mae's approach.

We pull back in front of Blooming Books, and I park across the street. There are still bright lights inside, but we can see most of the crowd has moved to the back of the store. We are free to open the front and go inside.

Susan greets us with a wave and shouts, "How's Missus?"

I roll my eyes at her and shush her. "No one's supposed to know!"

She rolls her eyes back at me but leans to laugh with the lead actor, Silas Pendersen, who's sitting on the arm of our sofa. "Si finds our little town adorable. Si, you've met Carolina, right?"

We both say we've met, then he stands up. "I'm going to get something to eat before the break is over." He weaves his way to the back, and I notice Susan watching him as he goes.

Out of the corner of my eye, I also see Susie Mae noticing her mother's focus. Has the girl always been this observant? Rattling my keys in my hand, I say, "Well, I have to go home. Bryan will be done with football practice soon and will need dinner. Let me go speak to my daughter."

Savannah is in the middle of the cast and crew, eating around the table. Leif had made sure to invite Savannah to the family-style meals particular to Leif's style of directing. He believes it helps the cast bond and keeps from having to round up the actors when he's ready to begin shooting again.

She stands as I watch her to talk to Leif and the main actress, Jenny. Her chin is high. Savannah holds her own with these people. Her sparkle is definitely back, and I'm glad this is working out for her. Gotta love when a teenager is obsessed with something other than who they're dating.

"Hey there," I beam. "How are things going?"

They open their circle for me, and Savannah actually gives me a side-armed hug. "Hi, Mom. It's great! Jenny and Leif are so encouraging about me being a professional actor."

"That's wonderful. Glad you're enjoying it. I've got to get home, so I just wanted to say hi. When do you think you'll be done here?" I ask, looking from her to Leif.

He says, "Savannah is done for the day, but we've told her she's welcome to stay and watch. Tonight we'll be doing more of the close-up scenes and the scenes in the store after it's closed."

"Homework?" I ask.

Her eyes dart to the clock over the register. "I'll be home by seven, okay?"

"Okay. We'll be done with dinner, but that's fine." Leif and Jenny both had begun to walk back up to the set. Savannah went with them in spirit as she was no longer even looking at me. "Bye," I say. She halfway answers with a faded goodbye and a wave.

I'm laughing as I turn to walk away from the set and slide out the front door. At the door I look to the side and realize Susan is standing in the window next to Silas. I do a double take when I realize his hand is on her back. It's not placed low or in a spot that's actually inappropriate, but still... Turning a little farther, I find what I expected—Susie Mae standing half-way behind a bookcase also watching her mom. She lifts her phone and takes a picture. She must feel my gaze, because she looks at me and grins before taking another picture. This time in my direction.

I give her a questioning look, but she grins bigger and waves at me. I wave back but give her a mean look with a swipe of my eyes toward her mother. A look that says, "I'm going to talk to your mother about this." She gets the message because she shrugs, then lifts her phone higher to take another picture.

I walk out into the dark. With a glance back at the lighted front window, I see Susan looking up into the actor's down-turned face, and I swear she looks so much like her sister.

My shudder is just because I'm cold. Don't you think?

"Anna, would you be interested in going to the shower for Shelby up in Kentucky? It's two weeks from Saturday."

Dinner is about over. Bryan is still eating, but he's slowed down from the frantic shoveling in of food he always begin with, especially after football practice. He's actually beginning to groan under his breath, but he pops one last piece of bread-stick into his mouth before leaning back and declaring himself stuffed.

Anna reaches for the salad bowl. "Anyone want the rest of this? I'm trying so hard to eat healthy, and the salad was really good. This is spinach, right?"

"Yes," I say. "And the dressing is light but with bacon flavoring. Feel free to finish it off."

Will's look at her is so sweet, and I'm touched to think they might just make it. Then he opens his mouth. "I can't hardly even remember what you looked like before you were big like that," he says with laugh. "Seems like you've always been pregnant, doesn't it?"

Anna's face crushes in on itself, and she stares at her plate.

"Will!" I practically shout. "What is wrong with you? She looks wonderful."

His mouth flies open, and he looks from her to me. "Of course she does! I was just saying that, well, um… I'm sorry. I meant it differently. That you look so good that you look normal to me. Or you know. I don't know. Sorry."

Even his little brother is shaking his head at him. "Dude," Bryan says.

Will reaches over to his wife and pats her hand. She's seated beside him on the corner across from me. Anna shrugs his hand off and speaks to me. "I don't know about going all the way to Kentucky this pregnant. I can check with my doctor, but… are you sure you want to go?"

"I'm absolutely sure I *don't* want to go," I say. "However, if it means getting away with you and Savannah for a night, then I'm up for it."

"See, they *do* think of you as family," Will says but the cut of her eyes at him tells me that he's sharing a confidence in public.

Again, Bryan is quicker on the uptake than his big brother. Bryan reaches for another breadstick and says, "Will, you might wanna stop talking. You're kind of an idiot."

"Bryan! Don't call your brother an idiot." I demand. Then, taking advantage of both of my sons being idiots, I instruct them to clean the table and kitchen.

"But I have homework," Bryan wails, accompanied by Will spouting the same lament.

"Then you better hurry," I say. "And start thinking about the words coming out of your mouths from now on."

Anna stands and says, "I'll help," but Will shakes his head. "No way. No how. You go sit down and finish your tea. The men have this. Right, Bry?"

Bryan nods, and I sigh. A glimpse. Every so often you get a glimpse that you're putting good people out into the world.

And a glimpse has to be enough.

Chapter 27

Perfect. After the rain and clouds passed Tuesday night, we had absolutely perfect fall weather in north Georgia the rest of the week. Even better, it's forecasted to last all through the weekend and into next week. Mornings are chilly, even cold, but the afternoon temps in the fifties and sixties seem to have everyone in a good mood.

"Definitely doing a bonfire tonight," I say to the guests checking in on Friday.

"Out front so we can see any trains going by?" the older gentleman asks, and the other two men look up hopefully as well. Their wives laugh, roll their eyes, and one smacks her husband's arm.

"Afraid not. But you said you brought your scanners, so you'll know when to expect a train, right? Here are your rooms," I say as each couple peels off into their assigned rooms. "Oh, and we will be having cheese and wine on the deck later. And before you ask, yes, you can take yours to the front porch. Plenty of seats out there."

One by one the doors close, and I return to the kitchen. This is the first time in a while we've had dedicated railfans in all three rooms. In the fall, many people come for the leaves.

The trains are an extra bonus. These men, though, as well as their wives, belong to a train club near Atlanta. The wives said their trips include a healthy amount of antiquing as well as train watching, and all six like both activities.

Jackson should be home soon. With the beautiful weather I'm anticipating a big turnout for our wine and cheese afternoon. The only person I know won't be here is the one driving me the craziest—Missus. She won't come home until she's completely healed, and yet she wants to know every little thing that's happening here.

Mostly she wants to know what everyone is saying about her being gone. "Where does everyone think I am?" Are they all worried about me?" She then adds, "Of course, I completely expect no one to notice my absence."

Yeah, right. The truth is that no one is asking because everyone *knows* where she is, but she still doesn't know that everyone knows. Her nurse quit yesterday (surprise, surprise), which is fine with the doctor, as he says she doesn't need round-the-clock care any longer. So, she's sitting in her room at the inn staring in the mirror and willing herself to heal while driving me and Anna completely crazy. It almost makes me want to tell her that everyone knows, so she should just chill out and come home. Except home for her is my house until the movie is finished. So…

"Miss Carolina?" Laney's daughter Jenna comes in off the deck. She's wearing her cheerleader uniform, and her hair is tied up in a big ponytail with a sparkly bow. "I'm supposed to ask you if I can put the cheese out now." The daughter voted most likely to follow in her mother's footsteps is the one turning out to be the least trouble. Her personality, her hair, her bounce all say Extreme Southern Belle, especially when she's wearing her cheerleader uniform. Savannah comes in the door after her, wearing the same uniform, the same high ponytail, but looking completely different.

"Mom, we need to leave. Are we done?" Okay, maybe it's that tone of voice and I'd-like-to-die look that make her look completely different.

"Yes. To both of you. Yes, Jenna, you can put out the cheese, and yes, Savannah, you girls are done. Thanks so much for helping out. Jenna, where is your mom?"

She smiles and shrugs. "I don't know. She just told me to get all this over here to you before going to the game." She heads out to the deck, and my daughter follows. I can't help but laugh. Jenna bounces out, her ponytail and skirt in motion. Savannah strides out, daring her hair or clothes to move one inch. She's in a bad mood, but she won't say why. Maybe it's having Parker coming back around? Or is the movie not as much fun as she thought it would be? The rash of college acceptances her friends are getting making her realize things are changing? She can only growl, "I'm fine!" so many times a day before I stop asking. I consider asking one more time, then I hear voices on the front porch.

"Come on in!" I shout. The screen door opens, and the ladies from Laurel Cove pile inside. Our overnight guests venture into the noise from down the B&B wing, and I motion for them to join the party. "Everything is ready in the backyard. Help yourselves. Susan Lyles is out there, and I'll join y'all in a minute," I say as I fight against the incoming folks in the living room. "My husband just pulled up and I'm going to go say hello to him."

I reach Jackson just as he gets out of his truck. "Welcome to the party," I say. He hugs me, and we kiss.

"Hope everyone doesn't get that welcome," he jokes. "Can you carry that? I'll get my suitcase." He hands me his laptop bag, and I take his empty coffee cup out of the holder. "Man, it's good to be home," he says, punctuating it with a sigh.

"It's good to have you home."

We walk up the sidewalk, and he says, "Saw Savannah and Jenna leaving. Where are they headed?"

"One of the playoff games is having the cheerleaders of teams that didn't make the playoffs come and cheer. Well, I thought they were cheering, but apparently they are just helping with tickets and stuff." I finally give in with a shrug. "I don't really know. Savannah just said they have to go. You know how hard it is to actually get useful information out of her, especially when she's in a mood. She's having a blast with the movie, I think, but who knows?"

I pull open the screen door, and he holds it for me to go in front of him. "That's good. She texted with me some about it this week." At the sound coming from the back deck and kitchen he looks up, then stops at the stairs. "I'm going up to get changed, and I'll be down in a minute. Make sure there's a cold beer. I can't wait to meet these railfan guests."

I lean into him and give him another kiss. "They are definitely your kind of people. See you in a minute."

In the kitchen, three of the ladies from Laurel Cove are in a tight little circle. Plastic glasses filled with wine in hand, each is wearing black pants, fall-colored sweaters, and big earrings. They take a step back when I enter the room.

"Oh!" Aggie says, then she looks at the other two. "Carolina might know." Aggie is the leader of the ladies who lunch at the Laurel Cove clubhouse each week. When Susan moved up there, she was invited, and then she invited me one week. I invited the ladies to our first wine and cheese afternoon, and now they have a standing invitation. Their word of mouth has resulted in several guests for our B&B, so it's a good relationship, I suppose.

"What might I know?" I say.

Aggie looks over her shoulder at the doors to the deck. "Susan and Griffin. Is it true?"

With a sigh and a nod, I say, "I guess. She's practically already moved out into a house her mother rents here in Chanc-ey. It's sad."

The ladies nod at each other. "But what about, you know…" One of the ladies raises her eyebrows at me.

"You know what?"

"Their housekeeper is my housekeeper, and she says, well…" The woman pulls back and closes her mouth.

"She says what?"

The woman, whose name I can't remember, which is true of both of the women not named Aggie, just shakes her head at me. The other one (who I believe is Marilyn? Marie?) speaks up. "It's really not much of a secret anymore, is it?" She shrugs a bit at Aggie, who rolls her eyes and sighs.

Aggie takes a deep breath. "He, Griffin. He has another woman."

"What?! No, he doesn't," I protest. "He's not like that. *They* aren't like that. They probably will be getting back together. This is just a temporary thing."

All three women shake their heads at me. Mrs. No-Name, the one not possibly named Mary, says, "My housekeeper says he told her. He told her himself."

"Why would he tell the housekeeper?" I blurt, probably louder and more defensively than I should. "That makes no sense."

This time they all three look down, then No-Name speaks in a whisper, with a little too much glee in my opinion. "He told her because… she's moving in."

The back door swings open, and we all gasp like we've been caught. And we were. Susan sails into the room with two emp-ty bottles of wine in her hands.

"Hey!" she says to me. "There you are. What are you doing in here? We forgot to put out a trash can…" Her voice trails off as she surveys our guilty circle. "What's going on?"

The three gossipers look at me, and I get a rush of heat.

"Nothing. I'll get a trash can. Y'all go on out." I turn into the dining room acting like the trash can I want is not sitting right there in the kitchen. The four women skedaddle out the kitchen with Susan close behind them.

In the dining room I lean against the wall. Is that what's really going on? All this talk about them growing apart, is that just a smokescreen for him having an affair? Would he really move a woman in with him and Grant? Now I'm not only hot at being caught gossiping about Susan, I'm also furious at Griffin. Furious.

"What are you doing in here?" Jackson says, sticking his head around the corner. He holds up his phone as he ducks back into the kitchen, saying, "Just talked to Griffin and told him to come on down. You coming out?" Luckily my husband didn't stick around to actually look at me or he'd have seen my mouth hit the carpet at my feet.

I close my mouth and swallow. "Yes. Oh, and we need that trash can out there. I'll be there in a minute."

"Okay," he says. I hear him grab the can and go out the back door.

Surely Griffin won't bring his girlfriend, right?

I push off the wall, shaking my head and coughing to press down the nausea that tries to rise in my stomach.

Who knows? Who knows anything at all anymore?

Chapter 28

"Sorry. Not my fault," I read out loud off my phone. What in the world is Anna talking about?

I text back, "What?" Putting my phone in my jeans pocket, I head back outside with two more bottles of wine. It's been a good thirty minutes, and Griffin still hasn't arrived. The fire is roaring, and several folks are trying to get close enough to cook their hot dogs. Others are using it for warmth. The sky is still light, but sunset colors are gathering in the west. With all the bare limbs, the sky appears wider, bigger, and the beauty makes my eyes water. Or that could be smoke from the fire.

Or maybe I'm emotional due to Griffin's imminent arrival. I can't figure out if I should warn his wife that he has a girlfriend. A moving-in girlfriend. That conundrum drew me to drink my first glass of wine rather quickly. The second glass went down with hardly a blink when our cute, cute movie star, Silas Pendersen, showed up and attached himself to Susan's side. She appeared to be very attachable.

That threw the ladies from Laurel Cove into overdrive. Then the other male lead, the older, bearded gentleman who looks familiar showed up, and I found out why Herbert Fisk looks familiar. He's been on the same soap opera for about a million years and is actually the *real* star in the movie.

Our railfan guests no longer wanted to talk about trains. They want to talk about how they've watched *Promises Made* since it began when they were teenagers. Apparently the Susan-Griffin drama can't hold a candle to the drama the ladies of Laurel Cove enjoy daily on the soap. Mr. Fisk's appeal became even more evident as he began telling stories that captivated us all.

Even Bryan and Zoe, who were seated together on one tiny log acting like they weren't together, were fascinated. I'm really uncomfortable with my son dating someone who can just walk here any old time. Sounds like extra vigilance (read: work) for me.

At the end of a story from Mr. Fisk about a location shoot in Las Vegas, I move around to check out the provisions of hot dogs, buns, plates, and drinks. That's when I see Griffin walk around the side of the house. My earlier anger sparks as I watch him. Because he is a good friend's husband, I never looked at him as a man, just a friend. However, I have to admit, he isn't bad-looking. He's solid, but not heavy. He dresses nicer than he used to. No jeans for him tonight, although every other man around the fire is wearing jeans. He has on khakis and a flannel shirt, but it's a nice flannel shirt. It looks like it was hanging in a gentlemen's store next to a rack of tailored suits and a display of shoes with the names of foreign designers on them.

The thing that makes my heart flip is that there is no woman with him. Whew. However, when I see him catch himself and stop dead, I look to follow his eyes.

Great, Susan is now sitting on Silas Pendersen's knee.

I told Jackson we needed more chairs.

"Hey, Griffin," I shout out. It's plenty loud enough for him to break his stare, look at me, and give Susan time to jump up from her new friend's lap if she will. Now my anger is back, but at her.

"Hey, Carolina. Thanks for inviting me," he says with a charm that looks even better in nice clothes. "You've got quite a crowd."

"Yes, we do. You know the drill. Help yourself. Beer, hot dogs, wine, whatever you want." My back is to the fire, but I can see he's watching something over my shoulder. I can only hope it's his wife *not* sitting on a movie star's lap.

"Thanks," he says, pulling his eyes back to me. "I'm having dinner out later, so I'd better not. Oh, there's Jackson." When I break eye contact with him to look where he's motioning, he takes the opportunity to wander off.

I watch him greet my husband with a handshake. Then he grabs a beer out of the closest cooler, and they stand with some other men near the fire. Susan and Silas haven't moved. She's so thin and his legs are so long that her sitting on his knee doesn't look sexy or risqué at all. Maybe that's why Griffin is completely unbothered. Or maybe he's as good an actor as Silas?

"If I'd known *he* was going to be here, I probably wouldn't have come," says a voice behind me. A familiar voice, but different. I feel the person is close to my shoulder. When they don't say anything else, I turn. Of course it's getting darker, but...

"Hello, Carolina."

"Laney? What's going on?" It sounds like Laney, but the thick Southern drawl, the sharp volume shifts, are gone. And wait, she doesn't look like Laney either. "What are you wearing?"

She looks like she's been shopping with Griffin. She's wearing a straight khaki skirt that falls well below her knee, along with flat loafers and cream-colored cable knit tights. She's wearing a slouchy dark-green sweater with a plaid shirt underneath it. She no longer has any curves, just lumps and bumps and…

"Oh my goodness! What did you do to your hair?"

"I've often wondered how I would look with gray hair," she says. Her grin jumps out for a moment, then she swallows it.

"Is this for the movie?" I stammer.

Now a very Laney look crosses her face, anger. "Why in the Sam Hill can everyone else change their looks but wh—" She stops herself, swallows again, then smiles, just a smile, not a grin. "Like others, I, too, sometimes desire a change."

"Laney?" Okay, well at least this got her sister off that actor's lap. Susan creeps toward us. "What are you doing?"

Conflict plays across Laney's face. She isn't supposed to be talking to her sister, but would her new persona not be talking to her sister? Talking wins out. "Decided to change my looks. You gave up your tomboy attire and no makeup lifestyle. It seemed time for me to let go of the Southern Belle routine. I'm the mother of three now, and all that seductive dressing is no longer appropriate." Her eyelashes beat up and down, but not in the old flirty, batting her eyelids way. In a trying-to-hold-tears-back way.

Susan and I both reach out to her, but she steps back. "I'm going to warm up by the fire," she says as she hurries stiffly away from us.

Susan and I turn and look at each other. I strike first. "What in the world are you doing sitting on Si Pendersen's lap?"

She narrows her eyes, then widens them and shrugs. "Bryan and Zoe just left the fire headed toward the river and *the tent.*"

I glare at her for a moment, then turn towards the fire and yell, "Jackson!" By the time I get his attention and have him moving in my direction, she's strolling back to the light of the fire.

Jackson is also strolling, hands in his pockets and a small smile on his face. "Hey. What ya need? More hot dogs?"

I start motoring down the hill toward Bryan's campsite. "Your son and his new girlfriend are headed to that make-out spot you thought was just fine for him to set up down at the river."

He grabs my arm and jerks me off my course. "No, they're not. See? They're still listening to Mr. Fisk." He turns me toward the fire, and I see them on their same log, roasting hot dogs with their faces turned to the old man.

"But Susan said—"

"Susan said wrong," Jackson says firmly. "Speaking of Susan, you didn't tell me she and that Pendersen fellow were together." He puts his arm around me and leads us back towards the fire.

I can't believe it. Susan threw me off on purpose. She sent me off so she could go back to that actor. She's acting more and more like her sister every day.

Jackson squeezes me as our strides match, and we walk. Then he asks close to my ear, "Since when did Laney go gray?"

Chapter 29

"Y'all plum broke Laney," Ruby says. We're meeting in the middle of her café on Saturday morning, me looking for a seat, her looking for a chance to laugh at Laney. They've been archrivals since Ruby's daughter and Laney were chasing Shaw back in high school. Ruby's daughter hasn't cared in a couple decades, but Ruby doesn't like to let things go. And Laney eggs it on every chance she gets. Well, that's what the old Laney did. I've no idea what the new Laney will do.

"I just want a cup of coffee and some peace and quiet," I say as I slide onto a chair at one of the middle tables.

She turns back to get the coffee pot (I hope), but she keeps talking. "Yep, everyone this morning been talking about that big shindig up at your place last night. Thought that was supposed to be some high-falutin' wine and cheese afternoon thing. I heard there were folks up there hootin' and a-hollerin' way past the moon coming up."

I look around at the near empty café. "Everyone?"

Carrying the coffee pot in one hand and a plate of muffins in the other, she doesn't miss a beat. She sways her skinny hips, which makes the big turkey with the shiny feathers on her chest look like it's doing a fan dance. As she gets closer I see the turkey has those glued-on googly eyes, and they are bouncing back and forth, too. I can't help but smile.

"Everyone who was not still up when good God-fearing people should be in bed was in here getting coffee 'fore now. Land sakes, Carolina, it's near nine o'clock. Pert near lunch time." She fills my cup. "Got three muffins this morning," she says with a tip of her head toward the plate she brought to my table. "Sweet potato with some little marshmallows on top, get it? That one there is my regular corn muffin, and then that's a gingerbread one I'm working on."

"I'll try the sweet potato one. Thanks," I say. I'm beginning to feel a little better until she pulls out the chair across from me and sits down.

There's not enough marshmallows and coffee in the world to fix that.

Her eyes are dancing more than the turkey's. "So, tell. Laney's gray and frumpy. Susan was making out with that good-looking actor. How young you think he is? Oh, and Griffin already has a new woman on the way in?"

The light brown crust on the marshmallow topping breaks just like on a sweet potato casserole. Underneath it's sweet and soft. The muffin is rich but spicy, and counterpoints the topping perfectly. I moan a bit as I take a sip of hot coffee. Every time I tried to get a cup of coffee this morning at the house, there was a guest wanting a refill, which meant making a new pot. I finally headed out saying I would pick up tomorrow's muffins knowing I could get a cup of coffee here. I take another bite and avoid looking at my table companion. Okay, so she knows about Laney, Susan, and Griffin, but so far…

"This muffin is really, really good," I say when my mouth is empty. I venture a look up at her. She's grinning from ear to ear. Could be about Laney, Susan, and Griffin, right? Okay, I'll try. "So what else were people saying this morning?"

"What I already mentioned."

My shoulders actually drop a good inch in relief. I lift my muffin to take another bite. She doesn't know. Maybe…

"And that Missus is back, read you the riot act, and then went high-tailin' it off with that famous actor. The one with the beard. I swear, Carolina, FM is rolling over in his grave. The whole town is liable to cave in." Her grin dissolves into a grimace. "I have been telling people for years she's a floozy. FM was a gift from God to her. He was a real gentleman. A real gentleman!"

The tension in my shoulders is back, and my stomach doesn't feel that good all of a sudden. It was just not a good night.

After I got the text from Anna saying, "Sorry not my fault," I stuck my phone in my pocket and didn't see her subsequent texts saying Missus had left the inn and was headed our direction. She'd found out that everyone knew where she'd been. And she'd found out it was me that spilled the beans. She arrived on our back deck in a tailored suit with a beautiful peacock-blue pashmina draped over her shoulders. She'd had her hair styled, and the firelight picked up the blond sheen. I didn't see a lot of structural change in her face in the shadows, but her makeup looked professionally, and dramatically, applied. It was a successful staging as she looked every bit like a queen standing above her court.

A vengeful queen, once she found me in the crowd.

She roared, "Carolina Jessup. Off with your head!"

I'm not joking. She actually said that. Out loud, like she meant it. Before I could say I was sorry and try to explain, our famous actor Herbert Fisk stepped away from the fire and towards her outstretched arm. Again, I'm not joking. Her arm was stretched out toward me in royal judgment.

"Madam. Am I to understand you've been wronged?" As he stepped to our deck stairs he actually bent his knee. Not all the way to the ground, but in a dip and at the same time he bowed his head. All he needed was a sword to lay at her feet. Wonder if he's been in that show *Game of Thrones*?

She raised an imperial eyebrow, and as he came to stand fully upright there were sparks. He offered his arm, and she descended the stairs holding onto him. I don't believe she let go of that arm all night. However, as you can imagine, I didn't hang out around her much.

Ruby slaps the table. "Carolina! I'm talking to you. Did they really leave together?"

My mouth opens, but I can't think of what should come out of it. They were there. Then they weren't there. Did I do a bed check around the house last night to see where everyone was? No. It was late. I'd had wine. I'd been sentenced for beheading. I had friends losing their minds, but acting like it was no big deal. Guests who apparently like railroading, antiquing, *and* playing guitars and singing old folk songs. Yep, it was a big, noisy night around the bonfire.

"I honestly don't know," I finally say to Ruby and watch as her forehead folds into a multitude of wrinkles that press down on her eyes and nose.

"Bah!" she says as she stands up. "I'll go get your order of muffins." She stalks off behind the counter where Libby has been busy. She sends Libby out to refill coffee, and I finish my cup while Libby checks on the few other customers. When she gets to my table she fills my cup and then sets the pot down and plants her thin behind in the chair across from me.

"Carolina, is it true?"

I take a sip of the fresh coffee and then sigh, but I smile as I look up at her. "Probably. But okay, is *what* true?"

She takes a deep breath. "It's probably not any of my business, but I just have to ask. I mean, I feel like I have some experience in this area. You know, with my Cathy and all."

"You mean with divorce? Or," with a smile I nod at her gray hair, "or with gray hair?" I lean closer to her. She's such a sweet lady, so I can't help but grin and say, "Or are you saying that you've run off with a dashing actor before?"

She shakes her head and actually blushes. "Oh my, no. Not any of that. I don't know anything about any of that but you know, is it true about... about Savannah?"

"What?" Immediately her daughter's high school pregnancy jumps to the front of my brain. I'm no longer grinning as I hiss, "Is *what* true about Savannah?"

"You know my son-in-law Stephen *is* her teacher, and well, he finds out stuff about the students. He tells Cathy, and sometimes she tells me. I am her mama, and well—"

"What?" I shout. Then I lower my voice. "What?"

She tsks and shakes her head. "It was just so awful with Cathy, and so I feel I can help, you know."

Now I'm just weary. "No. I don't know. What?"

After taking a deep breath she lets it all out in a rush. "Is it true Savannah isn't going to college?"

"College?" Lack of sleep due to nightmares of gray-headed queens running around my backyard and dismal amounts of caffeine have left my brain without the resources to say or think anything. Luckily, Ruby shouts for Libby. With a sympathetic look at me she jumps up and scurries back behind the counter.

Well, I guess I should've made time to think about what my daughter was mad about because not going to college sure wasn't on my list of possibilities.

But, hey, she's not pregnant.

As far as I know.

I look around the café. The seat at my table is empty. Anyone else want to sit down and brighten my day?

CHAPTER 30

I could go home. Or I could go to the grocery store. I always need something from them, and it opened at eight. Blooming Books won't be open for another half-hour, but I do have a key so I could always go there. Or I could just sit here in this nice, warm van and think.

The box of muffins is securely in the back so that it can't tempt me. My coat and the sunshine are helping the heater keep me toasty. There was a layer of frost on the roofs this morning, and I even had to scrape my windshield. I'm parked along the side of the square so that my view takes in Missus' house. Wonder where the movie people are shooting today?

Phoenix comes striding along the sidewalk in front of the library. She's all the way across the square, but with that red hair it's easy to know it's her. Her apartment with Colt is on the block behind the library, up by the church. She has on a long, dark coat and boots with high heels. Her hair is hanging down her back, but held back by a wide, knitted band on her forehead like I've seen Savannah wear. When I tried to wear one of those I looked like a Revolutionary War soldier with a head wound. You know, like in all the pictures, the one banging on the drum. Or is it playing the flute thing?

Anyway. Phoenix looks like she's doing a magazine cover. As she turns the corner and dashes across the street, her coat flaps open and I can see her emerald-green sweater. Wouldn't it be nice to have red hair and green eyes and know you could put on green anytime and look spectacular?

She stops at the door to the dance studio and unlocks it. With the big windows I can still see her as she moves from movie set to movie set, turning on lights. Maybe that's where they're filming today.

A van pulling up in front of Blooming Books catches my eye, and I try to make out the words on the side of it. Finally I pick out *Catering* and I realize this must belong to Margery. Yep, that's her jumping out of the driver's door. She runs around to the front door of my shop, and it's opened immediately. Andy blocks open the door and them joins her at the back of the van. I watch them unload boxes and tubs and wish I had a cup of coffee to sip while I watch.

Then Peter comes down the sidewalk from his house. He waves through the windows at Phoenix, stops to hold the door for an older couple coming out of Ruby's, and talks with them for a minute. He continues on to the door of his bistro and unlocks it. He doesn't have many windows, so I can no longer see him once he's inside, just the lights coming on. He has a neon sign that jumps on, saying, "Open," and I look at the clock on my dash. He's a bit early with the sign.

Andy finishes helping Margery unload. He lumbers down the sidewalk and over to Andy's Place. He's got a big smile on his face, but then, doesn't he always? Patty is such a Gloomy Gus that they make a good match, like a pair of complimentary bookends. He sure looks happy. I wonder if they are expecting yet? I know Gertie's ready, but I'm not sure if they've said that they're ready.

"Carolina? What are you doing?" a face close to my passenger window shouts. It's a good thing I don't have a cup of coffee because I'd have spilled it everywhere when I jumped out of my skin. I'd missed Peter leaving his shop, apparently, and walking this way.

"Peter! You scared me to death," I tell him as I press the button on my door to roll down the window.

"Sorry. Just saw your van out here. I usually take a walk around the block before I get any customers, so I thought I'd come check on you instead." He leans one arm on the open window and smiles. "So... big night up on the hill."

Oh man, wonder if he's heard about his mother. "Yep, it was. It's cold out there. You can get in if you want."

He opens the passenger door, and I roll up the window from my door controls. And I wait to see just what he knows.

He shivers and says, "It does feel good in here. So, Mother found out you let the cat out of the bag about her procedure." He's smiling big, so I smile back and answer with a question.

"You've talked to Missus?"

"She spent the night at our house."

"Oh! So that's where..."

He's laughing and seems to be in a pretty good mood for someone Missus descended on last night. "Mother looks right good, don't you think? She was pretty happy when she showed up. I think she might've stopped off and had a nightcap with Gertie. She'd gone to her house first and was going to just spend the night there, but the movie crew had her staircase blocked off."

"Missus was drinking with Gertie?"

"Well, that's what I assume. She seemed awfully happy. Except about you. Said she'd be dealing with you today. So, hiding out might not be that bad of an idea. She told us about Susan and that Silas guy and that Laney dyed her hair gray, just kept rambling on and on. I mean, you can see why we thought she'd been drinking."

He's laughing again, and he's not mentioned Mr. Fisk. *I'm*

sure not bringing him up. Peter checks his watch. "Better go." He opens his door. "What are you up to today?"

I shrug. "Just regular stuff, oh, and avoiding your mother."

He steps out and then looks back at me. "Oops, looks like that's not going to happen." He nods toward the gazebo area, and I see his mother headed our direction. She waves her hand at us to make sure she's been seen. He leans in the car and says, "Be nice. She really needs to not stay at our house tonight, okay?" He grins at me. "Although Shannon said trying to stay quiet this morning was kind of fun."

I glare at him. "Usually Missus is the first one up at our house, so we never have to keep quiet for her."

With a leer, he steps back. "I meant before we got up, if you know what I mean." He winks and turns to say "Good morning" to his mother as she approaches.

Yuck. People that brag about how early they get up are bad. People that brag about their sex life are bad. People that manage to do both? Luckily, those are few and far between.

Peter holds the door open and helps her into the seat he'd just left. He closes the door with another smile at me. I ignore him and turn to look at Missus.

She sighs and says, "I think I liked my son better when he was brooding and sad." Then she turns to me. She's wearing a brown herringbone wool skirt with boots and a cream turtleneck under another wrap like she wore last night, except this one is soft brown. Her hair is swept up in layers of swirls as it was last night, looking full and shiny. Her makeup is again applied with a professional hand, her lipstick is perfect and her lips look fuller.

"Did you get lip injections, too?" I ask.

Her hand flies to her lips. "No, just some new, uh, new lipstick. And I've started lining them. I bought all new makeup last week and learned how to line them and stuff."

Stuff? I don't believe I've ever heard her use that word. Except when she was telling me how stupid it made me sound when I used it. Her cheeks look warm, warmer than they were when she got in my van. She's blushing? Naw. "Okay, you wouldn't let me say this last night, but I am so sorry I let it out what you were doing with your, uh your face. It was completely by accident, and I feel horrible. Please forgive me."

"Oh, of course. You know I can never stay mad at you, Carolina. Plus, it would've been silly of me to expect you not to tell, correct?" She looks at me, and I don't think she's being facetious. She actually doesn't look mad.

"Okaaaayy." I'm not sure what else to say.

Luckily for me, she doesn't pause long. "So it might seem incredulous what I'm about to ask, but I need you to not tell my son about last night."

"Last night?"

She fusses with her shawl and looks down at her gloved fingers. "I could tell talking to Peter just now that you had not told him about last night. I must tell you, when I saw him get in your van as I was walking to Ruby's, my heart did jump."

"But, Missus, if you're talking about you leaving with Mr. Fisk, everyone at the party saw that. Not just me." If she had *any* idea she had been a topic of conversation at Ruby's this morning, her heart would be doing more than just jumping.

Her head snaps toward me, and she examines my face. "Are you saying that's all you, ah, saw? Me accepting a ride home from him? From Mr. Fisk?"

She studies me while I try to remember anything else, but she's apparently satisfied with my clueless look because she opens her car door. She steps out and closes it before I say another word. She's striding off across the square, leaving me wondering what just happened.

What else does she think I saw? Then I remember. In one of the strange cars in our driveway last night, there was a couple making out pretty heavily when I went into the living room to close the drapes. I was afraid it was Susan, so I closed the drapes quickly and didn't look anymore. It couldn't have been Missus, could it? Missus and Mr. Fisk?

I put the van in reverse and start backing out. I'm going to forget this entire morning. I do not want to know anything about any of this. How does all this happen when I was just trying to enjoy some peace and quiet? I'd have been better off staying home.

At the corner, I pause to look down the street to my left. The sun is no longer that early, muted sun but is bright. The frost on the roofs is steaming as it melts, and although it might not feel much warmer, it looks much warmer. More people are on the sidewalks, especially in front of the dance studio where they are in fact filming today. As I watch, my daughter's car passes in front of me. She pulls into a parking spot and shortly jumps out of her car. She has some papers in her hand ,and a coffee cup from the house in the other as she darts across the street. She doesn't pause at Blooming Books or Ruby's. She's headed straight for the dance studio. Could she have scenes there? She's supposed to be just doing background in the bookshop. She chats with the other movie people for a minute before disappearing inside. From this angle I can't see inside the big windows.

I look to my right and toward home. Then I look back down where Savannah is. Hmm. I pull down and look into the rearview mirror. Yep, not a lick of makeup, my hair looks like I thought it might, and I smell like woodsmoke. A big part of me wants to go see what's going on with my daughter and this movie and her going to college, but there's the embarrassment I'd cause.

Not to her. Embarrassing my kids is part of my job. Keeps 'em humble.

But me? I do just fine embarrassing myself when I don't try, so, home it is.

Besides, maybe letting her see how tedious this whole acting thing can be will change her mind for me. Then she'll never have to know I know about her thinking she's not going to college.

Quit laughing. It could happen.

Chapter 31

Before I pulled away from the stop sign, I got a text from Susan. "What's up with Laney playing Paula Deen?"

My reading the text was punctuated by a car horn. I tossed my phone in the seat beside me and pulled out and to the right, heading home. The car behind me was right on my tail, so I couldn't pause at the next stop. I headed up the hill to our house thinking about Laney cooking something like Paula Deen, the chef. Laney doesn't cook much at all. If she did, she would not have a problem with Miss Deen's liberal use of butter, so maybe she was going to use some of the recipes from the cooking show or one of Paula Deen's books for Thanksgiving?

Near the top of the hill, I see several kids and slow down as one of them belongs to me.

"Bryan, what are you doing?" I ask out the window. Zoe is walking next to him, but I see no cuddling or her hand in his coat pocket, like Brittani's always seemed to be. Of course, the lack of contact right now might be due to Zoe's brothers and sister walking in front of them. The baby Kevin is a year old. He's toddling between five-year-old K.J. and three-year-old Katherine.

He nods at the line of kids in front of them and says, "We're watching the little kids for an hour. Her folks are paying us five dollars to keep them outside."

Zoe looks at me with her wise eyes and smiles. "They wanted some time to themselves, if you know what I mean."

Lots of Saturday morning sex is apparently going on all over Chancey.

"So your mom and dad are doing well?" I ask decorously.

They'd been separated this summer. It was disastrous for not only their family, but mine as well. Kyle Kendrick moved in with my daughter-in-law, who was also his employee. He moved back home after Zoe got caught making some bad decisions of her own, and the whole family went into serious counseling. I'm happy Kyle and Kimmy are doing well, but I'm even happier Anna thinks it was all a huge mistake on her part.

"Yeah, they're doing pretty good, I think. How are Anna and Will?" Zoe asks. "I asked Bryan but he just shrugs."

"He is his father's son. Anna and Will seem to being doing pretty well. The baby is due in only a few weeks."

Baby Kevin stumbles and falls onto his diaper-padded behind, and Zoe steps forward to lift him up before there can be any tears. She soothes him expertly, and I'm reminded of how mature Zoe always acted before her vandalism episode. One thing the counselors hopefully talked to her parents about was that she acted more adult than they did. I'm not sure how adult it is to send your one-year-old out into the cold for an hour so you can stay in bed, but hey, it's progress that they are actually paying Zoe something for all of the work they make her put in.

"Y'all want to come up the house and have some hot chocolate?" I ask.

KJ and Katherine answer for them, and KJ reaches for the

side door on the van. He pulls it open, and he and his sister scramble in.

Mature Zoe looks inside and says, "There's no car seat for Kevin."

"Sit him in KJ's lap, and I promise I won't drive over five miles per hour. You and Bryan can walk."

My son's face lights up. He grins at me quickly before looking at Zoe. She's frowning, but then sighs and steps to the van to place Kevin on his big brother's lap. "I guess it's okay. Kev, you sit right here with KJ. Miss Caro is going to take you to her pretty house for chocolate milk. Okay? I'll be there in just a minute."

As we pull off, slowly, I look back to see Bryan offer his hand to Zoe. She takes it with a giggle. Good, she needs to get to be a kid sometimes.

The three little kids are sitting in the living room with their drinks and cups of dry cereal watching cartoons. Bryan and Zoe are having their hot chocolate in the front porch rockers. I abandon my return text to Susan and just call her. I'm fine with quick texts, but whole conversations? No thanks.

"Hey," I say. "So Laney's into cooking?"

Susan shouts, "What? Laney's cooking now, too? Seriously, what is up with her?"

"Where are you? Why are you yelling?"

"I'm at the lake park. They're cutting down some dead trees that had to get taken down before tonight. We have a big party booked for the pavilion, and the one dead tree from the storm started falling yesterday. Okay, should be better now. I'm in the office."

The background noise of saws and men shouting stops. I ask, "Who booked a party outside in November?"

"It's the Perkins family, Jim's on the park board. We put in that bonfire pit, remember? This will be the first time it's used. I'm planning on a community event the weekend before Thanksgiving if I can get it to come together. So you said Laney's cooking something?"

"No, you said she was. Like Paula Deen?"

Susan laughs. "No, I meant she looks like Paula Deen now. The gray hair and all. Even her clothes."

"I've never watched her much, but now that you mention it..."

"So spill. She's still barely speaking to me. Is it for the movie? Did they give her a role?"

"She says it's not, that she just wanted a change, but it just doesn't look like her at all." I can't hold back a giggle. "Wonder what Shaw thinks?"

"Oh Lord, I didn't even think of Shaw. My brother-in-law has always worshipped the ground she walked on, but I'm not sure he'll be on board for this. Listen, I've got to go. The tree guys are at my door. Bye."

Shoot. I didn't get to ask about Silas Pendersen or find out if she knows about Griffin's new woman.

Jackson comes in the back door and then into the living room where I'm seated next to the front window. "Hey, who're your friends? Hi, guys!" KJ and Katherine look over their shoulders for half a second, but Kevin pushes himself up to his knees and crawls around to pull up on Jackson's jeans leg.

"Hey, buddy!" Jackson says. Then to me, he asks, "What's his name again?"

"Kevin."

"Kevin. So what are you up to?" Jackson asks the boy as he lifts him up.

Jackson is good with kids. He was the best daddy to our

three, and a wave of emotion hits me when I think he'll be holding our grandchild in a matter of weeks. Seems like just yesterday our three were sitting like this in front of cartoons on a Saturday morning. Jackson sits on the couch near my chair. "You babysitting or something?"

"More something. Zoe and Bryan are actually in charge, but they're on the front porch."

He leans back, and Kevin settles against his chest, turned around so he can see the television. Jackson's voice is a tad husky when he says, "Seems like our three should still be this size, doesn't it?"

"I was just thinking the same thing."

With a background of cartoons, we sit for another few minutes enjoying our thoughts and memories. Guess that's part of what having grandkids does, it makes you remember when yours were little. I think of the looks in my parent's eyes as they watch Will, Savannah, and Bryan even now. I wonder why I never put together that they were thinking of me?

Life has ways of teaching you new things all along the way, doesn't it?

Kyle came and picked up the kids before he had to go to work. He's now also manager at another Dollar Store thirty minutes away. He seems to be learning to not be a bully, both with his family and his staff. When he left, he also took Zoe and Bryan to drop them off at the high school for a wrestling match.

Will and Anna are at work, and our guests are all out and about chasing trains. That's when you follow trains, but then get ahead of them so you can stop at a crossing, get out, and take pictures as the train rolls by. Then you get back in the car, chase it again, get out, and, well, you understand. Okay, maybe you don't *understand*, but I'm sure you have the logistics down. They have a spot for lunch picked out in a small town north of here, and the ladies told me this morning they were going to stay in town after lunch and shop while the men chased more trains. Sounds like they have this whole thing figured out.

Jackson is working in the backyard on our new decking with Colt. Well, he was until Colt left for the same wrestling match Zoe and Bryan are attending. Some of his football players are also on the wrestling team, and he wants to support them.

Showered and changed into gray wool slacks and a dark gray sweater, I walk outside to check on my husband. "I'm headed to the shop for a bit," I say as I walk out onto our deck, then cross over the little bridge to the steps for our new huge deck outside our bedroom. Jackson is sitting on the floor of that deck, but I can't just come outside our bedroom yet, as the door is still blocked off.

He looks up at me, squinting in the sunshine. "You look nice. Stopping by the filming, too?"

"Maybe." I walk out to the edge and marvel again at how those few extra feet give us such a view of the river. Before we could only get glimpses through the trees. "By the way, have you talked to Savannah?"

He shakes his head but continues his work on the bottom of the railing. "About what? Parker?"

Parker. I'd forgotten about him showing up. "Why would she be talking about Parker? I think he just happened to be in town that night."

"Happened to be in Chancey? Even with his uncle's cabin forty-five minutes from here, a boy doesn't come to Chancey for just no reason. Plus, you know Savannah. If she doesn't want you here, then..."

"Then you don't come here. So, has she mentioned Parker to *you*?" I watch him, and there's no head nod. No head shake. Matter of fact he's still. Too still. "What? What do you know?"

He looks up at me, again squinting in the sun, but more from what looks like guilt. "Guess I forgot to tell you."

"Tell me what?"

He lays his screwdriver on the deck beside him and stands up. "Um, you know Parker is at Georgia Tech this year, right? Well, he pledged a fraternity and their fall dance or whatever they call it is next weekend."

"Okay." I lean back against the railing and cross my arms.

"Well, he asked Savannah."

"To a college fraternity party?"

He takes one of my hands in his. "Did I tell you it's my fraternity? Isn't that cool?"

"Yeah, I guess, but how do you know he invited Savannah?"

"She had to get permission since she's not a college student, so she called me one day last week." At my face clouding up, he rushes on, "She said since it was my old fraternity she knew I'd want to know so she just called me."

I'm not convinced. "She just called you. At work. Out of town."

"Yeah, I thought it was kind of sweet, actually. I mean I'm gone so much, and well, it is kind of neat that he's in my fraternity. I still have some T-shirts somewhere, don't I?"

"I have no idea. So? What did you say to her about this party?"

He shrugs and then smiles as he steps to look off at the river as I did about a minute before. "I told her it sounded like fun."

"And you gave her permission to go?"

"Sure. I mean, why not, right?" He turns his head to look at me.

"Were you two even going to tell me?"

"Of course! That was the whole idea. Savannah said she

knew you wouldn't be able to give her an answer until you talked to me, so she just came straight to me." He has such a nice smile—for an idiot.

"But you didn't tell me."

His smile dies. "Yeah, sorry about that. Guess I got busy at work."

"Like she knew would happen."

"Who?" he asks, sincerely puzzled.

"Savannah. She knew you'd forget to check with me. She knew I'd say we needed more information. She knew you'd think it was cool it was your old fraternity, and since you were at work you'd be in a hurry and just say yes."

Still puzzled, he turns to face me and puts his hands into his jeans pockets. After a moment he scrunches up his face. "You think so?"

I can't even roll my eyes. With one last huff at him, I march off that deck, down the steps, and finally into the kitchen, with a good door slam to make sure he knows my thoughts. So Savannah has maneuvered herself into an invite to a college fraternity party.

I suppose this could work out. Get her on a college campus and let her see exactly what she'd be missing. Sure, that could work. Now I just have to keep acting mad. I can't let her know I possibly want her to go to the party. Also, I can't let Jackson off the hook that easily.

Our daughter's not the only one that knows how the game is played.

Chapter 32

"Shoot!" I say to myself as I lean on the shop's counter and look at the calendar on my phone. "No girls' trip for me and Savannah if she's going to that fraternity dance."

Shannon shakes her head and purses her lips. She's made it very plain she would never allow her daughter, which she doesn't have, to go to a college dance. Especially not a fraternity dance. She never went to college and she *certainly* never went to a fraternity party, but she's the expert. Pre-parents are *always* my go-to for advice on children—not.

She's at her worktable putting the finishing touches on flowers for one of the churches. I'm watching her when I remember Peter's comments about their morning activity. That gets me to straighten up and look in a different direction as I blurt, "I love what Bonnie did with the books in the window having a movie theme. The movie posters really add to it, too."

"We sure are lucky to have her," Shannon says. "She's been really helping me by making up some of the small bouquets I like to keep in the cooler. With the movie people in town, those have really moved and I couldn't keep up. She did a great job." Shannon sighs as she adds, "Peter needs someone like her. He's in that bistro all the time and still can't get it to turn a profit."

I walk back to her table. "Isn't the movie helping him at all?"

She looks up at me from under her fringe of dark bangs. "No. Ever since Alex moved on to the food truck, things just don't seem to be coming together." She checks to make sure the two people in the bookstore aren't near, then whispers, "Peter is not a good shop owner. He wants to be and thinks he can do it, but…" She shakes her head again.

"You're right. The bistro doesn't have the same feel as it did when Alex was there. Hope he doesn't have to close."

"Me too." She swallows, then swallows again, and I realize she's staring at the table.

"Are you okay? What's wrong?"

When she looks up, her dark eyes are swimming in tears and her cheeks are red. Her voice cracks. "What if he moves on? What if he fails at the bistro and finds something new to do somewhere else? He's not used to living in the same place for very long. Not since he's been an adult."

Peter not be in Chancey? Staring at her, I realize he's only lived back in his hometown for the past year. He feels like such a fixture to me because we've only been here a little over a year, too. "Oh, Shannon," I say as I reach across the table to pat her hand. "He has you here, and he's happy. He seems happy to me."

Now she's really crying, and her voice comes in jerks. "If he leaves, what will I do? My parents are so against us living together. If we don't get married, what will I do?" She darts between the craft services tables, set up but not in use right now, and escapes into our little bathroom.

Shannon has seemed so in control of the situation with Peter. Whenever her father drops I, she acts like everything is just great. She puts Missus in her place more than anyone other than Laney, and that's huge. I think we all pretty much expect a wedding in the spring, but…

I hear a throat being cleared and turn to see the two ladies standing at the counter.

"You ladies ready?" I say.

My hands are cold and shaking as I walk toward the counter. I clasp them together as I take a quick look back towards the still-closed bathroom door. Poor Shannon. I had no idea all that was on her mind.

With the customers gone, I straighten the shelves where they had been shopping. Out the window I see a crowd walking past on the sidewalk. It's the movie people, and I'm surprised to see them coming in our door. There's no food prepared in the back, and none of the crew are here.

"Hello," I call out as I step toward them.

Leif pushes to the front of the group, pulling Savannah with him. Some of the others stand around the two of them, while others begin walking around the shop or heading back to the catering area. I did notice that Margery left some packaged cookies and chips out earlier. Maybe it's snack time?

With his hands planted on his hips, Leif says, "We're taking a little break. Can I talk to you?"

"Sure." I say with a questioning look at my daughter. She lifts her eyes from the floor, right past me, and then to the ceiling. "What's going on?"

He smiles at me, but his eyes are narrowed. "Is it true? About Phoenix?" He draws back a couple inches and looks around. Then stretches his neck like he has a headache. In a lower voice he asks, "Is she a stripper?"

"Right now?"

"Now. Ever. I thought Mrs. Conner was just jealous when she said she was a stripper. But then, for her niece to say it."

"Savannah's actually not her niece," I say. "I mean, Phoenix is dating my brother-in-law, but they've not been together that lo—"

"Whatever. Look it probably doesn't matter but I'd like to know if some risqué pictures are suddenly going to appear all over social media when she shows up in my *family-friendly* movie."

Savannah is finally looking at me, but her mouth is firmly clinched shut. I answer. "Honestly? I don't really know. She was a dancer in Vegas. That's all I know for sure. You'll need to ask her."

"Yeah. Should have just done that right off, but..." he shrugs then laughs as he points a finger at me. "This is your fault. If you'd agreed to be our bookstore owner, we wouldn't have a problem. I mean, you've obviously never been a stripper!"

I laugh with him then put a hand on one hip. "Hey, you can't just assume something like that!"

"Really? So, were you ever a stripper, Mrs. Jessup?" He shakes his head. "Forget it. I'll talk to Phoenix." Then he turns to Savannah, "However, you'd do good to learn to not say things you don't actually know. That habit won't serve you well in *any* career, but especially not in one as rift with rumors as acting."

Hmm. Hollywood is growing on me. Leif winks at us both, then steps back towards the tables saying loudly, "Breaks over in five. See you back at the studio."

In only a matter of minutes, it's once again only me and Shannon in the midafternoon light.

"Well, that was a fast break," I say, but Shannon ignores me. She's busy with two big church-looking arrangements, so I ignore her right back. I pick up my duster and step to the window display. With only half the display dusted, I notice someone off to the side on the sidewalk, and I lean forward to look. Peter is standing there, scrunched beside the building, out of view of the front window. He's on the opposite side of our shop from his bistro, and he's motioning at me. When he sees that I've seen him, he motions for me to come outside. Then he puts his finger to his lips telling me to be quiet.

"Think I'll step outside and get some fresh air," I say. Since Shannon is ignoring me, I don't expect, or get, a response.

The sunshine fooled me into thinking it was warm out here, so I immediately wrap my arms around myself. My gray sweater isn't very heavy, and the cold penetrates it quickly. Peter is no longer beside our window, so I walk down another few steps and see he's hidden himself in the sunken entryway next to ours. It leads to some upstairs offices, including the *Chancey Vedette*, which don't get a lot of traffic.

"Peter, what are you doing?"

"I need to talk to you."

"You have my phone number. It's not near as cold in the store!"

"You want my coat? Here," He starts shrugging off his jacket.

"No. I'm not staying out here that long. This is silly. What do you want?"

Half out of his coat, he stops and looks at me. "I couldn't call you because you aren't really any good at subterfuge. You'd hem and haw, trying not to let Shannon know it was me on the phone and she'd know immediately something was up."

I bounce on my heels to keep warm. "True. But what is it?"

"I need you to write me a recommendation. As another store owner."

"What for?"

He sighs and finishes sliding his jacket back on. He chews on his lip above his dark brown beard, then pulls me farther into the entryway until we are against the doorway. "I have an opportunity that I just can't pass up. Closer to Atlanta. This town isn't ever going to be able to support the kind of store I want to operate. Besides, Chancey is a bit too, uh, too…"

"Familiar? Small? Crowded with people who really know you?" I'm ticked off. Everything Shannon said earlier is true. He *is* getting ready to bail. "What about Shannon? What about your mother?"

He jerks back at my vehemence. "It's not like I'm going to fall off the face of the earth. The Atlanta suburbs are close. You know. Lots of opportunities there and not all, all this."

"What about your mother? What about Shannon?" I persist. "Just this morning you were talking about you and Shannon making—uh, you know—being quiet."

His face flushes, and he looks away, staring at the dirty glass door beside us. "She's young. Younger than both of us. She knows how things are." He looks back at me and studies me for a moment. "You seem angry. I thought of all people you'd understand. Understand having to get out of Chancey. Weren't we having this very same conversation last year this time? Except you were the one wanting to leave?" He smirks. "Guess being a grandma has changed you."

I've gone from ticked off straight to really angry. I clamp my mouth shut and whirl around to leave.

"Stop, wait! I'm sorry. Please..."

I turn to face him, my back to the street.

His eyes are closed, and he sighs. "I'm sorry. This is business. Nothing to do with Shannon or Mother. I'm not moving, just changing jobs."

"So you've discussed this with Shannon?"

"No. Why?"

"You're living together! Aren't you a couple? A couple with a future?" My anger completely solidifies s as I remember the tears in Shannon's eyes.

"Maybe..." Then his eyes lift and he takes a step back, away from me and further into the shadows. His eyes tell me I should look behind me.

"If you wanted to be in the movie, why didn't you just take the role in the first place?" Phoenix demands as I turn around.

Her emerald sweater is even prettier up close. I smile and start to tell her that, but she doesn't give me the chance. She's tall and not happy with me.

"Colt is going to be so disappointed in you. He was enjoying getting to know you, but you're telling everyone I was a stripper? I *am* and *was* a dancer. A trained dancer." She tosses her hair with one hand, and the other rests on her hip as she looks down at me. "Of course, I didn't believe all I heard about you and him," she says that with a jut of her chin at Peter, "but here you are. I guess it's a good thing Colt and I are here to help Jackson get through this." Then with another toss of everything she has to toss, she marches back down the sidewalk in the direction of her studio. When I step out of the shelter of the entryway I look after her, then turn back toward the way I'd come.

Shannon is standing in our open doorway, half behind the heavy glass door, staring at me. I watch her put Phoenix's words together, then she steps away from the door, letting it fall heavy behind her. She heads straight for me. I look from her back to Peter, who once again holds up his stupid finger telling me to be quiet. I just shake my head at him and turn to follow Phoenix.

I don't think the finger thing is going to work with Shannon, but let him figure out that himself.

CHAPTER 33

"It was infuriating standing there outside the window, in the cold, watching Phoenix ignore me, but they'd closed the studio for shooting. Here's to having family in town." I toast my glass of Diet Coke, with a just a touch of peach cobbler moonshine in it, at Susan.

I'd stood outside the big glass windows watching the filming until I realized I was freezing. Then when I started back to the bookshop I saw Shannon closing the front door and locking it. She scowled at me and headed toward Peter's house, her home. This meant I was right in her path, so I hurried across the street and up the front steps of Andy's Place.

The old house sits high next to Missus' grand antebellum home. However, at the top of the front steps there isn't a gracious, comfortable porch or an ornate front door. There's a clean, freshly painted porch in the business' signature colors of neon orange, neon green, and neon purple. For a front door, there's a big window-door, like on the front of a Walmart store. Inside is all shiny wood flooring, modern furniture, and computers for digging through the massive online inventory Andy has accumulated. Gertie's side of the house is to my right, where she lives behind closed doors. Locked, too, I found when I tried to get a peek one time.

Yeah, I was snooping. Shoot me, the woman is a mystery.

Down the hallway and up the stairs are rooms full, full to the rafters full, of junk. Andy's specialty. I can't really complain because I have dibs on all the books he finds. However, I was not interested in any of that today, and so I sailed down the hallway toward the big sign saying The Cave. I descended the staircase, plush gray carpet under my feet, and entered Gertie's moonshine bar.

As I expected, there is football on the dozen televisions. As I did not expect, all but two of the tables have customers at them. I kind of thought it would be empty in the middle of a Saturday afternoon.

Gertie called my name from behind the big bar on my right, someone else called my name out from behind me, and as I glanced back, I saw Susan come bounding down the stairs.

So now we are seated at the end of the bar, my left side against the wall, with our drinks in front of us and Gertie leaning on the other side of them. She shrugs her big shoulders. "I guess I assumed she was a stripper. You sure you never said she was a stripper?"

"This peach moonshine is nice in my Diet Coke." I turn to Susan. "How's yours? You did the strawberry shortcake, right?"

"It's good. But I'm with Gertie. I do believe I heard you call her a stripper." She shrugs and waggles her head. "Not that that isn't an easy assumption to make with the way she looks and the whole Las Vegas thing."

"Okay. Maybe. See, this is why living in a small town is so stupid. There are so few people to talk to, and they have so little to occupy their time. Everyone remembers everything you say!" I finish my drink and then climb down off the barstool. Seeing as I don't have a stripper's physique, as was pointed out earlier, barstools are not my friend. "I'm going back to the shop to get my purse. Coast should be clear by now."

Gertie rises from her folded arms and hefty breasts that were resting on the bar. Her eyes dart to Susan's, and then Susan spins around on her barstool to face me. "What do you mean, 'coast should be clear'? Who are you avoiding?"

Gertie grins and with a tsk of her tongue says, "Shannon. Why are you avoiding Shannon?"

Susan nods. "Peter. He's texted you twice since we've been here. What's going on?"

I shove my phone into my pocket. I'd had it lying on the bar since I didn't have my purse or a coat and sitting with it in my pocket (due to my lack of a stripper's physique) is too uncomfortable. Should've known she saw. "He just needed some help. It's nothing." Ignoring my warm face, I look at them and say, "I've got to go. Thanks for the drink, Gertie. I'll pay you when I have my purse."

They aren't grinning now. Susan leans toward me and whispers, "Remember last winter. Do not get, well, *involved* with Peter again." Her words have Gertie's approval as she heavily nods.

"I'm not. He's with Shannon. He just asked for a favor. I have to go." Turning, I step along behind the people seated along the bar and head up the stairs. Susan has to put on her coat and Gertie is running a business, so I'm pretty sure I don't have to actually *run* to avoid them.

Good thing because, well, stairs.

I pass a couple on their way down, but the main floor is empty. With my hands on the metal bar to open the window-door, ready to step outside, I remember. Shannon locked the shop door, and I don't have my keys with me. Andy and Patty could open the door for me, but they are at his parents' house for dinner. Gertie has a key, but she's all the way downstairs and I'd have to bring her key back over here.

Jackson could bring my extra keys downtown, but he texted earlier he was heading out to Home Depot, then meeting up with our B&B guests for some train watching. Oh, shoot! He texted me so that I could pick up Bryan and Zoe at the high school wrestling match at, I check my phone, *now*. I dial Bryan and stare out the window. There's a sunset-pink glow filling the air, and the lights around town have started coming on. Bright lights from the dance studio say filming is still going on there. A young family plays in the leaves around the gazebo. As I watch, the mom holds out her hand for her son to grab it. The dad lifts his laughing daughter up onto his shoulders, and they walk away from my view as I listen to my son's phone ring.

Just great. As I hang up, I get a text from Bryan saying, "What?"

Okay, so he's holding his phone in his hand. I dial again. He texts back, "I said, what?"

I'm going to kill him. Right after I take that phone away. Mid-text writing, I stop when I hear Susan behind me asking, "What are you still doing here?"

As she steps up beside me, I explain. "I just realized I don't have keys to the shop where my purse is, and I'm supposed to be picking up Bryan and Zoe at the high school."

She pushes open the door. "Come on. I'll drive."

"Let me make sure they're actually there." I finish my text, shivering at the cold air Susan's letting in. "Yep, he says they are there and waiting on me." I look up at her. "You sure you don't mind?"

"Not at all." On the steps we both take in that gloaming time of afternoon, enhanced by the whiff of wood smoke in the air. Susan asks, "So, why'd Shannon lock you out? And why don't you have on a coat?"

When I don't answer, she tucks her arm around mine and pulls me close. "Here, this will help keep you from freezing.

My car's there across from Ruby's. We can hurry to warm up." We cross the street instead of following the sidewalk to the corner, which means we don't walk in front of the dance studio. But as we back out of her parking space, we are across from the studio. The darkness outside highlights everyone inside.

We both stare.

"It's like a display in a museum or play, isn't it?" Susan says as she puts the car into drive. However, she doesn't move forward. It's as if we're mesmerized. Then a car turns the corner ahead, and its lights swing at us. Susan jumps and presses the accelerator pedal. We pass the other car and then move toward the four-lane road.

All those people in action behind the plate glass stay in my mind, along with all the other watching I've done today. "A play. Yeah, it feels like this is all a play right now. So many moving parts, I can hardly keep track."

Susan is quiet and doesn't repeat her questions about Shannon and Peter. I stay quiet, too.

I want to know about Silas and whether she knows about Griffin's new girlfriend, but the quiet, and heat, is too good to ruin.

The front of the high school is lit up, but there are only a few people out front as we pull to where Bryan and Zoe are standing. Just as we pull up to them Susan decides we've had enough quiet. As Bryan reaches for the back door handle, Susan looks at me, takes a quick breath, and blurts out, "I slept with Silas." Then with a quick turn of her head, she says hi to the kids and tells them to put on their seat belts.

I'm still staring her direction.

What did she just say?

CHAPTER 34

"Where's your coat?" Jackson asks as I try to rush in the front door behind a dawdling Bryan.

"At the shop. Why are you home? I thought you were going to go train watching."

He motions out the front window. "It's kind of hard to watch trains in the dark. Who's that pulling out of our driveway?"

"Susan. My purse and keys are also at the shop."

Bryan comes out of the kitchen with a granola bar. "What's for dinner?"

His caretakers look at each other and realize they aren't doing a very good job. We both smile and sigh. Jackson gets up from the couch, looking at me. "How about you and I go get a pizza, and then we can go by the shop and get your things."

Bryan is already dialing his phone. "I'll call so it'll be ready. Will and Anna here?"

I look at Jackson. Again he just looks back at me. With another sigh, I say, "Order two large. Who knows if Missus will show up or what Savannah's plans are for tonight. Let me get a coat. My extra keys, too." After digging our extra key ring out of the kitchen junk drawer, I step to the coatrack and find a jacket for me and also hand Jackson his coat.

Bryan hollers from the kitchen. "Twenty minutes. Get garlic sauce."

With our coats on, Jackson opens the front door and steps back for me to go past him. On the porch, he wraps one arm around my waist as he closes the door. "Come here," he says as he pulls me into his arms. "I didn't get a kiss, and you look like you need one, too."

We kiss and I sigh again, but it's a good sigh. An "I'm happy I'm me and I'm happy you're you" sigh. He keeps his arm around me as we walk to the car.

"Feels like I'm watching everything today," I say. "From the outside of the fishbowl."

The lights on his car blink as he unlocks the doors with his fob. He doesn't let me go when we get to the car, but walks with me to my door, which he opens. I smile and reward him with another kiss before settling in the low seat.

I continue my thought when he gets the car started. "Like this morning. I sat in the van and watched people getting to the shops, Phoenix and Peter and Andy. Watched Missus, too. Then from inside the shop looking outside the front window I saw the movie people and well, Peter, again. And then from Gertie's front porch there was a young family playing in the square, and I could see the movie people in the studio windows. Susan and I watched them as we were pulling out, and it was getting darker." My voice trails off as my thoughts swirl faster, but I don't know where to even begin.

Jackson turns on the radio, but really low so it will be easy to talk over. I don't know what I want to say. I lay my head back and watch the lights of houses go by. When we get to the stop sign at the bottom of our hill, he reaches to turn the radio off and asks, "So what all did you see that's gotten you thinking so hard?" He chuckles, and as he hits the accelerator, he gives me a wink.

With my own chuckle, I say, "You know me so well. There is a lot to think about, but the biggest thing that keeps coming around is how I feel removed from it all. Like all these people are making these huge, life-determining decisions, but it's just not my life."

He's almost to the shop when I say, "Even Savannah. We can't make her go to college, can we?"

"Nope. We sure couldn't make Will go to law school." He pulls up in front of the shop.

As I'm unbuckling and opening my car door, I say, "No need for you to come in. I'll get my stuff and be right out."

I enter the dark, high-ceiling space. My purse is still under the counter where it usually sits, and then I go towards the back to get my coat. The tables are set up for breakfast for the movie people and I remember they are shooting tomorrow morning while pretty much everyone else is at church. Margery must've been in this afternoon while I was hiding at Gertie's.

"No need for me to hide anymore," I say with a strong voice full of confidence. "All of these people making problems don't have my life and I don't have theirs, and I can't do anything about it." What's that saying, "Not my circus. Not my monkeys"? Yep, that's my new motto.

Now, pizza with my family is all I'm thinking about. I lock the door behind me, but as I turn to get back in the car, I realize Jackson isn't in the car. Then I see him walking down the sidewalk toward me. Colt and Phoenix are with him. None of them look happy.

Okay, this might just be my circus *and* my monkeys.

Chapter 35

"Leif! Leif!" He turns at my yelling in the church parking lot. I'd tried calling him this morning, but he hadn't answered. I didn't expect to see him here, but coming down the church steps I saw him walking toward all the cars.

Even from this distance I can tell he's rolling his eyes at me, but he does stop walking. He even takes a couple steps in my direction. My maroon sweater dress comes below my knees and I'm wearing short boots, but it's still not easy to hurry. We meet in the grassy area surrounding the parking lot.

"What do you want? I got your texts. I even talked to Phoenix. It's all good." His words rush out at me and catch me off guard for a minute.

"I wanted to apologize to you in person. I don't know why I thought she'd ever been a stripper. I think it was more of a generic-dancing-Vegas-showgirl kind of assumption?" I smile at him and, Lord help me, I bat my eyes just a bit. "But it was all me. So, I'm sorry to have caused you that worry. Savannah is sorry, too."

He relaxes a little. "No worries, it's all good. I'm just preoccupied this morning." Then he tilts his head at me and asks, "Have you seen Herbert? Herbert Fisk?"

"No. Why?"

He looks around. "I need to talk to him, and he, well, he doesn't really believe in carrying a cell phone much. Thought he might be here at church this morning. He usually attends services when we're on location, but I didn't see him."

I shrug and look around as he's doing. However, I'm not looking for Mr. Fisk. I'm looking for Missus.

She didn't come home last night, again. I'm sure she just stayed another night at Peter's. Speaking of which, where's *he*?

Leif turns and looks down at me. "I've got to go. We're all good. No worries." He laughs. "Matter of fact, I probably overreacted on the whole Phoenix thing. The word 'stripper' just made my mind explode for a minute." He reaches out and gives my arm a squeeze. "Bye."

I take a deep breath and enjoy the sunshine that warms my face. I stretch to feel more of it and breathe deeply again as I close my eyes to the brightness. Colt and Phoenix actually even came up to the house and had pizza with us once I apologized profusely on the sidewalk outside the shop last night. It was very humbling, but they were so quick to respond that I'm wholeheartedly endorsing quick and thorough apologies from now on.

A smile breaks out as I think of how my just-issued apology to Leif shows I'm on the right path. One more deep breath, and I open my eyes to see a bull headed my way. A bull in navy slacks and a long navy sweater. A bulky, long, navy sweater with a light-blue man's shirt sticking out from under it at the bottom, the top, and the sleeves. And gray hair. How in the world she has let that dye job go this long is beyond me. This morning she looks less like Paula Deen and more like that actress. The really good one.

"Hi, Laney. Still playing dress-up, I see?"

"This isn't dress-up. This is me. The new me. I'm not cold like when I wore those dresses, and I no longer have to tiptoe around in the gravel." She flourishes her hand at her feet. "See? I can walk right here where you are in the grass and mud because I have on sensible shoes. Although for the life of me, why would anyone want to walk in the grass like an old brood mare!"

Her last line picked up all the twang and passion she'd left out of her other words. And I remember, Kathy Bates. She looks like the actress Kathy Bates, who happens to also be Southern. . Then Laney's eyes flashed a bit and she tossed her head like it was full of dark curls, not her plain ol' gray bob. The bob doesn't toss.

"Okay," I say, but I barely get that out before she cuts me off.

"Where is my sister?"

"Oh, y'all are speaking now?"

"She is breaking our mother's heart. I can't believe anyone could be so callous, disregarding her family's reputation so completely."

"Wait, wait, wait a minute. That's hilarious coming from you. Give Susan a break. You didn't seem to be all worried about your mother when you were gambling to raise money for the town. Besides, Susan deserves a little fun."

Laney gets quiet. Real quiet. And still. Real still.

"Fun? What kind of fun?" Laney gets closer to me. She may look like she's turned her back on being a Southern Belle, but the way her nostrils are twitching and her eyebrows are darting around, she's not given up one bit of her intuition. "*I was* talking about her letting Grant stay up on the mountain with his father and his floozy. What are you talking about? Susan is not to be having any fun *whatsoever.*"

Oops. I try to fix it, but with that gray bob in my face and my new policy of apologizing, all I can say is, "I'm sorry. I've got to go." I turn and hurry-walk toward our van. Jackson drove to church, but I get in the driver's seat and turn the van on. My husband is only a few feet away. When he hears the engine turn over he looks at me through the windshield to which I shrug and smile.

He wraps up his conversation with a couple of other men and waves at Bryan to come on. Savannah drove herself as she has filming today. Jackson climbs in the passenger seat.

"Okay. What's wrong now?" he asks.

"Nothing. Why?"

He gestures to me in the driving seat.

I ignore him, and as soon as Bryan is in the back seat, I put the van in reverse and step on the gas. Bryan lurches out of his seat. "Whoa, Mom. What's the hurry? Can you drop me at Zoe's? Her folks invited me to Sunday dinner, and since we don't usually do anything except the Chinese buffet or left-overs, I told her yes."

Staring out the front window, I feel my jaw settling into concrete. Now the Kendrick family is having Sunday dinners? While we do the Chinese buffet or leftovers? I feel Jackson looking at me as he says, "Sure, buddy. That'll be nice."

I let my jaw of concrete harden until we pull into Zoe's driveway and our youngest child is out of the car. His slamming of the van door breaks my silence. "He used to love going to the buffet. I tried the whole Sunday dinner thing, and I never knew who was going to be home to eat. We used to have Sunday dinner back in Marietta, didn't we?"

Jackson nods and pats my back. "The kids were little. They didn't have their own things to do." We sit there in the driveway for a couple more minutes. Then we turn to look at each other.

"Chinese buffet?" we say at the same time, then laugh.

Backing up out of the driveway I turn to go back down the hill.

Wonder of wonders, no one we knew was eating at the China Palace. With the restaurant's dim lighting and red carpeting, just the two of us in a booth felt like a date.

"I'm stuffed," I say as Jackson pushes his empty plate to the edge of the table to be picked up.

"No ice cream?" he asks.

"Nope. You go ahead. Going to just sit here and nurse my Diet Coke." He and the waiter, the owner's son, talk for a minute, then Jackson heads towards the ice cream freezer. A waiter takes our dirty plates. It's a tad warm in here, and now with a full stomach I'm feeling drowsy. I straighten up in the seat, take a deep breath, and blink my eyes. Jackson slides into booth with his little cup of ice cream. And two spoons.

"Thanks, but I'm really full. Hey, listen, I noticed something this morning, and I wanted to run it by you." I look for stray food on the table, then fold my arms on it me. The old, non-working springs in the cushion make the table a bit high for me, but perfect for laying my arms on. "I seem to all of a sudden be telling people secrets. Did it again this morning at church."

He studies me, then looks at his bowl as he scoops another spoonful of his strawberry ice cream. "About what? What secrets?"

I lower my voice. "Missus and her procedure. That got out because of me. Then this whole mess with people thinking Phoenix was a stripper."

He lifts his eyebrows at me. "Honestly? I was thinking about that. I'm thinking my mom might have said that. I'm sure folks up in Kentucky thought it. I mean, come on, the judge leaves his wife for her? I'm not sure that one's on you."

"But then this morning I let slip something that only I know. Well, me and the two people involved."

"Do I know this secret?"

Chewing on my lip, I shake my head at him.

219

He gets a sly look on his face and says, "Bet I can guess."

"Okay. Guess."

"Laney's hair is not really gray."

He looks so tickled with himself I almost want to let him have this, but, c'mon. I roll my eyes at him. "Really? That's a secret, you think? Of course that's not her hair color. She's in her forties. If that was her true color it would take weeks to grow out."

"Not if she had hair color on all this time and then she washed it off."

"Hair color doesn't work that way. It's permanent. It has to grow out. Besides, she's not gray. She's trying to get in the movie I think." I take a long sip of my drink. "Maybe if she was in the movie she could keep an eye on that Silas guy and make her sister behave."

"What's Susan done?"

I slam down my drink. "See! I almost did it again. I just keep saying whatever crazy thing I'm thinking about. I have to stop that." I start trying to slide across the sunken booth seat. "You ready to go?"

"Yes. Falcons are playing at one. I'll go pay. Don't forget your phone on the table there."

My mouth hangs open a bit as I watch him walk to the front counter. How can he not ask again about what Susan did? It's like he honestly doesn't care what everybody else is talking about. Maybe that's the ticket. Maybe I just need to not care. Walking to the front I decide I'll focus on my shop, my house, my family. That's all I need to do. Then I won't find out all this stuff that people want to keep secret and then I can't share it.

We step out onto the sunny but cold sidewalk. I tuck my arm into Jackson's, and we trot toward the car. He pulls it around, and as we get in front of the Piggly Wiggly a man dashes in front of us, headed for the grocery store's front door.

Jackson toots the horn. "There's Peter." He waves. I wave. Peter waves.

Then as he starts pulling forward again, I say, "You know, I need bread for lunches. You don't have to come in. I'll just run in and get some."

I'm free of my seat belt and opening the door almost before the car comes to a stop. Stop caring? These are my friends, and they are making huge mistakes. I can't just stop caring. I'll just have to be more careful about what I say. Yes. That's what I'll do.

Besides, that not caring phase was the longest five minutes of my life.

Now, I just need to find Peter.

Oh, and remember to buy a loaf of bread.

CHAPTER 36

"We've been invited to Hank and that Shelby's wedding!" my mother exclaims when I answer the phone. "Are you going?"

"Yes. Hi. He's maneuvered all the kids into having parts in the ceremony, so we all have to go." I'm unloading the two bags of grocery I picked up along with the unneeded bread. There's always that infernal running list in a woman's mind that jumps into action at the whir of the automatic grocery store door opening. "There's even a shower this coming weekend that I was thinking Savannah and I would go to. A mother-daughter thing. But now she's busy. Remember Parker?"

"I saw they were together last weekend some. Are they getting back together? Let me just pull up my Facebook and put you on speaker."

Of course my mother would be more high tech than I am. "I didn't think of checking there. He invited her to a fraternity dance next weekend."

"Good. She's getting a bit off track with this acting thing, don't you think?"

"I don't know. She really loves it, and she's apparently good

222

at it." What is that makes you automatically choose the opposite opinion when you actually agree with your mother?

"Would you let her skip college?" Alarm in my mother's voice comes across loud and clear. Loud especially since I also have her on speaker.

Anna and Will come up from downstairs and both immediately look at my phone. I snatch it up and turn off the speaker. Anna and Will wander around the kitchen, opening cabinets, getting drinks, looking out the windows, not even pretending to not be listening, so I put the speaker back on and lay the phone down. "Say hello to Will and Anna."

"Ooh," Mom squeals. "How's the baby? How's little Francie?"

They talk, and I finish putting the groceries away before I interject, "Grandma and Grandpa were invited to your pawpaw's wedding."

Anna wrinkles her nose. Will picks up my phone as I join them standing beside the table. He asks, "Are you going, Grandma? We're all going. Even Anna."

Hmmm, first I've heard that. Anna shrugs at me, then speaks to the phone. "The doctor said I'd be fine since we're driving. I just have to get out and walk around often."

Mother sighs. "Well, if you're all going, then we'll probably go, too. Let's all stay at the same hotel! Oh, that would be fun." My mother loves a good party. She's petite and pretty. Blonde, with blue eyes that she shares with Savannah. My father is tall with dark brown eye and what used to be dark brown hair, much the same color as Savannah's. I also got a combination of their looks, except it's a true combo, blonde hair and dark brown hair combined to make muddy brown hair. Sparkling blue eyes and deep dark brown eyes combined to make medium brown eyes of no distinction. Oh, well. Genetics. What are ya gonna do?

Jackson walks into the kitchen and talks toward the phone. "Hi, Goldie. What's Jack up to?"

"Hi Jackson. He's outside doing something. You know he's always got some project going. Sounds like we're going to be seeing all of you soon up in Kentucky."

He makes a look at me that says he's trying to forget about the wedding. "Okay. Guess that'll be nice." After a bit more chitchat with Anna, Mother hangs up.

Will shakes his head. "Why can't Pawpaw and Shelby just elope? Make it easier on everybody."

Anna lowers herself into one of the kitchen chairs. "I think you and I are the last people to be talking about making things easy on other people. We've made a mess of everything."

Will grunts under his breath and turns back toward the basement stairs. "I cannot talk about this one more minute with you. I'm going down to see about moving the couch. Again."

Jackson isn't stupid. He quickly says to his son's back, "I'll give you a hand."

With the door closed behind them and their steps fading, I sit across from Anna. "Feeling stressed?" I say with a little chuckle.

She turns to me with tears in her eyes. Not an uncommon occurrence with a pregnant woman. "Will just thinks everything will turn out fine. Nothing to be worried about. Have the baby and then we'll figure things out. I don't want to be controlling like Granmissus, but I need to know *something*."

By now she's openly crying, and I move around to sit beside her. "Honey, don't get upset. It's not good for you or the baby. We'll figure things out. We haven't pressed because we don't want to upset you or make you feel like you have to have answers. What do you want? Just tell me."

I wrap my arm around her shoulder and pull her close. Her tears slowly subside. Then I feel her breathing regulate. Finally she takes a deep breath and sits up. With a sniffle she turns to look at me.

Her face is mottled and swollen. She blinks to clear her eyes of tears and tries a little smile.

"What do I want? I want this to all be over. I want to not be pregnant. I want to be able to breathe and think and plan. I want to be able to bend over at work and stock shelves or stay on my feet for more than fifteen minutes without back pain." She laughs a bit, and I hug her as I join her laughter.

"Sweetie, that's what every woman wants at this point. It'll all come. I promise. But until then…"

"I know. I know." She stops and looks down at her undecorated hands—no polish, no rings—which are laying on her stomach. She lifts, then stretches her left hand. "You know, my rings actually still fit."

"Good for you. I never swelled a whole lot when I was pregnant either." We both look at her hand, and I wait.

Okay, I wait a little bit, then I ask, "Do you want to wear your rings again?"

Her answer comes immediately. "Yes. I think I do."

My heart lifts, and my smile grows. I lift up a quiet thank-you to God as I try to wait again, but "Does Will know?" comes spilling out of my mouth. I feel like a huge burden has rolled off my shoulders. I can't keep the joy out of my voice, but I try to stay calm. Finally! "Will must be so happy."

She drops her hand back onto her stomach. "You'd think so." She struggles to stand, and at the end of the table she looks down at me. "But he still talks to Rose. That's who he wants to be with, isn't it?"

"No, I don't think so. He wants you and he and Francie to be a family. He's told you that, right?" I reach a hand out toward her, trying to connect with her again.

She nods as she looks at my outstretched hand. "Yes, he

has, but I guess I'm not sure I believe him." She looks at me, then smirks a bit. "Guess it's your fault."

"My fault?"

"Well, Mr. Jessup's, too. You raised a good guy. Isn't that what good guys do? Be responsible whether they want to or not? Like my grandfather, FM. He was stuck with my grandmother all those years." She shakes her head at me as I try to interrupt. "No, I know he made himself happy. He loved her, I guess, but..." She shrugs at me, and this time her smirk is so sad. "Again, that's what good guys do. I can't do that to Will."

She pats her stomach and takes one of those pregnant women breaths where your whole body lifts. "Will is right, though. It'll be all over soon. Then we can all go on with our lives." She walks into the living room and turns on the television.

I'm still seated at the table. My hand is still stretched out to where she was standing. My lips are settled and unopened.

So much of life rests on little things. Moments that change everything pass by without a word. A phone call we accept—or don't. A look we let linger and turn into an idea. A denial falling on deaf ears. A realization we choose to ignore. The lives of those all around me flow through my thoughts. So many little things that the big things are now resting on.

And I have no idea how to help any of them.

CHAPTER 37

Usually I have the shop to myself on Monday mornings, but Shannon has a special order for a wine festival in Dahlonega this week so she had said she'd be in early. If she's still not talking to me, then today won't be much different than any other solitary Monday. I park down the side street behind the shop, and because it's cold, I hurry up the sidewalk. As I turn the corner I see Shannon unlocking our front door. I rush up to her, determined to find out where we stand on her speaking to me.

"Good morning. Cold out here, isn't it?"

She knows it's me, so she doesn't have to look, but she does say, "Good morning, Carolina." Then she pulls open the door and motions me in.

"Thanks," I say, but I don't move far inside the building. "How are you?"

She looks tired, but she smiles at me a little before she walks toward the back. "Do you know what the movie schedule is for this place today?"

I follow her. "Not sure. I don't think they'll be back here until one night this week to film. As for eating here, I have no idea."

She gets busy pulling buckets of flowers and greenery from her cooler, and after scooping coffee grounds into the machine the back, I get situated at my table, which is surrounded by small cardboard boxes of books from Andy's weekend flea market scavenging. Finally the coffee I'd started is done brewing and I get up to fill a cup.

"Can I pour you one?"

Shannon nods, so I fix hers the way she likes it, with a Splenda packet and a half-spoon of powdered creamer, and take it back to her. I lean one hip against her worktable, hold my cup in both hands to warm my fingers, and take a deep breath. "Listen, Shannon, I'm sorry. You know there's nothing between Peter and me, right?"

She doesn't look at me, only shrugs and keeps cleaning flower stems.

"Well, there's not. He just had a favor to ask me. That's it."

Still without looking up, she says, "Of course. I understand." Then she lays down her knife with a clunk and finally looks at me. "I also understand most of his attraction to you is your unattainability. You're married. You're happy. You're safe." She picks up her knife and continues as I mull over her words.

"Well, that's probably true." Harsh, but I don't say that. "Also, Shannon, I still believe what I said. Peter is happy with you."

Her fist and knife hit the table again with a clunk. "I have a lot to do for this festival, so I really need to get back to work. Everything is fine." She stares at me, practically daring me to say something else.

I stand away from the table and back up a couple steps. "Okay. That's good to hear. I'm, uh, I'm happy for you both. I really am." She doesn't return my smile, but she sighs and goes back to her work.

Near the front counter, I turn back for one more question.

It's not about her or Peter, so I think it's okay. "I didn't see Missus all day yesterday. How is she?"

This time she quietly lays her knife down and picks up her cup of coffee. After taking a sip, she shrugs again at me and says, "How would I know?"

My stomach sinks. "I just assumed she was staying with y'all. Where could she be?" I reach into my pocket to pull out my phone and call her.

But then Shannon says, "Maybe *she* is at Peter's."

Wait. I look up, finger poised to dial. "What? You just said you didn't know."

"No. I said, 'How would I know?'"

"Okay?"

We just look at each other. She starts back to her work, but then she sighs and says, "I wouldn't know because I no longer live there. I moved back into my parents' house yesterday. I'll have to find another place to rent, but until then I don't really have a choice."

The way her eyes cut to me, I see she wants no more conversation on this. I put my phone back in my pocket and walk past her to my card table and boxes of books.

Shoot.

Just as I finish the last stack of books and am ready for a break, Shannon steps toward me, her coat on and keys in her hand.

"I'm taking the arrangements over to the winery. Their first event is at lunch today. I'm not sure if I'll come back to the store or not. Bonnie will be here soon, right?"

I stand and stretch as she's talking. "Yes. I'll be here until she gets here, so take the rest of the day off."

She looks around as she licks her lips. "Okay. I restocked my cooler, and I don't have any appointments. Let me know if, well, if anyone calls." Then she meets my gaze. "Or stops in. If Peter stops in."

"I will. Are you okay?"

She seems sad, defeated. "Not really. Sure was hard to have to tell my folks they were right. My dad was good. My mom, she's still mad at me. Oh well." One side of her mouth curls up. "Peter just seemed grown up. Seemed to know what he wanted. I thought he wanted me, but how ridiculous is that?"

Her voice cracks, and I rush to hug her.

"Not ridiculous at all. He's the one that's ridiculous."

She lets me hug her just a minute more, then steps back. "I have to go. Thanks."

"Let me get the door," I say as I hurry to the front. She has a large tub she uses for carrying arrangements and I hold the door for her to carry it through. I watch her cross the street to her car.

"Peter is an idiot," I say out loud.

"Yes, he is." Patty's voice comes from behind me. "Good morning, Carolina."

I turn as Patty walks up to where I am. "So you know about Peter and Shannon breaking up?"

"I know he won't know what he's got until it's gone, and it sure sounds like she's gone. You know, everyone thinks her parents are just prudes, but..." The girl shrugs her shoulders. "I mean, they wouldn't like her living with any man before getting married, but it's not just about sex."

I smile when she lowers her voice and whispers the word "sex."

She grins at me and waves a hand at me. "Pshaw, Ms. Carolina," she says as she blushes. "People in Chancey know Peter Bedwell. Know he's used to getting what he wants, when he wants it. Then when he's through..." She waves her hand again.

"Wait," I say, "you're not from Chancey. You never lived here until this past year."

"But my momma is from here and everybody talks to her. Kinda like how everybody talks to you."

"Everybody talks to me?" I find this hard to believe.

She drops her coat off her shoulders. "It's hot in here. Wasn't planning on standing around talking. Want to go down to Ruby's?"

As I check my watch, the back door opens. "Oh, there's Bonnie now. Sure. Let's go to Ruby's. We haven't chatted in forever."

In the time it takes me to put on my coat, Bonnie has poured herself a cup of coffee and is lighting all the little candles around the shop, which I always forget about. She just brings the place to life.

"Bonnie's a good lady, isn't she?" Patty says as we walk down the sidewalk.

"Yes. I'm so lucky she came to work at the shop, but what were..."

Patty holds up a hand. "Wait. We're talking about Bonnie. She's a good lady and a good worker, but do people tell her things?"

I'm still thinking about that when we get to Ruby's front door. Patty waits with her hand on the door. "No. People don't tell her things. They don't tell me things. They tell my momma, and they tell you."

"So why do you think that is?"

Patty pulls open the door to let a couple of men come out. They're older, and you can see their confusion at having a woman open the door for them. They mumble their thanks, and one gives Patty a salute.

We enter the café with Ruby roaring from the back, "For the love of Pete! Close that door! It's colder than a metal bed pan in winter!"

Libby points us toward an empty booth. "Come back here. It's warmer than up front. It's supposed to get warmer this afternoon is what everyone is saying."

We say hello to a few people along the way, but then take seats at a table beside the counter at the back. No one is sitting at the counter, which faces the ovens where Ruby usually hangs out. Libby leans over our table and mumbles, "Ruby's home furnace went out, so she's in a mood. She came to work extra early, though, so you've got a good assortment of muffins to choose from. Chocolate almond ones are the sweetest, along with the Snickerdoodle one, but it does have cinnamon on top. There's a sausage cheese one and a sausage and sage one that tastes a lot like a pan of sausage dressing. I don't put sausage in my dressing, but I hear tell that some do. I'll bring you some hot coffee in a minute."

Patty screws up her face. "Andy and I are supposed to be dieting. Which one of the muffins do you think would be the lowest in calorie?"

Libby looks over her shoulder as she thinks. "Oh, I know. The apple oatmeal, I think. Yeah, Ruby's trying some healthier recipes, and that's the latest. It's pretty good I've heard. I ain't tried it."

I say, "Give me one of those, too. I love apple and I love oatmeal. Plus I should try to eat better."

Libby spins away from us to head back behind the counter.

"So, back to what I was saying," Patty says as she tucks a hank of hair behind each ear, then leans toward me. "People talk to you and my momma because you listen. Like, really listen. I haven't figured out *why* you do that, just that you do."

"Really? Doesn't sound like Gertie. Doesn't sound like me."

She nods quickly, then leans back when Libby strides to the table, coffee pot in hand. We wait for her to pour, then head to the next table. Patty leans towards me again. "Yes, ma'am. It is. Me and Andy were talking about how you seem to be the linchpin in so many things, and yet you've only been here a year and a half. Andy is real good at thinking about things."

"Apparently you are, too."

"You know, Andy said the exact same thing. He says he likes to talk too much to be a real philosopher, but that I don't have a problem being quiet and listening."

"So, people should like to talk to you, right?"

"Oh, no, ma'am. Not at all. I'm too quiet. Think about it. People want folks who'll talk with them right back. Not just sit like a bump on a log letting it all go in one ear and out the other." She shrugs. "With me people don't know if I actually hear them, you know what I'm saying?"

She's right. When I'm talking to someone that doesn't say anything back, I don't really feel like they heard me. Or that they really care.

Libby plunks down little plates in front of each of us with a light brown muffin on it. The muffin has pieces of oatmeal on top, and what looks like little chunks of apple poke from beneath the surface. "There you go. And I didn't bring you the butter since you said you were both dieting. Enjoy!"

She's off to the next table, and we grimace at each other.

Patty sighs, then whispers, "Doesn't look all that great, does it?"

"It is kind of light-colored, but it'll probably taste all right. So now, back to Peter, which is what got us off on the subject of people talking. I had no idea Peter has a reputation like that in Chancey. He seems pretty down to earth. And although I'm completely surprised, I think he and Shannon are good together." I take a bite of my muffin and find it moist, very moist. But there's not a lot of flavor.

"From what Momma hears, Peter just never has had to make a decision. Missus either made his decisions for him, or made whatever he wanted to do possible." She takes a bite and chews. Her wrinkled nose tells me her opinion. Even so, we both take a second bite.

She holds her hand in front of her mouth as she chews and says, "Maybe if FM hadn't died."

I nod. I'd thought of that. FM was so proud when Peter bought his house and when he started the bistro. This muffin is really tasteless, but at least it goes down easily. I pick up my cup of coffee. "Who knew how much things would change with FM gone? Missus has, well, has gone a bit crazy, I think. Who knows?"

Patty raises her eyebrows at me. "Yeah, well, I don't know about Missus, but the movie sure has changed things. Andy's Place and Momma's bar are doing great business. Looks like this place is busier, too."

I look around and have to agree. There do seem to be more people I don't recognize. Some look a little familiar. They could be people from the area I don't know, or folks from the crew.

"Patty, thanks for telling me all this. I didn't realize that about myself. Guess I just always thought of myself as kind of nosy."

I smile at her, and she smiles back.

"Oh, you're definitely nosy. Momma, too. I mean, why else would you be listening to everybody and everything!" We laugh, but I don't feel it. I don't want to be thought of as nosy.

When my name is called from the front door, I look up to see Leif headed my direction. He nods at Patty, but when he sits at our table, he turns to me. Speaking in a low voice he says, "I still can't find Mr. Fisk. Do you know where he could be?"

Patty sits back, smiles, and says, "See? People know you know stuff."

Leif looks at Patty and wrinkles his brow, but then looks back at me. "I really have to find him."

"There," I say as I look past Leif to the outside windows. "He's headed this way."

Leif whirls around, then stands. He thanks me over his shoulder, then he is on his way to his star. However his star has other plans, as he pushes past his director and comes straight to our table.

"Miss Carolina and—I don't believe I know you, ma'am."

Patty reaches for his outstretched hand as she says, "Momma and I have watched *Promises Made* since I was a little girl." She giggles. "I can't believe you're right here holding my hand!"

Herbert Fisk throws his head back and laughs. "That is the secret to my success. Hook the girls while they are babies." He envelopes her hand, then lays it on the table. "But Carolina, I need to speak to you. Privately." His eyes flash in Patty's direction, and she immediately gets up.

"Oh, I was just leaving. I'll pay for our muffins and coffee, Carolina, okay? So wonderful to meet you, Mr. Fisk." She's bundled up her coat, her purse, her coffee cup, and her half-eaten muffin and backs away, practically genuflecting. He gives her another royal nod, then sits down where Leif was sitting. Speaking of whom, Leif is now back and trying to loom, without looking like he's looming, over Mr. Fisk.

"Leif," his star says, "give me some space. Go on to the studio. I will be there momentarily. This is a private conversation."

Leif glares at me as if this is my idea, so I glare back. Rare to get the opportunity to glare these days.

He stalks off, and I turn to Mr. Fisk. "How can I help you?"

He's beaming at me when he says, "Flowers. I'm in need of flowers, and I know you are in business with the local florist. She wasn't in the store when I just stopped in, but the lovely lady there, Bonnie, I believe, told me I could find you here. And here you are!"

"Bonnie could've made a flower order for you."

"Ah, yes, she could have, but seeing as you are good friends with the flower recipient, I wanted some insight first. Do you believe red roses would be a good flower choice for her?"

"Of course. She loves red roses."

"As most do. It is such a classy flower. I was hoping you'd suggest it. I've heard you have impeccable taste. Now, about…"

"Who's your guest, Carolina?" Ruby says as she appears beside our table.

"Ruby, this is Herbert Fisk. He's with the movie."

Wide-eyed she says, "Really?" then she rolls her eyes at me and says, "No duh. Of course he's with the movie. He's a movie star, for crying out loud!" She sticks her hand out at him. "Ruby. Owner."

He rises and gives her his full attention. "Of course. Ruby, how delightful. However, I must be on my way. Movie to make. You understand, I'm sure." He shakes Ruby's hand with both of his, then turns to me with a wink and a wave. "Miss Carolina, it's been a delight. We will talk more in the future."

We watch him go, me from my chair, Ruby from beside my table, where she's caressing the hand that had just been incased in Mr. Fisk's hands.

She shakes her head, then licks her lips. "Now there's a man I'd let eat crackers in my bed."

"Ruby," I say with a frown.

One eyebrow arched, she cocks her head down at me. "If we even made it to a bed." She pats my table. "This here table would do just fine." She looks around. "Or the counter. Now that'd be something wouldn't it?" She cackles as she walks away, leaving me with a picture in my head that no tasteless, although moist, muffin can get rid of. I'd go straight to Gertie's for a tall glass of moonshine, but it's not even lunch.

Standing up, I put on my coat. Just as I'm heading for the door, Ruby calls my name. I turn and see that she's got both hands on the counter, rhythmically pushing against it. She gives me a big ol' wink. With a thumbs-up she yells, "Tell Mr. Fisk to come on back to Ruby's anytime!" She cackles again, and I shudder.

This town has lost its ever-lovin' mind.

Chapter 38

I pause to view the bookshop window as passersby do. Along with the movie posters and books, we've added a couple books about cooking to get ready for Thanksgiving, including a few colorful cookbooks and cozy mysteries with recipes in the back. It needs something, maybe a fake cooked turkey or something to tie it to Thanksgiving. Maybe dishes? Dishtowels? Bonnie will know. I look up and see she's at the counter with two customers I recognize as Pearl and Crystal Bennett from my new book club. Shoot. I still didn't get those books, and they look put out about it. The Bennetts have a good bit of temper to go along with their red hair.

I hunch my coat collar up and dunk my head inside it as I scurry past and then hurriedly dive into the bistro. Peter peeks out from behind the first row of specialty groceries, sees it's me, and with a look of disgust, steps back out of sight.

"Hello, Peter."

When he doesn't say anything, I walk back to find him. He's squatted down at a display of crackers with a red pen in hand. "What are you doing?"

"Putting these crackers on clearance. They'll be out of date soon. This whole picnic bistro idea is a bust. And in case you're interested, I didn't get that job down near Atlanta either. Next time I'll ask someone who actually can help me for a recommendation." He spits all this out without looking up at me.

"Sorry about that. Next time don't ask me while you're hiding in a doorway from your girlfriend and my business partner."

"You probably heard about Shannon, too, didn't you?"

"Yes."

He stands up, and as he jams the cap back on the red marker, he stares at me. "She just left. No warning. No talking."

"Maybe she thought it was a little late for talking."

"She's from the millennial generation. I thought they just did what they wanted and didn't worry about the future."

"Peter! She's not a little girl. She's a businesswoman, and she's part of this town." I shake my head and turn away, but then turn right back at him. "You know what people in this town think about you? They think you can't make a decision. That you never stick with anything and…"

The look on his face stops me. His mouth is actually hanging open, and his eyes bug out at me. Then the bell on the door dings, and our heads swing to look that direction. When I see it's the Bennett sisters, I dunk down behind him and then creep to the last row. Peter moves toward them.

"Hello, ladies. How can I help you?"

"Why, hello, Peter," one of them says. "We're looking for that delightful young man, Alex. He's not still piddling around with that food truck, is he?"

Peter's voice is as tense as it was when we were talking about Shannon. "Yes. That's exactly what he's doing. Piddling."

One of the women sighs and then squeaks out, "We were afraid of that. Are you even still selling lunch?"

"Hot dogs." Peter is not in the mood for this, and they seem to be getting the message.

I can hear they are moving towards the food area, so I sneak back to the end of the row away from them.

With several more sighs and some unintelligible murmuring, they move towards the front door. It dings again as they open it. However, along with the cold air rushing in, one of my book club ladies gets in a parting shot. "When every place in town, including our beauty shop, is having a surge of business due to the movie, you must be doing *something* wrong for things to be so woeful here." Clucking their tongues, they move out of the door and let it fall softly shut.

Peter laughs as I come out from the shelves. He's bent over the counter on his elbows with his head hanging between his hands. "I should've hidden, too. That family is…" He stands up and turns to me. "But you were saying it's not just the Bennett family which has disparaging things to say bout me. It's the *whole* town. Right?"

He storms past me and into the back room. I wait for a couple minutes, then he yells, "What are you waiting for? I'm busy."

"Okay. But Peter, I don't think… okay, I don't know *what* to think. You can call me anytime. Don't let all this get you down." Echoes of my voice die and there's no answer from him, so I head to the front door and open it. I step onto the sidewalk as the bell announces my departure.

In only a couple of steps I'm flinging open our shop door and stepping inside.

To where the Bennett sisters are seated on the couch.

"Oh, hi, Crystal. Hi, Pearl."

"Why, Carolina, there you are!" They both turn towards me. "Come sit down and visit for a minute. We knew you were around town somewhere, but we couldn't track you down."

Bonnie apologizes with a shrug and a small grimace as I sit on the edge of one of the chairs. "Really?" I say. "I've been around all morning. Y'all are probably looking for the books for book club, aren't you? I don't have them yet. I know I've been neglectful and can't—"

"Oh, no. Not at all!" Crystal exclaims. "We don't really expect you to find books for all of us. That's just Retta being a cheapskate."

Pearl nods. "We get our books from the library or sometimes online at one of the used book places. Retta never likes to pay for anything."

At the last book club meeting, I'd figured out a way to remember which one is Crystal and which one is Pearl. Crystal, Beau's mother, wears glasses with no frames so that they're clear glass, like her name. Pearl doesn't wear glasses, and that's about the only way they are dissimilar. They both have the Bennett red hair, cut in only slightly different styles. Now I look from one to the other and take a deep breath. All that hiding for nothing. Oh, and that fight with Peter because of the hiding. That makes me frown, and both women look alarmed.

Pearl gasps. "Oh, have we upset you? If you want to get all the books, please go right ahead. Don't let us get in the way. You probably counted on making some extra money, didn't you?"

Crystal leans over and pats my knee. "You are such a go-getter! Such a good business person. We are so proud of women like you! We will gladly buy our books here. Do you have them now?"

"No, silly," her sister says. "Remember she said she doesn't have them. That's how we got distracted with all this talk of the book club." She looks at me. "Enough about that. We will buy all our books from you from now on. We're here on a completely different matter."

"Wait! Stop, I don't want to get all the books. Please continue getting them how you did in the past." I smile, but they still look concerned.

They look at each other and share tiny shakes of their heads and barely heard sighs. Then in a voice that tells you the patient isn't doing well, Pearl says, "Whatever you say, dear."

I hear Bonnie let out a laugh, but I don't look her direction. Whatever, indeed. Let's just get this over with. With a smile plastered on and charm in my voice, I jump in.

"So, ladies, how can I help you?"

Chapter 39

"I've rearranged my schedule. They let seniors do that," Savannah says as she walks along the food table in the back of the shop. It's loaded down with lunch fare. Sandwiches, salads, and veggie trays alongside cookie trays. I'm trailing behind my daughter who minutes ago sashayed in the front door and walked right past me with just a little wave.

"School doesn't end for another two hours. Just how much rearranging did you do?"

She shrugs, picks up an apple, and turns to face me. "It's work-study. Everybody does it."

"Come here," I say to her. I walk back towards the front windows, but veer to my right, along the side wall. There's a ledge along the wall there that's wide enough to sit on, but it's kind of a dark, not very comfortable area, so no one usually sits there. We keep talking about possibly having a cushion made and getting some lamps or wall sconces, but never mind. Back to Savannah.

I sit and motion for her to sit down also. Our knees are pointed toward each other, then she crosses her long legs, crosses her arms, and crunches into her apple.

"So what's up with you changing your schedule?"

"It's not a big deal," she says, wiping apple juice from around her lips. She takes a minute to chew then swallow. "I dropped that art elective and another class. I don't need them to graduate, and they were boring. Besides, I get credit for work-study. Leif just had to sign that I have a paying job. I took care of everything." She takes another huge bite and looks completely injured when I roll my eyes at her.

"You have to eat that right this minute? We're talking. So you did all this, and your daddy and I didn't have to know anything at all? You don't need our signature?"

"Oh." She leans up on one hip, pulls a folded paper out of her back pocket, and hands it to me.

It's a parental permission form. A very vague parental permission form. Basically it says, just sign so we aren't responsible for whatever crazy thing *your* teenager wants to do.

She tilts onto her other hip and pulls her phone out of that back jean pocket and looks at it. "I have to go." She stands up. "I'm supposed to be on the set by one." She takes another bite of her apple, then with the piece held in her cheek like a chipmunk, she points at the form. "No worries. I'll get that tonight." She adds another little bite to her stored food and starts to walk away, then she steps back and mumbles, with the soggy, gnawed-on apple core in her outstretched hand, "Here. Can you throw this away for me?"

Mom instinct, patterned on my brain since she was only months old, when I was holding out my hand for her to spit out the cheerios that were gagging her, kicks in and I hold out my hand. "Okay, but wait, what's the other class you dropped? Art and…"

She whirls around in a swirl of black hair, flashing eyes, and an innocent smile. "Oh. Just chemistry," she throws back my direction as she continues on her merry way.

Now why am I thinking chemistry might be an important class for someone applying to college? Where would that silly,

silly thought come from? I'm mumbling as I creakily stand from the hard ledge. I'm still mumbling as I walk around the end of the nearest bookcase and find Susie Mae sitting in the floor, her back against the side of the case, a book opened on her raised knees.

"Susie Mae?"

"Hi there," she says as she continues reading for a minute. She repeats herself as she folds the corner down on the page (and creases my soul). Then she looks up at me. "I finished the book you gave me, and so I thought I'd come start the second one."

"Oh, glad you liked it," I say as I start away from her to find the nearest trash can. But she scrambles up from the floor saying, "And to come visit you. You said that was okay."

She's baa-ack goes through my head like the little girl in the movie *Poltergeist*. But, c'mon, Carolina, she's a teenager going through a rough time. Give her a break. "Good!" I say with a big smile directed behind me.

"So Savannah got a bigger role in the movie?"

"Looks that way. Did you have some lunch?"

"Some crackers, but I'm good. Or did you want to get some lunch?" She cocks her head at me, and her short, dark hair doesn't move a bit. It's stiff with gel, but looks cute, not punk rock. Her question comes through her eyes, too, and I'm stuck again on what in the world is going on with her. I've got to find some time to talk to Susan. About this and other things. As I remember what Susan said about Silas, I feel my face heat up and I move toward the food in the back.

"Come get a plate, Susie Mae. I know for a fact all this food will never get eaten. Right, Margery?"

Margery nods her head in agreement. "Plus, Mr. Leif said you and Miss Bonnie and Miss Shannon are to eat whenever you want seeing as y'all make this all possible. And you, sweetie, you're a guest of Miss Carolina's, so help yourself."

Susie Mae grabs a plate. "Don't have to ask me twice. Mom's pretty much quit cooking, but I know good food when I see it." She senses my concern and Margery's, so she laughs. "I mean she feeds me and all, but she doesn't *cook* like she used to. Remember?" She turns to me and I do remember. Susan and her big vegetable garden. She canned and froze vegetables; every meal was fresh and home-cooked. She even made her own bread. Her kids worked in the vegetable garden, and as matter of fact, my kids did, too. From that life, to living up on the mountain in Laurel Cove, to now settling into her grandmother's rental—that's a lot of changes for a teenage girl. Not to mention the divorce.

"This does look delicious." I gently pat Susie Mae's back. "Get a seat at one of the tables, and I'll join you there in a minute." She grins, and after grabbing a bottle of water, she goes to a table off to the side.

I take a dip of chicken salad and cut open a croissant.

Margery steps toward me. "Can I toast that for you?"

"Sure," I say. She puts it in the toaster oven and sets the timer. Then she leans toward me, pointing her chin towards Susie Mae, who's just sat at the table.

Margery is in her fifties, I'd say. She's from Canton, and since she's been catering in our shop, I've talked to her quite a few times. She whispers, "That girl? Susie Mae's her name, right?"

"Yes. Why? Do you know her?"

"Me?" She shakes her head as she steps to the toaster oven. "No, but she seems awfully hungry."

I laugh, or at least try to. "Really? But aren't all teenagers hungry all the time?" I try another laugh.

She meets my eyes and squints a bit. "I don't mean hungry for food." The timer dings and she turns as she adds, "But maybe I'm wrong."

However, my sinking stomach says she's not.

Chapter 40

"After hearing Susie Mae say her mom doesn't cook much anymore, I felt guilty about all the chicken nuggets and frozen pizza I feed the kids when you're out of town," I explain to Jackson over the phone. "So we had roasted chicken and vegetables tonight."

"Did you roast the chicken, or was it one of those rotisserie ones?"

"I wish. Piggly Wiggly leaves a lot to be desired in the ready-to-eat area. It was just chicken breasts on a pan with potatoes and even some squash."

"Sounds delicious. I grabbed tacos with one of the guys here."

"Well, you can try all my hard work this weekend as, except for what I ate, it's all in Tupperware in the fridge. Bryan went to the basketball game, which I knew he was planning on doing, but then he got invited to dinner at John's house. So, with dinner in the oven, I drove him over there. Savannah is still filming, at least I assume that's where she is since she's not answering my texts and her phone goes straight to voicemail. Will is working late. Missus is still a no-show and isn't answering my calls. I thought Anna was going to throw up when she smelled the roasting onions, so Will's bringing her a sub sandwich home and she can eat 'when the kitchen smells better,' which was her exact quote."

I take my coat off the rack by the door and lay it over the back of the couch as we are talking. It's too warm in the house to put it on while I'm still on the phone. I might as well sit down, so I perch on the edge of the couch as Jackson asks, "Why'd you let Bryan go before he ate?"

"Because apparently he sent me a text about going to John's earlier. I remember seeing it, but then I guess I forgot it. So... At least I no longer feel guilty about not cooking and I had a healthy meal, so we'll call it a win. Listen, did you know Savannah dropped chemistry? She says she doesn't need it, but I know some of the colleges required it when Will was applying. She's getting out of school early to do her acting thing."

"No, I didn't know anything about it. Shouldn't she have to get our permission?"

"She did give me a form today, but it's very generic. What are we going to do about her not wanting to go to college?"

"I thought she'd found some courses at Dalton State she was going to take. What happened to that?"

"I don't know. I'll try to talk to her. I know we can't make her go, but..."

We both pause, then I stand up and say, "Well, I'm going to go have coffee with Susan. She and I have a lot to talk about."

"Really? What?"

Oh yeah, I hadn't told him about the latest development with her and Silas. Hmm. "Susie Mae, for one thing. We had lunch together, and that girl was just plain old odd. I don't remember her being like this before. Also, I wonder if she knows who Griffin's new girlfriend is."

"Did you find anything else out about her?" he asks. "Did she really move in to the house?"

"I guess, but that's all I know. Can't you ask him? You're friends."

"Guys don't ask things like that. Well, at least not the guys I know. Plus, I don't believe it. He just wouldn't do that. I know what everyone is saying, but do you really think he'd move a woman in with him and Grant?"

I sink down onto the arm of the couch. "I don't know. Things are just so out of whack here. Since FM died, everything feels off. You know? Maybe it's the movie, too. When have I ever had to track down Missus and Laney? They were always underfoot with their noses in everyone's business. Especially mine! Now they come and go like ghosts or something, and they don't look like they should. Susan acts more like her sister than her sister ever did. Peter's become a stranger. He's surly, and now Shannon is living back with her folks and even more moody than before. And Ruby? She was crude even for Ruby this morning. Oh! And I didn't even tell you that Crystal and Pearl Bennett want me to run for president of the Chamber of Commerce to oust Retta! Can you believe that?"

"Wait. What? Run against Retta Bainbridge? You'd be an awesome president, hon, but Retta doesn't strike me as the type of person who loses gracefully."

I nod emphatically. "No kidding."

Then, as the empty air stretches a bit longer, he says, "Carolina?"

"I'm here. It's just, well, I told them I'd think about it."

"Really? Okay. Huh, I'm kind of surprised."

"Me too." I stand again. "But I really do need to go. Told Susan I'd be there by now."

We finish with I love yous, hang up, then I put on my coat and am out the door. I'm going to Susan's house because she's putting up the kitchen curtains her mom gave her and she wanted me to see them. Plus, Will is bringing home sandwiches for him and Anna, and this will give them some peace and quiet in the house. I've tried to talk to him about being more open with Anna, but I doubt he heard a word I said.

Maybe that's why I'm actually considering running for Chamber president—a group of people who *have* to listen to me. But, no, that doesn't really feel like it. All I know is when they asked I waited for the word 'no' to blast out of my mouth. However...it didn't. Instead I focused in on what they were saying about what all could be done and, well, I don't know. Plus they don't need an answer until January so lots of time to work on my 'no' muscle.

When I pull onto Susan's new street, there are kids on bicycles everywhere, even though it's dark. It's still early, but it's dark. Cars line the streets as the driveways are only long and wide enough to hold one car. It's a very busy street, and I wonder how Susan likes that. The difference between here and her house up in Laurel Cove is striking. Surely one day it'll dawn on her. I park in the street and then walk up the broken sidewalk to her front door. The wooden door is open, so I pull open the bent screen door, stick my head in, and say, "Hello."

Susan practically comes bouncing from around the corner. "You're here! Come in. Come in. We just got the curtains all put up."

"Oh, good, your mom is here?" Then I turn the corner and who should I see up on the little stepstool but Silas Pendersen, star of stage and screen. Okay, I don't know if he's actually ever been on stage, and star is a bit much, but... "Hi, Silas."

Susan lays her hand on the back of his thigh and looks up. "Don't they look great? Mom had these up in her house a few years ago, but she never liked them. She thought they were too busy. But they're perfect here."

Silas comes down the stool, stopping at the bottom to put his arm around her and kiss the side of her head. "Hello," he says to me.

"They look great." I agree with her mom that they are awfully busy, but in this house, with the wacky paint and every inch taken up with stuff, they fit right in. "You did a good job hanging them, Silas."

"Thanks. First time." He squeezes Susan again and looks down at her. "I'm going to go and let you ladies have your coffee. Nice to see you again."

I nod and move out of his path. "Good to see you again, too."

Susan rushes past me and grabs his arm at the door. "See you later? Want me to come to your trailer?"

He glances up at me, then down at her. He cups her cheek and bends down to talk into her ear. She giggles and then reaches up to wrap her arms around his neck. As they go in for a kiss, I turn to look at the curtains. I prefer this kind of busy to that kind of busy.

"Pour yourself some coffee and pour me one, too, okay? We can sit at the table. I'll be right there," Susan says as I hear the screen door close behind Silas. Then she goes down the hallway toward the bedrooms.

With our full cups, I sit at the table I assume she meant. The kitchen nook serves as the only dining space, so it's the *only* table. One end is piled high with a paint can, paint charts, newspapers, and mail. The other end appears to be clean because everything was pushed down to the full end. The linoleum floor is old and faded and dirty from last week's mud. The counters are crowded with newspapers spread under paint cans, dishes, stacks of disposable plates and cups, and unopened packaged food, some still in grocery bags.

"Here I am!" Susan dashes into the room and sits down. "Isn't Silas great?"

"Sure. Nice of him to help."

"He's enjoying it, he says. He's never made a home, been too busy building his career. I can't wait for you to get to know him better."

"So you feel this is a long-term thing?"

"Why not?" she says with a big grin.

Okay, I'm not answering that. "Glad you're settling in. I know it takes a while."

She looks around. "I actually feel we're pretty settled in now. Curtains were the last touch."

"But you're still painting?" I say with a look around at the paint and painting supplies.

"Oh, that. No, I'm done, just haven't had a chance to clean it all up." She jumps up. "Want some cookies?" She digs in one of the bags sitting on the counter and pulls out a box of Vanilla Wafers. "I love these. So much better than homemade cookies, I think."

"Okay. Stop." I hold up a hand and shake my head at her. "Who are you? You are not the Susan Lyles I know."

She concentrates on opening the box of cookies. "No, *that* wasn't the real Susan Lyles. This is me. All that other was me trying to be perfect. To be what I promised Griffin I was. To be my *mother*."

She starts pulling at the interior bag to get it open, then with a hard yank the bag splits and the little brown discs fly up and around her. For a moment, we stare in silent shock at the crumbs all over the floor and table. Susan's first look is one of astonishment, and then she's crying. Hard. Like dropping a glass jar on a tile floor, everything goes from nice and contained to explosion in one second. Guess she finally reached her breaking point. I reach over toward her, but she sits back and looks at me with tears streaming down her face. "Did you hear what Griffin did?"

"Griffin?" Oh, no. "Um, about, uh, what? What did he do exactly?"

She stands up and grabs the roll of paper towels on the counter. Ripping off one, she wipes her face, even though she's still sniffling and tears are still streaming. She leans back against the counter, her wadded-up paper towel in hand. "I can't believe he'd do that to me. We're not even completely divorced yet!"

I shrug. "Well, honey, it's not like you're sitting around waiting." With raised eyebrows I say, "Silas?"

"It's not the same. Not the same at all. Griffin will say he's doing it to make the *kids* happy. And of course, I'm sure Grant is delirious!"

"Now, Susan." I stand up and go over to face her. "You know that's not true. You need to calm down. It's just a woman."

She stares at me. "How can you say that? You know how I feel about her!"

Okay, I'm missing something here. "Are you saying you've known about this woman and Griffin for a while?" So Laney was right! I should've never doubted her. I reach over to hug Susan. "Oh, sweetie, I'm so sorry. I didn't know."

She rears back. "Of course you know. I've told you."

"Told me? About Griffin?" I shake my head at her and lift my arms in confusion. "About this girl? Or woman?"

She turns to the sink and throws her paper towel at it. Then she steps past me to the refrigerator and pulls out a bottle of wine. "Carolina, you're not helping. I don't know what you're trying to say, but there is no way in heaven Griffin's mother can be called a girl! Screw the coffee. I'm having wine!"

Wait a minute. Griffin's mother?

CHAPTER 41

Will lopes into the kitchen early the next morning.

"How was your dinner last night?" I ask. I'm drinking coffee and waiting for my other kids to appear. Will has an early class, so I knew he'd be first.

He stops and stares at me. "Dinner?"

"You and Anna? I tried to give you some space so you could talk. You know, about the future?"

"Oh, we watched football. Sandwiches were good."

He's collecting everything for a bowl of cereal, so I wait for him to sit across from me. Once his milk is poured and I know he won't get up and leave, I spring. "What is *your* plan? I think Anna wants you two to work it out. To have the baby and be a family. A family living *together*."

He stares into his bowl as he scoops spoonfuls of Lucky Charms into his mouth. Thinking about how much time and effort I wasted on thinking Griffin was moving another woman in with him when it was just his mother made me crazy last night. It's absurd how no one is talking about anything! I'm not playing the gossip game any longer, and I'm starting with my own children.

"Look at me," I say. His hunched position doesn't change,

but his eyes swivel up. "Are you still involved with Rose?" I'm safe to ask this because I know Anna is still in the shower downstairs. Old house noises let you know where people are.

He swallows, but his mouth was empty. He swallows again, then looks away. "Not really."

I try to hide my disgust. I am his mother, after all. "What does that mean? You are a married man. You don't get to be 'not really' involved with another woman." Guilt works across his face and he starts to speak, but I cut him off. "At least not in this house. I understand your attraction to Rose. Heck, I like her a lot. But you can't have it both ways. Again, as long as you're living here."

"Why do you think Anna wants to be a family?"

"Because she..." Wait a minute. Is this another thing I'm not supposed to tell? I feel my eyebrows dropping and I don't quite close my mouth because, well, why would she tell me if she didn't want Will to know? He needs to know, so I let my mouth open up even more. "Because she told me. She wants to make it work with you."

Now his eyebrows are scrunched down and he's looking at me. He's thinking and I'm feeling relieved, like a sack of cement has dropped from my shoulders. I'm sorry, but sometimes things just need to be said. Whether you have permission to say them or not.

"You and Rose were more than friends. If your marriage is going to work you've got to break off from her completely." I reach over and lay my hand on his. "Son, you have no idea how crazy you are going to be about little Francie. Get this settled *before* she comes."

He looks around, then leans closer to me. "But Rose keeps calling me. She says we should be able to be friends. She says..." He shrugs and leans back.

"What? What else does she say? That you shouldn't be tied to Anna just because of a baby? That Anna left you and was with Kyle Kendrick? That you don't want to be stuck in Chancey just because you made some mistakes?"

Now it's his mouth that's hanging open. "How did you know? I mean, uh..." Then his eyes widen. "Oh my god, did Rose tell you all that, too?"

I laugh. "She's like the only person in Chancey that doesn't tell me her woes. No, she didn't, but it's not that hard to figure out. You did make some mistakes, sure. But you've got to quit running from them. You and Anna and Francie deserve a chance."

"But..." He leans up and scoops up another spoonful of cereal. "But what if it's not good? What if Rose and I are..." He puts the bite into his mouth and chews, letting his questions hang.

With a shrug, I say, "I don't know. What I do know is you can't keep straddling the fence on this. Make a decision and commit to it. Or, well..." I emotionally and physically straighten my spine. "If you can't make a decision, you can't live here while Anna is here. She is the mother of our granddaughter, and I won't have her treated this way."

He continues scooping cereal into his mouth as I'm talking. He seems unfazed by my words, since he finishes by lifting his bowl and draining the milk from it. Then he scoots his chair away from the table. "Okay, Mom. Thanks. I've got some things to think about." He stands up and puts his bowl and spoon into the dishwasher, then wipes the table.

I want more information, but I can tell from the efficient way he moves around the kitchen that he's done talking. He fills a travel mug with coffee, and as he clips the lid on he smiles at me, but it's a closed mouth smile, revealing nothing. He tips his cup and his head at me, then heads through the living room to the front door.

It seems like a bad sign that he didn't go downstairs and tell

Anna bye like he usually does. He didn't even go down to get his backpack. Maybe it's in his car. Or maybe...

I slap the table. "Stop this," I say out loud.

Besides, I can't waste energy on him—there's another kid coming my way.

"Savannah seemed mad. Is that why I'm not riding to school with her?" Bryan asks from the passenger seat of my minivan. His head is cocked toward the window, but his eyes are focused on me.

"No. I wanted to drive you this morning." We're huddled in the van waiting for the defroster to clear enough of the windshield for me to pull out of our driveway. But he's right. Savannah was mad. Probably still is. No, wait. By now she's at school, and I'm sure has forgotten she even has a mother to be mad at.

"Why?" he asks as his eyes focus even more on me.

"I want to talk. Want to know what's going on with you. How are you liking high school?"

I put the car in drive and ease forward a bit. They talk more if you look like you're not paying attention to them. Unless you're trying to nail them on something, then the good old parental stare is required, but as far as I know, Bryan is in the clear. Again, as far as I know.

He takes a breath and eases back in his seat. He also stops staring at me. "It's not bad. I like the freedom. Everybody's not all over you if you're just walking down the hall during classes like in middle school." He pauses, then says, "I miss Grant."

"I bet you do. Did you hear his grandmother is moving in with him and his dad?"

"Yeah. He's not happy about that. Says he might even move down here with his mom."

Do not. Do not let your eyebrows jump like they want to. Keep your mouth closed, just gently nod. Inside, though, I'm screaming. Susan has no idea! After the appropriate amount of time I say, "Oh, really? But I thought he loves Darien Academy so much."

"He does. I think he's just threatening it to keep his dad and grandmother in line. You know."

Oh. Okay, never mind. "Sounds like you and he are talking more than you were."

"Yeah, some. He invited me to a party up at his house this weekend."

"Grant's having a party?"

"Yeah." Bryan laughs. "He says he has to do it before his grandmother moves in."

"Anyone else from down here invited? The usual guys?"

"I don't think so. I can go, can't I?"

"I guess. We just need to know what time to take and pick you up," I say as I pull up at the far edge of the high school parking lot. The line for drop-offs at the front doors is ridiculous, so I always drop the kids off here. It gives them a little exercise, and it's really not much farther than where they usually have to park.

He opens the door and steps out. As he swings his backpack over one shoulder, he says, "Grant said I can spend the night."

"Wait!" I yell before he slams the door. "It's just guys, right?" He shrugs and closes the door. His eyes almost meet mine. Almost.

Bet you dollar to doughnuts it's a girl-boy party.

I look down at my work jeans and sweatshirt. I'm not really dressed for work, but I don't work until eleven. Plenty of time for a cup of coffee at Ruby's.

The café's door isn't even fully closed behind me before Ruby yells out, "So I hear you're running against Retta for president of the Chamber of Commerce."

"Good morning, Ruby," I say as I move through the tables. I stop at an empty one in the middle of the room and sit down facing the street. Away from her.

Libby rushes to me, coffee pot in hand. "Are you really? Challenging Retta, I mean? Oh, how exciting! Cathy was planning on doing that, did you know? She wants to be the president in the worst way."

"Really?"

Libby leans against the chair to my side. "Oh, yes. She has such ideas. I know! You two can run together! Oh, you'd be unstoppable. Cathy's charm and your experience. Even Retta couldn't beat you!" With a quick wink and a nod at a booth, she darts over there with her coffee.

Hmm, Cathy. Pearl and Crystal didn't mention that. Wonder if they know? Wonder if that's why they asked me?

"Here," Ruby says as she spins a saucer onto my table. "This half is cranberry and dark chocolate chunks. This one is orange and dark chocolate chunks. Read about dark chocolate being good for ya, and then, cranberries and orange are fruit you know." Then she pauses and looks at the plate. "Are cranberries fruit? They come from a tree, right?"

"No, they come from bogs or something like that."

"Goldarnit! A bog? I can't advertise that as healthy. Are you sure?"

With a shrug I pick the cranberry one up to taste. "Oh, that's good. Really good. This is much better than the apple oatmeal muffin I had last week. Is this really healthy?"

She shrugs. "Let's just say I'm working on it. Now," she says as she pulls out the chair and sits down. "Tell me what made you decide to take on Retta Bainbridge."

"I haven't decided anything. Who told you I had?"

"Hmm, let's see." She folds one scrawny arm across her midsection and settles the elbow of her other arm on top of it so she can use that hand to rub her chin. "Beau Bennett when I went up and got my hair cut and rinsed last night. Then the mayor was right concerned about it when he was in here this morning." She drops her hand and leans toward me. "Just for the record, Beau wasn't concerned at all. She said she thinks of you as a forward-thinking woman."

"Really? That's nice."

"Plus, she says since your son and her niece are an item, it's like having all that power right in the Bennett family."

"Brittani and Bryan are not still an item," I correct her. "Plus, how much actual power can it be?" I say with the orange muffin in hand. I take a bite as she draws in a huge breath.

"Oh, you have no idea. No idea at all." She lowers her voice and her head. "And if you think a Bainbridge will easily give up power, you've got another thing coming."

"Well, even if that's true," I say, "Retta's term is up. Why everyone thinks it'll be some big battle is beyond me."

Ruby grins and stands up. "That's cute. You think a term ending means something to a Bainbridge. Yeah, that's real cute right there." Then she yells, "Libby! Carolina needs more coffee." She pats my back as she walks away.

Libby is filling my cup, standing between me and the front door, when it whooshes open, sending in a blast of cold air. Then Libby moves and Laney is almost to my table before she sees me. She stops, then her whole frame drops as she says, "Didn't think you worked until eleven on Tuesdays." She looks around, then down at my table. She sighs and gives up some invisible struggle. "Can I sit with you?"

I nod. "Sure, though it sounds like you were trying to avoid me."

She wrenches her mouth around as she takes off her big brown coat and lays it on one of the chairs beside me. Everything's the same as last time I saw her, except it might be worse. Her hair is still gray and short, but now it's not even styled. Her pants are wrinkled and the sweater is stretched out and looks like she might've slept in it. I'm getting kind of used to her face without a lot of makeup, but I'm not sure she's even got lotion on it today. Or has even washed it.

She sits down heavily and looks at me. Just looks at me. Then she finally says, "Guess I have been avoiding you." She holds her cup up for Libby who stops quickly to fill it and top mine off, then hustles on.

Laney takes a sip then says, "I'm right put out with you."

"With me? For what?"

She leans across the table toward me, and there's a bit of fire in her eye. "You're not from here. Why didn't you ever tell me what people, people not from here, thought of me?" Tears collect in her tired eyes. "Floozy. A Southern belle floozy. No, a *stupid* Southern belle floozy. You were laughing, too, all the time, weren't you?"

"Laney? Are you serious? No." I scoot over to sit in the chair to her right. "I always thought you were beautiful and fashionable. Why would you think anyone thought all that other stuff?"

She motions with her hand to her left, I guess through the wall and toward the dance studio, and shakes her head. "The movie people. They thought I was playing a part when I was just in my regular clothes! I heard them laughing at me." She sniffles and digs at the table with her plain, unpolished nails. Her sad purple-blue eyes finally look up. "Why didn't you tell me?"

Laying both my hands on hers, I give her a smile. "I promise. I never thought any of that." I motion to her outfit and hair. "Is that what all this is about? I thought you did this for a part in the movie."

She closes her eyes and sighs. "I did all this to be taken seriously. I don't want to be a, a caricature. You know, one of those people in Southern movies or books that everyone laughs at."

"Here ya go, honey," Ruby says as she sets another saucer with two muffin halves in front of Laney. "Carolina will tell you what they are." She pats Laney on her back and walks away, but as she leaves we hear her mumble, "Poor thing."

I point to the saucer. "That half is cranberry and dark—"

"What the hell," Laney mutters under her breath. Then she stands up yelling, "What the hell, Ruby Jean Harden, do you think you are doing?"

Ruby is back toward the counter, but she stops in her tracks and slowly turns around to stare at Laney who is just getting started.

"Sympathy muffins? *You're* giving *me* sympathy muffins?" Laney picks up the saucer. "The day *I* need sympathy from the likes of *you* will be the day they put me in the ground, I'll have you know." Then she turns around speaking to the rest of us who are gathered in the restaurant. "Yes, I may look like something the cat drug in, but I'll have each and every one of you know it's because I *chose* to look this way! It was way more work to *not* fix my hair. To *not* put on makeup. To hide all the qualities God gave me under this, this mess." She looks down at her clothes and shudders.

Then she holds the saucer high and then she wraps her arm in front of her like she's going to toss a Frisbee.

Ruby screams, "Laney Troutman, don't you dare!" while everyone else ducks. We have no illusions about just how much Laney Troutman Conner dares.

But then Laney straightens up. She sits the saucer down on the table. Despite the gray hair and frumpy clothes, it's the real

Laney looking at me. "What do I care what anyone thinks of me? Right?"

My smile jumps right into a big grin. Laney twirls around and sashays toward the front door like she's wearing a tiara and a sash, carrying a huge bouquet of roses.

"Wait," I shout at her. "Your coat."

She doesn't even turn around.

"Give it to Goodwill."

CHAPTER 42

Off the road into our driveway, there's a small wooded area before I get to the railroad right-of-way. At the edge of the gravel on each side of me, there are weeds, bushes, and tree branches full of brown leaves. It's dark in that little space, but as I near the tracks everything opens up and I see something I've been looking for—Missus' car.

I park, close my door quietly, and sneak up the porch steps then through the front door. Inside, the house has that morning quiet when the bustle of everyone getting out the door is over. Bryan and I were the last ones in the house when we left.

Creeping through the downstairs, I don't find her. She must be up in her room, Will's old room. The one next to mine and Jackson's. Halfway up the stairs I hear voices.

Voices? I stop. If she brought that man here? Wait, she's not my child, I remind myself. I try to breathe. She's a grown woman. She, uh, she… but FM!

I stomp up the rest of the stairs to let her know she's been found out. I don't slam my bedroom door, but I'm not gentle. She wants to sneak around? Fine. I'm not playing that game with her. I flip on the radio part of my clock radio and turn it louder. I don't want to hear anything else.

In only fifteen minutes, I'm dressed and ready to go down-stairs. After I turn the radio off, I wait inside my closed door and listen. Nothing. Good, maybe she heard me and left. Even though I've been trying to track her down the last few days, now I hope I *don't* see her. Sometimes I say I don't want to know something when I actually do kind of want to know, but I don't mean this. I don't want to know anything about this. Me and the rest of Chancey, we're still mourning FM whether she is or not!

The store is entirely too warm. I cannot keep my eyes open. Margery is working in the back setting up a late lunch for the movie people, but she's not making enough noise to bother me. Even standing at the counter, I keep leaning over on my elbows, propping up my head, and taking a snooze. I hate how those efficient, get-a-lot-done mornings turn into barely func-tioning afternoons.

"They're all headed this way," Shannon says as she pushes through the front door. "Wake up, Carolina." She nudges me over with her hip as she stuffs her pocketbook under the front counter. "Why is it so hot in here? I'm going to block open the front door to get some fresh air in here," she says as she goes to do just that.

I watch her and try to wake up.

She's wearing a black tunic shirt over gray leggings and burgundy suede short boots. She's got a burgundy scarf on and some cool jewelry. I'm glad to see her newfound fashion sense didn't depend on her close proximity to Peter. I had my doubts she could pull it off without him there to dress her each morning. She is just getting the door propped open when the first folks from the movie appear. They wave hello, but dash back to the tables set up for them.

Savannah sails by without even a wave. Yep, she's still mad. You know, it makes a mother feel warm all over to know she can still get to her kids.

Silas walks in and gives me a wink as he passes. Why in the world Susan thinks her fling with him is a long-term thing is beyond me. Leif holds out his hand as he enters and comes straight to me.

"Carolina! Come have lunch with us! Or do you have customers?" He takes my hand in his and then pulls me into a quick hug across the counter. "Great morning of shooting! Absolutely everything went as planned. Even better!" He laughs and looks around. "I think we'll shoot here later today, if that's okay. It's not scheduled until tomorrow, but we are actually ahead of schedule. That's a miracle in this industry. What do you think?"

"Okay. We'll probably just go ahead and close early. Let you have the whole place, but I'll need to check with Shannon."

He rises up on his toes and looks toward Shannon's work area. "There she is. I'll go run it by her." He starts off. "Come eat. I'll save you a place."

He's gone before I can tell him I've already eaten. As the last few folks wander in, I walk over to the front area and then look out at the gazebo across the street. Phoenix is striding down the sidewalk. When she comes in the open doorway, she turns immediately toward me. Her eyes are wide and her mouth is set as she comes up to my side, grasps my arm, and whispers, "I need your help."

I try to take a step away, get a little breathing room, but she pulls me close. "It's out now, and I can't figure out how it got out. I've got to find out who it is."

"What's out? What's going on?"

She doesn't release me, but looks me straight in my face.

Her green eyes look a bit wild, and now she's holding both my arms. "You were right. I *was* a stripper. But it was a long time ago and I didn't think anyone could find out."

I keep my mouth shut\ and manage to give her my "Oh, no! Whatever shall we do?" look.

She shoves a piece of paper in my hand and says, "Read that. I'll go pretend to eat something and then I'll come back up here, okay? Thanks." She strides off. I stay turned toward the windows to see what the paper she gave me is, but before I can get it open, Savannah comes to stand beside me and stare out the window, too.

"What's that?" she asks.

I shove the paper into my pants pocket. "Nothing. How did school go this morning?"

"Fine. I just wanted you to know I did what you said. I set up an appointment with the guidance counselor for Friday for you and dad."

"And you."

She rolls her eyes. "Of course." She stands next to me not saying anything for a bit. Then her posture softens as she takes a deep breath and turns a little in my direction. "I should've told you about Parker inviting me to his fraternity dance."

"Thank you," I say as I also turn in her direction a bit. I add a smile, and she smiles back. She then adds a shrug as her smile gets bigger.

I exhale. "I know. Your dad is just *so* easy." I put my arm on her shoulders. "He's got a serious soft spot when it comes to you, but you cannot abuse it. I honestly have no problem with you going to the dance, but I do have a problem with you using your dad like that."

She leans her head towards me and says, "I know. I sometimes forget about how y'all are."

"Mean? Old-fashioned? Fuddy-duddies?" I laugh and give her a squeeze before she steps away just a few inches. Her head is tipped forward, and she looks at me halfway through a curtain of dark, shiny hair.

"No. Together." She pushes her hair back and gives me a lopsided grin before she heads back to the tables and her co-workers.

Well, now, that's about the nicest thing my daughter has ever said to me.

Checking over my shoulder to make sure she's gone, I pull the piece of paper out of my pocket. Don't you hate in movies where a person is given a note, told it's important, and then they stick it in their pocket and forget it? I mean, how can they not be curious? Do people give you strange things to read so often that you are just used to having your pockets full of secrets?

Yeah, not me.

It's a sheet of regular printer paper, but what's printed on it looks like a newspaper or magazine column however it's way off center. Maybe a blog? The title is done in bright pink with black writing. Cute, but nothing special. It's called *Taking Chances*.

I don't see a name or a byline, but I do see what has gotten Phoenix's nude leotard in a twist. "Stripper on Main Street?" the headline questions. There's a picture of Phoenix standing in one of her big windows with one leg jutted out from underneath her short pink dress. I remember her wearing that, but I don't remember when it was. It's a shirt dress, which should be very sedate, but hers was really short and she wore patent leather boots with it. It didn't look that sexy in real life, but this picture is pretty suggestive. Especially the way she's pressed against the glass. She was probably just arranging things in the window, but... I scan the article and see that there are dates and a strip club somewhere in Arizona called the Pink Pony. Ah, the pink dress really makes that jump out. I look at the top again to see where this *Taking Chances* thing is from. The picture was taken here, but where I've never seen anything like this around here.. Wonder how she found it?

I turn around to see if I can spot her and see that she's still eating. She's seated beside Leif, and they don't look like they have a problem in the world. Shannon waves to me and nods toward the counter, so I meet her there.

She bends down to get her purse as she says, "Leif says they want to film here this afternoon. I'm good with closing early if you are."

"Yeah, it's been slow today. I think the weather is just too nice for people to be inside."

"It's supposed to get colder again this weekend. What's that?"

I've folded the paper so only the pink header at the top shows. "Have you ever seen this column? Or I guess it's a blog thing?"

She reaches for the paper, but I don't hand it to her. I don't want her to see the story.

"Yeah, it's that gossip blog. About all the kid stuff." She's still digging in her purse and not looking at me.

"Gossip blog? Kid stuff?"

"Where are my keys?" she says then adds, "You know. Who's dating who around town and who had a party get out of control over the weekend. Stupid kid stuff. We had a secret zine like this when I was in school, but no one printed it out. Never wanted it to get in the parents or teachers hands." She jerks her keys out and then slings her purse over her shoulder. "You'll lock up?" she says as she heads toward the front door.

"Sure."

She's gone, followed by a steady stream of movie folks headed off to their next scene. I wait until there's only a few people left in the back before I lay the paper out flat on the counter and really look at it.

I see what Shannon means. Besides the article about Phoenix, there's just some stuff about kids. The names are familiar, but I only know a couple. There's nothing really concrete. There are a couple of pictures from a sporting event in the gym, a 'look who's sitting with-who.' I study the pictures, but they don't tell me much.

Then my eyes bug out at the last picture. This one wasn't taken in the gym. These are not students.

The story is cut off, and I flip the paper over to see if it's continued on the back. There's nothing. No names, but no one will need names if they look very long. The location might be harder to nail down, but I was there. I saw this in real life.

Missus and Mr. Fisk are making out in the front seat of his car in my driveway.

"Hey, Shannon still here?" Peter says as he pushes through the door.

"No!" I shout. "Sorry. You scared me." I scramble to get the paper back in my pocket. I clear my throat and look up at his puzzled face. "No, we're closing early and she already left."

"Okay." He looks toward my pocket, where my hand – and the paper – are buried. "Are you all right?"

"I'm fine. How are you?"

He shrugs and looks around. "Might as well close the bistro, too." He looks back at me, but I'm saying nothing. "Okay. Tell Shannon I was looking for her."

"Okay."

He leaves and then Phoenix comes up to me. "Sorry. Got to talking back there." She waves and we say goodbye to a couple of her fellow actors. Then it's just the two of us in the front area. She whispers, "What are we going to do?"

"Where did you get this?" I ask pulling the paper out of my pocket.

"In the studio this morning. It was laying there, just out in the open. What if Leif had seen it?"

"He will soon. Get out in front of it. Tell him. Does Colt really not know?"

She looks at me, halfway rolling her eyes. "He's such an easygoing guy. You know. He's like his brother."

"Tell him. Tell him now."

She takes the paper and folds it several times until it's reduced to a small rectangle. "Maybe. Or maybe I'll just see what happens." She tightens her fingers around it, then lets it drop off her fingers and onto the counter with a shrug. As her shoulders slowly roll back down, she smiles and says, "I've found truth has its place and its time. Bye now." She leaves, and I can't help but look at the back where she was. She came in here so frantic, but that's not at all the way she's leaving. Is Margery doctoring the food with tranquilizers? Was there vodka in those water bottles?

Shaking my head, I repeat her words out loud, "Truth has its place and its time?"

Yeah, right. I've watched enough soap operas to know how that philosophy works out.

Chapter 43

"You. Carolina!" a woman yells from behind me as I head across the street to my car. Only Margery was left in the store, setting up a light dinner for the crew that would be filming in the store later. I turn after I get to the parking spaces, so I'm not in the middle of the street.

The woman is crossing behind me from the corner at the bistro. She's short and heavyset with dark hair, but with the sun behind her, that's all I can tell. As she gets closer I realize who it is and know that I should've kept going. "Mrs. Lyles," I say and even smile. "Hello!"

Griffin's mother. I've only met her a couple of times, but she's one of those people you can't forget. The spike of fear they engender is burned into your brain to warn you of impending danger. Everything in me says, "Run. Run far, far away." However, manners say, "Stay and be nice." Southern manners go even further and say, "Give her a hug—she just needs some lovin'," so…

But Mrs. Lyles glares at my opening arms like I'm armed with butcher knives. My arms slowly fall to my side.

She has the jowl of an old-time judge. Her mouth is dark-wine-colored and turned down, as are her thick, highly outlined eyebrows. She'd've been a hanging judge. A guilty person looking up at that face would volunteer to be hung.

"I was just coming to your shop," she says as she crosses her arms and arches one eyebrow.

"Oh, we closed early today. They're filming a movie here in Chancey. Isn't that neat?"

She turns and looks at the shop. "Closed? It's practically the middle of the day. Whatever kind of a way is that to do business?" She turns back to me and stares.

So, I volunteer to be hung. I mean open the shop, or whatever she wants. And I smile. I smile a lot and, after a while, stop talking.

She looks me up and down. What she sees settles her mouth into an even deeper frown. She throws up her hands and her mouth opens. "I suppose we can talk here as well as in your shop. It's about your book club. I will be joining it and want to know what book I need to read so as to be ready for the discussion."

"Oh, well. I'm new to it, and from what I understand there's a waiting list."

"Balderdash. What book are you reading?"

"It's by Fannie Flagg, something about a girl's gas station?"

"I know it. When do you meet?"

"Like I said, I think there's a—"

Her eyes bulge at me, and she has a hand on her hip. "When do you meet?"

"Second Tuesday of the month. Seven."

She pulls back, then looks at me with more confusion than judgment. "Tonight? Your meeting is tonight?"

"No, the… shoot."

Oh, no. How in the world did I do this? How did I forget about the book club? I look across the street in panic, to where the movie crew people are already setting up. *That's* why filming in the store was marked off for today. Shoot. To add insult to injury, I don't have anything ready to serve, and I didn't even finish the book. "I need to make a phone call," I say with an abrupt turn. As I walk to my van, I pull out my phone and dial Retta Bainbridge. She answers as I open the van door.

"Retta. It's Carolina. I made an awful mistake. They are now filming and serving the crew dinner in the store tonight."

There's a pause, but not a very long one before she says, "And how are you planning on remedying that?"

"Uh, meet next week?"

No pause this time. "No, that will not do."

There's a pause now, but I don't plan on filling it, so I wait.

"Put her on speaker phone," says a voice at my side. A demanding voice. A judgy voice. So I put the phone on speaker. "Um, Retta. I've put you on—"

"Ms. Bainbridge, this is Rachel Lyles, Griffin Lyles' mother, and I have a solution to your problem. I'd like to invite your club to meet at our home. Mine and Griffin's home in Laurel Cove. There will be a catered meal, and if transportation is needed, I can have the club bus bring you ladies up to the house."

My mouth is hanging open. I'm staring at the lady beside me who is now holding my phone, whose first name is apparently Rachel. However, no pause is necessary for Retta.

"What a delightful suggestion, Mrs. Lyles. We would love to take you up on your invitation, but your gracious offer of transportation is not necessary. My car and Carolina's van will suffice nicely. We will contact the other members. Besides, we couldn't possibly put you out any more after you've stepped in to fulfill Carolina's responsibilities."

The dark eyebrows dart my direction and lift just a bit as if to say they aren't surprised at all at having to fulfill my responsibilities. "No worries whatsoever, dear, and please, call me Rachel. I look forward to meeting you in person this evening."

Retta matches her oh-so superior voice. "I do as well, Rachel."

Before I can get a word in, they both say goodbye and my phone is handed back to me.

Rachel Lyles takes a deep breath through her nose and looks up at me. "Well, that worked out nicely. Glad I could be here to fix your mistake." With a shorter sniff, she turns and heads back across the street.

This really stinks.

Rachel used to be one of my favorite names.

CHAPTER 44

"You let her into the book club!" Susan yells when I pick up my phone. I haven't even had more than a sip of coffee yet this morning.

"I didn't," I groan. "I mean, not officially. I forgot it was Tuesday and—"

"I know. I've heard all about it. She had to rescue one of *my* friends. Isn't it lucky she's here? Everyone in her book club is *so* welcoming and *so* glad she's living here now."

"You talked to her?"

"Of course I talked to her! She's the gateway to my son now," Susan yells, then her voice catches like she's crying.

"Susan. Calm down. Where are you?"

"Sitting in my car outside the Laurel Cove clubhouse. Wednesdays I've been taking Grant to school. I pick him up, we have breakfast at the club, then I drive him to school." The steam disperses in her words as she talks. "*She* called and told me I could meet the *two* of them at the club this morning so we could discuss Grant's schedule going forward. Can you believe that?"

"Where's Griffin?"

"He's out of town. That's why she moved in apparently. He's

been put on some big committee that requires him to spend more time at their headquarters in North Carolina. Of course, no one mentioned that to me, but that's why she moved in."

"Can she just take over like that? What does your lawyer say?"

Susan says something so quiet I have to ask her to repeat herself.

"We don't have anything formal, and I moved out, so yes. Yes, she can."

"How did Grant seem?"

She laughs a little. "He was seated beside her and he kept rolling his eyes at me when she couldn't see. Apparently he had to cancel a party he wanted to have so he was upset, but he's not one to make waves and I understand that, but how did *you* let her in the book club? Thought there was a waiting list."

"I don't honestly know. It snuck up on me somehow, and she was right there to jump in. She's rather, uh, crafty, isn't she?"

"Very. She makes everything she wants to do sound completely reasonable and anything outside of what she wants sounds selfish and goofy. Plus," Susan takes a breath, "she knows about Silas. At least she knows *something* about Silas, she was very cagey when she hinted at it. I'm not sure how she already knows, and maybe she doesn't. I can't risk it." She seems to remember how she yelled at me by way of greeting and adds, "Oh, and I'm not mad at you. I'm just... I don't know."

"You headed to work?" I ask.

"Yes. You?"

"Yep. Maybe we can get together for lunch. Chinese buffet?"

"Noon sound good?"

"Yes. And I promise I won't invite Laney. That's all between you and her."

Susan chuckles. "I should probably get back into Laney's good graces. She's the only one Griffin's mom doesn't play for a fool. See you at noon."

We hang up, and I pick up my coffee cup. They'll be filming in the store all day, so I'm in no hurry to get there. Shannon is opening up. Bonnie doesn't work today so I have to go in at some point, but not right now.

Last night's book club was interesting. I did finish the book yesterday afternoon since I didn't have to get food and drink ready for book club. The discussion was lively. Rachel didn't allow us to get off-topic, but before she smacked down that rule, I did hear something I need to think about.

Crystal and Pearl were all atwitter about Beau's new beau. A guy from the movie. They said he's an actor, but maybe they're confused. I mean, maybe he's in the crew and they assume he's an actor. There just aren't that many actors here Beau would be interested in. They wouldn't give me many details, but they did get ticked off when I suggested it could be an actress. I mean, it is Beau.

"He is most definitely a man!" Pearl exclaimed. Then they giggled and got Rachel involved in the conversation. It was hard to follow from there, since they were talking in whispers behind their hands. However, I'm sure that's how Susan's mother-in-law knows about Silas. His name slipped out a couple times, and Rachel looked appropriately horrified then. This worries me for Susan, and not just because of her mother-in-law. My friend is going to get her heart broken sooner than I imagined.

Is Beau's new beau Susan's beau? I look at my reflection in the mirror near the stairwell and tug at the back of my hair. As I walk into the kitchen and sit down, I muse, "I could stand a haircut. Wonder if Beau can fit me in?"

"Mom?" Savannah calls, coming down the stairs. I don't

answer because she turns the corner and sees me seated at the kitchen table. "Mom, where'd you get this?"

It's the paper Phoenix brought to the shop. The last time I saw it it was still folded in a small rectangle and laying on my bathroom counter. Now, it's unfolded and in my daughter's hand.

"Why? And what were you doing in my bathroom?"

She drops the paper on the table and goes to the refrigerator. "I can't find my hairbrush."

"Did you put my hairbrush back where you found it?"

She doesn't answer, which means no, it's in her backpack. She pulls out the carton of orange juice. "Did you see that story about the stripper? Is it true?"

"How would I know if it's true? Phoenix would say it isn't true, right?"

"*Taking Chances* used to be just about the kids at school. Kind of stupid to have a story about old people in it." She pours her glass of juice, snags a cup of yogurt, and comes to sit across from me. She cocks her head at me. "What? What's that look for?"

"Cherry yogurt and orange juice? Just makes my mouth pucker. Phoenix isn't exactly 'old people.' But go ahead with what you were saying. So you've seen this, uh, this thing before. *Taking Chancey*?"

"Chances. Yeah, not printed out like this and I didn't see this one yet, but it's a blog. Everybody at school reads it."

"Who writes it?"

She shrugs. "Probably a lot of kids. Or maybe not. It's usually about half right."

"How long has it been around?"

She sits back and thinks. "Since this summer? Maybe last school year. First time I was in it was with Alex. It was correct that I was wearing more dresses. Remember all those frilly things Mee-Maw sent me?" She looks up at me and I nod. "Well, that part was right. The part about me not wearing panties wasn't exactly true, you know."

"I hope to goodness not!"

The way her eyes slide toward me and then focus hard on her yogurt makes me not want to know exactly how true it was.

"And Bryan made it in. Pretty good for a freshman, especially when it made his camp down by the water sound so busy."

"Busy?"

"You know, like with girls and guys…" She pops up and drains her juice glass. "But everyone knew it wasn't like that. I mean, freshman guys? Bryan and his friends were so goofy when it came out. And no girl would admit to actually going there." She throws away her yogurt cup and grabs a banana while she's talking.

"Wait, was that after that picture of Zoe and Bryan?"

"Nope. Before. That's why Brittani flipped out. She thought it was all made up until that picture."

Bryan growls from the doorway. "Are y'all still talking about that? Give it a rest." Then I see him get a glance at the *Taking Chances* paper. "Oh," he says as he goes to the refrigerator, passing Savannah on her way out of the kitchen.

"I'm going upstairs to finish getting ready, but we are leaving on time, so be ready!" she says. He grunts something back at her but his head is stuck in the fridge.

"So who do you think writes this?" I ask my son.

He shrugs as he pulls out the jug of milk. Then he's opening Pop-Tarts and putting them in the toaster. He props his elbows on the counter next to the toaster, then rests his head on it and flops forward like he's taking a nap. Which he might be. My sleeping genes are pretty strong.

I get up and freshen my coffee with a small pour. Leaning back on the counter, sipping my coffee, I wait for the toaster to pop and wake him up. It pops, he takes them out, then falls into the chair Savannah perched in earlier. There is no semblance of perching with my youngest, and it makes me smile. He's wearing an olive-green long-sleeve shirt, dark khaki pants, and his hair hasn't been combed. If I looked closely I bet there's sleep in the corner of his eyes. After his glass of milk, he'll probably have a milk mustache over the semblance of hair he's cultivating on his upper lip.

Savannah's right.

Freshman boys are in a class all to themselves.

I leave him to his breakfast since communication with him at this point isn't going to happen. I take my coffee into the living room.

"My hairbrush?" I ask as Savannah plows down the staircase, headed for the front door. I meet her as she steps off the last stair.

"Mom, I have to have a brush at school. I'll bring it back, I promise, and if you need one there's got to be one in my room somewhere. I didn't have the time to find it. Okay? Just let me use it today?"

"Fine." At least this gives me a reason to snoop around in her room. Not that I need a reason, but it feels more noble to have one.

She grins and gives me a hug. Definitely worth a hairbrush. Then in my ear she bellows, "Bryan!"

He comes flying out of the kitchen. "Bye, Mom."

The house is once again quiet, but far from empty. Will and Anna are still downstairs. Missus is upstairs. Alone. She came in last night, and it was sickening how happy she was. Even Anna was cringing. Anna and I were watching some sitcom, and after Missus spent a few minutes telling us of her "exotic" dinner and "romantic" drive with Mr. Fisk, she then whisked herself upstairs for her "beauty sleep."

Anna made a gagging sound. "I can't stand all that."

"Me either," I said. "But I guess it goes along with her new looks."

Anna sniffled, then wiped her eyes. "I miss FM."

I reached over and gave her a side hug. "Me too. And I know Missus does, too, but... I don't know. Mr. Fisk seems like a nice man, and I guess I should be happy she's happy."

Anna nodded just a bit. "That's what I keep telling myself. Guess I can't believe she's really that happy, but she seems to be." Anna stroked her stomach, then sighed and said, "I just wish she was around more. Where do you think she is all the time?"

I moved my stare from her to the TV even as I felt Anna staring at me.

Then she said, "Oh." She turned to face the TV, too. "You think she's with him. I guess he does have a trailer out there at the park. I mean, he is one of the stars."

We sat, letting the commercials roll by. When I chanced a look at her, it was to see her chin quivering and tears rolling down her cheeks. I hugged her again, then she pushed her way up off the couch.

"I'm going to bed. Francie and I have a big day tomorrow. The district manager is going to be in, Mr. Kendrick's boss. I've never met her, but I hear she's really tough and I want to impress her." She stretched her hands over her stomach. "Kind of hard to do when you look like this, but it is what it is."

"She'll love you. And honey, maybe this is just some weird stage of grief with your grandmother." I reached out my hand for one of hers. "But I miss her, too. Feels strange to say it, but I guess I got used to being her *best friend*." That made us both laugh. She was still chuckling as she walked down the stairs to where Will was studying.

"Hey, Mom." Will sticks his head in the living room, where I'm leaning against the back of the couch and remembering last night. "Good morning. Anna and I are going to Ruby's on our way out." He disappears into the kitchen, and I follow him.

"That's a good idea. I know Anna's nervous about the big boss being in the store today."

He's fixing himself a cup of coffee to go. Guess he wants one for the five-minute drive. "Yeah. Did she tell you she'll get her grades on manager training Friday?"

"No, she didn't. I'm sure she did great, but I know she's nervous. We should celebrate. I'll think of something. There she is!" I say with a big smile as Anna joins us, hoping she's feeling better about things than she did when she went to bed.

With a groan she laments, "Are those stairs getting steeper? I swear I need a rope to pull myself up them in the morning." She laughs, but it's a nervous laugh.

Will laughs with her. It's just as awkward as hers.

I give them each a little hug. "You two have fun at Ruby's and have a great day. Anna, the district manager is going to so enjoy meeting you. I just know it. I have to go get ready. Love you guys."

By the time I reach the second floor, they are heading out. From inside my room, I hear the front door close and the house grows quieter. I pause to see if I can hear Missus, but there's no sound from her room. I decided last night to try and be happy for her. She's happy, so why shouldn't we be happy for her? After all, if this is just a stage of grief, then it will end. If it's meant to be, then, well...

Oh, a hairbrush. I first check the back of our bathroom cabinet to see if I have any stashed back there, but like I thought, my stash is empty. I'm still in my robe, so I dart out and up the stairs to Savannah's tower room. It's actually just a dormer room under the eaves, but being the princess she believes herself to be, calling it a tower stuck. It's a mess, of course, but it doesn't smell like a teenage boy's room when it's a mess. This smells like her. Body wash, perfume, powder. No food scraps as she saw a mouse up here once and that took care of that.

I look around, but I don't feel like snooping. I'm struck with how alive the room is, and at the same time, I'm struck with how this time next year she will probably be living in another room. This one will fade into a museum, full of things she can't throw away, but will never again want with her every day. Necessities turned into memories. Except she won't know that right away. She'll think she lives in both places.

I know that's not possible. I can't fool myself with her like I did with Will.

Luckily, with my short hair, a hairbrush isn't always required, so I reach out for the short stair railing, since, well, it's kind of hard to see right now and I don't want to stay in here any longer.

After stumbling down her steps, wiping my eyes and sniffling, I make it into the hallway and close her door behind me. Suddenly, Missus is standing in front of me. "Oh!"

"Carolina! You scared me. Are you okay?"

I tilt my face away from her and maneuver around her in the hallway. "I'm fine. Have to get dressed." I'm in my room leaning against my closed door before she can get fully turned around.

"Okay," Missus says loudly. "I'm going down to have some coffee. We can talk when you're dressed. I need you to do something for me."

Great. Now what? I take off my robe and fling it onto the bed and enter the bathroom.

I'm in the shower when I remember that the *Taking Chances* paper is on the kitchen table with the picture of her and Mr. Fisk making out.

Well, at least she won't be so happy now.

Chapter 45

Rushing into the restaurant, I spot Susan and go straight towards her. "I have to eat fast. I have a hair appointment at twelve-thirty." I don't sit down, but I hang my purse on the back of my chair and wait for Susan to stand up. As she does, I turn to make my way to the buffet area. Once our plates are full, we meet back at our table and sit down.

While we were getting our food, I tried to gauge how Susan was feeling. She looks perfectly normal, not upset and sad, but not giddy like she's been a few times since she moved back into Chancey. "How are you?" I ask.

She chews, then says, "Good, I think. I calmed down from this morning. Griffin's mother can be a royal pain, but she's here, so..." She shrugs.

"Do you think she'll tell Griffin about Silas? Maybe you should cool it with him for a while." I focus on dipping my egg roll in the hot mustard and don't look at her.

"Silas suggested that, too." She grins as she looks down at her plate. Then she looks up quickly and catches my eye, whispering, "But I managed to convince him otherwise this morning." She waggles her eyebrows at me.

"Oh, that's why you're not as upset as you were earlier. How convenient to have the movie crew's trailers, not to mention your boyfriend's, right outside your office."

"Oh, you are so right!" she purrs.

She completely missed the cattiness in my statement, but *her* feline tone can't be missed.

"Susan! For crying out loud, he's an actor. He's got to have, you know, other girlfriends in, uh, other places."

"You would think so, wouldn't you? But he's different. He's a one-woman guy." She grins like a kid in an ice cream shop. "He's actually crazy about me. I mean, he agrees, well, agreed with you that we shouldn't see each other for a while. Would a player say something like that?"

I can't believe she's not seeing this. "Yes! That's exactly what a player would say. Ugh. Player. Can't believe you got me to use that term, but it's right. Playing with people is exactly what a player does, right? Tell them what they need to hear to make them think you care about them."

She keeps eating. Her smile never dims. "Everyone thinks they know what's best for a person, but none of you knew how boring my life with Griffin was. Like living with my brother all these years." She lifts her head and straightens her shoulders. "I deserve to be treated like this. I deserve it!" Her eyes are full of fire, and her cheeks full of color. Her haircut is bouncy and lively. Her turquoise sweater dress is both businesslike and classy.

She looks like an entirely different woman than the gardening mom with dirt under her fingernails, constant ponytail, and tanned skin I met when we moved here. The one who wore only jeans or shorts as she ran the church youth group and tended her massive garden. I'd thought she had everything under control, but apparently that impression came because she held everything in her life very tight and very close. She definitely seems happier now—at least she will be until she finds out about Beau and Silas. Oh, well. Like I decided with Missus last night, if she's happy…

"Okay," I say. "If you're happy, then I'm happy."

She reaches over and pats my hand. "Sweetie, I am happy, but it's not all to do with Silas. I'm not making that mistake again. Poor Griffin would've been so much happier, and so would I through the years, if I didn't try to force him to be happy the way I wanted him to be happy. Does that make sense?"

I nod, and I eat for a bit. "It does, I guess." Finishing my last bit of rice, I swallow and look at her. "Don't take this the wrong way, but I'm not only talking about Silas either. Everything in your life is kind of upside down right now. Your mom and Laney and your kids. Cooling things down might help with everything, not just Silas."

"Carolina, don't worry so much. The kids are all right where they want to be. Leslie leaving for college showed me just how quickly they move away and start their own lives. Susie Mae and Grant will be fine."

"But Leslie was always so self-sufficient." I hadn't thought of Leslie having just left for college this fall. Is that what started all this? "Susie Mae and Grant are different."

"I thought you had a hair appointment," Susan says as she stands up. "The kids will all be fine. Griffin is already fine. My mother and Laney will come around, and I'm, as I already mentioned, more than fine." She forces a wide grin at me. It feels fake.

She moves toward the front counter and I follow.

I don't feel so fine.

"I don't usually kiss and tell," Beau says to my reflection in the mirror at her station. Her short red hair is spiked high to-day, almost as high as the heels she's wearing. She has on tight black jeans and a light-blue tunic shirt. "But yes, this movie has meant I don't have to go looking for a, well, a *friend*. I wasn't sure I even wanted another baby, but Raphael is already four, plus I'd really like to have another girl. Angel is just about as precious as they come, but she's already in first grade."

Beau is tall and dramatic, very different from me, but we've become pretty good friends. The romance between her niece Brittani and Bryan has made our friendship stressful at times, though. The Bennett women are a bit ferocious when it comes to defending their own. Their little queendom centers on Beu-lah Land Beauty Shop where they all work. The outside of the building is all sky blue and white with touches of shiny gold. It's about as hillbilly stereotypical as you can get. However, the dark walls, black porcelain, abundant greenery accented with bouquets of roses, low lighting, and soft music inside set an entirely different mood. It's a mood I'm trying to enjoy while I get some information on Beau's new "friend."

She bends down closer to my ear. "Never thought I'd want five kids, but then I never thought a movie star would be de-livered to my doorstep." She straightens up and winks at me in the mirror.

"So he *is* an actor? Not one of the crew?"

"Pshaw. I don't pick just anyone for a daddy. Has to be someone special."

"Do none of the guys ever come around wanting to find out about, you know, the kids?" I'm keeping my voice low, though I don't know why. Everyone knows Beau wants kids but no men. Except for, well, the process of getting a kid.

She waves a hand at me. "They don't know anything. For all they know, the men, that is, they aren't the only one I'm sleep-ing with. They have no idea they've been selected." She winks again. "This one I could tell right off was hot to trot, so I let him trot on over to my place when he gets a chance. He's really been busy on this shoot. Not much free time. He won't give me another second of thought once he's moved on. Just how I like it."

She's got me turned away from the mirror so I look directly up at her and suggest, "Maybe he's got another girlfriend in Chancey."

Beau, who is never still, suddenly goes still. "You think? Hmm. That would explain a few things."

I'm a bit afraid to ask. "Like what?"

She's studying my hair and then turns me to face the mirror as she checks places and makes little snips. "Lack of time for one thing, and then he is often kind of tired."

Thinking of how happy Susan was at lunch, my anger builds. How dare Silas do this to her. He and Beau, well, I'd expect that. She wants a baby daddy that's an actor, and he wants some fun on location. But why involve Susan? Especially now?

"How's that look?" she says.

"Fine," I say without really looking. But then as I'm getting up, I look at her tight jeans. She still has her model's figure. "You really want to have another baby?"

She shrugs as she begins sweeping around the chair. "If it happens, it happens. Just thought the opportunity was too good to pass up. Plus, he just threw himself at me." She leans on the broom and looks at me. "You know, though, I bet you're right about him having another girlfriend."

"Wouldn't you feel bad about her? It could even be someone you know."

"Of course, it'd be hard to imagine us not knowing each other, as small as Chancey is," she says with a laugh. "But feel bad? No way. You get involved with a guy who's in town for only a couple weeks, you should know what to expect, right?" She leans the broom against the wall, takes a sniff of the roses on her station, and leads me to the desk that serves as their office.

She's right. Susan *should* know what to expect.

But I don't think she does.

Chapter 46

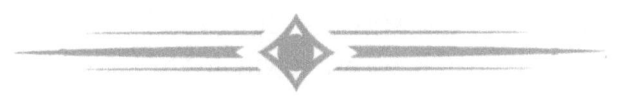

Midafternoon sunshine pours through my windshield as I drive from Beulah Land back to the shop. Between the sunshine and an open parking spot directly across from Blooming Books, I should be feeling great. However, all I can think about is Susan. She's feeling so confident, but what will she do when she finds out all this faith she's put in Silas has been misplaced?

I'm not out of the van before Savannah is standing beside it, motioning for me to hurry.

"Okay, okay," I say as I get unbuckled, grab my phone and purse, and get out. "What's going on?"

She has on jeans, boots, and a sweater. Her hair is pulled to one side, and I can see by the amount of makeup on her face that she's been filming. It's heavy, but her eyes look even bigger and prettier. She's tugging her sleeves down over her hands and shaking her head. "Mom. Parker is going to kill me. The wrap party is Saturday night. I have to be here!"

"Saturday? This Saturday? Wrap party. Does that mean it's all over?"

"Yes. The good weather has sped stuff up, and Leif just told us we'll be through Friday."

"Well, honey, you don't have to be at the wrap party. Leif will understand."

Her eyes get even bigger. "Mom! There is no way I'm missing the wrap party. The fraternity party is nothing. I just hate to let Parker down, but well, he'll just have to understand. I'm going to be an actress. My career has to come first."

"Oh, well, then. Okay. Parker will just have to understand." I look at her standing there like there's more. "Are you done filming for today?"

"No." She just stands there, and at first, I think it's the sunshine that's making her eyes sparkle or the eyeliner making them look so big, but then I realize she's beaming. "Mom. Leif wants me to audition for another film!"

"Honey! That's amazing," I say as I grab my daughter in a big hug.

"He says there's no promise, but he thinks I'm perfect for the part!" She steps away from me and hugs herself. "I've got to get back inside, but get this. It's being filmed in Atlanta, so I'd be on location! How cool would that be?" She gives a little squeal then darts across the road as I watch her.

Well, all that sadness this morning about her going away to college next fall might have been wasted.

Apparently she's not going to wait that long to leave.

I follow Savannah. She's holding the shop door open for me and holding a finger to her lips to let me know they are shooting. We both ease inside, and she weaves into the crew standing to the side. I move in the other direction, back towards Shannon's worktable where she's arranging red roses in a clear vase. The roses are beautiful. Usually we don't have so many long-stemmed red roses in, but with the movie people in town, they seem to be everywhere.

I mention the roses, but she only sniffles and doesn't acknowledge me, except by moving to the side a bit so I can't see her face as clearly. Men are clearly not high on my like list right now. I never imagined Peter could be such a rat! Just as I lift my hand to pat her back, a voice cuts through from the filming area and the fake counter where the scene is being shot.

"Laws-a-mercy!" I hear Laney yell. I step that direction to see what's going on. I can comfort Shannon later.

Laney's voice rings loud and clear. "This here argument has gone on long enough, I'm telling you. Stop it! Stop it right this very minute and behave like the grown adults you are." Laney has a glow about her—the glow of movie lights. Looks like she made it into the movie after all.

Leif is letting her steal the limelight, but what really makes me smile is that it's the old Laney doing so. Well, kind of. She's wearing a peplum purple suit jacket. Her skirt is tight, but not too tight, so it's a recent purchase. Don't tell her I said it, but she has not gotten down to her pre-baby weight. Her hair is no longer gray, but her "natural" dark color. Those masses of curls are gone, of course, but instead of just hanging around her face, her hair styled to really frame her eyes. They look brighter than even Savannah's did.

Everyone watching is grinning as she goes on to castigate Silas and the lead actress, Jenny. They are seated at the table across from each other with stacks of books surrounding them. Laney has one hand on her hip and is letting them have it. She references the Civil War a couple times, compares their argument to "two dawgs fightin' over a hambone," and says, "It's as ridiculous as iced tea without sugar." Then she settles her pocketbook on her forearm, sticks her chin in the air, and sashays out of the scene.

Leif shouts, "Cut!" and everyone breaks into applause. Laney immediately sways back into the center and bends over to kiss Jenny's cheek, saying, "Darlin', you know I'd never yell like that at you." Then she stands straight and looks across the table at Silas, her one eyebrow telegraphing her thoughts before she opens her mouth. "You, however, I do have some words for."

Leif clears his throat and strides toward his actors. "Wonderful job, Laney! Exactly what we needed. Now, let's get that last scene set so we can have dinner." He steps closer to Jenny and Silas and talks in a low voice. I can't help grinning as I think, *Well done, Leif, that was the best block I've ever seen thrown at an oncoming hissy fit.*

"Laney," I shout over the others. She takes a breath, fixes that eyebrow, and walks toward me.

"You saw me?" Her face is lit even without the big lights, and she rushes to me for a hug.

"Yes! You were wonderful, what happened?"

"Yesterday morning, in Ruby's when I got bent all out of shape and stormed out? Well, that young woman over there," she points back toward the movie crew, "she was there and saw it all. She looked up my number, called me, and then came out to the house yesterday afternoon. She's one of Leif's assistants, and she's also worked on makeup and wardrobe for other movies. Well, she told me the movie was missing something. She said my little scene in Ruby's was better than an audition tape!" Laney giggles, and she hugs me again. "She flat-out told me to stop looking so old. She did my makeup and colored my hair back to normal, then she styled it right there in my master bath!"

Leif hurries over to us. "Well done, Madam Mayor! Lisa was right, you were perfect." He grabs one of her hands and leans over to kiss her cheek.

"Mayor? You're playing the mayor?"

Laney nods as Leif explains, "We needed a touch of the South and couldn't figure out how to add it until Lisa saw Laney in action yesterday morning." He leans back and looks at Laney. "You look so much better than when we first arrived and you were trying to play a Southern belle."

He laughs and Laney's eyes meet mine with a small roll. He grabs her hands and holds them out to the side. "You are the epitome of a modern Southern woman, and you'll make the movie pop." He leans in for another kiss on her cheek, waves at me, and is gone before I can ask about Savannah's audition or the wrap party.

We watch as he goes back to the set, where his actors are looking at scripts. Laney sighs. "I really do want to give that Silas Pendersen a piece of my mind. Susan is acting like a schoolgirl, but you and I both know he's going to be moving on at the end of the week."

"Yeah, Savannah just told me the wrap party is Saturday night. Wonder where they're going to have it?"

Laney turns to look at me. "Didn't you know? It's at your house."

I gasp. "Over my dead body! We have a house full of guests. There are already far too many people. No way!"

She grabs my forearm as she bends over laughing. "Gotcha. Remember how we had so many things up at your house when you first moved here? I knew you'd blow a gasket."

Laney's laugh is loud and infectious, and it's so good to hear again. Everyone is looking at us and smiling, so I join in with a laugh. Then I ask again, "So where *is* the wrap party going to be?"

Shannon speaks up from behind us. "Here. Figured the food is already here anyway, and we have plenty of room. Gertie said it was fine."

The shop is much better than the house. "Sounds good to me."

Laney leans on our counter. "These shoes are killing me. I'm going home to my baby."

The woman she pointed to earlier walks up to her. "Laney, you did fantastic."

"All thanks to you, Lisa. You've met Carolina, right?"

Lisa sticks her hand out at me. "Yes. A couple times. Good to see you again. I have to get back over there, but I just wanted to say how great I thought you did, Laney. You look really good." She turns to me. "Savannah did great, too. She said she'll be eighteen soon?"

"Yep, middle of December."

"Perfect. She looks young, and that's good with actors. She tell you she's been specifically asked for with our next movie?"

"She did. That's quite an honor."

Lisa looks at me a little awkwardly, then nods. "Oh, okay. Good. Gotta get back." Then she walks away.

"Next movie?" Laney asks.

I shrug. "Yes, she just mentioned it when I got here." I grin at her. "Are you interested?"

Laney pushes away from the counter and shakes her head as she walks toward the door. Over her shoulder she says, "No! I've been here all afternoon saying the same thing over and over and over. I'm done with acting. However…" She stops and faces me, pulling herself up tall. "I do believe my new look would fit the role of mayor rather well. Don't you?" She winks at me. "Jed better watch his back!"

Then she throws open the door, setting the bell to jingling. Before it closes I hear her try the title on like a girl writes her name connected to the boy she likes. "Mayor Laney Troutman Conner," she says, then she marches down the sidewalk like she's already leading a parade.

"She looks great," Phoenix says behind me.

"Oh, hi!" I turn to her. "Didn't see you. Listen, that newspaper thing. The blog?"

"Yeah?" She whispers.

"It apparently some high school thing, but that particular one isn't out as far as I can tell. You don't know who left it in your studio?"

"So that's the only copy?" She brightens up immediately.

I sigh. "Possibly, but if it's true maybe you should just not worry about it. As long as you tell Colt."

She shrugs as she chews on her lip. "It's just going to be so hard admitting it. I've told everyone it was a lie for so long that I'd started believing the stripping didn't really happen."

She looked so cool, so confident when she first came here. Now, wrinkles around her eyes make her look older, and her clothing, which usually is so put together, looks like she's actually playing *me* as the bookstore owner. Black pants and a caramel-colored shirt, but without that crispness that usually defines her look. Her hair is just plain old red hair, missing its gloss and care.

"If that article never comes out, maybe I *won't* have to tell Colt." She peers at me. "You wouldn't tell him, would you?"

"Me? No, but if someone found this once, it can be found again." Of course at this moment I'm wracking my brain to remember if I told Jackson last night. And what about Missus? I assume she has the paper since it was missing when I came downstairs this morning. But Will or Anna could've also found it. Why do I end up holding all these secrets?

Suddenly, Phoenix hugs me tight. "Thanks, Carolina. I knew I could count on you."

Seriously? Wouldn't you think by now she'd know better?

CHAPTER 47

It's Thursday morning. I hear Patty leaving her apartment, so I walk toward the back of the shop and greet her at the bottom of the stairs. I'm here early as Bonnie took off for a day trip to Chattanooga with the ladies from Laurel Cove.

"Good morning," I greet her. "Andy said you'd be coming down in a few minutes. He looked like he was in a hurry to get to work."

Patty chuckles. "He's always in a hurry. Everything he does." She's beaming, and I watch her carefully descend. At the bottom she stops. "He didn't tell you, did he?"

"Tell me what?" I ask, but from the way he was bouncing and the way she's glowing, I'm pretty sure I know.

She steps to me and hugs me as she whispers in my ear, "We're going to have a baby!" We hug tighter, then she steps back. "But we haven't told our folks. We want to do a big surprise tomorrow after church. We're taking them all out to dinner."

I press my lips together. "I won't say a word. Gertie is going to be beside herself!" I link my arm in hers. "Margery has the coffee ready. Come have a cup, or some juice, and we can visit a minute."

As we'd been talking, the movie people started arriving for the breakfast spread. I motion her ahead of me as I say, "This is our last few days with Margery here, so we might as well take advantage of it." Leaning towards her I say, "Besides, you're eating for two!"

She nods and takes some cantaloupe and a croissant, and I point to a table where we can sit. I join her with my coffee, half of a cheese Danish, and some strawberries.

Herbert Fisk approaches our table. "Miss Carolina, may I join you and the lovely Miss Patricia?"

"Of course, Mr. Fisk," I say. "Are you slated to shoot early today?"

"Indeed I am." He sets a bottle of water and a bowl of oatmeal on the table, then sits just as Lisa, Laney's new style guru, calls my name.

"Carolina? You have a customer up here," she says.

I get up with a shrug. "Sorry. Duty calls." I take my plate and cup with me and hurry to the counter where a woman is waiting.

Whenever the movie people are in the store eating, our business picks up. People wander in to be among them. Then they feel bad just gawking and pick up a book or a bouquet or both.

Usually their time stargazing time here isn't wasted. Mr. Fisk always takes time to sign autographs and chat with his fans. Jenny is often recognized and Silas is occasionally, but I think most people (read: women) just want his autograph because of his looks. According to Lisa, Silas and Jenny are currently filming in Phoenix's studio, so Mr. Fisk has no competition this morning. He's very charming. I have to admit that he and Missus do make a very attractive couple, but he's as different from FM as night from day. I groan and turn away to look out the front window. Every thought of FM hurts, but if this is Missus' chance at happiness, how can she let it pass? She's not getting any younger.

Speak of the devil, there she is. Missus is walking through the park, headed in this direction. Her blonde hair picks up the sunlight, and her sweater set is the color of the deep blue sky. She has on gray tweed slacks and suede boots. She looks like she could be one of the actors. She sees me through our front door and waves. On the sidewalk she stops to talk to a couple of ladies from town. They appear to be gushing over her. She does seem a lot more approachable these days.

"Good morning, Carolina," she says, pushing through the front door. She says my name, but her eyes wander about. I think I know who she's looking for.

"He's in the back with his fans," I say and then she looks at me.

"Of course he is, but I was talking to you." She comes to the counter and then around the end so she's behind it with me. "Thank you so much for leaving that delightful article with our picture in it for me yesterday morning." She giggles.

Yep, folks, you heard it here first. We've moved into giggles. "Well, I didn't, um, but if you're happy, then…"

"And the roses!" she exclaims. "Oh my, they were glorious. It's been ever so long since anyone sent me roses. Herbert is so, oh, just so thoughtful. When I called to tell Shannon how beautiful they were, she told me you delivered them for her last night. Sorry I was out so late."

Now we have a giggle *with* a blush.

Smiling tightly I say, "They were beautiful. Shannon does a wonderful job. Mr. Fisk is very thoughtful."

Missus moves to where she can see the back area. Mr. Fisk walks toward us talking to a couple of ladies who hold bags from our store. He's obviously flirting with them, which comes with being an actor I suppose. I look to see how Missus is taking it, but she only has eyes for him. When he sees her, he steps forward and kisses her cheek, then wraps her arm in his.

"Ladies," he asks his admirers, "have you met Ms. Bedwell yet? She practically runs this charming town and has quite stolen my heart." He takes her other hand and bows to kiss it. Both ladies say, "Aw" and practically curtsey as they move away. What I've just realized, and now can't seem to get over, is that there is no glove on her just-kissed hand!

From the back area, Lisa announces the time and says shooting will begin in ten minutes. Mr. Fisk and Missus turn toward me, and he says, "I believe that means I should head down the street." He untangles his arm as he kisses her cheek again. He leaves with a salute for me, and we watch him stride down the sidewalk. He's so confident and charming as he greets everyone.

"Isn't he wonderful?" Missus says with a sigh.

"When did you stop wearing gloves?" I ask.

"Oh, I don't know." She folds her hands together and looks at them. "They seemed old-fashioned suddenly." Then she looks up at me. "Did you hear tomorrow is the last day of film-ing?"

"Yes. The wrap party is here on Saturday night."

"I know," she says with another sigh. "I so wanted to have the party in my house, but things will not be back in order in time since they are filming there tonight and tomorrow." She folds her arms, and I notice how she tucks her hands inside. "I would like your opinion on something."

"Okay?" Where in the world are all the customers and movie people now that I need a good interruption?

"Mr. Fisk, Herbert, he's asked if, well, if he should stay in Chancey after the filming." Her speech is breathy, like her mouth is completely dry despite her licking her lips. Her blush from earlier is gone, and she's sort of pale.

"Do you want him to?" I grasp her elbow to pull her closer

301

to the counter. At least this way I can grab her if she starts to faint.

"Do I want him to?" she repeats. A smile crosses her lips, and this time, when she licks them, they glisten a bit. "I believe so, but..." Then pain settles on her face. "But FM."

"Yes. I know. We all miss him, but if you're happy..."

"Herbert is a dear man and he does make me happy, but FM... But I'm afraid if I send Herbert away now he won't come back. He has the next few weeks empty, and I think I'd like to try... try something new. Should I?"

I rub her shoulder. "Oh, Missus, I can't answer that for you."

She unfolds her arms, then rubs one hand along the back of the fingers on the other hand. Then she switches hands, but her eyes never lift off them.

After a long silence, I say, "Anna gets her scores from her management course tomorrow. Jackson and I were planning on taking everyone out, including you, and, uh, Herbert... if you'd like to invite him."

She tips her head up at me. "Yes, I would love to join you. I'll ask Herbert if he would as well." She grasps my hand. "In fact, that will be wonderful. I'll go invite Herbert right now before he's preoccupied." She's all smiles again and hurrying down the sidewalk before I can even process what she was asking me.

Herbert Fisk living in Chancey? Even if only for a few weeks that will be huge. Wait, living where? "Oh, no," I say out loud. "In our B&B?"

Then my mind races on, and the words come tumbling out. "She wouldn't move him into FM's house, would she?"

CHAPTER 48

"Why are we taking eleven people to dinner?" Jackson asks as he buttons the cuffs on his shirt. "And why do we have to go all the way down to Woodstock?"

I grin as I hug him from behind. "And here I thought if I got you all loved up you wouldn't find anything to complain about."

He turns in my arms. "Definitely not complaining about *that*. You were awfully good, Mrs. Jessup." We kiss, but like the man said, we have a dinner to get to, so I push away. "I'm not sure everybody is going, but better safe than sorry. Only ones I'm sure of are you and me, Will and Anna, Savannah, Bryan, Missus and Peter. Whether any of them bring someone, we'll know when we know." I pick up my phone and look at it. "Still nothing from Savannah. She said she may have to film tonight."

"Do we know how Anna did on the course?"

"Nope. Will picked her up, and they came in through the basement using the outside door when they got home. All I know is he texted me a thumbs-up when I asked if dinner was still on, which is more than I've heard from Savannah."

Apparently all the good luck the movie people had been

experiencing ran out yesterday morning. From broken equipment to a stomach virus, everything careened off the tracks. Shortly after Missus left Blooming Books, there was a fire alarm in the dance studio. Fire trucks showed up. It was discovered that some wiring was smoldering and had actually singed a portion of the back wall. Consequently no one was allowed in until a thorough inspection was completed, which took the rest of the day.

The stomach virus turned out to most likely be food poisoning, as it was discovered that the four sick crew members had all eaten hot dogs from Peter's Bistro. I've got to say, I wasn't really surprised to hear that. However, Peter is no longer serving any food and has gone into hiding. He did return my text, though, saying he'll join us for dinner tonight.

Due to the dance studio fire alarm, Leif moved everything to Missus' house early. That's where the broken equipment came in. A large piece of equipment, a crane or something, was set up to film on the staircase. It got stuck and wouldn't move up or down. Missus, despite being warned not to, had snuck up the stairs past the equipment, and she was stuck up there all yesterday afternoon. She didn't sneak up there alone. She and Mr. Fisk were both stuck up there for several hours.

She was just giving him a tour. That's her story, and I'm sticking to it.

Anyway, all of these SNAFU haven't made things pleasant in Chancey.

Until Jackson got home earlier. Then it at least got better for me.

As he dampens his hand and smooths down his hair at the bathroom mirror, he asks, "Who's riding with us? Bryan, I assume."

"Yes, and I told him he could invite Zoe. Everyone else is meeting us at the restaurant as far as I know. You ready?"

"Yep. And I'm just being a grouch. It'll be great to be with everyone." He flicks off the bathroom light and gives me a lookover. Seeing as I'm standing with one hand on my hip and another on the wall, in his path to the door with every body movement from my eyebrows to my posing feet asking how I look, I guess the lookover was to be expected.

"You look great." He gestures at my outfit. "Is, uh, that new?"

Poor thing. There's really no winning for guys and their wives' clothing and/or hair changes, so I help him out. "Just the sweater. Found it at Target on sale. I think it's supposed to be a dress, but with the leggings it works great, and I knew you'd like the boots. Your mom gave me the scarf for Christmas."

The sweater dress is dark maroon, and my tights and boots are black. The large scarf is paisley in rich tones of maroon, green, and gold. Jackson follows up his lookover with another kiss. I open the bedroom door, and we step into the hall. I lean over to knock on Bryan's door as Jackson yells, "We're ready to go," and we begin down the stairs.

"Speaking of your mom," I continue. "We have to nail down our plans for the wedding week."

"Oh, Emerson and Abigail have it all laid out. They even made reservations for us all to have Thanksgiving dinner at some old inn on a horse farm. I told Emerson whatever they decide is good with us. I'm actually kind of looking forward to it now. Oh." He stops talking and walking, so I also stop on the landing and turn.

"What? What's wrong," I ask.

"Should we have asked Colt and Phoenix to come tonight? It *is* kind of a family thing."

I turn and keep going down the steps. Through careful questioning I've figured out I apparently didn't tell Jackson about that *Taking Chances* exposé of Phoenix's past as a stripper. I've also found out that was apparently the only copy. It never did appear on the *Taking Chances* blog page. Yes, I also figured out how to find that. The old blog posts are as Savannah described. They are very much focused on how it is to be a teenager living in a Southern small town, including some rather interesting but harmless vignettes of life in Chancey. The last entry is about upcoming changes to the blog "COMING SOON." The author is only listed as Small Town Girl.

I enter the kitchen and then say over my shoulder to my husband who's stalled in the living room, "It's kind of late now, don't you think? We can invite them next time."

I get my purse and do a little straightening as I wait for Bryan to come clomping down the stairs. Jackson, still in the living room, hasn't said anything. I didn't intentionally forget to invite Colt and Phoenix, but I'm really glad I did—accidentally. Can you imagine how awkward it would be having Missus, who I'm sure read the article above the picture of her and Herbert making out, and Phoenix at the same table? Especially since Phoenix thinks I'm the only one who knows.

I'm making sure the back door is locked as I hear Bryan on the stairs, so I leave the kitchen for the front door.

"Good news," Jackson says from where he's standing in the middle of the living room, his thumbs working his phone. "Colt and Phoenix will meet us there."

Bryan jumps from the landing to the entryway. "Zoe couldn't come, so I invited Brittani. Told her we'd pick her up." He jerks open the front door and heads out. Jackson follows him, but I turn around and go back in the kitchen.

I'm going to need more ibuprofen.

"Can I get a glass of wine while we're waiting?" I ask the hostess. As if worrying about Phoenix and Missus wasn't enough, Brittani never shut up once after she got in the car. I remember telling Bryan he could invite Zoe. I do *not* remember telling him he could invite Brittani if Zoe was a no-show. The hostess points to the bar around the corner, and I motion to Jackson that I'll get him a beer. He nods, well, he nods specifically at me. He'd already been nodding because Brittani was telling him something. Something that was going on and on and on. Remind me to ask him if he wants some ibuprofen.

Around the corner, the restaurant opens up so it's not as loud as the waiting area. They said they'd have our table set in about ten minutes, so I prop myself on the barstool at the end and wait for the bartender to see me.

"Hey," someone says with a tap on my shoulder. With a slight turn, I see it's Peter. He looks ghastly.

"Did you eat the hot dogs, too?" I ask.

"Very funny. No, but maybe if I had, it would've killed me and things would be better. Is Anna here yet? Any word on how she did?"

"Just thumbs-up texts from Will, although I'm sure she did fine. She sure studied hard enough." Just then the bartender stops by and we order.

Turning, I ask Peter, "Your mother with you?"

"Yes." Then he grins. "You heard about her and Mr. Fisk getting stuck upstairs yesterday afternoon? He seems like a nice guy, I guess, but I'm ready for the movie folks to move on. Mother's a tad infatuated with it all, and with her getting her face done and that blonde hair. But it'll all be over soon."

The stool next to me opens, and he sits on it. "I've got to figure out what I'm doing with the bistro." He pauses and then revises his words. "Yeah, right. I've got to figure out what I'm doing with my life." He plants his elbows on the bar and props his head in his hands.

He's moved on to the bistro, but I'm still thinking about Missus. So he thinks his mother is over this? I know he's been preoccupied, but surely he knows his mother and Herbert Fisk are a thing, right? But, hey, whatever. "Have you talked to Shannon?"

"She won't talk to me, and I don't blame her. I have half a mind to ditch all this and move to Atlanta or maybe further."

"Start over again?"

"I don't know."

As the bartender sets our drinks on the bar, I hop off my stool. "This is for Jackson," I say lifting the beer. "You going back out there?"

He looks at me and then nods. "Guess I should." He pauses, and our eyes lock. "I miss my dad. A lot more than I thought I would."

I match his nod and smile. As his eyes start to glisten, I look away, but then quickly I turn back. "Peter, maybe you should just slow everything down. Take some time off and re-lax. Maybe you're pushing yourself too hard."

"Maybe." He takes a sip of his beer and stands. "I'll come with you. Our table should be ready soon." He's behind me as we move toward the front, and he bends down toward my ear. "Just a warning. Mother is in a foul mood."

Before I can ask why Missus is upset, a group of departing guests has foisted its way between us. Oh, dear. I need to see if I can manage to keep her and Phoenix at opposite ends of the table.

"Our table's ready," Jackson says as I hand him his beer. "Savannah is here. Did you know she was bringing Leif?"

Savannah brought Leif? The director? The thirty-some-thing director? Jackson directs me to start walking with his hand on the small of my back. At the table I'm too busy trying to get a glimpse of my daughter to see where anyone else is sitting, which is how I end up between Brittani and Missus.

Leif gives me a wave as he pulls out Savannah's chair. She looks up at him through her lashes with a little smile. I'm too far from them, and the restaurant is too loud for me to hear what they are saying, but they are talking entirely too closely down at their end of the table. Jackson is across the table from me. He's getting Colt situated beside him, directly across from me, which means Phoenix is directly across Missus.

Then Will and Anna join us. Jackson saved them seats at the other end of the table from where Savannah and Leif are whispering. Jackson points them toward the seats and then says loudly, "Here's our guest of honor. Congratulations on finishing the management course, Anna!"

We all clap, and she takes a small bow, then sits down. Brittani is yapping in my right ear. Missus is sulking on my left. I asked if Mr. Fisk would be joining us, and she didn't answer, only glared at me with her idea of an evil eye. He can't be filming since the director is here. Peter is across from his mother and already ordering another beer, which is probably not a good idea, but he does look a little better than earlier.

As we get ordering underway, it seems we might as well all be here at separate tables. It's so hard to hear anyone not right beside me. Colt and Jackson are talking. Phoenix and Peter talk once in a while, but they both seem pretty intent on their drinks. Brittany is talking, but I have no idea who's listening to her because I'm not. However, both ends of the table seem to be enjoying themselves. Will and Anna. Savannah and Leif. They're certainly not concerned with talking to the rest of us.

I'm left alone with my thoughts. Leif is the one who said she should audition for this new movie. The movie being shot on location in Atlanta. The movie assistant lady, Lisa, said Savannah had been asked for specifically. What do you want to bet it was Leif that asked for her? Tyler, his business partner, has a fiancée, but I've never heard Leif talk about a girlfriend. Why would he have a girlfriend? Just shoot a film in a little town and romance one of the teenagers there with talks of being a star. Of course he seems nice, but of course, that way the good girls and their mommas believe you.

"What, Brittani?" I shout as I flip around when she won't stop tapping my arm and saying my name. Of course, the table had already quieted down, and the restaurant seemed to be experiencing a lull, too. Now it's gotten real quiet as everyone is staring at me. Brittani looks scared and I roll my eyes. "I'm sorry," I say, adding in a sweet tone, "What?"

She bats her eyes and squeaks, "Anna wants to say something to us all."

Jackson shakes his head at me and smiles, then looks to where Anna is standing, her stomach draped in a pretty red maternity dress. Will is standing beside her, and she takes a deep breath.

"Thank you all for being here tonight. It means so much you putting this together, Carolina and Jackson. All of you have been so helpful with me taking the management course, and I found out today I passed with the highest marks!"

We all cheer, clink glasses, and clap. She looks up at Will. As he looks at her, she smiles at him and gives him a nod.

With one arm around her back, he pulls her close and pulls himself up taller. "We, Anna and I, want to also say that we appreciate everything y'all have done for us as a couple and as a," he laughs and looks down at Anna's belly, "as a family. We want to let everyone know that we *are* a family and we're going to start acting more like one."

He's interrupted with laughter and more cheers. Then Anna says, "I'm going to be named the co-manager of the Chancey Dollar Store after my maternity leave is over and..." she looks up at Will and he says, "And so we put down a deposit on a house this afternoon!"

Anna glows as she says, "It's the cutest thing ever. We're renting, but they may sell it in the future." Both of them are beaming, and there maybe one or two tears around the table.

Then Will holds up his free hand. "One more thing. Y'all know how crazy our relationship has been. We've gotten off track more than once, but we've been meeting with the pastor and doing some counseling, and we are trying to be more intentional about our lives. So even though Anna is already my wife…" As he says this, he steps away from her. Holding her hand he kneels to the sound of gasps.

His focus is solely on her as he says, "Anna, this may be backwards, but I want to ask you if you'll agree to still be my wife. We didn't have an engagement last time, so I never bought you a ring. I can't believe it never occurred to me and you never even asked. He unfolds his hand to reveal a black box, which he hands to her.

She's crying as she opens the box. Her hands are shaking, but she manages to say, "Yes," then adds, "It's so beautiful." He slides it on her finger, atop the wedding ring I'd noticed she'd been wearing again lately. As he stands up, we all leave our seats and cheer, along with those at tables nearby who'd been watching.

My heart is so full. I look over at Jackson who also has tears on his cheeks.

I lean across the table to grasp my son's hand. He also has to lean because his other arm is wrapped tight around his wife and child. Our eyes meet, as they have thousands of times since that first moment I held him, and I so clearly see the man he's becoming. No, wait.

The man he is.

Chapter 49

I waited up for Savannah to come home last night. Well, I waited up in spirit, but in body, not so much. Waking up on the couch in a dark house, I was a little stiff as I stumbled my way to the front window to see her car neatly tucked in the driveway. I get the feeling my ability to sleep through anything is why my babies seemed to learn to sleep through the night fairly early.

I did, however, text her last night that I wanted to see her in the morning. Of course, when I got up a bit ago I saw that she'd texted back this morning that she had to be downtown early and she'd catch up with me later. I'm showered and dressed, and the front door opens as I am halfway down the stairs.

"Oh, that wind is cold!" I exclaim to Jackson who looks up at me. His cheeks are red, and his hair is nearly standing up straight.

"It's freezing out there. Guess that cold snap came in last night." He opens his arms, and I step into them. He tightens his grasp as I feel the cold on his jacket. He says, "You're so warm," and laughs as he won't let me go. Our laugh turns into a longer kiss before he lets me go.

"I'm not ready for cold weather," I say. "Do you already have coffee?"

"Nope, I just walked Will out to his car. I'm so proud of the two of them. Did you know they were getting counseling?" he asks as he comes into the kitchen.

I hand him a cup of coffee. "I didn't. I actively tried to stay out of their business. I can't wait to see their house, though that feels so weird to say. I'm going to go sit in the living room."

We barely get settled before I ask, "Did you talk to Savannah or Leif much last night?" I never seemed to get close to either of them, and I can't decide if they were being evasive or if that's just how it worked out. I'm trying to not be suspicious, but, well, I'm not trying *that* hard.

Jackson shrugs. "I talked to Savannah for a minute. Something about a new film she's auditioning for?"

"Yeah. I'm worried she's getting in over her head. What if Leif has ideas about her?"

"Ideas? You mean parts she'd be good for?" He's so cute when he's confused and innocent.

"No! Like as a girlfriend or something even less. You know what they say about young actresses in Hollywood."

"This isn't Hollywood." He laughs a bit. "And I like Leif. He's much too old for her. I think he just sees a young person that has dreams and he wants to help her."

"That's what I was thinking, but why'd she bring him last night? They seemed entirely too friendly." I set my cup down and get up. "Feels like that wind is coming right in the house. I'm turning up the thermostat."

"Aren't you leaving soon? Don't turn it up too far, or I'll be roasting here. I'm going to work on the B&B bathroom before the guests check in this afternoon."

"Since I'll be downtown when they get here, you're going to be here, right?" I stand at the thermostat until I hear the heat kick on. I still have trouble trusting the new system.

"I promise. Besides, they're with a train club out of Alabama and are spending the morning at a big train show on their way here. Can't wait to talk to them. How long are you working today?"

Back in my seat, I sip my coffee. "Until two, then I'll be home to change for the wrap party which is at four. Seems early, but Lisa told us today is for closing up the trailers, so a lot of the crew won't be staying here overnight."

We sit in silence then Jackson says, "Peter looked rough last night. Is he okay?"

"I don't know. I think FM's death really hit him, and he's just not thinking clearly about things. I hope to see him today."

Jackson doesn't say anything, just watches his thumb rubbing the lip of his coffee cup.

"What are you thinking?" I ask.

"Nothing." He takes a deeper breath, and as he lets it out, he looks at me. "Just be careful he doesn't try to lean on you too much."

"Oh, of course." I stand up. "Well, I better get going." I lean over and kiss Jackson. "Good luck with the bathroom floor. I'll be home in the afternoon. Are you going to have some breakfast here or are you going to Ruby's?"

"Here. I told Bryan I'd make bacon and eggs for us this morning when he gets up."

"Oh, he'll like that." With my coat, hat, and gloves on, I step out into the cold. I wait until I'm inside the car and have it started before I check my phone, even though my text tone rang while Jackson and I were still talking, the tone responding to the text I sent earlier.

My phone reads, "Okay. See you at Ruby's."

Peter already has muffins at the table and my cup turned right side up, ready to be filled.

I mean, a girl has to eat, right? But I do say, "I can't stay long," before I sit down.

"Sure," he says, then he cocks his head at me with a smile. "That was something with Anna and Will last night, wasn't it?"

"Yes. What are these muffins?"

Libby swirls to a stop at our table to answer before he can. "Caramel apple, and cinnamon apple is the one with that red on top. It's those little cinnamon candies."

She fills my cup, refills Peter's, but doesn't stop talking. "Aren't these movie people just the sweetest? Smells just like Valentine's in here this morning. They brought over all the flowers from the trailers since they're packing up." She extends the coffee pot out to point around her, and I see the small bouquets that look a few days old situated on several tables, including ours. On the bar are some bigger arrangements. Along the wall in the booths there are several vases holding long-stemmed red roses.

Libby smacks Peter's shoulder with her empty hand. "Shannon sure is going to miss all those folks buying flowers, isn't she? Even Cathy got some roses, although she brought them to my house since she said Stephen probably wouldn't appreciate her getting flowers from another man." She blows out an exasperated breath, saying, "That girl is going to be the death of me!" as she whirls on along her way.

I bend closer to Peter. "Shannon's been doing great business, but she's not very happy these days."

He harrumphs, grabs the caramel apple muffin, and bites into it. He's wearing a gray tweed sport coat and dark gray sweater with a button-down shirt underneath it. His beard and shaggy, dark hair makes him look even more moody and distant when he's all hunched over into himself. He has his small plate with the muffin and his coffee directly in front of him, and he reminds me of some sulking English poet. For the first time, I realize how he reminds me of the professor I had that awful affair with in college. I actually gasp as I see it. He rolls his eyes up to look at me and scowls at my fast-blinking eyes.

How did I not see the resemblance before?

I jump up from my seat. "I have to go." I can't get out of here fast enough. My heart is pounding, and although I remember to grab my coat, I don't take the time to put it on. The cold hits me like a bucket of ice water, and I draw in a long breath. Fumbling with my purse, I manage to have the store key in hand when I reach our front door. I open it as quickly as possible.

Leaning against the closed door, panting, I feel like a character in a horror movie, trying to outrun the monster. My breathing slows down finally, and my shoulders relax. How did I never see that before?

I think I'll call Jackson and see how things are going at home.

CHAPTER 50

Savannah stopped by the shop just before noon to tell me my long, concerned text about Leif was silly. He was her mentor and friend with no romantic thoughts at all. With a sweet, condescending look for her old, addled mother, she said, "Besides, it wasn't Leif who requested me for the audition. It was Mr. Fisk." She also informed me she'd let Parker down easy as she no longer has time for all that dating nonsense.

She then sailed on, busy with her day as all teens are, unless they are lying on your couch with a bag of chips. Then they are *totally* busy.

A little later Laney didn't exactly sail in. It was more like the god of war arriving on your doorstep, blowing down the doors while throwing lightning bolts.

"Did you know Alex and Angie had some crazy idea about her moving into his apartment? He said you knew!"

Customers stepped out of the bookshelves to watch as I tried to corral my friend toward the back. "Laney, hold on. I told him you'd never agree to it. I told him he was crazy, and if you'll remember, I did try to ask you if they weren't more than just friends."

She stopped near the back where Margery ignored us and went on with setting up for the party tonight.

Laney looked marvelous, but then drama always does that to her. She had on a lime green wool suit with a short jacket. Her silk blouse was a creamy white and her short, dark hair bounced around as she tossed her head and words at me. "I told that daughter of mine in no uncertain terms that she is over that young man and she will be moving *on*, not moving *in*! How dare she use that business as a cover for their, their, well, you know!" She suddenly deflated and slumped against the wall. "It was awful last night. We were all still at the dinner table when they made their little announcement and the world blew up. And then, she left with him. Just got up and left. She won't answer my calls. Her daddy's either. We didn't sleep a wink last night."

My heart hurt for my friend. "I'm sorry, but you know she'll come around. She's really a smart young lady. You'll talk things out when you've both cooled down." I reached out and squeezed her arm. With a laugh, I said, "Maybe you didn't get any sleep, but you still look good. That's one thing in your favor."

I tried to get her to look at me and smile, and finally she did.

"I had to get up and get dressed." She straightened herself and gave me a full smile. "I called some people I know from all the pageant PR I did, and I have a television interview this afternoon."

"Really? What for?"

She checked the clock on the wall and started walking towards the front, talking loud enough for everyone in the shop to hear. "Well, Carolina, it's for that local feature thing on Sunday mornings. They were very interested in the story of an area pageant queen acting in a major motion picture."

Major? I thought about rolling my eyes, but I just said,

"Oh," as I followed her. "I'll have to remember to tape that." Along the way I smiled at the customers and held up a finger for the woman standing at the counter ready to make her purchase. "I'll be right with you."

I jumped ahead and opened the door for Laney since she was obviously headed that way. She stopped before crossing the threshold and turned to me. Speaking in a normal voice she said, "I'm not really mad at you for the Angie situation. I'm mad that I wasn't paying attention, but *now* I'm back to my old self." She leaned closer and whispered, "And there is no way my daughter is going to be living with her boyfriend on the town square, especially not now."

I'd been trying to smile and give my customer another nod, but then I was jerked back to what Laney was saying. "Why especially not now?"

Laney winked at me, lit up like a sparkler on the Fourth of July, and announced, "I'm doing it, Carolina. I'm running for mayor!"

Poor Jed. Poor Chancey.

With the closed sign turned out to the sidewalk, Shannon and I huddle at the door, me blocking the wind off her as she locks up. "You did remember to give Margery your key to get back in later, right?" she asks.

"Yes, I already told you a million times." Immediately I regret being snotty with her. "I'm sorry. You are still coming to the wrap party, right? Please come."

She tugs to make sure the old door is locked, then shrugs as she turns. "I want to. I feel like I should since the movie people virtually made this my best year ever in business."

We cross the sidewalk, then look before we start across the

street. I shout since my face is buried in my coat collar. "I saw all the flowers in Ruby's from the movie trailers. I knew you were busy, but I had no idea."

"Some were used on the sets, and the little bouquets I made up were popular. However, the roses are where I really made out." A stiff wind causes us both to hurry. As we get to our cars, Shannon waves at me and shouts, "Hate the idea of coming back out in this, but I really should. See you later!"

I wave at her and get in my car. With this wind, I'll be lucky if the car warms at all on my way home.

I don't care how cold or how windy it is, I can't wait for the party tonight. I want to see with my own two eyes that Mr. Leif Nelson doesn't have designs on my daughter.

Plus, it means I don't have to cook.

CHAPTER 51

"The guests checked in and immediately left for some train watching before it gets dark. Then they're getting dinner." Jackson met me at the door with a glass of iced tea. Now we're sitting in the living room just as we were this morning. "It's all guys. Should be no muss, no fuss. They said all they want is beds to sleep in. I told them about the muffins, and they said those and coffee in the morning will get them on their way home."

"You weren't tempted to go train watching with them?" I stretch my feet out to rest on the coffee table. I've already pushed off my shoes.

"I wasn't invited. They are all driving together in one SUV, so there wasn't room anyway." Responding to my cocked eyebrow, he adds, "Plus I would *never* miss the wrap party. Remember Tyler from the movie company, Leif's partner? He's coming up for the party, and he called to see if he could bring his fiancée up here to take a quick look at the B&B. He said something about wanting to stay sometime."

"Oh, he's coming here?" I look around, but things look pretty good so I relax. "Sure." I lean up. "Guess I should go get ready. Bryan say if he's going or not? I know Will and Anna aren't planning on going." Pretty much anyone remotely involved in the movie has been invited to come to the party. Leif mentioned these parties are more for the town than the movie crew and actors, although they are all encouraged to make an appearance.

"He walked down to Zoe's house a while ago, but he didn't say." He pulls out his phone as we both stand. "I'll check with him. Tyler said they'd be here around three-thirty."

I head upstairs as he steps into the kitchen. From the stairs I holler, "How did the bathroom floor turn out?"

He groans, then sticks his head out of the kitchen. "It's going to need to be replaced. Water got under the flooring and made a mess. I've got it covered, though, and they'll fix it while we're in Kentucky. We don't have to cancel any guests, so that's a good thing, right?"

"Right," I say with a big smile at him. What could possibly go wrong with letting strangers have the run of our house while we're out of town? But I'm not getting involved. He's handling it, and I'm letting him. See? I *have* learned a few things from all these years of marriage.

In our room, I look in the closet, then over at the chair where I lay all my clothes for the maid to hang up. I'm going to have to fire her, because all the clothes I've worn all week are still laying there. Examining the pile, I'm tempted to wear what I wore last night.

I go through my test of seeing if I remember what everyone was wearing last night. Okay, about half and half, so let's say half the people there remember what I was wearing. Do I really care? If I had money to bet, I'd bet even Jackson won't remember what I was wearing. Only Missus would be ornery enough to mention it, and she's in a funk, so I doubt she'll notice. Okay, that was easy.

Just then I hear a clunk next door. Jackson didn't mention Missus being home. I thought maybe she'd moved back to her house since filming is over. I step into the hall and knock on her door.

She whips it open and spits, "What?"

I startle back. "Oh. Sorry. Thought maybe you'd moved back into your house."

"Not hardly. Besides, well…" She looks past me, then up and down the hall. "You know what I told you about Herbert staying in town?" I nod, and she continues. "He's getting ready for the party at my house." She looks at me as if I should know something.

"I don't understand. Isn't that what you wanted?"

She shakes her head, then stops to think. "Did I?" She steps back into her room, and I move in past the doorway, too. "Everything's happened so fast."

I frown sympathetically. "You seemed to not be happy last night either."

"Well, I wasn't, uh, I couldn't be. He wouldn't answer my calls or texts yesterday afternoon, but he's a busy and popular man. He can't be at my beck and call like…" Her voice dwindles to silence, and she sits on the edge of her bed.

I step closer and ask, "Are you okay?"

She looks up at me, and when she does, she doesn't even look like herself. Her makeup is perfect and her blondish hair styled, but I'm getting used to all that. What's strange is that she looks confused. Like she doesn't know what to think. Then she bounces up and I jump back.

"Of course I'm okay, Carolina." She looks in the dresser mirror. "Don't I look okay? I'm lucky to have Herbert, and if people want to talk about him staying in my house while he's in town, well, people talking has never stopped me before, right?"

"Right. Okay, well, I need to get ready." I turn, and as I do I look down and see green stems sticking out of her wastebasket. I look back at her.

"Oh, those. Well, I guess I was irritated yesterday. Probably shouldn't have taken it out on the roses." She laughs a bit and follows me to the door of the room. "I'll be moving back into my house, probably tonight."

Hearing shakiness in her voice, I turn to her. "Missus, if you're not ready to have a relationship with Mr. Fisk, then you don't have to. Stay here. Let him stay in your house."

"I'm not a child. I know that!" she spouts at me, her hand poised on the door to close it, then she softens. "But Herbert is a very special man and he's put a lot into this relationship. Wait until you see the outfit he helped me buy. It's quite something. Like I'm a whole new person." She swallows and puts on a big smile as she says, "Well, you better get ready."

She slowly closes the door just as Jackson yells from downstairs. "Bryan says he's going and has something to tell you. We're to pick him up at Zoe's. Tyler will be here soon, you ready?"

"Soon." I start for our bedroom, then I remember I don't have a hairbrush, so I turn in the other direction and go up the steps to Savannah's disaster of a room. It would be easier to yell at my daughter about the state of her room if I didn't have my own chair laden with clothes. She'd gotten dressed earlier and had already left by time I got home. I can smell her perfume, but just barely, because a huge bouquet of opening roses is on her dresser. Their scent overpowers everything else.

When did she get those? There's no card. Man, if bit-part actors like Savannah all got these humongous arrangements, Shannon must be rolling in money. Jackson has never given me roses like this. Mine tend to come with a plastic grocery store bag wrapped around the stems.

Hairbrush in hand, I leave the flowers and mess behind and dash into my room and get ready. I'm walking down the stairs when I see Tyler pull in our driveway.

"Jackson, they're here."

He comes to the bottom of the steps and looks up. "There you are. You look great!"

As I step onto the floor beside him, he tips his head at me and says, "I like that scarf."

I can tell he doesn't remember it from last night. Not a clue. Good thing he's cute.

Chapter 52

"Mom! You're not going to believe it!" Bryan spurts out as he bounds up into the van, Zoe on his heels. Then he says, "Oh, Missus." She's riding to the party with us and sitting in the seat behind Jackson, who's driving.

Bryan goes to the back seats, and Zoe sits behind me. Pulling down my visor with the mirror, I look back at our youngest son and ask, "What is it?"

He points at Missus' back and then says, "Nothing." Okay, I get it. I find Zoe in the mirror. "Hey, Zoe. How's your mom and dad?"

"Fine." She and Bryan are both staring at the floor. I move my head to see Missus in the mirror. She's also looking at the floor. Okay, I'm good with a quiet ride.

We park next to Tyler and his fiancée, Ashley, who are just getting out of their car. They seem like a nice couple, but I don't think she was impressed with the B&B. She's more of the resort type, I believe. She rolled her eyes a lot and kept sipping from her monogramed Yeti cup on her tour of the B&B.

We all walk in a group across the street. Blooming Books looks so festive in the late afternoon light. Lots of folks are inside, and the extra lights used for filming are still up. They really light up the whole inside so you can see the high ceilings and how deep the building is. It looks huge. Jackson sees the same thing apparently, as he says, "You may need to look into some more lighting. It looks really impressive."

Ashley brightens up. "Oh, I love cute old stores like this. This is yours? Oh, how absolutely precious!" She threads her arm with Tyler's and pulls him ahead. Jackson offers an arm to Missus who is wearing the highest shoes I've ever seen her in. She's wearing a dress that doesn't look like her at all. It even has jewels on the large collar, and it's too form-fitting. I mean, it fits her and she looks good in it, but it's not her. I'm at the rear of the group with Bryan and Zoe, and suddenly they are holding me back. They each have hold of one of my arms.

"Mom, you have to see this," Bryan says as he holds up some papers. "We printed it up. It's all online and has like a million hits."

I step closer to the side and more into the light coming out our front window. I say, "It's that *Taking Chances* blog. I didn't look at it today." The first headline I see is the stripper story about Phoenix. I grimace, but right beside it is a big picture of Silas Pendersen with no shirt on. He's kissing someone with only a bare shoulder showing that looks an awful lot like Susan, but maybe it's Beau? It's hard to tell, especially in black and white and in this light. There's another picture of Silas' co-star Jenny with her kids outside her trailer at the lake park. The headline is one word: "Germaphobic???"

I unfold the papers, then Zoe grabs them and shuffles them. "There, that's the one you've got to see."

But before she can hand them to me, the door to the shop opens back up and Jackson looks out. "You coming in?"

There are more people walking down the sidewalk towards us, so Zoe folds the papers and says, "Let's go inside."

She and Bryan pass funny looks at each other, but it's too

cold for funny looks. "Come on. Show me inside, it's freezing out here."

It's warm inside, but really loud. Everyone is talking, and everything feels different. Several people are staring at their phones.

As soon as I walk in the front door, Missus leans on me. "My apologies, Carolina. How do women walk in these shoes? Oh, there's Herbert, finally."

Zoe and Bryan are hanging on my other side anxiously rattling their papers, but with Missus holding onto my arm, I can't just abandon her. She launches herself across the floor headed for Herbert leaving me behind. Her dress is a bright gold, almost like lamé. She is trying to hold herself tall and regal, but she doesn't look too steady on her heels. Either way, she has everyone's attention.

Ashley sashays up, straw from her Yeti still in her mouth. She's also looking in Missus' direction. "So she's the one?"

I turn toward her. "Pardon?"

Still speaking around the straw, she shrugs and says, "She's older than he usually likes, but it's the money that matters, right? Tyler was so hoping Herbert would behave this time."

"Are you talking about Mr. Fisk?"

She waves a hand at me and rolls her eyes. "He seems so sweet, but whoa, honey! Leif said he was hanging around with an older woman on this shoot. Oh, looks like they're opening the bar. Can I get you anything?"

"Uh, no, thanks." She scurries off, and I watch as Missus approaches Herbert. He kisses her, caressing her shoulders, then he steps back from her. Even over the din, I can hear him exclaiming about her dress and shoes.

"Here's the rest of it, Mrs. Jessup," Zoe says as she hands me more sheets of paper. "Look at this." She's pointing toward the bottom of the page, but then I hear my name.

"Hey, Carolina!" Gertie says loudly. I look up to see her

headed my way. She doesn't look happy. "Why would you do that to Patty? You couldn't wait two days for her and Andy to surprise all of us with their news? Couldn't hold onto her secret for just one more day?"

That I blabbed about this secret is news even to me. "I didn't tell anyone. Why would I tell?" I stammer.

"You're the only she told. *Only one.*" Gertie is hurt and mad. She glares at me and shakes her head.

Zoe is shuffling papers again, and Bryan tugs on my arm. "Mom, it's right here." He hands me a sheet of paper from the *Taking Chances* blog. Here there are just bullet points. Bryan points to the third one down. It says Patty is pregnant and then says something about the baby's heritage including a preacher and a moonshiner.

I look up at Gertie, my mouth hanging open. Of course Patty thinks I told. No one else knew. "I didn't tell anyone, Gertie. I promise. I have no idea how this got in here."

Peter sidles up to me and spits, "Really? How about that line there that I'm planning on selling everything and running away? How did they find that out if not from you?"

Ruby who has up to this point been quietly listening nearby says out the side of her mouth, "But really, is that a secret?"

Peter's mouth drops open. He turns around and stalks back toward the front of the shop.

Jackson makes his way through to me. "What is this blog they're all talking about?" Bryan shows him the papers while I just shake my head and close my eyes for a minute.

Zoe speaks up. "Nobody knows who writes it. It's never had so much adult stuff before. It's always been fun stuff about high school things. This was posted this afternoon, and it went viral."

Staring at his phone, Leif strides up to us. "Jenny, Silas, and Herbert are all tagged in everything so it's spread all over." He looks at Zoe. "You're saying you've seen this before. This Taking Chances in Chancey thing?"

Zoe and Bryan frown at each other and then look at the paper. "It didn't used to have Chancey in the title. It was just *Taking Chances*."

Jackson had been reading one of the pages. "Says here Savannah has a starring role in an upcoming film and something about her having a special 'Sugar Daddy'? What is all that about?"

Leif holds up his phone. "Must be someone with inside knowledge to get this picture of me and Richard."

"Who's Richard?" I ask.

Zoe whispers in my ear, "Says it's his boyfriend right here."

Oh, so he's not after Savannah. Good to know. But then who's her supposed sugar daddy?

Leif's phone rings, and he steps over to the side to answer it. I look at Jackson and grit my teeth, saying again, "I did not tell all this."

My phone had been buzzing, but I was ignoring it. I pull it out of my purse and see I have a string of texts, mostly from Susan and Laney. Last one says, "B there soon" so I decide to just wait for them to get here and not bother with trying to read everything. "I need something to eat and drink," I say. "I'm not going to act guilty. I didn't tell this stuff, and I sure as sugar didn't write it."

Pushing forward, ignoring everything else, we finally arrive at the tables and the beautiful spread of food. I am determined to have a good time. "Margery, this looks amazing and I'm starving."

She smiles. "Thanks. Sure has been a good gig for me. I've been busy, what's got everybody all upset?"

Tyler steps up behind me. "Gossip. Somebody spreading half-truths and flat-out lies. Par for the course in this business."

He sounds a little accusatory, so I flip around to plead with him. "But I didn't tell all this." I lower my voice. "Some of this stuff is true, but it wasn't supposed to be told. People are really hurt!"

Ashley laughs. She laughs really loud. "That's the stuff they'll go to any lengths to find out. I'm just amazed the playboy didn't get exposed. That's usually what the small towns get the most upset about. Right, Ty?"

"Shut up, Ashley," Tyler says.

I don't care if she thinks it's funny. I explode at her. "He's right there on the front page with no shirt on. That's pretty exposed. He also took advantage of my friend." I grab the front page from Zoe and shove it towards Ashley and Tyler. They both look at it, then Ashley laughs again, even louder, and I realize things have quieted down. I also realize Ashley is a little drunk. And I just thought she was being friendly up at the house. She takes the page in hand and waves it around. "Silas? Mr. Too-Good-for-Anybody Silas Pendersen? Not hardly. Wrong star!"

Tyler grabs her hand and takes the paper away from her. "I'm serious, Ashley. Be quiet."

She, however, takes another long sip through her straw and says, "Okay, okay. I'll be quiet. You'd think in a place this podunk they would've noticed him sending roses to all his conquests. But if they don't care, I don't care!"

Roses? I turn further and meet Missus' eyes. I didn't realize how close she was standing to me. I have a feeling we're both remembering all the roses we've seen lately. She draws in a shocked breath, swallows, and lowers her eyes. Wait, Herbert is Beau's friend? And Cathy got roses from a man she didn't want her husband to know about. Looking around, Lisa the production assistant nods and shrugs at me. Savannah, too?

I whirl to my daughter where she's standing behind Mr. Fisk talking to Leif. "Who gave you those roses in your room?"

She looks confused for a minute, then says, "Mr. Fisk. He said he wanted to help me in my career and that we'd have more time on the next set since we'd not be in my hometown."

Leif is standing behind her. He just puts his head down.

When I turn to look at Missus, she no longer looks guilty. She looks furious. I'm not sure how she manages in her heels, but she pulls her hand back and lets it fly, connecting with Herbert Fisk's face. Then she straightens her back and says, "You are scum and are no longer welcomed in Chancey. Get out."

With a few quick glances around the room, Herbert Fisk sees leaving as his best option, so he bows to Missus and to all of us, then ambles to the front door.

Before the door can close behind him, Laney and Susan come pushing in. "Where's Carolina?" I hear them asking.

Ignoring them, I turn to my daughter and put my hands on her shoulders. "He didn't try anything with you, did he?"

Savannah recoils. "Ew, no! He's old!" She shrugs off my hands. "I'm fine."

Susan and Laney are quickly followed by Silas and Susie Mae. As they pass by us, Susan points and blurts out, "Back there where it's quieter." Jackson and I move back to the back wall, and the four of them meet us there. Susan pulls her daughter in front of her into our little circle.

She says, "Tell her," and prods her daughter forward.

Susie Mae's eyes are swimming with tears when she finally looks at me. "It was me. I write *Taking Chancey*. I just thought including the movie people would help it go viral. Sorry."

Over her bowed head, Susan and I meet eyes. She shakes her head and mouths, "I'm sorry."

Then I hear someone on the steps to Patty and Andy's apartment and see Gertie staring at our little group. "Susie Mae," I whisper. "How did you find out about Patty being pregnant? I didn't tell anyone."

She shrugs and mumbles something. I lean closer and she mumbles, "I hid recorders here in the shop." She looks up and points to the tables where Margery has been serving everyone not only tonight but for weeks. "One's under that table, and the other one is up at the front counter."

We all take a step back, trying to wrap our heads around it all. I meet Gertie's eyes. She nods, then says, "I'll tell Patty," as she starts up the rest of the stairs.

Susie Mae sniffles. "I don't know why I put that about Patty in there or Peter or Aunt Laney. It was just all so interesting how everyone seems to come here to tell you their secrets." She looks up at me and apologizes again before adding, "I really did enjoy getting to hang out here with you and the books we read. Those were great. I'm sorry I ruined all that."

Reaching out to grasp her upper arm, I squeeze and say, "It'll be okay. You've got more than me to apologize to, but, well, you have been under a lot of stress lately."

Susan takes her under her arm, and as they turn, she shakes her head and frowns. "Did you see that picture on the front of me and Si? Thank God my face isn't showing, but still anyone that knows me will know." She smirks as she says, "I'd be completely mortified if he didn't look so hot." She winks and I smile at her a bit.

Of course it's her in the picture.

I knew it all along.

Missus is still on the Blooming Books couch where she sat down after Herbert Fisk left the shop over an hour ago. She's smiling as she holds up her plastic glass still half full of wine. "I've never been drunk before. No wonder people do this."

There's a bit of laughter from those of us close by and I

reach out to take her glass. "Then I believe you've had enough. Matter of fact, I've had enough of this whole evening." I sit forward. "Think it's time for me to go home." The movie people have all been gone for a while, but the few of us left just haven't gathered the energy to leave.

Shannon showed up a little late, but she's been caught up on everything that happened. She had been leaning against one of the bookshelves, but she stands and walks toward the couch where Missus is sitting. "Missus, I'm sorry I didn't put together what all those roses meant. He just seemed like a nice guy." She shakes her head and sighs. "I guess I was so busy that it never dawned on me."

Missus shudders, then moans. "Roses will never be the same!"

Savannah, who is seated next to Missus, lays her head over on the older woman's shoulder. "Oh, let's not blame the flowers."

Shannon laughs. "No, let's not ever blame the flowers!" She places her hand on my shoulder. "You've had a long night, Carolina. You go on home, and I'll close this all up." She smiles down on me, and I realize she's truly become a friend.

I pat her hand. "You don't have to do that. We'll all help."

Peter stands up from where he'd been sitting on the front window ledge. "Yes, we'll all help. That's what we do here in Chancey, right?" He grins and looks more like his old self than he has in a long time. "Last night was such a big night for my niece, Anna, and her husband, Will. They should be an inspiration to all of us that even when we hit rough patches we must keep moving forward. I look around and see people I trust and love and know we are lucky to have each other." Okay, maybe it's not his old self. Maybe he's had more wine than usual.

Jackson sits on the arm of my chair and I drape my arm across his legs. Missus and Savannah snuggle a bit closer, and behind us I hear Bryan and Zoe playing video games on his phone. Susan and Silas took Susie Mae home, probably to a very long grounding sentence, and Laney left with them. Having her mayoral run announced in *Taking Chances* wasn't exactly her idea of an appropriate launch, so she didn't feel like staying around. Instead, she wanted to go home and think about how to make it work for her campaign.

Jackson looks down at me and says, "You're right, Peter. We are very lucky."

I scoot to the edge of my seat and say, "Lucky we all have homes to go to. Time for this party, and *movie*, to be over!" There's agreement from everyone, then groans as we start getting up.

As we begin moving around, Peter walks to the open space between the chairs and the counter. He's behind Shannon, who is standing, still facing me and Jackson. Suddenly, Peter drops to one knee. Shannon, seeing the shock on our faces, turns around.

"Peter!" she gasps.

He reaches out and takes her left hand in his. "I was inspired by Will and Anna last night. I, too, want to be intentional about my life from this point on. Shannon, will you marry me?"

Shannon starts crying, then I realize she's pulled her hand from his and is covering her face with both hands. Was there a yes in there somewhere? She's shaking her head, and finally in the midst of the sobbing, she says loud and clear, "No."

Peter's face falls. He lets down his other knee, too. Shannon runs to the bathroom in the back and slams the door behind her.

Her would-be fiancé jumps up to his feet and, without looking at us, darts out the front door.

We are all left staring at each other. Missus stumbles a bit and rests a hand on the chair where she's standing. As I step towards her, I realize she's staring at her hands. Is she missing her gloves? Is everything from this night finally hitting her? Is she worried about Peter? I lean toward her and softly ask, "Missus, are you okay?"

She slowly nods, holds her one hand up, and looks at me. "Carolina, didn't I have a glass of wine just a moment ago?"

Hesitantly I answer, "Yes. Why?"

She sighs and grimaces with a nod toward the bottles sitting on the florist table. "I'm thinking I might not be *quite* drunk enough for all this."

Amen, sister.

"Jackson, can you get us some fresh glasses?"

Visit Kay's website at www.kaydewshostak.com
or friend her on Facebook or Twitter.

Character List

Jackson and Carolina Jessup – Moved to Chancey one year ago. Operate Crossings, a bed-and-breakfast for rail-fans in their home. They have three children: Will, 22, a recent college grad; Savannah, 16; Bryan, 13. Jackson works for the railroad and is out of town often. Carolina also runs the bookstore side of Blooming Books.

Jackson's family – Mother Etta lives at the beach in South Carolina. Father Hank is married to Shelby and lives in Kentucky. Two brothers, Emerson and Colt. Emerson is the oldest, and he and his wife have three daughters and live in Virginia. Colt is the youngest, is single, and lives in their hometown in Kentucky.

Carolina's family – Parents Goldie and Jack live in Tennessee. Carolina is an only child.Missus and FM Bedwell – Lifelong residents of Chancey.

Peter Bedwell, 45 - lives two doors down from his parents. Owns Peter's Bistro on the square.

Anna Jessup, 19 - Missus' granddaughter. Her mother was given up for adoption and died when Anna was 16. Anna found Missus and came to Chancey. Married Will Jessup when she got pregnant. They are currently separated.

Laney and Shaw Conner – Both from Chancey. Shaw owns an automotive dealership. Laney partners with Carolina in the B&B. They have three children: twins Angie and Jenna, 17; Cayden, 4 months.

Susan and Griffin Lyles – Susan is sister to Laney and manages the Lake Park. Griffin recently got a big job with the electric company and moved his family to the well-to-do community on the mountain of Laurel Cove. They have three children: Leslie, 19; Susie Mae, 15; Grant, 13. Laney and Susan's mother is Gladys Troutman.

Gertie Samson – She has one child: Patty, 28, married to Andy Taylor. Gertie was raised in Chancey and returned after her daughter, Patty, settled there. She owns a lot of property in town. She lives in the house she, Patty, and Andy run their businesses out of.

Ruby Harden – Owns and runs Ruby's Café on the town square. Lifelong Chancey resident.

Libby Stone – Works with Ruby at the café and is married to Bill Stone. Daughter

Cathy Stone Cross – Libby and Bill's daughter is married to Stephen Cross, a teacher at the high school. They have a young son, Forrest. Cathy sells lingerie through at-home parties. Her previous role as a high school cheerleader still has a profound impact on her life.

Kendrick family – Moved to town for father Kyle to open new Dollar Store where he hired Anna Jessup as assistant manager and then began an affair with her. Currently he lives with Anna. Wife Kimmy and their four children live in Chancey. Kyle's daughter, Zoe, from a previous marriage lives with Kimmy and cares for the younger three children.

Shannon Chilton – Operates florist part of Blooming Books. Lifelong Chancey resident. She's 30 and in a relationship with Peter Bedwell.

Bonnie Cuneo – Works in Blooming Books. Retired teacher who lives in Laurel Cove.

Books by Kay Shostak

The Chancey Books

Next Stop, Chancey
Chancey Family Lies
Derailed in Chancey
Chancey Jobs
Kids Are Chancey
A Chancey Detour
Secrets Are Chancey

Florida Books

Backwater, Florida
Wish You Were Here

www.ingramcontent.com/pod-product-compliance
Lightning Source LLC
Chambersburg PA
CBHW031149120726
47905CB00006B/1868